THE SHIP IN THE WOODS

Published by the Navillus Press   *www.oregonhiking.com*
1958 Onyx Street
Eugene, Oregon 97403

Front cover: Tombstone in the Visby Museum in Sweden; Saint Sophia in Novgorod. *Back cover:* Model of the *Vasa* in Stockholm. *Frontispiece:* Runic tombstone from Gotland, Sweden.

This book is a work of fiction. Significant historical personages in this book (presidents, emperors, celebrities, and the like) are based on actual historical descriptions. All other characters are strictly products of the author's imagination. An Author's Note at the end of the book includes information about historical details.

THE SHIP IN THE WOODS

By
WILLIAM L. SULLIVAN

ILLUSTRATIONS BY
KAREN SORENSEN SULLIVAN

NAVILLUS PRESS
EUGENE, OREGON

IN MEMORY OF
KAREN "BITTEN" WESTERMANN

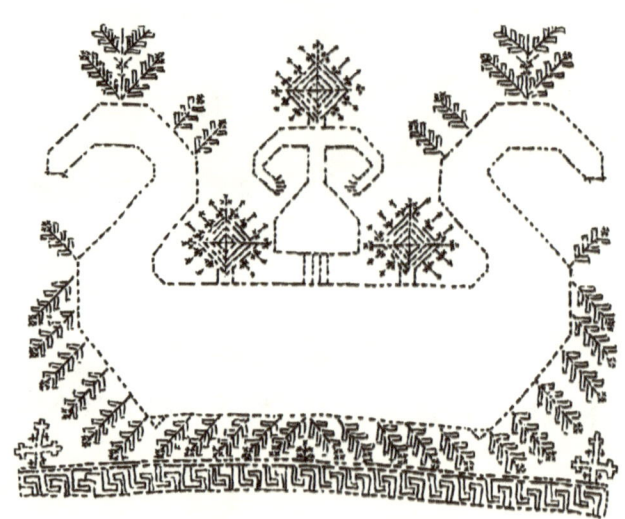

CHAPTER 1
TUNSBERG, NORWAY, 882

The sorceress who sold jewelry had seen many a longship sail into Tunsberg in the months since King Harald Fairhair defeated the Viking Alliance in Norway's western fjords. Amidst the blue-striped sails of local fishermen and the white sails of Harald's own fleet, there had been the tattered red and black sails of the beaten jarls—either those who had accepted Harald's offer of amnesty in exchange for relinquishing their titles, or the defiant losers who had come merely to regroup before setting sail for Iceland, where Harald was permitting them to found homesteads beyond his immediate rule.

But yellow? Groa looked askance at the strange yellow sail tacking tentatively around the skerries towards Norway's trading harbor. Long and low, the ship might have been a visitor from Sweden, but it was not flying the mandatory blue pennant of the Svea king.

A prickling of foreboding at the back of her neck made Groa lock up the iron shutters of her tiny booth on Kingsgate. She hobbled slowly down the planked street to the beach.

Every bone in her bent body ached with age. Her hands, once so nimble, had shrunk to claws. No woman was meant to weather so many winters. People laughed when she told them she had helped her husband forge the sword that launched the Viking Age. Halfdan Whiteleg's raid on the Lindisfarne Abbey had been six generations ago. The ancient Vestfold king had wanted a sword of power, and, foolish young sorceress that she had been, she had summoned the evil wolf god Fenris for the task. But now that Harald had buried that sword together with his grandmother Asa—the last person who remembered Groa from those days—hadn't the gods made her do penance enough?

By the time Groa made her way to the harbor a crowd had already

5

gathered. The foreign longship, like dozens of others along the harbor, was clinker-built, with iron rivets fixing the overlapped strakes into the long, elegant curve of a dragon's body. But the mast was short, as if this serpent rarely flew on open seas. And the twenty oarlocks along each flank were not holes, but rather notches carved directly into the gunwales. This was obviously a ship whose crew preferred to row.

"We are the Rus!" A giant man at the prow bellowed to the crowd. Stringy blond hair hung from his acorn-shaped metal helmet, but his bushy eyebrows, monstrous mustache, and beard were a fiery red. A shawl of chain mail draped his massive shoulders. "We bring treasure and opportunity to those daring enough to seize it."

A skeptical voice from the crowd asked, "Are you Swedes?"

The foreign captain's gray eyes scanned the faces. "Once, like you, we were thralls to a king. But now we are building our own empire in the forests beyond the Baltic. Behold the trade goods of Russiya." At a wave of his hand, half a dozen men carried chests onto the pebble beach. The captain climbed ashore with two heavy leather bags.

Groa was so shriveled with age, and the crowd was so thick, that it took a long time before she was able to see what the captain poured out onto the planks for display. Crewmen with axes allowed only a few people at a time near enough to see—and fewer still the privilege of touching.

What she finally managed to glimpse between shoulders was a treasure indeed—a pile of silver coins and a mound of colorful beads. But a

closer look revealed, even to her clouded eyes, that this hoard was still more wondrous. The coins were not stamped with the crosses and heads of Frankish kings, but rather with alien squiggles. And the beads were not clay, but genuine glass.

"Where did you find such things?" she asked, her voice little more than a croak.

The captain held up a coin. "These are silver dirhams, mined in the mountains of Persia and stamped in the mint of the Arab caliphate in Baghdad."

The men in the crowd wrinkled their brows at such strange place names.

Next the captain held up a green glass bead—precisely the kind of impossibly rare ornament so hotly desired by Viking wives. "And this is Greek glass, smelted in Miklagard, the stone-walled city at the center of the Earth, known to the emperor there as Constantinople."

A man in front of Groa ventured, "You say, captain of the Rus, that these treasures belong to whoever dares to seize them?"

The captain laughed, but also drew a rusty short sword. "Our opportunities may be seized. Our treasure, however, is for trade."

One of King Harald's helmsmen, a cautious guard with a gilt breastplate and a large, shiny ax, spoke loudly from the edge of the crowd, "What is your name, Swede, and what is your business in Norway?"

"I am Oleg of the Rus, and this is Vlad, my purser." The captain held out a hand to a strikingly handsome, dark-haired young man. The youth was beardless, of moderate stature, with teeth as perfect as the foreign coins. Groa's ancient heart sometimes beat erratically, but this time when it stumbled she glimpsed one of her presentiments—that the handsome lad would ask her to sail away with him, escaping the miseries of her life in Tunsberg.

No one believed her prophecies anymore, much less that she could read minds. This time Groa herself guffawed at the absurdity of her waking dream. The wheezing cackle made a tear run down her cheek.

"Steady, hag," a man beside her said, stepping away.

Oleg continued, "Vlad will pay for any amber or furs you bring by tomorrow noon, when we set sail for the east. We will pay particularly well for blades of fine Norse steel." He glanced at his own sword disparagingly and slid it back into its sheath. "As for opportunity, see me if you would dare to leave with us for Russiya, where we rule the Slavs. You will not need to bring cattle or grain to live as jarls there. Bring only your ships, weapons, and women."

Groa raised a shaking claw. Her voice croaked, as if by the will of an invisible power, "I will go."

At once the serious mood shattered. Men roared with laughter. Women giggled into their hands.

Oleg's face flushed as red as his beard. "No crones! Russiya is a land of bravery and promise—"

But his words were drowned by the sea of mirth, and the crowd began to disperse. Rough men shoved Groa as they passed. Boys threw pebbles at her, jeering "I will go!" as she hobbled slowly back

7

up Kingsgate.

It was too late to reopen her jewelry cupboard, and no one bought her old-fashioned trinkets anyway. Wearily she limped inside the wattle-walled hut that had once been her husband's blacksmith shop, hoping that she might find refuge from the insults of the day. But Thorleif had been dead for fifteen years, and although the hut still technically belonged to her, she had gradually been reduced to the role of an unwelcome guest. Forges had been banned in the old part of town because of the fire danger, and she had no children to carry on the trade anyway, so she had invited Bjarne to run the place as an inn. She had felt sorry for him then, a scarred orphan who had lost a hand in battle.

Today the dirt-floored rooms were crowded with travelers who sat on stump chairs, ladling mutton soup with horn spoons. Bjarne hurried about, balancing bowls between his left hand and the fleshy knob that had been his right. The scar on his face had sliced his mouth sideways into a permanent smirk. Still, his lips twitched downward at the sight of Groa.

"We're full up, hag," Bjarne whispered fiercely. "No meat. No chairs. Fetch your own broth and keep out of the way. Where's the silver you promised?"

"I had no sales today—" she began, but he cut her off angrily.

"Just don't look anyone in the eye. You scare the customers."

Groa sighed. Her oddly mismatched eyes—one green and one blue—had once been deemed beautiful. And as for food—well, she didn't eat much anymore.

The kitchen was just as crowded, with strangers standing about the open hearth so closely that it would be hard to reach the big iron kettle suspended from a tripod. Worse, she had to pass beside the water trough on the way.

"Oops, Your Highness. Underfoot, are we?" As usual, the slave maid Solveig had chosen just that moment to dump a bucket of water into the trough, and as usual, it had sloshed onto Groa's leather shoes. Once Groa had made the mistake of confiding how painful her joints became when they were wet. Now even the slave girl had learned to make her suffer.

Still she managed to reach a bowl from the stave wall with shelves. There was no need to take a knife from the rack if she could have no meat. She dipped up some broth and cowered against a corner post to sip her meager meal.

More than once, overlooked in the shadows, she had learned secrets of value to an old sorceress. That evening the conversations proved to be especially interesting. Nearly all of the travelers at the inn were Viking refugees from Harald Fairhair's war to unify Norway. And nearly all of them were talking about the strange yellow-sailed ship on the beach.

"They're Swedish," a black-bearded, heavy-set man growled. He thumped the table with his fist, clanging his iron armband. "You can hear it in the sing-song way they talk Norse."

A tall, thin man in an elegant red jacket countered, "Yes, but not from Sweden. I've heard of this place, Russiya. It's a colony in the marshy forests across the Baltic. The Slavs there are short, dark, and leaderless. To them we are as gods."

"Marshy forests?" An older man with a square white beard asked. He wore the thick silver rings of a noble but had drunk enough ale that his speech was slurred. "What kind of place is that for Vikings? Iceland would look more like home. Fjords, mountains, and grass as deep as a horse's withers."

"Have you been to Iceland?" The red-jacketed man asked, lifting an eyebrow.

The older man grumbled. "No, but we've all heard—"

"Well, I visited your Valhalla last winter. That island has mountains of liquid fire, wastelands of black rock, more ice than grass, and no woods worthy of the name. Do you know what Icelanders say to do if you're lost in one of their forests?"

The older man shook his head.

"Stand up."

Even Groa laughed, her cackle lost amid the men's voices.

"If you're building ships or houses," the man in the red jacket continued, "You'll wish for marshy forests instead of Iceland's scrub."

Just then Bjarne came by, clearing empty bowls from the table. When he reached for the older man's drinking horn, however, a flattened palm chopped at his wrist. "Stop, thief!"

Bjarne withdrew his hand in alarm. "A thousand pardons, Jarl Bork. I thought you were done."

The old Viking squinted at him from beneath bushy white eyebrows.

"I've still a little ale in this horn, Bjarne. Be careful, thief, or you'll lose your other hand as you did your first. Bring us refills!"

"Yes, of course." Bjarne's scarred lip twitched as he retreated.

Groa nearly dropped her bowl, struck by a sudden realization. Bjarne's hand had not been cut off in battle, as he claimed, but rather as punishment for theft! How could she—a sorceress—have been so blind? All these years she had been tricked into letting him steal ownership of the inn. And now how could she claim it back?

A younger man standing behind the table crossed his arms. "Forest or not, I'm still taking my family to Iceland. There I can start my own farm on land that isn't overrun with small, dark foreigners."

The red-jacketed man turned to study him. "Yes, you might do well on a farm. Why would silver dirhams or glass beads tempt a plowboy like you?"

The young man wrinkled his brow. "Riches can't be plowed up from marshy forests."

The overweight, black-bearded man asked, "How do these Swedes reach lands with silver and glass?"

"By rowing a thousand miles on rivers," the man in the red jacket explained. "That's why they're called the Rus—the rowers. Their leader is the most famous oarsman of all, Rurik."

"Where do they get such names?" the jarl asked.

The men at the table shook their heads, silent for once.

"Well, I'm not rowing with them to the end of the earth," Jarl Bork said. "But I'll sure as Hel trade for their treasures."

"Me too," the fat man agreed. "I have some amber and a few furs to spare."

"What they really want is Norse steel." The white-bearded jarl finished his mead and banged the table for more. Drink had made him incautious. He lowered his voice, as if this would suffice to keep his secrets. "My slaves at Jarlsberg have been digging for treasure too. Closer to home, at Asa's hill."

Groa couldn't help but gasp. Fortunately the murmurs of the men hid her startled wheeze. Norway's king had buried his beloved grandmother that winter in a dragonship four miles north of Tunsberg. He had topped the grave with boulders and a gigantic earthen mound to discourage looters. Jarl Bork, with an estate on a nearby hill, had been a rival to King Harald before the Great War. The thought of his

10

men violating such a tomb made Groa's blood run cold. She tried to read the jarl's mind, but found it too muddled to hear. What was mind-reading, anyway, but the mundane skill of listening to people?

"How is this possible?" the fat man whispered back. "The king posted guards."

"Guards can be bribed," Bork bragged. "And the king himself is away in Horthaland, wooing some princess. My men have worked on moonlit nights, tunneling in from the side. They hide the dirt in a pit and cover their entrance with sod."

"But there was no treasure buried with Queen Asa," the man in the red jacket objected. "What would you want with old wooden sleds and looms?"

"My men have found their prize," Bork replied darkly. "A blade of fine Norse steel."

"Fenris!" Groa said in horror. This time her voice was clear enough to be heard. But it echoed every man's thoughts, as if one of them had spoken. Bork slowly turned his head, as if searching for the voice. For a moment, as his gaze swept past the shadows concealing Groa, his eyes gleamed red. Outside, a wolf howled in the night.

"What use could that sword be to you?" the man in the red jacket asked quietly. "Every man in Norway can recognize the cursed sword Harald took from the Vikings at Hafrsfjord."

The jarl replied, "You know the verse, 'Fenris vests the Vikings' fate.' Did our cause die at Hafrsfjord? If what the skalds say is true—that the sword will swing at Ragnarök—then the blade must see the light of day once more." He chuckled. "Tonight my men are selling it to a Swede in exchange for a treasure."

"Ale all around!" Bjarne exclaimed, barging into the room with a pitcher in his good hand. "On the house, to show we have no hard feelings toward the noble jarl. Solveig, bring a candle so I can see where I'm pouring."

Bjarne's slave followed him with a taper as he made the rounds. When the men made room for him to refill Jarl Bork's horn, the candle lit the corner where Groa crouched with her empty bowl.

"It's the crone from the beach!" the fat man exclaimed.

The young man mimicked her words at the harbor that afternoon, "I will go!"

All the men laughed except Bjarne. "She will go to bed, is where

she'll go," he said scowling. He took her roughly by the arm and nearly dragged her out of the room. "I told you to stay out of the way."

"This is my house," she objected, but her words were feeble.

"Not anymore, and it's full. You'll have to sleep in the courtyard on
the forge stone."

"It's not covered. I'll catch my death."

"If only," Bjarne muttered. He shoved her out the doorway.

Groa fell hard to her knees on the cobbles of the dark yard. She
cowered there, hurting inside and out, too weary even for tears.

"And take your cursed box!" Bjarne pitched an iron-bound chest
after her and slammed the door.

Why had she lived so long, she wondered, if only to suffer? Even
her sorcery now seemed like a sham. Her spells had worked no miracles—certainly not for her. Her prognostications had come to pass
more often than not, but only because any half-wit could guess what
was likely to happen.

Odin, the god who knew all and saw all, may have given the gift
of second sight to Asa, Harald's blind grandmother, but the prankster
seemed to have granted Groa nothing but the curse of endless life.

In all these years her one great joy had been Thorleif. She clutched
her hands together, feeling the silver ring he had made for her—two intertwined biting beasts, locked as tightly as she and Thorleif had been
in love. She reached out for the box, another small reassurance. Her
fingers traced the iron curlicues and rivets that Thorleif had wrought.
Smaller than the sea chests that sailors used as seats on their voyages,
the box held more than just her few nice clothes. It held memories. It
held love.

She took a deep breath, gathering what strength she had left. Then
she crawled to her feet and set about preparing for the night.

Thorleif's forge was circular because he had built it atop a discarded
millstone. Still black from fires, the stone might be large enough for a
bed if she stood the chest at one end as a footrest. The only cushion
would have to be straw. She took some from the pile beside the privy,
where it had been left for those who cared to wipe themselves. Bjarne
had installed a rail to keep drunks from falling into that hideous pit.
Not only did the stench pervade the courtyard, but she knew men
would be staggering out at all hours to relieve themselves.

Groa looked up at the sky. No stars. It might rain, and it would surely be cold. She took an old sailcloth from a stack of firewood. Then, after squatting to use the privy herself, she climbed up on the millstone and wrapped herself as tightly as possible against the humiliation of being forgotten by the gods.

* * *

The god that appeared to Groa in her dream that night was not the one she wanted. Wolves raced down from the fjells, their eyes red and their fangs white. When they reached Queen Asa's grave the largest male stood atop the mound, howling. The others burrowed in from the side, digging a den. As an icy moon rose across the fields, the howl slowly changed into a deep-throated laugh. The wolf atop the mound stood on its hind legs. Its hair whitened. Its snout and ears shrank, turning into the grizzled features of Jarl Bork. Only the glowing red eyes remained unchanged.

"Bring forth my progeny!" Bork commanded. At once young wolves began emerging from the burrow beneath him—curious, slavering, and eager.

Groa wanted to stop them, but her legs were leaden and her hands crippled. Fenris was loose, and she could do nothing. "Odin!" she cried in despair. "Help me, All-Father! Help us all."

Bork laughed at her. Then he roared to his countless wolf-pups, "Devour the world! End the age of men! Go and destroy!"

Already some of the young wolves had begun loping off into the night. A dozen others circled closer to Groa, snarling and snapping. Gleaming teeth nipped at her tunic.

Then a shadow flew across the moon. Black wings slowly circled the black sky above the burial mound.

"KRAAAK!" the raven cawed, studying Groa with a single yellow eye.

Were the wolves becoming smaller? No, Groa realized, somehow she was growing larger. Her legs straightened. Her hands unclenched.

"Stop her!" Jarl Bork cried, the loose flesh on his face trembling with rage.

Wolves lunged at Groa, trying to sink their teeth into her legs.

But she had grown so tall that she easily kicked the attackers aside. She grabbed half a dozen others with her hands and hurled them across the fields. Soon she was so tall that Bork himself seemed no bigger than a pup. When she bent down to pick him up, however, she found that the jarl had turned as hard as steel. And when she opened her hand, all that she held in her fingers was a cold light.

* * *

Groa awoke in the cold light of an early Norwegian dawn with the strange feeling that she was somehow larger. Certainly her legs and arms now hung out over the rim of the millstone, but that might be because she wasn't curled so tightly under the sailcloth. She stretched, fearing that everything would ache after her night outdoors on a stone.

Miraculously, nothing hurt. In fact, she felt wonderfully renewed. She sat up, swinging her feet to the ground. Then she pulled aside the sailcloth and stared at herself in disbelief.

She really was bigger! Or no—now that she felt herself through her tunic, she was merely straighter than before. And more muscular too.

She stood up, marveling that this must still be part of the dream. And yet the dream itself was fading. And here she was, standing in a cobbled courtyard beside a privy. The tunic that had once nearly hung to the ground scarcely reached her knees. Her hands were unwrinkled. Her fingers no longer curled into claws.

Dizzily she sat back on the edge of the millstone. What could have happened? Never before had her attempts at sorcery produced such astonishing results—with the possible exception of the day she had summoned Fenris in Thorleif's shop. But that had been long ago, when she was twenty.

Struck by a sudden thought, she put her hands to her face. The wrinkles of age were gone. Her hair was long, thick, and as ashy-blond as it had been on that fateful day. Quickly she unpinned one of the two keys dangling below the shoulder strap of her tunic. She unlocked the box beside the forge and rummaged through the clothes until she found the little silver mirror that Thorleif had given her.

The face that looked back at her from the tarnished plate was flush with youth, as if she were looking through time. She still recognized herself—one eye was emerald green and the other a piercing blue—but this was the face she had worn at the age of twenty.

14

Suddenly the door banged open and the young man from last night shambled into the courtyard yawning. He stopped before her as if struck by Thor's thunder. "By the gods! I beg your pardon, miss. I was just—I need to—"

"Go ahead," Groa said, her voice wonderfully musical. She waved him toward the privy. "I've seen bigger men than you before."

He swallowed hard. "If you say so, miss." Blushing, he stepped to the rail and lifted his tunic. When he was done he dared to wink on his way back to the inn. "Lovely morning for a lovely girl."

Groa sat back on the millstone and slapped her forehead. This would never do! Even if she was dreaming, she would have to come up with some explanation before Bjarne and the others showed up. What would they think? That she had abducted Groa and stolen her clothes?

The fact that her eyes still seemed to be mismatched gave her an idea. No one would believe she was Groa, but per-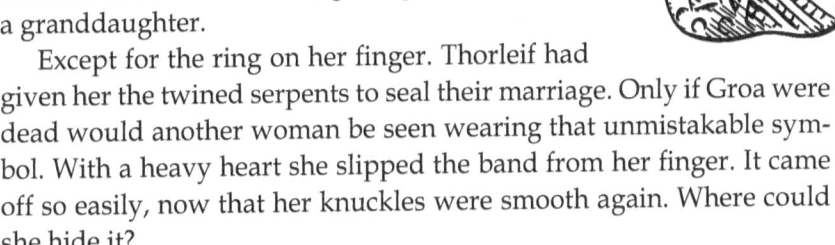haps she could pass as the granddaughter Groa never had? As she thought out the details of her plan she went to use the privy herself.

Just fifteen minutes later she was ready. She had hurriedly changed her old tunic for a light blue woolen shift from the chest. She hadn't worn it for years because it hung so poorly. Now it fit marvelously, with a saucy cling. After combing out her hair and tying it over her shoulder, she checked in the mirror. Yes, perhaps she could be a granddaughter.

Except for the ring on her finger. Thorleif had given her the twined serpents to seal their marriage. Only if Groa were dead would another woman be seen wearing that unmistakable symbol. With a heavy heart she slipped the band from her finger. It came off so easily, now that her knuckles were smooth again. Where could she hide it?

Not in the box. If someone found it there, they would know. Then she thought: What if it were to return to the forge where it was made? She smiled sadly, thinking of Thorleif. Because he had built his forge on a millstone there was a small square hole in the middle. Safe in that stony cache, even the most precious ring might while away the years until it could be reclaimed.

The instant she dropped the ring, the door from the inn banged open again.

"What the—?" Bjarne sputtered. "Then it's true!"

Groa paled, her fears rushing in upon her. "What is true?"

"The kid from Thelamork said there's a beautiful girl at the privy. Everyone's been afraid to go pee."

"Oh! Well, you can tell them to come on out."

Bjarne crossed his arms. "Who are you? And where's Groa? I told her to sleep out here last night."

"Did you really?" Groa crossed her arms to match him. "You sent my grandmother, the owner of this house, to sleep on a millstone in the courtyard?"

Bjarne hesitated. "Your grandmother?"

Groa leaned forward, pointing to her own mismatched eyes. "Recognize this look? It runs in the family."

"But how—why—"

"We're going to Russiya. I've just come back to pick up a few of grandmother's things."

The innkeeper's mouth, sliced by his scar, opened and closed crookedly.

Groa suggested, "You could make yourself useful by preparing us a packet of provisions."

When Bjarne finally found his voice he bellowed, "Solveig!"

The maid peered out anxiously from the doorway. "Yes, master?"

"Do you know anything about this?" He pointed to Groa.

Solveig covered her mouth with her hand. "No, master! I had no idea a noble lady was at the inn." She bowed. "Would you care for breakfast, my lady?"

Groa bit out the words, "Your Highness."

A look of confusion crossed the maid's face.

Bjarne explained, "This is Groa's granddaughter, come to collect her things."

"Her—? Oh my!" Solveig stammered, "D-did your noble grandmother tell you about her happy life here at the inn, Your Highness?"

"She did." Groa advanced slowly, feeling her old balance and strength return. At twenty she had been renowned as an athlete in Vestfold, shocking everyone by defeating men at wrestling. That

notoriety had pushed her into the equally notorious profession of
sorcery.

The maid backed through the doorway, mumbling nervously,
"Then you know that we were only fooling, Your Highness."

Groa's hand shot out like a viper, clutching Solveig's wrist. In an
instant she had bent the maid's
arm backwards. Groa hesitated,
considering what level of punishment the girl deserved.

"Oops," Groa said, untwist-
ing the arm while swinging the
girl backwards into the water
trough. Water splashed across the
kitchen, sending a cloud of sooty
steam hissing up from the hearth.
"Underfoot, are we?"

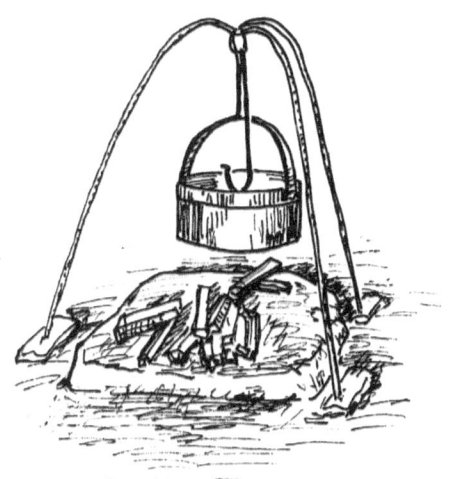

By now everyone in the inn
was awake, watching this show
with amusement.

Bjarne approached, his hand in the air. "You can't just come in here
and—"

He stopped short when Groa scooped half a dozen knives off the
wall rack. The blades were Thorleif's work—sharp and finely balanced.
She weighed one in her hand, remembering her old skills.

"Give back my knives," Bjarne demanded, facing her from the
stave wall.

"Very well." She flipped a knife end over end. It thunked into the
wooden wall, pinning the left sleeve of Bjarne's tunic.

While he tugged at this sleeve, unwilling to tear the wool, she
flipped a second knife. It caught his other sleeve, trapping him against
the wall like a beetle.

"Ow!" Bjarne cried, although he had not been cut. "You're no
granddaughter. You're a brigand!"

"No, Bjarne. You are the brigand." Groa aimed a knife at his left
leg, and succeeded in pinning his pantaloon to the wall. "You lost your
hand as a thief, not as a warrior." A fourth knife whirled across the
room, but he moved his right leg just in time.

Groa clucked her tongue. Even at the age of twenty her aim had not

17

been perfect. She balanced a fifth knife in her hand. "You came here to rob my grandmother of her home."

She aimed at his crotch, squinting.

"No!" Bjarne cried.

The knife flashed end over end. The people who had been watching gasped.

Thunk! The knife pinned a flap of pantaloon just half an inch from Bjarne's manhood.

The innkeeper's eyes rolled back in his head and he fainted, sagging from his pinned clothes like a sodden scarecrow.

Groa tilted the sixth and final knife between her fingers. "Does anyone else have a problem with my grandmother?"

Heads shook vehemently.

"Very well. Then we're off to Russiya, the land of bravery and promise. But remember—this inn is ours, and I will be back."

She slipped the knife inside her shift and fetched the iron-bound box from the courtyard. On the way back through the inn she stepped on Jarl Bork's toes.

"Oops."

The jarl sputtered, "You will pay for this."

"Send the bill to Russiya." She stalked past him to the door.

On the street she paused, unpinned the second key from her shift, and opened the iron door of her little jewelry booth. The trinkets were silver, after all, and perhaps their old-fashioned patterns would be more popular in the colony of Russiya than they were in Norway, where styles changed so quickly.

She scooped everything into her iron-bound box and strode down Kingsgate, balancing the box on her hip as if she owned the world.

If this was a dream, she never wanted to wake up. Already she could imagine Oleg welcoming her aboard the ship that would take her away. Or no—she would bat her eyes at the handsome young Vlad. Perhaps yesterday's presentiment would come true after all.

Ahead lay another lifetime of adventure. And yet, at the back of her mind, a niggling worry remained from the wisps of a different dream. Why had she been granted this gift? And what payment would the gods eventually demand?

CHAPTER 2
STOCKHOLM, 1960

"I will go." Helen Gustmeyer was only fifteen, but her mother Mette had long since realized that the willful girl was able to cook up more than her share of mischief.

Mette sighed. "I thought you didn't care about the *Vasa*." In fact, there wasn't much to see at the archeological site. The sunken ship she had come to Stockholm to raise would still be underwater for at least another six months.

"But you're taking the American ambassador."

"A *candidate* for ambassador." The man was little more than a tourist at this point, but even Mette felt the warmth of his reflected fame. Mr. Jay Bonworthy, a Texas oil derrick manufacturer, had been suggested for the post of American ambassador to Sweden by his friend, the newly elected President John F. Kennedy. The world was swooning before the glamor of the Kennedys, as if they were American royalty—a ray of hope in dark times.

"Please?" When Helen pouted, tipping her head so her shoulder-length golden hair framed her face, it was difficult to say no. Helen had the tall, noble forehead that ran in the family, but while her mother's eyes were blue and just slightly askew, Helen's dark brown eyes were as straight and wide as an owl's, as if she were always staring in wonder. What Mette envied most, however, were her daughter's beautiful blond locks. Her own brown hair tended to frizz out sideways like a fright wig, even with hats and hairbands. Some days it was hard to look as professional as her position required.

"Then put on something nice. And no nonsense."

When the girl dashed to her room, Mette shook her head. Raising a daughter was every bit as mysterious as raising a sunken ship. Until the girl emerged from her teens and broke the surface of adulthood you really couldn't be sure what you'd got.

* * *

By the time Mette was driving her Saab across the stone bridge to Gamla Stan, the island at Stockholm's historic center, Helen had tuned the car radio to Elvis Presley's "Jailhouse Rock." A sugar coating of frost lingered in the long shadows cast by the low November sun. The tires thumped on cobblestones. As they approached the front of the palace courtyard, Mette leaned over and switched the radio off.

There could be little doubt that the man with a white cowboy hat and bolo tie was the American she had been asked to take on a tour. Who else would wear white socks with a black suit? Beside him a Swedish attache with a narrow tie was smoking a cigarette.

Mette parked by the curb. While she was getting a portfolio of papers from the back seat Helen opened the passenger door, boldly walked up to the American, and asked in English, "Are you Mr. Bonworthy?"

"Well!" The Texan swept off his hat, revealing a flat-topped crewcut. He looked like he'd been shaved by a lawn mower. "This is indeed an honor, Mrs. Gustmeyer. If I'd known Swedish scientists are all as pretty as Liv Ullman I'd have studied harder in school."

Mette closed the car door firmly, holding the portfolio to her breast like a shield. "*I* am Mrs. Mette Gustmeyer. May I introduce my fifteen-year-old daughter Helen?"

"But—" Bonworthy looked from one to the other, perplexed. Then he laughed. "At first I thought she was driving the car. Forgot you Swedes drive on the wrong side of the road."

"The government is considering having us switch from left to right," Mette admitted. Why did it bother her so much to be confused with Helen? Was it that the girl was already taller than her? Or that Helen really was cleverer at dressing to advantage? While Mette had put on a standard pin-striped skirt suit, Helen had worn a snappy

20

white dress with a black belt, black lapels, and a hem that barely covered her knees. Wasn't she cold?

Helen broke the awkward pause with a smile. "So have you been to meet the king?" The girl nodded toward the palace. Two stiff soldiers with blue uniforms and gold helmets stood at attention beside the entry.

The American turned his hat in his hands. "Not yet."

The Swedish attache put in, "Mr. Bonworthy will present his credentials to the king after he has been confirmed by the U.S. Senate. In the meantime he is here to learn as much about Sweden as he can." He motioned with his cigarette to Mette, dropping ash on the sidewalk. "The Ministry for Foreign Affairs would be grateful if you could show him your work and see him back to the Grand Hotel by six."

Mette nodded. "Yes, of course."

The attache nodded back, said "*Hej då*," and turned to go, almost as curt in his manner as the palace guards.

Helen took Mr. Bonworthy by the hand. "Come on. We'll tell you about my Mom's boat."

Mette's Saab was the color of an eggplant and nearly the same shape, with smoothly rounded fenders. Mette held open the passenger door for Mr. Bonworthy, leaving her daughter to get into the back seat.

"Have you seen much of Sweden so far?" Mette asked, sliding in behind the wheel.

"Just churches and old buildings," the American replied. "Only saw the outside of the king's place. Looks more like a courthouse than a castle to me."

"It's as elegant as Versailles on the inside," Mette assured him. "Parquet floors and high ceilings. Gilt everywhere."

Bonworthy sighed. "My wife wanted Paris. She stayed home in a snit because France was taken."

Helen leaned forward eagerly from the back. "Have you really met Present Kennedy? And Jaqueline?"

"Oh sure. I got a summer place next to theirs in Massachusetts, on Martha's Vineyard. Donated a few million to his campaign."

Helen gasped.

"Pocket change in our circles, sweetheart. Jack's a popular guy back home in Dallas. The rest of Texas, not so much."

"Really?" Mette turned right along the waterfront in front of the

Grand Hotel. A line of white swans was paddling along the nearly waveless bay. "Why?"

"Folks worry that Kennedy is secretly a socialist, like you Scandahoovians. Is it true the Communist Party's legal here?"

"Sweden *is* a democracy," Mette replied cautiously. Sensing that it would be best to change the subject she asked, "Have you had lunch?"

"Sort of. I asked for a hamburger. The closest thing they had were these dinky meatballs in gravy. The State Department guy said you've actually banned McDonalds here. What kind of country allows Communists but not hamburgers?"

This time it was Helen who saved the conversation. "Someday I'd like to go to America. My uncle Lars sometimes lives there."

"Oh? Where?"

"All over," the girl replied cheerily. "He's a spy for the CIA."

Mette laughed out loud.

"What? He might be, Mom."

Mette shook her head. This was exactly why she shouldn't have brought Helen. "You'll have to forgive my daughter's overactive imagination. My brother Lars works for LogistEx, an American import-export firm. He's currently based in Berlin, so Helen dreams he's secretly involved in international intrigue."

Mr. Bonworthy cleared his throat. "You seem to have a diverse family, Mrs. Gustmeyer."

Mette shifted the Saab to third gear. "My grandfather was a professor of archeology at Cornell. The rest of my heritage is Norwegian, although I grew up in Denmark. Helen here has been raised Swedish."

Helen piped in, "And Dad's a Jew."

The Texan whistled. "Only in America. I suppose that's why they picked you as my tour guide. You talk English like a Yankee. Last night when I turned on the TV in my hotel they had a Perry Mason show with the voices taped over in Swedish. Raymond Burr sounded like Donald Duck with a slide whistle stuck in his craw."

"Actually, they chose me as your tour guide because of the *Vasa*." Mette drove across the iron bridge to the island of Skeppsholm. A decorative gold crown perched atop the bridge's railing, as if the king had left his royal hat while passing by. Pleasure boats bobbed in the bay. Beyond, the spires of Stockholm rose from a horizon of yellow stone buildings.

"What's a Vasa?"

"A ship. To understand Sweden you need to understand our history." Mette drove across Skeppsholm, an island with a wooded park full of old schools and museums. Then she slowed to cross a much smaller bridge to Kastellholmen, a smaller island topped with a turreted orange fortress. Lying at anchor to the right was a gigantic gray destroyer, its deck bristling with gun turrets.

"Holy cow," the Texan muttered.

"Sweden has the fourth largest navy in the world," Mette said.

"But you don't have the bomb. Why aren't you in NATO?"

"We've been neutral a long time. And cautious. Our navy has hollowed out caves into the solid rock of sea islands so the fleet can survive even a nuclear attack. But the warship I'm taking you to is older. Much older."

On the far side of the bridge they turned left past a small marina. Mette parked at an empty dock. Bonworthy got out, looked around, and scratched his head.

"Weird, isn't it?" Helen said, squirming out of the back seat. "All this fuss about a boat you can't see."

"The *Vasa* sank more than three hundred years ago," Mette explained. She pointed to a pair of barges offshore. "A team of divers has been working from those barges to seal the gunports and clean out the debris so we can start lifting her. She's in thirty-two meters of water, but everything inside seems to be intact. It's a time capsule from a lost age when Sweden was a superpower."

Mr. Bonworthy frowned at the otherwise empty bay.

"There's a model inside I can show you," Mette suggested. But when she turned toward the office she was embarrassed to see that vandals had struck again. During the night someone had spray-painted three clumsy, upward-pointing arrows on the brick wall beside the door.

"Weird," Helen said. "Always the same graffiti."

"Looks like someone's pointing out where to put your ship," the American commented.

Without reply Mette unlocked the door. She had no answers about the graffiti. Cleaning the brick would take one of her workers all day. For now she would simply continue the tour.

"Watch your step on the wet floor. This first room is where we store the air tanks, wet suits, and other diving gear. We estimate the project will require about two thousand dives. Our first task was to clear a tunnel through the mud under the ship for the cables. We used specially designed spray nozzles and suction tubes."

"Sounds as dangerous as oil derrick work."

"We haven't had any serious accidents." Mette opened a door to a second room. Office desks, blueprints, and nautical charts lined the walls. "Here's our command center. And this—" she paused dramatically before a table with a three-foot-long model of a fully-rigged ship. "This is our holy grail." Two decks lined with cannon portals striped the ship's sides. The stern rose up to a four-story officers' cabin decorated with gilt carvings of lions.

"Wow. Were all Viking ships this fancy?"

"Viking ships?" Mette repeated, nonplussed.

"Sure. That's what Sweden's famous for, isn't it? The Vikings used ships like this to terrorize Europe."

Even Helen was hiding a smile.

Mette explained slowly. "The Vikings lived seven hundred years before the *Vasa* was built. Viking longships had one mast and a single deck. They had no guns. The *Vasa* has sixty-four cannons, three masts, thirty sails, and five decks. She was built during the reign of King Gustavus Adolphus in 1628, when Sweden ruled the Baltic. The king built a hundred ships like this to flaunt his power."

Bonworthy tipped back his cowboy hat. "Don't you have any Viking ships?"

"They haven't been well preserved in Sweden. I've helped excavate a few in Norway and Denmark."

The Texan examined the model more closely. "So why'd this one sink? Was it outgunned?"

"The *Vasa* just tipped over. On her maiden voyage she sailed about a kilometer. As soon as she got a little wind in her sails, she keeled over."

"Looks top-heavy with all those cannons."

"The weight of the guns shouldn't have mattered that much. It's a puzzle we won't solve until we bring her up."

Helen interjected, "If."

Mette gave her daughter another warning glance.

Bonworthy noticed the exchange and raised an eyebrow. "If?"

Mette was about the explain the technical obstacles that lay ahead—that no one had raised such an enormous wooden structure from the seafloor before—when she noticed a rapid movement outside the window. The lead diver, Per Fälting, was stumbling across the dock in his heavy diving suit. Had there been an accident after all?

"Excuse me a moment." She hurried back to the building's entrance to meet the diver at the door. "What's wrong, Per?" she asked in Swedish. "Is someone hurt?"

Per shook his head, trying to catch his breath. He had removed his diving helmet, but water dripped from his thick, awkward diving suit. "No, it's just—"

"Take it easy. Sit down." She motioned for him to come inside. "Helen, make some coffee."

The girl sulked, but began filling a pot at a sink nonetheless.

The diver sat down heavily and wiped seawater from his eyes. "We've found a body."

"What! Where?"

"On the lower gundeck. I was inside, clearing mud by a porthole, when I started coming across bones. They look human."

Jay Bonworthy had understood none of this Swedish, but he recognized the solemn tone. "What's up?"

"They found a dead guy," Helen explained in English, taking coffee cups from a shelf.

"Helen!" Mette objected.

Mr. Bonworthy took off his hat. "I'm sorry to hear it. Who was it?"

"We don't know," Mette said. "The *Vasa* had a crew of 145 sailors and 300 soldiers. Dozens must have gone down with the ship. These are the first remains we've found."

The diver switched to English as well. "I noticed an artifact near the bones. I would have left it in place for you, but I was afraid it might be lost in the mud." He opened a pocket of his diving suit and withdrew a handful of mud with a glint of silver.

Mette carefully picked a silver medallion from the diver's muddy palm. She turned it over in her fingers, mesmerized. "Incredible."

"Cool," Helen said, wide-eyed.

"Looks like your time capsule could be a treasure chest," Bonworthy put in.

"No, don't you see?" Mette wiped the metal clean with her fingers. "It's from the wrong era. A design with a pair of intertwined biting beasts? This is Norse, much older than the seventeenth century."

"Maybe it's a Viking ship after all." The American suggested, "Can you tell the age with carbon dating or something?"

Mette shook her head. "It's not easy to date silver." She turned the medallion in her hand. "But this looks like an Arab dirham that's been stamped with a different pattern. Then someone punched a hole to use it as a necklace."

With the sharp eyes of a fifteen-year-old, Helen was the first to notice the inscription. "Look! The same markings as the spray paint."

Mette examined the medallion more closely. Baffled, she saw that three arrows had in fact been scratched across its face. "How on earth—?"

The American guffawed. "That's rich! Your vandals are pulling your leg, leaving graffiti everywhere."

"On silver?" Mette doubted that whoever spray-painted the arrows on the office wall could afford this kind of prank. But the alternative—that the same puzzling symbols had been used here 333 years ago—seemed impossible.

"Maybe these arrows are pointing down instead of up," Bonworthy said. "Hard to tell with a necklace."

Mette took a magnifying glass from a drawer, walked to a window, and inspected the medallion in better light. Beside the arrows was a fourth symbol—a line with two faint but unmistakable branches: ᚠ.

For a moment a flush of fear made her heart stand still. She stared out the window, her lips pale.

Helen stopped pouring coffee. "What is it, Mom?"

"A rune. *Fehu*."

The American asked, "And that means what?"

Helen had learned enough about her mother's work to know. "The F-rune stands for cattle, wealth, — or Fenris."

"Who?"

"An old wolf god."

Mette was still looking out the window, lost in thought. "Then the other symbols aren't arrows at all. They're runes. T-runes."

Her daughter nodded. "For Tyr."

Mr. Bonworthy arched his eyebrows.

Mette explained. "The god of war."

CHAPTER 3
TUNSBERG, 882

Boarding the yellow-sailed ship to Russiya did not go as smoothly as Groa had hoped. Still swaggering after her victorious departure from Bjarne at the inn, she had imagined using her new, mysteriously youthful beauty to seduce Vlad. After all, she had foreseen that the handsome, black-haired purser would invite her to sail away with him. But when she neared the harbor there were two other ships beside the Swedish one, and the crowd of people loading and trading goods was so thick that it took her quite a while to find Vlad at all. When she did, he was so busy weighing out silver and amber that he didn't give her a glance.

"I'd like to go to Russiya," she said, pouring honey into her words. Vlad's dark eyes and protruding jaw were every bit as attractive as they had been the day before.

"Sorry, fully up. Twenty-eight single women already."

A little desperately, Groa added, "I can row." Perhaps it was a mistake, thinking she could run away to a wondrous land where silver dirhams grew on trees. But after storming out of her own house, throwing knives and stepping on toes, it would be hard to turn back.

The purser finally looked up. His expression softened. A slow smile revealed even rows of white teeth. Vlad looked from one to the other of Groa's mismatched eyes. He was used to women offering themselves to him—sometimes with a subtle flirt and sometimes with a more obvious suggestion. He took pride in his looks, carefully shaving his square chin and oiling his black hair before a mirror each morning. Perhaps the young woman before him was worthy of his attention. There was more of interest here than just her strange eyes— an attitude that suggested a challenge.

"Well," Vlad said, "We Rus are always looking for people who are handy with an oar."

Groa tossed her hair. "Then will you beg me to come?"

"What is your name, wench?"

"I'm Groa."

"And what's in the little box?"

"Silver jewelry. Some clothes."

Vlad tilted his head. The girl really was a besotted neophyte. No real oarsman would presume to row while sitting on a jewelry box. It was touching when a girl couldn't help herself. He enjoyed having that effect. He lowered his voice to a whisper. "Yes, my dear. I beg you to come away to Russiya with me."

She eyed him skeptically. "Really?"

He patted her on the head. "Really, little Groa. But first you'll need to get yourself a proper sea chest." He waved a hand dismissively. "Go ask the carpenter at Thorkell's prow."

Groa was so angered by the purser's arrogance that she couldn't think of a reply. A man with a bundle of furs shoved her aside. She stumbled out of the way. Despite everything, her young body felt drawn to the purser like a bear cub to honey. But her older self was repelled by his smug, patronizing manner. She wound her hair angrily into two braids, as if her nervous hands belonged to a different person too. When she was done she felt calm enough to focus. What she needed, apparently, was a sea chest.

The two other ships on the beach belonged to Viking jarls who had otherwise been planning to accept King Harald Fairhair's amnesty by taking their clans west to Iceland, but now had been persuaded to sail east instead. Where the front of the first boat had been run up onto the gravel a stocky young man was standing on a stump, sawing a notch into the top of the blunt, square prow.

"Hello?" Groa said.

The young man turned to look at her and nearly dropped his saw. He had almost no neck, so his square, beardless head sat like a block of wood almost directly on his broad shoulders. His nose appeared to have been notched in place. It wasn't a completely ugly face, but because his mouth hung open he looked like a wooden statue.

"Are you the carpenter?" Groa asked.

"Oh!" He appeared to gather his wits. "Forgive me, miss. Yes,

I'm—I'm a carpenter."

"You don't seem sure about it." Groa had seen this startled expression in men before—in fact, just that morning she had been ogled by a swain in the inn's courtyard. It was gratifying to be considered pretty, even by a man as homely as this.

"Vlad," she said, and then caught herself. She had been thinking about the purser. She cleared her throat. "Vlad says I might sail on Thorkell's ship if I have a sea chest. What are you carving, carpenter?"

"I'm fixing the prow to match the other two ships. Oleg wants us to look like a fleet." He set down the saw, blew sawdust from the notch, and fit two short boards into the top of the prow at an angle. Together they formed an upward-pointing arrow.

"It's the T-rune," Groa observed. "For Tyr, the god of war."

He lowered his voice. "Oleg says he has a secret. A sword he won't show anyone until we're underway. He worries me. I'm not sure I really want to go along. Are—are you going?"

She sidestepped the question. "Why are you so unsure?"

He looked down. "I'm a third son. My eldest brother got the farm. The next got a ship. I got a box of woodworking tools." The three-foot-long chest at his feet was as wide and plain as a bench.

"What's your name, carpenter?"

He still stared at his feet. "Hrolf."

"Rolf?"

"No, H-rolf." He kicked at the gravel of the beach. "I know. It sounds like someone throwing up."

"It's a fine name." She gave him a smile. "My name's a little strange too. I'm Groa."

"Groa?" He looked up at her. "That's so old fashioned. You're not from here, are you? I mean, I'd remember if I'd seen you before."

"Originally I'm from Skiringssal. At the Vik."

He cocked his head, although without much of a neck he couldn't tilt it very far. "The old Viking outpost? But that place has been abandoned for forty years. How—?"

Once again she changed the subject. "I'm ready to leave Norway behind. Vlad says Thorkell is short of rowers. Can you make me a sea chest?"

"This morning? Before we leave?" He bit his lip. "There's no time. You can take my box instead. I'll—I'll stay behind."

"What! You'd give up your place for a girl you've just met?"

He swallowed. "Your eyes. They're different. They're beautiful."

"No, no, no. Your toolbox is long enough to seat two. We'll share it, Hrolf."

To her surprise, he burst out laughing.

She put her hands on her hips. "What's so funny?"

"You must be a sorceress!"

Well, she was, but she didn't want to admit it now.

He shook his head. "Otherwise it makes no sense. Who would believe that the most beautiful girl in the world would want to row to Russiya beside the homeliest carpenter in Norway?"

He laughed again, so helplessly that she couldn't help but laugh as well. And she decided that sitting next to this humble young craftsman might not be so horrible after all.

Before long Groa's laughter ebbed. The man she really wanted to sit beside—despite herself—was Vlad.

* * *

For all her boasting, Groa had never actually been to sea. She was sick for the first two days. Fortunately a westerly breeze filled the sails of the three longships, pushing them across Oslo Fjord toward the straits of Denmark. Groa sat on the toolbox with her elbows on the gunwale, watching the endless waves peak past. Each roll of the ship reminded her of the carpenter's gut-wrenching name, Hrolf.

While the others on board played dice or chess, she gaped at the sea like a dying fish. Her mouth tasted as if she had been chewing her own silver jewelry. But her miraculously young body proved to be much more resilient than that of a withered hag. When the wind slowed along the sandy shore of Halland she managed to keep down some flatbread and water. She didn't dare touch the dried fish. She smiled weakly as she took her place behind an oar. Hrolf kindly let her sit on the outside so he could do most of the work, dipping and pulling the end of the oar's handle in large circles while her hands rested nearer the oarlock's pin, moving in smaller circles.

To keep the rhythm without crossing oars, everyone sang the most tedious ditty Groa had ever learned.

> We're sailing up and over,
> And sailing back down again.
> That was such a lovely song,
> We'll sing it again, all day long.
> Oh, we're sailing up and over—

Hrolf seemed never to tire, either of the stupid verse or of the endless rowing. Groa's right hand soon reddened with such a painful blister that she had to arch her palm with each stroke to keep a torn flap of skin from rubbing. By nightfall her back was so sore that she lay down on a deck plank, moaning as she tried to straighten her spine against the hard, flat oak. She fell asleep like that.

In the morning she awoke to discover that someone had wrapped her in a reindeer hide. Hrolf denied that he had access to such a luxury. Apparently Thorkell himself, the jarl who owned the ship, had taken pity on her and pulled a hide from his store of trade goods. She made her way back to the tiller to thank him, but the jarl merely waved her back to her seat with an ominous, "You'll find a way to repay me one day."

The wind had come up with the sun. To hold pace with the other two ships they had to keep the sail fully raised. To Groa's dismay, this meant they would not be stopping ashore that morning to wash themselves and refill the tubs of fresh water. Instead everyone—man and woman alike—took turns squatting over a bucket, concealing things as best they could with their tunics. Disgusted, she took her turn, dumped the waste into the sea, and rinsed the bucket in seawater for the next in line. Then she hung her head overboard, awkwardly washing her face and hands as the waves slapped past. Somehow, after this baptism in saltwater, she felt sufficiently part of the sea that chewing on a dried fish for breakfast seemed possible.

Groa felt so much stronger that morning that she took the inside seat, where the rowing would be harder. Hrolf bit his lip, watching as the blister on her right palm made her wince. He reached inside his tunic—a gray woolen cloth that was always flopping open at the shoulder—and withdrew a leather glove. Wordlessly, he held it out to her.

Groa tried it on. The glove fit her perfectly, armoring her tender palm with stiff leather.

"Where did you—" she began.

Hrolf grunted dismissively. "Rowers always have them. I don't need it for now, so I thought—" He touched her hand, blushed, and pulled up the shoulder of his floppy tunic.

Groa unpinned a key from her shirt, unlocked her little jewelry box, and took out a small silver pin. She leaned over and pinned the shoulder of his tunic in place. "I don't need this for now, so I thought—"

Hrolf flushed such a bright red that she was afraid his stubbly, straw-colored hair might catch fire. He pursed his lips as if he were holding his breath, and his eyes grew damp.

"Prepare to stroke!" A gruff voice called out from the stern. Thorkell raised a fist over his head. Twenty-two oars rose into the air, wobbling as the wooden blades aligned into two rows.

"We're due in Gotland in two days, despite the headwind," the jarl growled. "Stroke!"

The oars came down, as if the ship had two great handfuls of fingers clawing the sea to either side.

"Stroke!"

The sea splashed as the prow sliced forward. This was no morning for song. Fighting the wind, the rowers had only enough breath for a few words between each stroke. Hrolf, who shunned long speeches, did well with this interrupted, staccato style of dialogue. It gave him time to compose his thoughts and choose his words.

"You're no oarsman," Hrolf said.

Groa let several strokes pass without reply.

"Are you a silversmith?" Hrolf continued.

"My husband was." At once Groa regretted this incautious reply.

"You had a husband?"

"No," she said, but the word hurt. She had always been skillful at lying. Denying her love to Thorleif, however, felt shameful.

Five strokes later she said, "Yes. Once."

The carpenter eyed her from the side. Her green eye stared straight ahead—a gaze that seemed to penetrate the rowers, the ship, and the horizon itself.

"You are not what you seem," Hrolf commented.

"A widow? Why not?"

"From Skiringssal," Hrolf replied. And then after another stroke, "A lost city."

Neither spoke for a long time. Groa still stared straight ahead.

"What do you see?" Hrolf asked.

She shook her head and lowered her eyes. She couldn't lie to Hrolf. The man might be homely, and he was not particularly bright, but he was honest. He would always sense the truth.

"I'm never sure," she whispered.

He caught his breath. At the next stroke he exhaled the words, "I was right."

"About what?"

"You *are* a seer." And then, suddenly able to compose whole sentences, Hrolf said, "I felt it from the first. Your beauty is inside, as well as out."

She turned to him in confusion. "What?"

"Tell me, does the blue eye see the future, and the green the past?"

"Stroke!" The helmsman shouted their way. "You two, pick up your pace."

Groa sighed, pulling harder. "That's not how it works."

Hrolf's mouth had opened into an O—the same stupefied expression she had seen when they first met.

"Tell me," Hrolf whispered, "Will I come back from Russiya rich? Will I get my father's farm after all?"

She scoffed. "No. You'll build ships." She had said this without thinking. Where had this image come from?

"Ships?" he repeated, puzzled.

It made sense, that a carpenter sailing to a colony with forests might build ships. Perhaps that was how the picture had formed in her mind. "Ships like this," she said, "But lighter."

"Not oak?" he asked.

"I don't know." She pulled on the oar, shaking her head to dispel the vision. "Ships in the woods."

* * *

34

On the fifth day, with a breeze behind them again, they sailed across the choppy Baltic from the low, sandy island of Öland to the larger, rockier outpost of Gotland, where Oleg was apparently expecting to be welcomed by a Geatish jarl named Wiglaf.

Groa sighted the island late in the day, when the midsummer sun was skimming the horizon like a red, half-closed eye. At the same time, watchmen from the shore must have spotted the three incoming sails, because a bonfire roared to life on a headland. Then a second, and a third fire lit in the distance, a string of warning lights passing word ahead that longships were approaching.

"Is Oleg sure the Geats are friendly?" Groa asked Thorkell. Beacon fires were usually intended to alert a garrison. Most of Thorkell's crew were colonists, not warriors keen on battle.

"The Geats are uneasy vassals of the Swedish king, Eirik Eymundsson," Thorkell replied. "Yellow sails make them nervous. Wait and see."

As they rounded the rock skerries that rose from the sea like the backs of whales, Groa's sharp young eyes could make out half a dozen warships in the twilight, each docked before a boat shed with crews at the ready. Two hundred men with spears, bows, and gaffs were waiting for the order to attack. Shoulder to shoulder, the grim soldiers wore identical black leather armor plated with iron.

Oleg sailed his ship onto a gravel beach directly in their midst, leapt ashore, and strode alone up toward the army.

A gray-bearded man in the center of the troops began laughing. The burly man opened his arms and stepped forward to embrace the visitor. "Oleg! You old river-paddling dog. What's this I hear about you getting married?"

Groa couldn't hear the reply because by then Thorkell's ship was crunching ashore and everyone was talking. Soon the Rus crews were being escorted up a boardwalk to a gigantic stave hall. Outside were troughs where Groa and the others washed up after the long sea voyage, stacking their sea chests and their weapons in a pile. Inside the hall's massive wooden doors, two rows of torches lit dozens of plank tables and benches around a central fire pit where an ox and a pig were roasting.

"Mead for our guests from Russiya!" Wiglaf called out, taking his place at a high seat between dragon-head pillars. Then, motioning for

Oleg to take a seat to his right, he added, "Now repay our hospitality with news of your adventures. Why, my old friend, have you left your bride in Sweden this past month?"

Groa was curious enough that she moved closer to hear. Hrolf followed, sliding onto the bench near her.

Oleg took off his metal helmet and wiped aside his stringy red hair with a brawny hand. "It wasn't my choice, Wiglaf. Rurik is the leader of the Rus, not me. Before we sailed from Russiya, Rurik assigned his sister to round up colonists in Sweden. I was left to see what I could find in Denmark and Norway." He cast an eye toward his volunteer crews. The glance strafed Groa and Hrolf. He sighed. "I hope Helga did better."

"I'm sure she will," Wiglaf said.

Oleg lowered his bushy red eyebrows at the Geatish jarl. "Do you think so little of my skill with words?"

Wiglaf laughed again. Groa was beginning to realize that the Geat laughed too easily, even when it was not appropriate. "No, Oleg, you're an adequate poet, but the Swedish king has given your bride-to-be an advantage in her efforts to enlist recruits."

"Oh?" Oleg pulled his red mustache. "And what mischief has Eirik Eymundsson been up to now?"

"He wants to tax Birka."

"What! Birka is an island of free trade. The Rus, the Geats, the Swedes—everyone meets there to barter. It's been that way since the first of the Svea kings."

Wiglaf's smile dimmed. "But now King Eirik has built a rival town, Sigtuna, on a fjord closer to his capital at Uppsala. He's asking that traders and craftsmen move there, where he can *protect* them." The way Wiglaf stressed the word "protect" made it clear, even to Groa, that the word he actually meant was "tax."

Oleg scoffed. "Eirik may be a scheming dullard, but that's no concern of mine. Let him drive his subjects into our arms. In two days' time I'll have Helga in my own embrace. We'll celebrate our marriage with a grand feast in Birka and sail off to Russiya. Good riddance, I say, to the politics of Sweden." He raised his eyebrows. "Now where's this mead you promised?"

Wiglaf laughed long and loud, but he also waved to his servants to bring the drinking horns. The horns were carried in by a procession of tall blond girls in identical floor-length white linen gowns. Each maiden wore a crown of woven flowers—blue, yellow, or red.

Oleg stroked his beard, marveling, "Your Geatish mead-bearers are enchanting."

"More so in winter," Wiglaf laughed. "Then they parade into feasting halls with crowns of lit candles."

For the next hour everyone in the hall ate and drank their fill. Groa could hardly believe her appetite. In her former, nearly toothless life, she had subsisted on broth and crumbs. Tonight she astonished herself by devouring the entire ankle of a roast pig and washing it down with four horns of mead. Even then she still had room for a bowl of curds with lingonberries. Had she really been this gluttonous at the age of twenty? Or was her body trying to slake the hunger of the intervening ninety winters?

Two young men with flutes piped tunes during the meal. As the tables were being cleared, Wiglaf clapped his hands. "Come! Bring out your skalds. Recite us a tale about the Rus."

Oleg raised his bushy eyebrows toward Vlad. "My purser is the nimblest wordsmith for that task."

Vlad walked to the open area before the hearth, slicked back his dark hair, and tossed one end of his cloak over his shoulder in preparation for his performance. Groa recognized each of these moves as signs of the man's vanity. But it was no use—Vlad was simply so confident that her heart beat in her throat. His sheer physical beauty defeated all logic. Could it be that he was also an accomplished poet?

He was. With lines sweetened by alliteration and colored with clever *kenning* metaphors, Vlad wove a word-story from the history of the Rus.

Countless winters ago, Vlad recited, the oarsmen of the Rus had ventured out from their fjord east of Uppsala, curious about lands beyond the rule of the Svea kings. They found a string of islands like stepping stones that led them to Finland, the land of Lapps. Rowing east along that shore they came to the forests of the Slavs. Unlike Sweden, with a single king, the countless Slavic clans had hundreds of rival leaders. Petty raids and feuds hindered trade, leaving them poor and powerless. The Rus built a trading post in a fortress with a wooden palisade along the Volkhov River. They named their outpost Ladoga, for the huge lake that lay a few miles to the north. The Slavs who came to visit Ladoga were amazed. They could trade safely while armed guards kept the peace. The wealth of metals, furs, and art in Ladoga was unlike anything they had ever seen. And the Rus themselves seemed as gods—tall, strong, and blond.

The elders of three Slavic clans were so impressed that they asked the Rus to send them leaders who might bring this prosperity to their people. That challenge was taken up by Rurik and his two brothers, Truvor and Sineus. Rurik stayed in Ladoga to rule the lands there. Truvor built a hall at Pskov, two days' ride to the south, while Sineus founded his estate on the shore of Lake Beloye, to the west.

Vlad paused in his recitation, his eyes scanning the audience with a suspenseful challenge. Everyone knew that Rurik was sole ruler of the Rus. What had happened to his two brothers? Each time the tale was told, the story seemed to change.

> For treachery, trust no man
> Who offers fealty for free.
> Sineus was slain while sleeping,
> Truvor was poisoned at table.
> Rurik, resolved on revenge,
> Merged his might at Novgorod,
> A new fortress on the Volkhov.
> Now, to link his lands,
> He sends his sister Helga
> And his helmsman Oleg
> To gather the gallant
> And help him rule Russiya.

Vlad bowed in conclusion, holding out his cloak to each side like the wings of an eagle. Throughout the hall, fists thumped on the tables in approval. Hrolf stomped his feet enthusiastically. Beside him Groa was trying to hold back tears of admiration—or was it love? Skillful skalds were the most esteemed of men.

Wiglaf laughed. "I see you have a proper poet for your wedding feast, my old friend. But do you have a proper wedding gift?"

Oleg's eyebrows lowered until they nearly hid his gaze. "I had thought a silver band might do, in the old dragon style. Or better, two bands. The English exchange rings at marriage, a tradition I think Helga admires. But I've yet to find a worthy smith."

Hrolf jumped to his feet. "There's one right here!" he cried out proudly. To Groa's embarrassment he was pointing to her, hopping slightly from foot to foot like a boy before a race. "Her name is Groa. She sailed with us on Thorkell's ship."

"Is this true?" Oleg demanded.

The handsome Vlad cast a slow smile to Groa that made her heart swell. "I believe this young oarswoman did bring a jewelry box." Was his smile a smirk, Groa wondered?

"Then fetch it," Oleg said. He waved a hand at her as if he were brushing away dust. "Hurry, woman."

Groa felt every eye watching as she walked from the hall. In the dark outside it took her a while to find her small box amid the stack of sea chests. The hall was silent as she walked back and set the box on the table before Oleg. She unpinned the key from her tunic, opened the lid, and withdrew two old-fashioned silver rings that she had been unable to sell for years. Her old husband Thorleif's work had been masterful, but his motifs were hopelessly antiquated.

Oleg turned the rings over in his fingers. "Remarkable." He squinted at her. "And have you the sorcery to inscribe them with runes? I had imagined three Tyr-runes to match the first three prows of my fleet."

Silently Groa reached under the hem of her tunic and withdrew a sharp knife—the sixth and final blade from the Tunsberg inn. It was the knife she had not thrown.

Wiglaf drew in his breath. "Only Oleg and I may wear weapons in this hall!"

"This is a silversmith's tool," Groa replied coolly. She took the rings one at a time and held them firmly against the tabletop with her left hand while she scratched three tiny arrows inside the bands. Then she slipped the knife back under her tunic. Finally she spun the rings on the table before Oleg—two twirling silver tops that slowed, spiraled, and fell with the *kling!* of tiny bells.

Oleg picked up the rings, studying them in amazement. "How is this possible? How could an oarswoman have the rings I seek, in the dragon style I want, and yet know the wizardry of writing runes? Are you a sorceress?"

"Yes!" Hrolf declared. "She's a seer. She foretold my fate, that I would build ships in the woods of Russiya."

"A seer?" The red-bearded Viking stood up, towering before Groa like a bear. He pulled his sword from its scabbard and held it upright, inches from her face. "Have you seen this?"

Groa pulled back her hair, feigning calm. But inside, her heart was racing. Her emotions wrenched back through the decades to a distant forge fire where a foolish silversmith's wife had summoned an evil power to aid another ambitious Viking.

"It is Fenris," she said. "A sword of fate."

"And what fate do you see for me?" Oleg demanded.

The etchings on the blade danced before her eyes. There was the wolf-god, loosed upon the earth. There was Thor, striving to bind the demon with a desperate chain made from the footfalls of cats and the breath of fish. And through it all, the dread runes: *F E N R I S*.

"What fate, I asked?" Oleg bellowed. "I've heard the tales, that there is power in this old Norwegian steel, but also a curse. Tell me! Will I die by this sword?"

"No," she said, as if in a trance. "You will die by your horse."

The silence in the hall was as deep as in any troll-cave in the fjells. Why had she said such a thing?

Wiglaf was the first to laugh. "Oleg will die by his horse? But he doesn't have a horse!"

And then, as if an icy dam had melted, laughter burst through the hall. Oleg leaned back and roared. Vlad shook his head. Hrolf chuckled until tears came to his eyes.

"You have the best skalds and the best jesters," Wiglaf exclaimed, patting Oleg on the back. "More mead!"

Oleg sheathed his sword and fished a gold coin from a pouch at his waist. "Here is payment for your rings, oarswoman. And for your witty words."

Groa took the gold coin—a princely fee, a hundred times what the rings might have fetched in Norway. Then she looked up at the Viking chieftain. Suddenly Oleg's eyes seemed like dark doorways into a house. Inside that Viking hall, unknown figures crouched beside the embers of a hearth-fire, plotting destruction. What had she done?

When Oleg returned her gaze, his smile died.

CHAPTER 4
GOTLAND, 1960

My name is Helen Gustmeyer, and I'm a spy. I'm like my Uncle Lars, but for the other side, and they have no idea because they think I'm just a fifteen-year-old girl with an imaginary friend named Lenny.

In fact, I'll be sixteen in March and Lennart Bronsson is a very real nineteen-year-old guitarist at The Hammer. That's a coffee shop in the basement of a dormitory building at the University of Stockholm. I pass for a student there because I can look older when I want. We secretly call it "The Hammer and Sickle" because it's a hangout for activists. The place has red tablecloths and posters of Lenin. Everyone talks English because of the foreign students and, well, just because.

When I tell Mom I'm going roller-skating with Lenny or that I'll be doing my homework with him at the library she just smiles. I make sure she's seen me roller-skating alone or studying by myself, too. Sometimes I even ask for an extra cup of hot chocolate for Lenny. She thinks it's cute. But for God's sake, I'm almost sixteen! The real Lennart chopped up his roller skates, nailed the wheels to a rocket-shaped board, and does tricks on the concrete loading dock of the abandoned washing machine factory. He's played backup guitar at a revolutionary café in East Berlin and at a sailors' dive in Hamburg. The amp on his electric guitar rattles windows. When we study, it's Mao's *Little Red Book*, not *Pippi Longstocking*.

We've kissed a little, Lennart and me, so I guess I'm his girl. He's got nice cheekbones and light brown hair that hangs down almost to his eyebrows. He's really interested in me, always asking questions about my family and Lars and Aunt Sasha. Not everyone has real-life relatives who might secretly be working for the American CIA. And that's what might make this Christmas vacation a bit less unbearable.

41

I can't invite an imaginary friend with us to Gotland, of course, but I can act as his secret agent. I'm a girl on a mission.

Let me explain why my family goes to Gotland. It's a big island about a six-hour ferry ride from Stockholm. The whole Gustmeyer-Andersen clan, all six of us, meets there for Christmas because our apartment in Stockholm is way too small. When my grandparents in Canada died, they left Dad enough money that he bought the house of an old sea captain in Visby. It was supposed to be a summer place, a cut above the boat sheds that most Stockholmers rent in August. But because Mom's work on the *Vasa* is busiest in summer, her only time off is when it's freezing outside and you can only dream of swimming at the beach. Even now she'll be working, meeting with a farmer who says he's dug up something valuable in a field. Actually, that part sounds mysterious enough that I'm a little interested.

What I'm really looking forward to, though, is *Bedstemor*—Grandma Kirstin. That old lady has stories to burn your ears. She smuggled the Danish physicist Niels Bohr past the Nazis in World War II. Her lineage may go back to the first Viking king of all Norway, Harald Fairhair. She'll turn ninety when I'm sixteen, but I swear, she's the coolest girlfriend I've got.

* * *

When Kirstin saw her granddaughter waiting for her at the Gotland ferry dock she briefly wished she could be fifteen years old again. Ever since her beloved, crusty, Norwegian husband Magnus died she had felt ancient—a lonely widow in her big, empty apartment, and everywhere else, an underfoot crone. What a thrill it would be to wake up one morning in such a vibrant young body! How wondrous to have smooth strong muscles that never ache!

As the ship raised its hinged prow and churned whitewater to align its car deck with the amputated road in Visby's harbor, the girl on shore waved, bouncing a little with excitement. Helen was wearing pink slacks under a tailored blue coat that should have been too cold, but apparently wasn't. Her blond hair curled up on her shoulder epaulettes in a flip. Was that lip gloss? Little Helen, Kirstin's only grandchild, looked like a twenty-something from a men's magazine. And that was why Kirstin's envy remained so brief. No amount of lip gloss could cover up the fears, the insecurity, the sheer cocky desperation of being fifteen.

After crewmen had secured the ropes and opened the gate, bicyclists were the first to cross the metal ramp to the pavement, followed by a crowd of bundled-up pedestrians. Behind them cars and trucks

waited in the ship's dark cavern, impatiently turning on their headlights and engines. A businessman tipped his hat and offered to carry Kirstin's suitcase. She smiled a thank-you. Then she steadied herself with her cane and made her way across the ramp to solid ground.

"Bedstemor!" Helen cried, hugging her so tightly that she nearly knocked the cane loose. The girl had always used the Danish word for "grandmother," because Kirstin had always been her Danish *bedstemor*, even though they had spoken English together from the first. Kirstin had taught her to play pattycake while singing, "Bedstemor, apple core, who's my friend? You!"

The businessman set down the suitcase, smiled, and walked on.

"How's my Helen Juul?" Kirstin asked—another inside joke. "Juul" was a fictitious last name that punned closely with the words for "wheels" and "Christmas." The girl had been both "Hell On Wheels" and "Hell On Christmas" since the year Kirstin had given her roller skates.

"Less bored, now that you're here."

"Where's everyone else?"

Helen sighed. "Mom and Dad have been waiting all day for Uncle Lars and Aunt Sasha at the airport."

"The airport?" Kirstin asked, puzzled. Gotland had an airstrip, but there were no commercial flights.

"Oh, it's a military plane, from Berlin to Stockholm. I guess they talked them into stopping on the way. Or maybe they didn't. Who knows?"

"I see." Kirstin disliked flying. She herself had made the trip to Gotland in thirteen hours using a taxi, a train, and two ferries. But her son-in-law loved planes. In the war he had escaped Denmark and run away to the United States in order to pilot a B-17 bomber. He was probably chatting up every mechanic and crewman at the airfield.

"We could call a taxi if you'd like," Helen suggested.

"No, the walk will do us good." It was only two kilometers to the villa. There would be just enough daylight if the fog didn't thicken. Kirstin set out, thumping with her cane while Helen carried the suitcase first in one hand and then the other.

At the end of the dock Kirstin suddenly stopped short. She pointed her cane toward a row of overturned dinghies. "Look at that, child!"

"What?" Helen saw only rowboats.

"Those rowboats are clinker-built, with riveted strakes. That technology hasn't changed in a thousand years."

Helen hid a smile. Her grandmother often did this sort of thing, drifting into daydreams from the Viking Age. She had earned the quirk fairly, excavating the famous Oseberg ship and building a museum for it at Bygdøy, an island in Oslo Fjord.

"This was once a beach, you know." The old woman's gray-blue eyes scanned the marina, the harbor-front shops, and the fog-shrouded spires of churches beyond. "Viking longships would land here to trade at the halls of Geatish chiefs."

"Yiddish chiefs?"

Kirstin laughed and kept on walking. "The Geats were a Gothic tribe that settled Gotland. Haven't you read *Beowulf*?"

"No."

"How about *The Hobbit*?"

"The Tolkien story? Sure."

"It's a gussied-up version of the Old English poem about a Geatish king. Beowulf slew a dragon that had been ravaging the countryside in search of a thief." She looked at Helen from the side. "Any dragons you need me to slay?"

"Um—"

"Don't tell me yet. First, how's school? What subject do you hate the most?"

Helen tried carrying the suitcase in both hands, but it made her walk like a penguin, so she went back to lugging it with her right arm. "Religion class is really dull. We get it twice a week."

"Not math?"

"Naw, algebra's OK."

"Favorite subject?"

"You want me to say history, don't you? But English class is easier. I could do it in my sleep." She stood the suitcase on end and sat on it. "Why don't we leave your stuff here and have Dad come back for it later in the car?"

"Your Christmas present is in this bag."

Helen huffed and stood up. She yanked the suitcase along, thumping it on the cobblestones of the waterfront street. The two-story stone and brick buildings of downtown had given way to smaller half-timbered houses painted yellow, red, and even blue. A few had thatched roofs instead of the usual tiles.

"You've been writing me beautiful letters in English," Kirstin said. "Thank you for that."

"That's OK." Helen wrote to her *bedstemor* so often because Kirstin always responded with a letter that included a Danish hundred-crown note. At the bank Helen exchanged them for 112 Swedish *kronur*—enough to buy two records or three paperback books.

"I've told Mom I have a new pen pal," Helen went on, as if to prove that she didn't just write to her grandmother. "An Italian girl named Celeste. She lives in Syracuse, in Sicily."

"That's wonderful. What do you write about?"

"Lots of stuff. Music I like." Helen tried to shrug, which was hard while carrying the suitcase. She was already sorry she had brought up this subject. The idea of getting a pen pal had come up at The Hammer. The students there had urged her to connect with young Communists in other countries. You were supposed to write about solidarity and the people's struggle. Helen didn't. In fact, she didn't have an actual pen pal at all. She had invented "Celeste" as a way to assuage her friends at The Hammer and tease her mother. Someone who thought her real boyfriend was imaginary deserved to think that an imaginary pen pal was real.

"That reminds me. I tried to buy a record with music from that British band you said you like, The Beaters?"

"You mean The Beatles?" Helen looked at her with wide eyes. "Really?"

"Yes. But it seems they don't have a record out yet. You wrote that you heard about them when they played in Hamburg. Did you take a trip to Germany?"

Helen blanched. This was dangerous ground. She had never been further south than Copenhagen. Her parents avoided Germany since the war. "I meant, a friend of mine heard them playing in Hamburg."

"I see." Kirstin didn't want to reveal too much about her investigation. She had called a friend in Hamburg and learned that the British group had played at the Indra Club on *Grosse Freiheistrasse* two months ago.

Kirstin said, "I'm told they mostly sing about love, love, love, and holding hands."

"Pretty much, I guess."

By now they had passed Visby's medieval city wall, an ancient stone divider that climbed into the darkening fog. In the distance along the shore, a light in a villa window suggested that the rest of the family had returned from the airfield.

Kirstin stopped. Her granddaughter turned around uncertainly, a fifteen-year-old girl trying to act older.

"You have a boyfriend, don't you?" Kirstin asked. "He's the one who heard the band in Hamburg."

Helen closed her eyes. She was good at lying, but not to her *bedstemor*. She took a deep breath. "My mother thinks he's an imaginary friend."

Kirstin managed to keep a straight face for five seconds. Then she laughed, "Isn't your mother a little old for an imaginary friend?"

Helen laughed too, despite herself. She dropped the suitcase. They sat on it together, shoulder to shoulder, laughing until tears came to their eyes.

"She calls him Lenny!" Helen said, laughing even harder.

Kirstin put her arm around the girl's shoulder. Gradually Helen's

laughter faded. And then only the tears remained.

"You won't tell Mom about Lennart, will you?"

Kirstin patted her shoulder. "Not unless she asks. It's all right to have secrets, as long as you tell the truth."

Helen swallowed hard. This was the moment when she should have confided her doubts about The Hammer and everything. Why was Lennart so curious about her family? Was she doing the right thing, with her secret mission? Maybe she wasn't cut out to be a spy.

Kirstin stood up. "Are you ready to go home?"

Helen wasn't. But she nodded. "OK."

* * *

Gotland may have a youthful party scene in summer, but in winter it's an island of old people. Helen had tried riding a bicycle around Visby in search of someone her age. She had found old fishermen in dark bars, black-coated women shopping for groceries, and farmers buying parts for their tractors.

Her parents were smart enough to recognize this problem. They proposed to counter it by having each of the five adults in their villa pick one of the five days leading up to Christmas and organize holiday activities that would interest everyone—including a fifteen-year-old girl. The adults welcomed this suggestion because Christmas really is more fun when seen through the eyes of a child. Helen accepted the plan, ostensibly because she would get presents every day, but in fact because it would give her time with Lars and Sasha to surreptitiously complete her spying mission. Ironically, the breakthrough Helen sought would come only on the day organized by her mother, late on Christmas Eve itself.

Aunt Sasha took the first day, December 20, announcing that it would have a Russian theme. Helen threw herself into the festivities, hoping to learn enough about the mysterious doings of her Russian aunt that she could impress the crowd at The Hammer.

Sasha and Helen spent much of the day making borscht, boiling chicken in the morning and chopping vegetables in the afternoon. The old villa had a brick-floored kitchen with two stoves—one fired by wood and one electric—so it was easy for two cooks to work side by side. Helen discovered that her aunt was not truly Russian, but rather Ukrainian. Sasha's parents had fled Stalin's Jewish pogroms in the early 1930s. Sasha had ended up teaching Russian to American G.I.s at a university in Eugene, Oregon. That's where she had met Lars. He had drifted away from his parents in Denmark, joined the U.S. military, and been assigned to Army Intelligence. After the war Sasha had gotten a job as a travel agent and had wound up working for the Soviet Intourist office in Minsk.

"Tell me the truth, Aunt Sasha," Helen said. "The real reason you're in the Soviet Union is because you're with the Central Intelligence Agency, right?"

Sasha laughed so hard she had to dry her eyes with her apron. "Oh, Helen, you've been reading too many spy novels." She shook her head and sighed. "Working for Intourist isn't glamorous, but it's what I do."

"And that's all?"

Sasha smiled and nodded. With her red lipstick, her clear skin, and her long black hair pulled back so tightly that her face showed almost no wrinkles, she looked thirty years old instead of fifty. Helen wondered what kind of bra Sasha wore to make her breasts aim out from her tight black sweater like nuclear weapons.

"I think it's time to cut the cabbage," Sasha said.

That evening after dinner Helen unwrapped the presents Sasha had brought, all of them obviously from Russia. There was a set of stacking dolls, each one containing a different coin, from ten rubles to one kopek. This was something she could show off to her friends at The Hammer. Even better was a recent issue of *Pravda* and a copy of

Sputnik, the Soviet Union's English-language magazine. Sasha served shots of vodka (which made Helen sputter) and led everyone out into the cold night air to watch for the real Sputnik. But the stars were hidden, and the satellite's battery must have run down after three years, because Sasha's radio only picked up static on the designated frequency, instead of the *beep-beep-beep* that had astonished the world.

The second day of the family's holiday festivities was December 21, which was in fact Hannukah, so the planning fell to Helen's father Julius. There was no synagogue on the island, and Julius' observance of rituals had pretty much lapsed since the war, but they still ate fried potato latkes, spun dreidels, and gambled with chocolate *gelt* coins. Why, Helen wondered, did her father think it would be fun to play charades? And why did he laugh so hard when assigning Uncle Lars to act out *The Seven Year Itch*?

Lars had his revenge the next day, when he orchestrated an American Christmas. The family awoke to discover that each of them was missing a stocking. The stolen footwear was found hanging by the chimney with care, stuffed with a bottle of Coca-Cola for Helen, bottles of Cuban rum for most adults, and a lump of coal for Julius.

Helen's father responded to the coal incident with the wry Hollywood smile that had once won him comparisons to Clark Gable. As far as Helen was concerned, her father just looked old, with his antiquated narrow mustache, silvering hair, and the beginnings of a paunch. It was hard for her to believe that Lars was the same age. Lars' long, clean-shaven jaw gave him horsey good looks. Lars had thick sandy hair and a well-muscled build.

With nothing but frost on the ground outside, Lars' plan for a coal-eyed snowman named Parson Brown gave way to a thousand-piece jigsaw puzzle on the living room's trestle table. The puzzle he had chosen was a hopeless photograph of a birch forest. Endless autumn-yellow leaves dappled endless white trunks. By evening, when they had completed only the frame and a small red farmhouse, Lars attempted to make piña coladas using canned pineapple juice and a tired lemon. He then attempted to conjure up tacos using flatbread, rice, beans, and a can of diced tomatoes.

Mette eyed her brother's efforts suspiciously. "Let me guess: LogistEx has started importing things from Latin America."

He grinned. "*Feliz Navidad.*"

Helen felt like slapping her own forehead. Cuba! The corrupt bourgeois dictatorship there was being threatened by Fidel Castro's revolutionary forces. Of course the CIA would want agents to keep an eye on the Communist uprising. The island was probably as close to the mainland U.S. as Gotland was to mainland Sweden.

"What's it like in Cuba?" Helen asked breathlessly.

"Afraid I'm stuck in Berlin," Lars replied. "But I tell you, the Germans are going nuts for cigars and rum."

And that was all she could pry out of him.

The fourth day of festivities was orchestrated by Helen's grandmother Kirstin, who had apparently missed the memo that the day should be for children. Bedstemor had stayed up late the night before baking Santa Lucia buns. With the enthusiasm of someone who had never actually participated in the Swedish tradition for December

13, she cajoled an unwilling Helen—as the eldest daughter of the house—to get up early, put on a long white gown bought for the purpose, wear a wreath of flaming candles on top of her head, and balance a tray of buns through the doorway of her parents' bedroom in order to bring them breakfast in bed. Mette and Julius applauded as if their daughter had just sung Mozart's Queen of the Night at the Royal Opera House, when in fact the only singing had been a badly warbled version of "Santa Lucia" by Bedstemor.

The ultimate proof that Helen loved her grandmother followed when the girl agreed to repeat the whole performance for Lars and Sasha. But this ended abruptly when Helen pushed open their bedroom door to find them sitting up in bed, naked to the waist. Had they never heard of pajamas? Helen dropped the tray and fled, having learned more than she wanted about her aunt's chest.

Bedstemor surprised herself by managing not to laugh. Instead she announced that they would skip over Saint Lucy's Day and move right on to Little Christmas Eve, which is what she called the day before Christmas Eve. Accordingly they drove to town and bought a Christmas tree. They sewed together straw ornaments in the shape of stars. They wove strips of red and white paper into little heart-shaped baskets, which they then filled with candy and hung on the tree. In the evening Kirstin and her granddaughter cooked a rice pudding that contained a double handful of chopped almond slivers and exactly one whole almond. When it came time for dessert, Kirstin announced that whoever found the whole almond would win a fist-sized candy pig made of pink marzipan.

Everyone took turns serving themselves a dish of the pudding. Then they watched each other across the table as they ate, occasionally crunching bits of almonds. Lars and Julius took seconds, and then thirds. Only when the bowl was empty did Helen reveal that she had found the intact almond in her first spoonful and had kept it hidden in her cheek all the time. She retired with the marzipan prize, satisfied with the day after all.

The fifth day of their vacation was Christmas Eve itself, with Helen's mother in charge. She had called the telephone number left by the farmer who claimed to have found something valuable in his field. The man had informed her that he would reveal the hiding spot only if she attended the noon service on Christmas Eve at his local church in the small country village of Eskelhem. Mette apologized that this didn't seem like a very kid-oriented holiday activity. But the farmer's mysterious demand had made Helen curious enough that she asked to come along. Her *bedstemor*, herself a veteran archeologist, said she wouldn't miss it for the world.

And so, while the others stayed home to finish the jigsaw puzzle, three generations of Andersen-Gustmeyer women put on their Sunday best and drove the family's Saab south fifteen kilometers to Eskelhem.

The spire of a whitewashed stone church dominated a frosty landscape of rolling farm fields and bare-limbed trees. Other than the church the little village consisted of six half-timbered farm houses, each flanked by low, thatch-roofed barns so as to enclose a cobblestone courtyard. The air smelled of manure as the three women got out of the car and walked past crooked tombstones toward the church.

Helen tugged on her mother's arm. "Look! On the hill behind the churchyard."

Mette and Kirstin squinted to make out what the girl's sharp eyes had noticed. The hill had two curving rows of standing stones.

"A ship burial," Kirstin said.

"Without an actual ship," Mette replied. "Vikings of modest means generally arranged stones in the shape of a ship rather than go to the trouble of burying a real one."

"Still, maybe that's where the farmer found something," Helen put in. "You know, in a grave."

"I hope not," her mother replied. "Amateur excavators are trouble. And they don't find much in that kind of tomb, anyway. Charred bones. Perhaps some melted metal. Norse myths suggested that the dead could travel to Valhalla in smoke, so Swedish Vikings were usually burned."

The main entrance to the church was not beneath the tower, but rather in a small side vestibule with a stone step. Mette pushed open the heavy, creaking door. It closed behind them with an echoing clunk. The three women stood in the gloom uncertainly. When their eyes became accustomed to the dimness they noticed a large model of a sailing ship hanging from the ceiling. Beneath the ship perhaps twenty people were sitting on wooden pews.

"Which one is the farmer?" Helen whispered.

"Shh," her mother admonished. In an even quieter tone she replied,

"He said he'll reveal himself after the service."

Helen rolled her eyes.

They sat near the back. For most of the next hour they sang numbered Christmas hymns led by a priest in a black robe. Helen thought the man's pleated white collar looked like a vanilla bundt cake. The priest read a sermon about the true Christmas spirit—which he felt consisted of renouncing the temptations of money.

Finally, as the organist played a few benedictory chords, the parishioners stood up and filed past the priest, mumbling their thanks at the door. Helen, her mother, and her grandmother stood in the vestibule like wooden statues of saints, waiting for someone to approach them. But no one did. At length even the organist left through a back door.

"Fru Gustmeyer?" The priest asked, standing at the door beside a burly custodian with a broom.

"Have we met?" Mette asked.

"My name is Johansson."

Mette hesitated. "I was told to meet a farmer here after the service."

The priest nodded toward the janitor. "That would be my part-time assistant, Sven."

Mette studied the janitor. He certainly seemed strong enough to do more than push brooms. "Then you're the one who found an artifact in a field?"

"No." The man shook his head. "I lied."

Mette's face flushed red. "You had me come all the way out here, on Christmas Eve, with my family, for nothing?"

The priest cleared his throat. "We were being cautious. You didn't sound like a real archeologist on the phone. And I have to admit, you don't exactly look—"

"Because I'm a woman?" Mette cut him short. "Pastor Johansson, my archeological degree is from the University of Copenhagen. I am currently in charge of raising the *Vasa*. My mother here is the former director of antiquities for the University of Oslo."

The priest tapped his fingers together. "In that case, I suppose Sven should tell you what he has found."

The big farmer's eyes sparkled. "There's nothing in the field, see? That was all a trick, in case of thieves."

"Then where did you find this—this valuable thing?" Mette asked.

"It's right under your feet. Come outside, all of you."

As soon as they were out the door the janitor pointed to a small round hole beneath the stone step. "That's a mouse hole, see? Pastor Johansson asked me to do something about the mice that keep chewing the hymnals. So I thought to myself, maybe I should look in the old entryway."

"This area is prone to problems," the pastor admitted. "It is the oldest part of the church."

Helen's grandmother stepped back, surveying the building. "Yes. I see that now. The tower is from the sixteenth century, and the main nave from the fourteenth. But the vestibule must have been the original church, probably from 1200 AD."

Mette touched her chin, thinking. "I bet the original church was wood, a century earlier, and was replaced with stone on the same site."

"But rotten wood leaves holes for mice, see?" The janitor jammed his broomstick into the hole and pried up the handle. The stone step lifted just enough that he could get his fingers under the edge on one side. Then, squatting like a weight lifter, he began tilting up the stone. The step was part of a six-foot-long slab that must have weighed several hundred pounds. The man's eyes bulged and his brawny arms flexed. Dirt fell from the edge of the massive flagstone as it rose. A mouse darted to safety. With a final grunt, the farmer heaved the stone upright against the oak door.

Beneath the stone, in a cavity in the compacted dirt, lay the moss of a mouse's nest.

Helen was about to comment on the value of this hidden treasure, but her mother held out her hand.

"There." Mette pointed to the underside of the threshold slab. "You see? It's actually a Norse gravestone."

Mette brushed the surface lightly with a finger. Dirt fell away, revealing the ancient carvings. Cast in sharp relief by the raking light of the low December sun were a square-sailed longship and a horse. Near the top of the stone, men battled with swords while a woman brought them a drinking horn. Around the edge, two braided snakes writhed until they bit each other's tails.

The priest cleared his throat. "Evidently they used this pagan stone as construction material for the church. No proper Christian would allow such a thing today."

"I need my camera," Mette said. "Leave everything as it is." She hurried back to the Saab. When she returned she took flash photographs from various angles. "Only a dozen Viking Age gravestones as beautiful as this have survived in all of Gotland. This one has been protected by the doorway." She turned to the pastor. "I'm sorry I doubted you. This is truly a valuable find."

The farmer scratched his head. "But the stone isn't why I called you here."

"It isn't? Then whatever for?"

"Why, for the treasure." The farmer reached down. He picked up a handful of moss from the mouse nest. Glinting beneath were a jumble of silver coins.

All three of the women gasped. They knelt in the dirt, oblivious to the damage this might do to their holiday clothes. Mette took more photographs. Then she reached out for one of the thin silver disks.

"Are they Roman?" the priest asked.

"No." Mette turned the coin in her fingers, revealing the squiggled lettering of Arabic words. "These are dirhams, from the silver mines of Afghanistan, forged for the glory of Allah."

"Merciful heavens!" The priest covered his mouth with his hand. "How did this heathen lucre end up here, in my church?"

"That," Mette replied, "Is the stuff of sagas."

* * *

Christmas Eve in the Gustmeyer villa turned out to be especially festive that year, celebrating not only the family's annual reunion but also the discovery of a Viking silver hoard. Throughout the dinner of roast goose, potatoes, and creamed cabbage, Mette took turns with her mother and her daughter telling the story of their visit to Eskelhem. The farmer had groaned in dismay when he learned that all buried treasure in Sweden belongs to the king. Mette had, however, promised a finder's fee. The priest had somehow expected that Mette would remove the pagan gravestone from his church at once. He was upset that his parishioners would have to continue walking across the stone for months, until an archeological team could be sent to transport the stone to the museum in Visby. As for the silver hoard itself, Mette had spent an hour photographing and examining what proved to be a disintegrated leather pouch with 213 dirhams. Then she had packed it up in a plastic shopping bag and had taken it back to the villa, where she had locked it in the old sea captain's safe.

After dinner the family lit candles on the Christmas tree and sang carols. Then they blew out the candles, turned on the electric lights, and settled down to the business of opening the remaining presents. Because Helen had already opened most of hers on previous days, she received only one. It was not the moped she had wanted, but rather merely a helping motor that could be bolted onto her bicycle.

By eleven o'clock Grandma Kirstin was so tired that she wished everyone a *gledelig Jul* and retreated to her back bedroom. At this point the other adults brought out Lars' Cuban rum. Incautious after the victories of the day, Mette made the mistake of telling her daughter that it was time for her to go upstairs to bed.

Helen complied too easily—with a simple "Good night" that should have alarmed everyone.

Helen seethed all the way up the stairs. She was not a child, nor was she tired. She had come to Gotland with a secret mission that she now resolved to fulfill.

In her bedroom Helen took off her shoes, dropping them loudly on the floor. Then she wrapped herself in the down comforter from her bed and crept back into the upstairs hallway in her stocking feet. She had planned to spy on the adults from the top of the staircase. But the living room was already dark. Where had everyone gone? She located the adults with a trick she had learned years ago. Because the upstairs of the villa had no heat, the rooms on that level each had a small floor vent that allowed some warmth to filter up from below. If you crept around carefully, avoiding creaky floorboards, it was possible to open the vents and spy on people below.

The adults had gathered around the kitchen woodstove, where they were busy mixing rum cocktails. Helen enveloped herself in the comforter. She lay down beside the floor vent with her head propped up on an elbow. Spying had never been so convenient, nor revenge so sweet.

Because the only view the vent offered was of a brick chimney, Helen imagined the voices below as part of a playscript—much like the Strindberg drama her class had been forced to read aloud in school, only more interesting.

ACT I, SCENE 1—The kitchen of a villa in Gotland on

Christmas Eve, 1960.

FATHER: That warms all the way down! Do you remember the Christmas Eve in Sasha's Eugene apartment, when we sat in her kitchen drowning our worries about the war with akvavit?

UNCLE LARS: We stuck pins in a map to show how much of the world the Nazis had overrun.

AUNT SASHA: Hard to believe that was almost twenty years ago.

FATHER: In the year 3 BC.

MOTHER: BC?

FATHER: You know, Before Child. (laughter)

Upstairs, Helen winced. Did they think she was such a burden? Maybe they should try walking in her shoes for a while. She shifted positions, propping her head with the other elbow.

UNCLE LARS: We might as well be sticking pins in the map again. Except this time it's not just a few B-17 runs at stake. It's nuclear Armageddon.

MOTHER: Do you really think the Cold War could come to that?

AUNT SASHA: The Soviets got a late start testing atomic bombs, but I think they've caught up. You hear rumors when you work in Russia. Apparently Stalin threw everything he had at the A-bomb project. They say his top bomb designer died last month of radiation poisoning in a secret Moscow clinic. And the new premier, Khrushchev, is just as brutal.

FATHER: But the Americans have nuclear submarines, right? They can stay down for months and launch warheads from anywhere. That's got to be a deterrent.

UNCLE LARS: Haven't you been reading the newspapers? The Russians have nuclear subs too. They claim they're for scientific purposes, looking for sunken ships to rival the *Vasa*.

MOTHER: That could be a good thing.

UNCLE LARS: More likely it's a ruse, to get a jump on World War III.

MOTHER: Hush! You shouldn't be talking about such things out loud.

FATHER: What? You think the Russians have spies in Visby?
UNCLE LARS (laughing): Gotland isn't exactly Berlin.
FATHER: Are you in danger in Germany?
UNCLE LARS: LogistEx has talked about pulling out of
Europe altogether. The Warsaw Pact and NATO both have
plans for another war in Europe. Germany and Sweden
would be the nuclear wasteland in the middle. They've
carved the rest of the world up into "spheres of influence."
It's the propaganda game we played in World War II, times
ten. Whoever has the most impressive technology wins.
MOTHER: If you're talking about the Russians winning the
space race, that's nonsense. Who cares if they sent a dog
around the world?
UNCLE LARS: How about if they send a man? Or a satellite
with cameras to watch you? Or nuclear weapons to annihilate
cities?
MOTHER: Lars! Please, this is Christmas.
FATHER: She's right. Let's not give everyone nightmares.
(Pause. A bottle clinks as glasses are refilled.) One more toast
before bed.
UNCLE LARS: *Gledelig Jul*, everyone. (Glasses clink)
AUNT SASHA: Here's to hoping that we all live another year.
(More clinks)
EVERYONE (somberly): *Gledelig Jul*.

Helen sat back from the vent, terrified. What if her parents were already making their way upstairs to discover her eavesdropping? She scooped up her comforter, shuffled on stocking feet to her own room, and quickly composed herself on the bed, pulling the covers to her chin. If her mother discovered that she was still wearing her Christmas dress, she was doomed.

Helen lay with her mouth half open and her eyes nearly closed. Through her lashes she was able to make out the shadow of her mother opening the door. The shape stood there a moment, and then, inexplicably, blew her a kiss.

* * *

Helen awoke early on Christmas morning with a troubling memory that almost seemed like a dream. She had been unable to sleep, still excited from the adventures of Christmas Eve. On a hunch she had tiptoed downstairs and put her ear to the keyhole of the bedroom of Uncle Lars and Aunt Sasha. They had been talking so quietly that she missed some of the words.

> AUNT SASHA: —in Vilnius, and then Minsk. They've got me wasting my time with a U.S. Marine named Lee Harvey Oswald. They want to know why he defected. He's getting disillusioned about the wonders of Communism. The Soviets gave him a rundown apartment and a stupid job. I think he's found a Belorussian girlfriend, though, so maybe—
> UNCLE LARS: (unintelligible)
> AUNT SASHA: And you? Cuba?
> UNCLE LARS: Since September, too late to make a difference. The Russians trained Castro's insurgents with Kalashnikovs. Havana will fall in weeks, barring a miracle.
> AUNT SASHA: An American miracle?
> UNCLE LARS: It won't be Santa Claus. Eisenhower doesn't want to do anything before leaving office. Everyone thinks Kennedy will be weak because he's young. But if he's pushed, I think he'll push back.
> AUNT SASHA: Push back with what?
> UNCLE LARS: With a little red button. My sister would name it Fenris.
> AUNT SASHA: Don't say such things out loud. Just kiss me.
> UNCLE LARS: Kiss you? Now?
> AUNT SASHA: (unintelligible)

Helen had retreated to the darkness of her own room.

When she awoke on Christmas morning the windows were still dark and she was uncertain how much she had dreamed. The horrors of the Cold War seemed to flutter about her like bats, trapped in her bedroom, circling on stiff little wings. Such secrets were exactly what Lennart had asked her to report. She was proud to have attracted the attention of such a prominent nineteen-year-old activist. Her spying mission had been exciting. But now she was afraid. If her aunt and uncle really were spies, their lives would be at risk.

How sure could she be that Lennart had her best interest at heart?

CHAPTER 5
BIRKA, 882

"There were spies on Gotland," Groa whispered to Hrolf between pulls on the oar. The three Rus longships with the Tyr-rune prows had sailed a full day and a night north of the Geatish island on open seas, but now, with dawn, they had lowered their masts and begun to row westward through the maze of skerries that guarded the hidden inlet of Lake Mälaren, Birka's inland sea.

"How do you know?" Hrolf asked, frowning.

"I don't." She never knew such things for certain, but she had learned to trust the prickling sensation at the back of her neck that warned of trouble. "I just wonder, if the Swedish king is as powerful as they say, perhaps he has his own Hugir and Munir."

Hrolf glanced up fearfully at the sky, as if their ship might be followed by Odin's all-seeing ravens, Thought and Memory. The only birds he could see were white gulls.

High tide had passed when they reached Holm, the rock island between the salt sea and the freshwater of Mälaren.

"Stroke!" Thorkell called out. "Harder!" Pulling for all they were worth, the oarsmen made slow headway against the current of the ebbing tide. According to a legend retold by an old sailor on the ship, the lake had once been salt, and the entrance had been open even at low tide. Since then the sea level had dropped, the sailor said, because of Thor. Apparently a frost giant had challenged the thunder god to a drinking game. But the giant had tricked Thor with magic, secretly connecting his bowl to the oceans of the world. When, after two tremendous draughts, Thor had managed to lower the water level only a little, he had admitted making a poor showing. But the frost giant had backed away, terrified by Thor's power. Ever since, the sea had lowered twice a day, and the resulting tides had been known as Thor's Draught.

As far as Groa could tell, all of the islands in Lake Mälaren were covered with birch woods, so how was she supposed to recognize Birka—literally, "Birch Island"? Ironically, it turned out to be the only island with almost no trees. Fields of freshly plowed black earth surrounded a collection of perhaps a hundred thatch-roofed huts. Groa found it odd that smoke wafted only from a few of the roof holes. And only half a dozen ships lay pulled up on the cobble beach. If Birka was Sweden's rival to the Norwegian trading port of Tunsberg, shouldn't it have been busier?

As at Gotland, Oleg's ship was the first to beach, and he was the first ashore. But this time, instead of facing a line of suspicious troops, he was welcomed as a homecoming hero. A cheering crowd waved yellow banners. To Groa's surprise, one of the burliest of the Birka Vikings gave Oleg a hug that lifted him off his feet. The welcoming warrior wore so much armor—chain mail, a metal cap, and metal gauntlets—that it took Groa a while to realize this was none other than Helga, Oleg's betrothed. As if to prove her identity, the big woman took off her helmet and shook loose a cascade of golden hair. Laughing, Oleg put his arms around her and lifted her off her feet in turn.

Groa and the other Norwegian colonists were left to watch as two groups of Rus warriors, those led by Helga and the ones brought by Oleg, exchanged greetings and swapped stories. The townspeople of Birka joined in too, obviously well acquainted with the Rus.

Eventually a middle-aged woman in a white fur cloak tapped Groa on the shoulder. "I'm Astrid. I can show you to a hall with bedding for women guests. Did you bring a sea chest?"

"Just a small box."

Astrid eyed the ornate clasps on the box. "I'm told you're a silversmith."

"My husband was," Groa said, and then added, "He passed away."

"And you so young! Once we had a dozen smiths here in Birka, most of them single. You could have had your pick."

Groa followed the woman along a crooked pathway between empty huts. "What's happened to everyone? Birka looks like a ghost town."

"It's the king," Astrid said. "He keeps trying to move everyone to his new town, Sigtuna. The population here has dropped from more

61

than six hundred to under two hundred. Some of us don't want to leave. Not even to go to Russiya, although believe me, the Rus have begged us to put old King Eirik behind us."

"Is the king so unpopular?"

"The Sniffler?" Astrid stopped and lowered her voice. "He's not like his father Eymund. For two hundred years the Svea kings ruled

from Uppsala in peace. But there's evil in Eirik's heart. The man is greedy, capricious, and mean. If anything, his son Björn the Bent is even worse. If the graves of my family's ancestors weren't anchoring me to this lonely old island, I'd be tempted to join the Rus."

"Has Helga convinced many of the Rus to become colonists?"

"No. She's had the same problem recruiting in Ruslagen as here. I hear she's enlisted five shiploads. Ten times that many Rus people said no. They're tied to their old farms. Why start a new estate from scratch across the sea?"

Astrid pushed open a wooden door to a hut. A smoke hole in the roof dimly lit rows of wall benches that could serve as beds. "Make yourself at home. And you might doll yourself up a bit for the wedding feast by the harbor tonight." She winked. "I reckon you could find a swain, if you're interested."

* * *

That evening Groa tried a trick she hadn't used in years—mixing black soot with a drop of oil to widen the shadow of her eyes. She washed, dried, and brushed out her hair, and then tied it up in a proud golden knot. Only as she was making her way back to the harbor did she ask herself who she was trying to impress. Not Hrolf, not really—after sharing a bench for a week the poor carpenter already seemed besotted with her. Vlad? He was so arrogant, and had so many women admirers.

At the harbor she discovered that the wedding was being celebrated outdoors around a gigantic bonfire. The Rus had pushed together the ruins of one of the abandoned huts and had lit the whole pile on fire. Apparently the townspeople wanted to clear up space by the waterfront, and didn't mind letting visitors burn an empty house. People brought out stockpiles of food and drink. They sat around the fire on stumps and sea chests while Oleg and Helga sat on thrones to one side. As a flattened red sun skimmed toward the horizon in the northwest, a nearly full moon rose from the dark waters of the lake in the other direction, paving a wavy sea-trail toward Russiya with liquid silver.

Oleg clapped his hands. "Now for the entertainment. Who's first to wrestle?"

Helga shook her head. "Not yet. First they're supposed to weave a wedding pole."

"That's right." Astrid stepped forward. She gave Oleg a wink. "You can wrestle with your sweetheart later tonight. Now let's bring out all the unmarried swains and maidens. Come on, you know who you are. Here's your chance to make a match."

Groa tried to shrink back into the shadows, but Astrid called her out. "You too! Or have you found a husband since I saw you last?"

Unwillingly, Groa stepped forward to join a cluster of a dozen girls—most of them younger and more eager than she was. Hrolf and Vlad were among the eligible young men who came forward.

"Gather round the pole," Astrid said, leading them to a grassy area overlooking the beach. From a distance Groa had assumed the thirty-foot pole was some sort of mast. Now she saw that two dozen colored ribbons hung from the top—thin linen strips of alternating yellow and blue.

"Boys take yellow on the outside," Astrid said. "Girls stand toward the middle with blue. Ready to sing?"

Groa didn't know an appropriate song, and neither did the others from Norway. A boy asked, "What do we do?"

Astrid put her hands on her hips. "Boys dance to the right, of course.

Girls to the left. Each time you pass someone, weave a different way—over, under, and over again. The one you're with when you run out of ribbon gets a kiss. More if you both want, but a kiss for sure. Ready?"

Without waiting for an answer, Astrid began to sing. The crowd of onlookers quickly joined in, clapping their hands. Among the dancers themselves, however, giggling chaos reigned. Boys collided with girls, each trying to figure out who should go under or over next. Groa understood almost nothing of the song itself, other than the words "Freya," "children," and in a louder voice at the end of each verse, "Oleg and Helga!"

As Hrolf passed he held up his streamer as if it were a triumphal arch for a queen. Behind him, Vlad had to duck beneath Groa's ribbon. In passing he intentionally bumped her hip. She glared back at the purser and found herself running straight into the arms of the next boy.

Despite all the confusion the ribbons gradually shortened, weaving a checkered tube around the pole. As the circle of dancers tightened it became harder not to bump in passing. Eyes glanced forward around the ring, estimating where the ribbons would run out and the dance would end. Soon only an arm's length of cloth remained. And then scarcely a hand's width. Finally the dancers were packed in a tight circle, nearly holding each other's hands over their heads.

Hrolf stumbled past Groa—or had he been pushed? She was left wedged directly between Hrolf and Vlad.

"And now the kiss!" Astrid announced.

Hrolf and Vlad both grabbed for Groa's hand. But instead of looking at her, they were glaring at each other. Groa pulled her hand away, a little disappointed in the two young men. She turned the carpenter's head toward her and kissed him on the lips. Then she turned the purser's face and kissed him too. And with that she walked back to the bonfire, considering which kiss had tasted best.

"Let the wrestling begin," Oleg called out.

"First the gifts," Helga countered.

"Wrestling!" Oleg insisted.

Helga stood up, pulled her chain-mail vest over her head, and flexed her muscles. "Very well."

The crowd cheered, egging Oleg on from behind. He stood up uncertainly. "The two of us? Now? I thought some of the men—"

"The two of us. Now." Helga dropped to one knee and put her elbow on a stump, holding out her palm in challenge.

"*Arm* wrestling?" Oleg lowered himself to a knee. He grasped her palm. "Is there a prize for the winner?"

"You bet there is." She looked him in the eye. "Ready?"

"Ready."

"Then go!"

Oleg pressed her hand halfway to the stump. But then his progress slowed. His brow furrowed. He growled and his arm began to tremble.

"Have you been rowing?" Helga asked. "Or have you just been giving commands while the others worked?"

With her jaw set firmly, Helga slowly straightened the Viking chieftain's hand upright.

The crowd hooted approval. More than half the Rus were from Helga's ships, and clearly took her side.

Growling fiercely, Oleg managed to sway her hand a few inches back. But then he began to chuckle, and his strength faltered. In another moment she had pressed his palm all the way down to the stump.

Groa joined the crowd in a cheer.

"Ow." Oleg rubbed his bicep. "Did I win by losing?"

"No, you lost. Where's my prize?" Helga looked at him sternly. "Or did you forget to bring a wedding gift?"

"Oh! Yes." Oleg fumbled for a pouch at his waist. "I managed to find two silver rings, one for each of us." He took out Groa's rings and put one on the fourth finger of his own right hand. Then, apparently realizing that he should have given Helga first choice, he tried to pull the ring off his finger. But his knuckle was large, and the ring was stuck. So instead he simply offered Helga the other ring. "Here. This one's for you."

Helga examined the band. "Just the style I wanted. It's hard to find nowadays." She tried to slip it on, but without success. "It's a little small."

Oleg gave it a try. Finally he managed to get it over the knuckle of her little finger.

"All right," Helga said. "I'll wear it proudly on my little finger." She gave him a long, passionate kiss. Her voice was husky. "And now, my love, I have a wedding gift for you."

"Yes?" He looked at her expectantly, as if he could see through the linen of her dress.

Helga snapped her fingers. "Bring us Norna."

Two of her crewmen ran into the shadows behind a nearby hut. A moment later they returned, leading a horse.

"A horse?" Oleg frowned.

The horse was no larger than the average Norse pony—hardly more than waist-high to a man—but it had a noble bearing, with sleek reddish-brown fur and white shaggy tufts above its forehead and hooves. The horse nickered and nuzzled up to Helga's outstretched hand.

"Norna is the surest sign of my love." Helga's words seemed to be directed toward the horse, rather than to Oleg.

Oleg swallowed. He had laughed at Groa's premonition about a horse, but that was before his wife gave him one. "I don't understand."

Helga stroked the pony's nose. "As a child in Ruslagen I rode Norna's mother, Urda, every day. We conquered armies of thistles in pretend battles. I beheaded many an attacking cow parsnip. Urda is gone, but when I returned to the old family farm this summer I discovered her daughter, Norna. In Russiya we have had to leave many memories behind. That makes Norna more precious to me than ever." She turned to Oleg, her eyes damp. "By giving her to you on our wedding night, I am entrusting my dreams to you."

Oleg put his hand to his forehead. Refusing this gift would doom his marriage. But would accepting the horse change his own fate? Surely the silversmith's words had been in jest. Still he suggested, "I suppose we could leave Norna where she grew up, at your old farm."

"In Sweden?" Helga shook her head. "No, Norna will come with us on our ship to Russiya."

"But we can't ride into battle on Norse ponies. The Huns have horses twice this size."

"Norna is a pet," Helga said, as if this were obvious. "Now she's *your* pet."

Oleg held up his hands as if to object. But then he simply clapped his hands. "Time for wrestling!"

"What about Norna?" Helga demanded.

"Let's tie our pet to the wedding pole for the night. In the meantime, I wonder if there's anyone here who is interested in wrestling with more than just one arm?"

Several of the crewmen raised their hands, and soon a match was organized. Groa bit her lip. She had been famed as a wrestler at Skiringssal long ago—not because of her strength, but for her speed and her wiles. Tonight, however, was no time to wrestle men. The prickling at the back of her neck warned that she should find her way to her bed—alone. Sometimes the gods explained things through dreams. Perhaps she would learn why she had told Oleg to be so afraid of his horse.

* * *

Groa did not sleep well that night, itchy from the straw on her plank bunk—or was it the tingling of fear? Other women came into the hut much later, drunk and disheveled, to fall asleep in their clothes. The dark was dreamless, and so was the long, slow dawn. Stale smoke lingered in the air. Birka drowsed under a wedding hangover.

And then a man's cry jerked Groa upright. At once she was putting on her clothes and lacing her shoes. Now a second voice called out, a shout of alarm. Groa hurried outside. In the morning light the labyrinth of passageways between huts seemed unfamiliar. She wasted time with several wrong turns before she emerged by the smoldering ashes of the wedding bonfire.

Five yellow sails were nearing the beach. Unlike the solid yellow of the Rus, however, each of these sails had a blue band through the middle. Blue pennants flew from the mast tops. Strangely, the five ships seemed understaffed, with half the usual crew. But the men on board were all heavily armed warriors.

Astrid came hurrying out of a passageway behind Groa. "It's the king! By the gods, it's old Eirik himself."

"Where is Oleg?" Groa asked. At the same moment the big, red-bearded Viking stumbled out of a waterfront hut, strapping his sword belt over a rumpled tunic. Behind him Helga emerged, tying up her hair. Wearing an unimaginably valuable night shirt of red silk with silver threads, she looked like a goddess from the Orient.

Already men were jumping from the ships and wading ashore. Soon they had formed a line along the beach. Three of the largest men carried Eirik to dry land. The Swedish king wore a blue cloak over a full suit of heavy chain mail. Although age had begun to whiten his beard and wrinkle his face, he was still muscular.

The king wiped his nose with the back of his glove. "Did I wake you, Oleg?"

"What do you want?" Oleg demanded.

The king sniffed. "I'm sorry to have missed the wedding of two of the Baltic's most notorious pirates. It will be my pleasure to see the sterns of your ships retreating to the swamps of Rurik's outpost. I hear you failed to recruit as many of my subjects as you had planned."

"I asked what you want," Oleg repeated.

"Just the tribute that is my due."

"Birka is a free island. There are no tributes here."

"Everyone in Sweden pays tribute to the king. My realm has no room for freebooters." He turned to his men. "Archers? At the ready."

A dozen men with bows notched their arrows.

"What the Hel are you thinking?" Oleg looked behind him desperately. Twenty people had assembled so far. They were mostly unarmed villagers and colonists, not fighters. Oleg turned back to face the king. "Would you slaughter your own citizens?"

"It's more of a threat, really." Eirik held up his gloved hand, motioning the archers to hold. "You see, the time has come to remove the last of Birka's population to the safety of Sigtuna."

Astrid called out, "But we don't want to go! The Rus will defend us. They honor free trade."

King Eirik wagged his finger. "That would be a poor choice. I do not tolerate pirates who linger. The Rus need to sail at once, if they are to sail at all. I've decided that Birka will become a hunting preserve, if not for deer, then for fugitives. The accumulated tribute will be whatever I find here."

A murmur rose from the villagers. Groa felt their confusion and anger. Were the people who stayed to be hunted like animals? Were their possessions to be confiscated as "tribute"? Groa noticed that more of the Rus warriors were arriving from the huts all the time. Nonetheless, they would be no match for armored Swedish troops.

"Björn!" The king called to a young man wading up behind him. "I'll give you first choice. What would you like as tribute?"

Björn's neck tilted forward oddly—perhaps, Groa thought, because of an accident at birth. The prince's head craned like a turtle as he surveyed the shore.

"The horse," Björn said, pointing to Helga's roan pony, still tied to the wedding pole. "I'll take the horse."

68

"You will not!" Helga cried. "I gave Norna to my husband as a wedding gift."

"A fine-looking animal," Eirik commented. "A small tax to pay for your safe passage home to the swamps."

Oleg rested his hand on the hilt of his sword. In a low, steady voice he said, "The horse is mine. We owe no tribute."

"I will have the horse," Eirik replied in the same steady tone.

Oleg looked behind him again. Sixty armed men had now gathered from the ranks of the Rus. The Swedes had twice that number, but they were downslope, with their backs to the water.

Groa's heart was beating fast. She stepped forward uncertainly. Is this how the saga of the Rus was to end, with Oleg battling impossible odds for the honor of a horse?

Oleg drew a breath that filled his barrel chest. "You will never take this horse, Eirik the Sniffler."

The king wiped the mucus from his matted mustache. Then he raised his hand. "Archers! On my command, kill the horse."

"No!" Helga ran toward the wedding pole, her arms outstretched.

The king lowered his hand as if it were a blade. At once a dozen arrows arced across the beach.

Groa screamed. The pony itself reared up, shrieking like a demon. It broke its rope and ran awkwardly toward the plowed fields with six feathers in its flank.

Meanwhile, Helga had simply stopped. The big Viking woman turned, her eyes wide with astonishment. She put her hand on a feathered shaft protruding from the silk at her side. She opened her mouth wordlessly. Then she sank to her knees and fell sideways into the grass.

Oleg was the first to reach her. He cradled his wife's face in his hands, whimpering like a child. "Stay with me! Stay!"

But Groa could see the light already fading from the eyes, revealing the darkness of Niflheim beyond.

Oleg ripped the silk at Helga's side, exposing the bloody shaft. He gasped in horror. Then he turned to Groa. "They say you are a sorceress. Save her!"

Groa had learned enough of the healing arts, however, to know there was no sorcery to repair this wound. The arrow had entered at a rib and had aimed slightly upward toward the heart.

Groa put her hand at Helga's mouth to feel for breath. There was nothing. Groa gently lowered Helga's eyelids. "I'm sorry," she said, as if it were all her fault. And in truth, she felt the fault was hers. If only she had seen this fate more clearly!

The rest of the crowd had stayed at a distance, held back by fear and respect. Helga, the sister of Rurik, had ranked as a queen among the Rus.

The Swedish king advanced with three of his men and his son. For once Old Eirik had lost his haughty stance. He lowered his eyes.

Perhaps there were no words the king could have spoken to give Oleg solace. But Eirik chose the wrong ones.

"I only meant to take the horse."

Oleg turned, wiping the tears from his eyes to focus on this man—this snot-nosed sniffler—this snake who had murdered his bride on their wedding morning.

The king added, "I'll pay the proper *wergeld* fee to compensate you for the loss."

A growl began deep in Oleg's throat, the rumble of a landslide in the fjells of giants.

Eirik took a step backward. "Be reasonable, Oleg."

The Viking raised himself to his feet. He unsheathed Fenris so quickly that the steel sang. "Here is my payment, Sniffler."

"Stop him!" the king commanded, retreating behind his three guardsmen.

Oleg advanced, gripping the sword's hilt with both hands.

Prince Björn called out from behind his father, "Cut him down!"

Groa thought: This battle is madness. The king's men have two swords and an axe. They are wearing full armor—steel helmets and chain mail. Except for his nightshirt and his anger, Oleg was naked. Or did he sense that the sword in his hands might serve as an uncanny shield?

The first of Eirik's guardsmen took a tentative swipe. Oleg clanged the blade aside, swung again low, and sliced off the man's foot at the ankle.

The second Swede wore longer mail. He parried half a dozen blows in quick succession, backing up step by step. Then Oleg roared, swinging Fenris at the narrow gap between the man's helmet and his chain mail. With a sickening gurgle, the man's head flopped backwards, his neck severed to the bone. Blood splatted Oleg's white tunic with a red stripe.

Next the king's axe-man raised his weapon. Oleg managed to jab him in the chest. Chain mail stopped the blade, but the blow knocked the man backwards to the ground.

Oleg turned his bloody sword to King Eirik. "Now, Sniffler, fight me fairly."

The king drew his own sword. "Very well, pirate. You will find that anger is no match for skill."

Groa quickly realized that the king's lighter sword was in fact better suited to this kind of duel. Eirik had only to land a glancing cut to deal the armorless Viking a mortal wound. Oleg, for his part, could win with nothing less than a massive, lucky death blow. Worse, the fallen axe-man had gotten to his feet and was raising his weapon behind Oleg.

"Behind you!" Vlad cried out from the crowd of onlookers.

Oleg must have trusted his purser profoundly. Without taking the time to look, Oleg swung Fenris two-handed in a full circle. The sword sliced off the axe-man's arms above the wrists. But Fenris also stuck fast in the axe's wooden handle. The seconds when Oleg struggled to free his sword were all the time Eirik needed. The king raised his sword for a final blow that would split Oleg's head in two. None of the Rus' warriors was close enough to intervene.

And yet when Oleg finally wrenched Fenris free of the axe handle, he turned to see the Swedish king seemingly frozen, holding his sword over his head. The man looked as if his hands were hanging from an unseen rope.

"Ah!" the king moaned, dropping his sword. His left hand swatted at his side, as if to claw away an insect. And there, in the gap his chain mail had exposed when he lifted his arms, was the hilt of a small knife. The finely wrought handle had an old-fashioned motif of intertwined biting beasts.

The king looked up, puzzled. The closest person facing the knife was a girl five paces away. Somehow the blade had been thrown so that it sank beside the same rib as Helga's arrow. He staggered back, collapsing into the arms of his son Björn.

The prince pulled loose the knife and threw it aside. He held his father's head in his lap, seemingly unsure what to do next.

The old king's lips struggled to form words, "If I die—"

"You won't die, father."

Eirik's eyelids sagged. "If I do, burn Birka and—" the king lapsed into silence.

"And what?" Björn shook his father's shoulders.

The old man suddenly opened his eyes wide. "And kill the Rus. Kill them all."

Björn swallowed hard. A drop of sweat ran down from his helmet. Blinking it away, he called to the men on the beach. "My father needs the care of a healer. Bring him to the ship."

After the crewmen had carried away the wounded king and the bodies of the three slain guards, a Swedish helmsman asked, "Where to, Prince?"

"We sail for Sigtuna," Björn told his troops.

Before he left, Björn cast a dark look at the villagers of Birka and the crews of the Rus. It was an ominous glance that said he would be back.

CHAPTER 6
BIRKA, 1961

Mette didn't want to spend a day examining a horse's grave, but she didn't really have a good excuse. A month remained before the final lift of the *Vasa*, and all the arrangements had been made for the celebratory reemergence of the old warship. The Ministry of Defense was orchestrating guest lists and media coverage for April 24, when pumps were scheduled to lift the wreck after 333 years beneath Stockholm's harbor.

Mette also felt a bit guilty about neglecting Per Gertula, the post-doctoral student she was supposed to be mentoring. This was the second season that Per had taken half a dozen undergraduates to the island of Björkö. She had read his reports and had talked to him in Stockholm, but it was time she paid a visit to the actual site, even if all they had found there was a dead horse.

That morning Mette packed the usual three lunch boxes with rye-bread sandwiches of thinly sliced eggs and pickled herring. She kissed Julius goodbye on his way out the door to catch the tram to his real estate office downtown. She surreptitiously checked to make sure Helen hadn't forgotten to put her homework in her knapsack for school. Then Mette put on her wool overcoat and drove the Saab fifteen kilometers to the west, on smaller and smaller paved roads, to the Björkö ferry landing.

Although the equinox was just a few days away, the only signs of spring were a light green haze of tentative grass shoots in the fields and the even fainter pastel whisper of buds among otherwise barren birch woods. The ferry landing wasn't a dock, but rather just a ramp at the edge of a field, as if the highway engineers had miscalculated and built a road that angled straight into Lake Mälaren. The ferry, when it

finally arrived, was simply a motorized barge with a steel deck hardly large enough for a milk truck, Mette's Saab, and a farmer's rusty Volvo. She paid the few *kronur* fare and stood by a chain at the square prow, watching the glassy water vanish beneath her feet.

Mette closed her eyes, breathing the cool, sweet air. She could understand why the Vikings had loved islands so much. There was something liberating about a place surrounded by the sea, free from the worries of the mainland. The Cold War's superpowers might be threatening the world with nuclear missiles even now, but they would never notice Björkö, "Birch Island."

On the far shore Mette drove up to a farm house. There, following Per's directions, she turned left on a gravel lane. After a kilometer she crested a rise with her first view of the eastern end of the island. On the horizon an orange pall of smog hung over Stockholm. But overhead the sun was climbing into a sky as blue and wide as if time had stopped a thousand years ago. She could almost imagine that the horizon was smoky from the hearth fires of Birka, Sweden's first town.

Mette parked by a trailer and walked past several tents to a patch of black earth where students were working in a rectangular pit marked with string.

"Doctor Gustmeyer!" Per Gertula climbed out of the pit, extending a hand to shake. He was a short, square-shouldered young man with the roundish face of a Finn. His Swedish had no noticeable accent, something Mette envied. Per had grown up in the western, Swedish-speaking part of Finland while Mette had been raised in Copenhagen.

No matter how carefully she pronounced Swedish words people smiled and said, "Oh, you speak Danish so clearly!"

Mette shook Per's hand. "I should have visited last season, but the *Vasa* took all my time."

"Of course."

"I hear you've started off the new season with a find. A ritual horse burial?"

"That's the problem," Per said, wrinkling his brow. "It doesn't look like a sacrificial offering. It's more of a—I don't know—a peculiar counterpart to grave Bj 581."

Every Swedish archeologist knew about Bj 581, the burial chamber of a Viking warrior excavated by Hjalmar Stolpe in the 1870s. Stolpe had found a complete skeleton sitting in a large wooden box with an ax, a sword, a spear, a knife, two shields, and even a game board for *hneftafl*, the early Viking form of chess.

"Where was that tomb?" Mette asked.

"You're standing on it."

Mette took a step back. She nearly bumped into a waist-high boulder.

Per pointed to one side. "Originally there must have been two grave mounds here, each marked with a large rock. When Stolpe was researching Birka he ignored the grave with a horse. He must have assumed it had been looted in antiquity. The boulder had been rolled aside long ago and part of the mound was missing. Instead Stolpe excavated the mound where you're standing."

Mette considered the side-by-side burial sites. "Could the horse have been a decoy—a trick to make it harder for looters to find the warrior?"

"Possibly. But we've found complications to that theory. Take a look."

Per asked the workers to climb out of the dig. Mette watched the students—such bright young faces! She couldn't help but think of her own daughter. Every year Helen seemed older and university freshmen seemed younger.

The students waited politely while Per and Mette climbed down into the rectangular excavation. Only the front half of the horse's skeleton had been exposed—the upper rib cage, two hooves, and an elongated skull. Reduced to bones, the horse looked as alien as a dinosaur, with an eerily empty eye socket and grinning yellow teeth.

Per pointed to the ribs. "Here."

It took Mette a moment to recognize the angular shapes among the bones. "Arrowheads?"

Per nodded. "The shafts have rotted away, but I don't think this horse died of old age. And there's more."

"What?"

"I've got a copy of Stolpe's report in the trailer. He wrote that the warrior was buried with virtually every kind of Viking weapon except

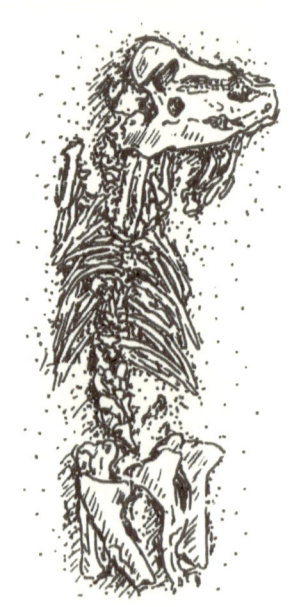

for a bow. Stolpe wondered why, if the warrior wasn't an archer, he had an arrow lying beside his ribs."

Mette drew in her breath. "He was shot. Both of them were shot with arrows. The warrior must have been riding into battle on the horse." She stopped. "Or wait. It's more complicated than that, isn't it?"

"Much more, I'm afraid." Per sighed.

"That's why you wanted me to see the site for myself." Mette studied him. "What are you thinking?"

"I'm wondering, where's the armor? According to Stolpe the warrior had no helmet and no chain mail. His only defense was a silver ring on his little finger. A man might do that, but for God's sakes, this warrior was wearing a dress—a silk gown with silver threads. That cloth came all the way from China. You don't wear silk into battle."

"Are you suggesting he wasn't a warrior? Or that this wasn't the grave of a man?"

"I don't know." Per shook his head in exasperation. "I haven't yet looked at the skeleton itself. That's stored in an Uppsala archive. But I've been studying Stolpe's sketches. The width of the pelvis, the shape of the femur—I swear, it just doesn't look male."

Mette glanced up at the students. Was this a discussion they should overhear? Per obviously kept no secrets from his team. It was a good policy. Mette insisted on open dialogues with her own workers, and with her family.

"I assume you realize, Per, that grave Bj 581 has long been considered the archetype of Norse masculinity. Richard Wagner is said to have based the hero of his *Ring* trilogy on the man from Stolpe's excavation."

"I know." Per blew out a breath. "If I tried to publish a theory that the warrior was female, I'd be laughed out of academia."

"That depends on the evidence you've got." Mette herself had once excavated the grave of a Viking shield maiden near the old Danish capital of Hedeby and had survived the resulting criticism. "If your work is solid, Per, I'll back you up."

"Thanks, Doctor. We've just gotten started here this season, and already we're digging up more questions than answers."

"Let me know what else you find." She looked about the unfinished dig. "There may yet be something here that ties everything together."

* * *

Mette spent the rest of the morning getting to know the students. After eating lunch together in a field above what must once have been Birka's harbor, Per walked Mette back to her car.

"Oh, and thanks for sharing that *Pravda* article about the submarine. I didn't realize you speak Russian."

Mette tried not to reveal her perplexity. "Actually, I don't speak Russian." What was Per talking about?'

"Oh, that's right. It's your sister-in-law. Amazing, isn't it, that the Soviets are using their nuclear submarines for research instead of war?"

Now Mette really was alarmed. How could Per know about Sasha? Suddenly she made a connection, although it seemed impossibly remote: Sasha had given Helen a copy of *Pravda* as part of a Christmas present on Gotland.

"Didn't you know about the article?" Per asked.

Mette shrugged noncommittally.

"Well, it seems the Russians have been using sonar to scan the seafloor for anomalies. Off the coast of Estonia they've found an interesting wreck."

"A Viking ship?"

"They're not sure. I can't believe your daughter didn't tell you about this."

Mette managed to hide her own disbelief with a small laugh. "She's so independent these days." Then she added casually, "So how do you know Helen?"

"From the university, of course." They had reached Mette's Saab. Per turned to her earnestly. "I don't know what Helen's major is, but she belongs in the archeology department. That girl has talent."

Mette gripped the handle of the car door so tightly that her knuckles whitened. Had her daughter been impersonating a university student after school, instead of roller skating?

"I'll talk to her about it."

"And what a voice!" Per smiled, singing a verse in English that Mette did not recognize:

> Love, love me do!
> You know, I love you.

Per aimed his finger like a gun and winked. "You've got a star on your hands, Doctor."

CHAPTER 7
BALTIC SEA, 882

When Oleg first sighted land after crossing the Baltic he turned about in the Tyr-rune prow of his flagship to reassure himself that his fleet really existed. Sixty-four sails! Two thousand warriors and a thousand colonists! This was the army that Rurik had dreamed might expand his realm in Russiya. Even Rurik must have thought it unlikely that such a force could be assembled in a single summer. And, like Rurik, Oleg would have wished it all away if only he could bring Helga back to life.

There had been so little time to mourn. The day after Prince Björn had departed from Birka with his wounded father, everyone had gathered on a rise behind the village to say their farewells to Helga, uncrowned queen of the Rus. Hrolf, the Norwegian carpenter, had built two stout wooden boxes, more like grain bins than coffins. In one they had laid Helga's beloved roan pony, Norna. In the other Helga sat upright, her eyes closed and her arms defiantly crossed, as if she were merely napping, biding her time until the call came to wade into battle for the glory of the Rus. Oleg had insisted that she wear no armor. He himself had fought the Swedish king in a nightshirt. Oleg wanted to remember his bride as she had been then—a strong, beautiful woman in the red silk gown of an empress.

As soon as the wooden chambers were nailed shut, Helga's crewmen began carting dirt for the two burial mounds. Oleg sat on one of the marker stones with his head in his hands. No one dared disturb him. With Helga's death, Oleg had become the ruler of seven Rus ships. But the crews could only guess what orders he might give once he awoke from his grief. Would he seek vengeance against the king? Would he fortify Birka? Or would he flee to Russiya?

The evening after the burial Groa was walking back to her hut through the town's crooked passageways when she felt a hand on her shoulder. She spun about to discover Oleg in the shadow of a doorway.

"I owe you something, sorceress." He motioned her inside. When

he closed the door behind them with a shoulder, his chain mail jangled. The hut was smoky and dim, but Groa could see that the big Viking's eyes were as red as his beard.

"You paid me well for the silver rings," Groa said.

"But I haven't yet paid you for my life." Oleg sat down heavily on a bench by the hearth. "How did you manage to strike Old Eirik?"

Groa reached under her tunic and slipped out her husband's knife. After the Swedes left she had picked it up from the beach and cleaned the blade. Now she balanced it in her hand, took aim at a pillar across the hut, and threw. The blade whirled through the smoke, glanced off the wood, and fell to the floor.

Groa shrugged. "Sometimes the gods guide my hand with more skill."

"For one so young, you are full of mysteries, woman."

"My name is Groa." She retrieved the fallen knife.

"Very well, Groa. Cutting down a Svea king is a deed that comes with great risk. My sword was stuck in an axe handle, so I never got in a blow against him. Somehow you did, and saved my life."

"But not Helga's life." Groa sat down opposite him.

The Viking rubbed his eyes for a long time. "That debt is not yours, Groa. The debt to you is for my own life. What is your price?"

She picked up the knife. "That depends on what you are planning. Will you seek vengeance against the king?"

80

"No. Eirik's wound might already be mortal. If Björn takes the throne he can call on the allegiance of thousands of fighters. Confronting him would be worse than foolish. It would dishonor Helga's memory. She had no quarrel with Björn. She was raising a force to help her brother in Russiya."

"Then you plan to sail back to Novgorod after all?"

He nodded. "We'll stop in Ruslagen along the way. Eirik's threats may win us a few more volunteers than Helga was able to enlist."

"They will indeed."

Oleg eyed her suspiciously. "Is it true that you can see the future?"

Groa couldn't answer this question, and in this case, she didn't need to. "I've been talking with Astrid, the woman who organized the wedding dance. Astrid seems to have more than her share of influence here in Birka. She tells me the villagers are afraid Eirik's troops will come back to burn the city. Astrid says nearly a hundred townspeople are now willing to leave for Russiya."

"Do they have ships?"

"Six small ones. And they would sail as colonists, not warriors. Their ships would be full of tools, cattle, and belongings."

Oleg stroked his beard. "This can be useful too. But it doesn't answer the question of your payment, Groa."

Groa sighed. "You won't like the fee I ask."

"Name it."

"It does have a name," Groa said quietly. "It is the evil wolf-god, Fenris."

Oleg narrowed his eyes. "Explain yourself."

She held up her knife by the blade, so the biting beasts of the hilt caught the firelight. "My first husband was the cleverest smith of his age. He forged both this knife and Fenris, the sword you are wearing."

Oleg withdrew his sword from its scabbard. The etchings on the blade did in fact suggest similar workmanship to the knife. "But that's not possible. I bought this sword from a jarl in Norway. He said the blade was old—very old."

"You bought Fenris from a thief, a grave robber. Stolen goods are always cursed."

Oleg ran his finger over the runes on the steel. "The jarl said Fenris has the power to win battles. So far that seems to be true."

"Luck has its price. Eventually Fenris obeys its evil origin. You admitted this yourself, Oleg, when you asked my price."

"Is that your fee?" Oleg demanded, growing angry. "You'd ask for my sword now, just when I need the luck to win battles?"

Groa sat back, considering. He was a strong man with a strong sense of justice. He could use some luck. "All right. I won't ask for your sword yet. But you must promise me that one day, when I ask, we will trade these two blades. In exchange for the knife that saved your life, you will relinquish Fenris."

They eyed each other through the bluish smoke of the dying fire. Groa was still holding her knife by the tip of its blade, a reminder that the knife had once been thrown to bring down a king.

Oleg looked down and nodded. He turned the silver ring on his finger, admiring the old pattern. "You ask a lot for your trinkets, silversmith. Still, I doubt that you are really a seer. You said my horse would kill me. That didn't happen."

"Not yet."

"Not yet? The horse is dead."

Groa shrugged. Why had she not simply admitted that she had been wrong?

* * *

Three days later when they sailed from Birka, Oleg had insisted that Groa row on his ship rather than on Thorkell's. "I want to keep an eye on her," Oleg told his purser Vlad. Because Groa still had no sea chest of her own, it was agreed that she and Hrolf would make the move as a team, sharing his carpenter's toolbox as a seat.

The smallish fleet—seven Rus longships and six boats of Birka villagers—slid through the rapids at Holm on the tide. Then they spent a day threading their way north amongst the islands to Norrtälje, the home fjord of Ruslagen. Oleg told lookouts to keep a sharp eye out for the blue-banded sails of the Swedish king. As the flotilla neared the end of the twelve-mile-long inlet they rounded a bend and suddenly saw dozens of ships ahead—their masts up, but with no sails.

"Armor up!" Oleg called out. Warriors took their shields from the gunwales and dug into their sea chests for helmets. The colonists, trembling and uncertain, took out axes. Vlad found an extra helmet for Groa. "The only weapon you've got is a knife?" he demanded.

Hrolf offered, "I've an extra adze she could use."

The purser shook his head in disgust. He handed her a fishing gaff with a metal hook.

"Hail Rus!" Oleg shouted toward the shore.

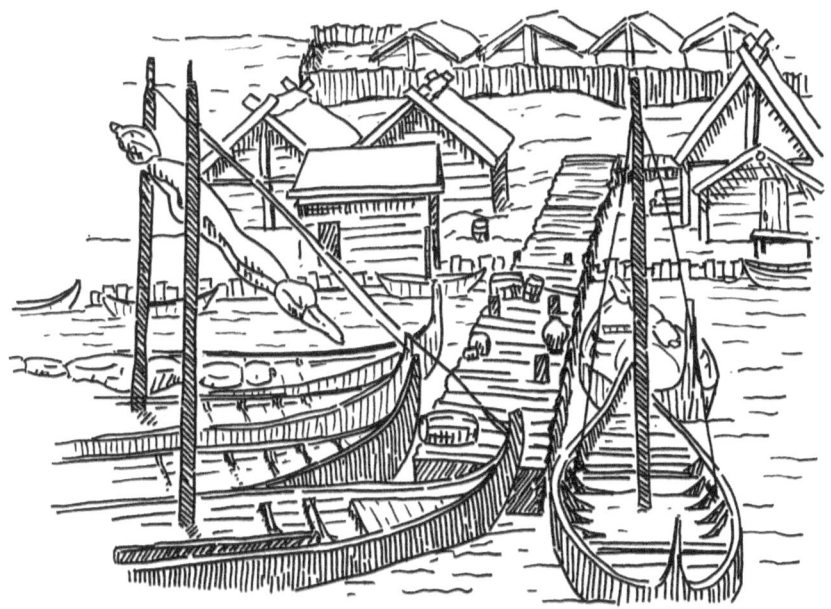

Ahead on the beaches were hundreds of men. An entire army had crowded near their ships. Was this an ambush, and if so, was it too late to turn about and flee?

"Hail Rus!" Oleg shouted one more time. He glanced back at his crew, preparing to give the command to turn about.

"Hail king-killer!" a faint voice called from the shore.

Oleg frowned, unsure how to respond.

"Eirik must be dead," Groa said behind him.

Vlad asked, "Then Björn is the new king. Are these his troops?"

Oleg squinted at the shore. Among the men were cattle, carts, and women. "No. They are Rus. They must be fleeing Björn's army. I doubt that will make us any more welcome."

The first of the Rus to meet them on the beach were angry women. A crone marched up to Oleg and pounded his chest, wailing that he had slaughtered her three sons. Another woman accused him of burning her farm and stealing her cattle. Oleg stood there, enduring their shouts until the angriest had vented their rage.

Oleg raised his voice to the crowd. "Old King Eirik murdered my wife at Birka. He told his son to burn Birka because it was an island of free trade. Do you know why Björn is attacking you?" He paused a moment, but no one spoke. "Because the Rus, too, love freedom. We have never gladly submitted to the tyranny of the Svea kings. Fighting the armies of Uppsala will only bring us more suffering and more loss." He pointed to the fjord. "Freedom for the Rus lies in the east. Your cousins have already founded a realm of riches there. Join with us and sail to freedom. To Russiya!"

"To Russiya!" At first only a few voices from the crowd echoed Oleg's call. But gradually the chant spread, "To Russiya! To Russiya!"

* * *

Within days the people of Ruslagen had readied forty-eight ships. An entire Swedish garrison in Norrtälje turned against Björn the Bent. Rus soldiers managed to slow the young king's march toward the fjord. After most of the settlements had been evacuated the garrison's soldiers boarded their own ships, reefing the yellow sails to hide the king's blue band. By then word had arrived that ships were sailing from Gotland as well, although no one knew why. The Geats had not been targeted for revenge by King Björn.

At the Åland islands, when eight white-sailed Geatish longships joined the Rus' fleet, Oleg learned that Wiglaf had brought his warriors on a business venture. The decline of Birka, the Geatish chieftain reasoned, would leave Gotland as the logical port for goods traded between Russiya and Western Europe. Wiglaf was willing to help the Rus in order to stake a claim to the trading routes of the Baltic.

The key to securing trade in the eastern half of the Baltic Sea was the Estonian island of Hiiumaa—nearly as large as Gotland, but low, forested, and riddled with dark bogs. Every ship bound for Russiya would have to pass that shore, and most would want to stop to resupply water and food. Twenty years ago Rurik had struck a deal with the Finnish tribe there allowing Karl the Lonesome to staff an outpost. It had been named Karlsgard.

Now Oleg scanned the fields behind the beach. The Finnish huts at Karlsgard were still there, although they seemed deserted. And Karl's stave hall was gone.

If Oleg had been sailing alone he might have been more cautious. With the sea full of his sails he landed his flagship on the beach, left some men to guard it, and took the rest of his crew in search of the lonesome Karl. The settlement appeared to be inhabited only by dogs, goats, and terrified children. All that remained of Karl's house was a smoldering ruin. A cluster of children, cowering behind a woven willow fence, pushed a taller boy forward.

"What has happened here?" Oleg demanded of the child. "Where is everyone?"

The boy glanced to the sails in the bay and swallowed. In heavily accented Norse he stammered, "They're in the bog."

"The bog? What bog? Why?"

"They're learning the secret of iron."

Oleg frowned. "What does that mean?"

"I don't know!" The boy's eyes were wide. "How can anyone make iron out of water? It's a Varangian secret."

Groa knew all about bog iron, but was fond of secrets. She asked, "Who are the Varangians?"

The boy turned toward her, more puzzled than alarmed. "You are, my lady. Va-Rangians, Way-Rangers. That's what everyone calls the Norse who travel to Russiya and beyond."

Oleg spoke with less patience. "If the adults are hiding in a bog, go and bring them here."

"I can't!" the boy said. Then he added, "But I suppose I could take you to them."

Vlad shook his head. "I don't like it. This could be a trap."

"Agreed. Gather a troop of sixty." Oleg waited while the purser assembled a force of fighters. Soon they were setting out behind the boy. Axe-men led the way, with spear-men to either side and archers in the back.

The footpath the boy followed into the forest was tangled with roots and branches. With the passage of this axe-wielding troop, it became a road. After a mile the forest gave way to what looked like a meadow—except that the moss-covered ground was springy, and each footstep soon filled with reddish-brown water.

"A peat bog," Vlad called out to the soldiers. "Spread out, or you'll sink in your armor." A few small pines had struggled to grow in the bog. Their trunks wobbled as the men marched past, evidence that their roots were not in soil, but rather in the floating moss of a hidden lake. The boy at the front was light enough that his feet weren't even wet. Groa wondered if this was in fact a trap—a ruse to sink an army.

The boy led them around the edge of the bog to a cove where several dozen adults were working. Or rather, only about eight people were actually digging with spades. Watching them were old men with swords and black-haired women with colorful skirts. As Oleg's troop approached, the workers threw down their shovels. A woman cried, "Thank the gods! It's the Rus."

Only then did Groa realize that the workers were shackled with chains. The workers were taller and blonder than the others. They were Norse.

"What is the meaning of this?" Oleg demanded.

A dozen voices began talking at once: "We thought—" "They took—" "How did—"

Oleg silenced them with a wave of his brawny arm. Then he pointed to the woman who had spoken first. "Where is Karl?"

She lifted her head. "The Finns have burned my husband in our hall."

Oleg aimed his finger at the elder men with swords. "Why?"

From the confusion in the men's faces, it was clear that none of them spoke Norse. Instead one of the younger women, with a black vest over a red-and-blue patterned skirt, answered in a stuttering accent. "I am Anni, and the boy who led you here is my son. We thought the Rus had become weak. We learned that Rurik is dying."

Oleg turned to Karl's widow. "Is it true that Rurik is dying?"

She nodded. "Half of him is dead. His entire left side is useless. He lies in Novgorod's fort, unable to walk."

"Perhaps he has suffered a stroke," Groa mused aloud. "It is a sickness of the heart, the center of thought."

The widow continued, "Rurik's son is only three, and his wife is no leader. The realm is collapsing. Everywhere the Finns, Slavs, and Huns are moving in to plunder what they can." She held out her hand to the cluster of dark-haired women. "For twenty years we had lived in peace with these people. They were our neighbors—our friends. We traded milk and iron for their bread and vegetables. We brought them prosperity and peace. We gave them a connection to the outside world. Now they have slaughtered our cattle and murdered my husband."

The widow paused and added, "Karl died because he would not tell them how we smelt iron from rusty water and peat."

Oleg scanned the villagers disparagingly. "I see no warriors. Where are your men?"

Anni lifted her chin. "My husband is among those sailing to take Ladoga. Then they will move on to Novgorod. Once we had imagined the Varangians were as gods. Now that we have seen the weakness of your leaders, a dozen tribes are rising to reclaim their riches. I have heard of you from visiting traders, Oleg. You cannot stop us with the shipload of pirates you have brought to Hiiumaa."

The little boy cleared his throat nervously. He said something to his mother in a language the Norse could not understand.

The woman's face darkened. She looked to Oleg uncertainly. "How many ships?"

Ignoring her, Oleg turned and spoke to a white-haired chieftain in black leather armor. "What do you think, Wiglaf? Is this a job for the Geats?"

Wiglaf laughed. "We've been hoping for a trading port on Hiiumaa. I think four of our ships could secure the island. That will leave you four other Geatish ships for further projects."

"Good." Oleg turned to go. Over his shoulder he said, "Switch the shackles to the Finns. I think they have earned a taste of slavery for a while."

The old Finnish men and the women in colorful skirts began exclaiming in outrage as their feet were chained.

Vlad hurried behind Oleg. "Are we sailing?"

"We'll camp for three days in Karlsgard to build a proper stockade." He stroked his red beard. "And then we'll sail to Ladoga. Along the way I think we may find a shipload of Finns that needs sinking."

* * *

With a force of three thousand, construction of the stockade required less than three days. Teams of men cut trees from the forest and hauled logs to the site. Others dug a rectangular rampart to support walls of pointed posts. Hrolf was part of a crew that laid out a large central hall—not of split staves as in Sweden, but of whole logs notched together horizontally, in the quicker style of cabins in Russiya.

Groa served as a messenger for Oleg. She quickly realized that the Viking chieftain's goal was not merely to fortify a trading outpost for the Geats, but also to organize his haphazard army. Oleg divided his force into sixteen battalions—each consisting of the crews of four ships, and each led by a single captain. Wiglaf's Geats formed two battalions—one contingent that would sail onward to Ladoga and another that would stay at Karlsgard. In the meantime Oleg made use of the Geats' strict military discipline to train the other teams. For one hour every morning and evening the Geats drilled troops with weapons. They marched into mock battles. People without shields were helped to build their own. Regardless of age or sex, every colonist and recruit took part.

The few who shunned these rigors were not flogged. But on the morning of the fourth day, when the Rus fleet prepared to sail east, Oleg ordered seventeen of the least obedient recruits into the smallest of the ships and sent them rowing back to Sweden. No one wanted to imagine what would become of the disgraced shirkers when they returned to face Björn the Bent.

As the rest of the Rus boarded their ships, Oleg told Groa, "Bring Anni and her son onto my flagship."

"In chains?" Groa eyed him warily. The Viking chief had not drawn his sword since leaving Sweden. He had dealt with the insurgent Finns without bloodshed. But she was watching to see if Fenris would turn his heart.

"Remove the shackles. They've had a taste of slavery. At Ladoga I'll need them as translators."

"Or as hostages?"

Oleg turned without answering.

* * *

With a wind from the west, the Rus fleet raised its sails and sped through the waves toward Russiya. Groa could feel the planks vibrate and flex, as if Oleg's flagship were an eager horse, galloping across the sea. The mood of the crew seemed to have changed as well. After the stay at Karlsgard they no longer thought of themselves as refugees. They were an armada with a mission—to restore the realm of Russiya. They jested with Anni and entertained her son with knot tricks. But the haughty Finnish woman responded with an aloofness that spread a flicker of doubt. Bringing order to the outpost at Karlsgard had been almost too easy. How large, really, were the battles that lay ahead?

The wind behind them proved to be the front of a storm. For two days dark clouds pelted the fleet with rain. The flagship's crew stretched sailcloth across the gunwales, but the makeshift tent leaked and flapped in the wind. Groa shivered all night, wrapped in a cloak on wet deck planks. When the rolling of the ship pushed her against Anni on the one side, or Hrolf on the other, she was glad for the warmth.

The sun returned when the ocean ended. The Baltic shores on either hand narrowed to the marshy mouth of the Neva, the first of the rivers of Russiya. The sails came down and the oars came out. For a day they rowed against the current of the Neva. The next day they rowed against the wind on Lake Ladoga. Then they turned sharply right, following the Volkhov River upstream. Finally their goal came in sight—a palisade of dark, sharpened logs on a grassy promontory where a smaller river joined the Volkhov.

"*Alode-Joki*," Anni said quietly.

"What does that mean?" Groa asked.

"Lowland river." The Finnish woman kept her gaze fixed on the fortress. Smoke rose from rooftops within the walls. Eight ships lay beached near the river mouth. "*Alode-joki* was a Finnish village before the Varangians came. The Norse called it *Aldeigja*. And the Slavs, with ears like cabbages and tongues like snakes, heard that as *Ladoga*."

Vlad leaned back from the prow. "It's Old Ladoga now." He winked—to Anni, or to Groa? For the first time it struck Groa that the black-haired purser did not look entirely Norse. Had a mix of Finnish or Slavic blood given his features their extraordinary attractiveness?

"Why do you call it old?" The question came from Hrolf.

Unwillingly, Vlad shifted his gaze away from the young women. "Because it is. Ten years ago Rurik moved his capital south to the head of easy navigation on the Volkhov, closer to the treasures of Byzantium. Holmgard is his island fortress there, and the new city that grew up nearby is named just that—New City."

"Novgorod, to the Slavs," Anni explained. "Novgorod was never truly Norse." She squinted toward the wall of sharpened logs on the rise. "I do not know if the Slavs have taken the fortress of Holmgard yet, but the Finns have captured *Alode-joki*."

Anni's young son pointed to the beach. "That's my father's ship!"

Oleg had overheard the entire conversation from his position at the prow. He commented grimly, "An armed fortress will be costly to re-take."

"We could sail past it," Vlad suggested. "Our main goal is Novgorod, to help Rurik at Holmgard. We could leave a small force to besiege Ladoga and row the main fleet up the Volkhov."

Oleg frowned. "An army that leaves unfinished business behind risks an attack on two fronts."

"There's one obvious solution." Anni's dark eyes flashed. "You could threaten to kill my son and me unless my husband opens the gates. Then, of course, you could slaughter everyone."

Oleg turned silently to meet her gaze.

The Finnish woman lifted her chin. "That's why you brought us, isn't it?"

The Viking nodded slowly. But Groa could feel the struggle raging within him. His right hand touched the hilt of Fenris, as if drawn by its power. Then he placed both hands firmly on the gunwale of the ship.

"No," Oleg said. "The Rus were invited here a generation ago to rule Russiya, not to destroy it. We bring order, not chaos."

"You may think that, but—"

"Enough." Oleg cut her words short. He raised his voice to the crew. "We land at the beach to let our visitors go. The mother and her son will take a message to the Finns in the stockade. They are free to sail home. They may keep their arms and any plunder they have found. Oarsmen, row us ashore!"

Groa and the others took up their positions. At Oleg's signal they dipped their oars in unison. As they approached the beach, Oleg took Anni aside. "Remind your clansmen of the reason the Rus were brought to this land. Tell them to go home and take care of their farms. There is now a garrison of Geats at Karlsgard to make sure you do not slaughter each other's cattle, burn men in their halls, and enslave your friends. You will obey the law of the Rus."

Anni tossed her black hair. "And if my people refuse to leave Ladoga?"

"Then we will encourage them." The ship's prow ground into the gravel of the shore. "You have until nightfall."

Somehow even Groa doubted that the Finns would retreat. As soon as Anni and her son were ashore Oleg ordered his ship pushed off the beach. Then he shouted for the fleet to follow him to a different beach on the far side of the fortress. That position would allow the Finns to leave by the stockade's main gate and sail north to Lake Ladoga without interference.

"You've offered the Finns more than they deserve," Vlad said. "What if they refuse your offer and stay to fight?"

"We outnumber them ten to one."

"But we'd still lose hundreds attacking a stockade."

For a while the only sound was the creak and splash of oars.

Between pulls on his oar Hrolf asked, "How old is Ladoga?"

Oleg frowned at the question. "What?"

"The stockade," Hrolf said. "How long ago was it built?"

"Twenty winters." Oleg cocked his head. "Why do you ask, carpenter?"

"Because logs that old would be rotten at the base. If it's like the stockade we built at Karlsgard, they're only braced from the inside." Hrolf pulled again at his oar beside Groa. "A wall like that might be winched down. Back in Tunsberg we winched whole ships out of the water for repair."

Oleg stroked his red beard. "Pull up your oar, carpenter. And tell me what you know about winches."

By the time the fleet landed on the southern beach, Oleg was ready with new orders for his captains. The battalions were to set up camp two arrows' flight from the stockade, arrayed in a semicircle to the south of the fortress. If the Finns had not left Ladoga by nightfall, the crews were to secretly bring the stoutest anchor ropes and oars from the ships. Every warrior—man and woman—was to be battle-ready at dawn.

The Finns did not leave. All night they paraded the catwalks of the stockade, taunting the Norse in the darkness. Occasionally the Finnish guards heard the footsteps of scouts, but sent them fleeing with random arrows in the night. Fog from the river dampened the cool air with a fine mist.

When the first light of dawn pinkened the clouds, the Finnish guards heard a distant voice cry, "Now!" To their bewilderment, dozens of thick ropes rose from the ground outside the stockade. Each rope had been looped around the point of a sharpened log. The ropes tautened, splayed out like the strands of a gigantic spider's web. A few guards attempted to lift off the loops, but by then the ropes were already too tight. Other guards hacked at the ropes with swords, and managed to chop several loose.

But then the entire southern wall of the Ladoga fortress began tilting outward. The old wood groaned and creaked. With the massive thud of a forest felled at once, the wall collapsed outward across the earthen rampart.

Throughout the fortress village, people awoke with a start. Doors were flung open. Dark figures ran out to see what had happened. The guards who had been thrown from the catwalks picked themselves up and blinked into the graying fog before them.

Marching out of the mist was a solid row of round shields. Nearly three thousand Rus were advancing on Ladoga. And the barrier that had blocked them was gone. A roar rose from the Vikings, a war cry that shook the last of the Finns from their beds.

The Finnish guardsmen turned and ran. Everywhere people grabbed what they could and fled to the northern gate, pounding on its planks until it swung open.

By the time the wall of Vikings reached the settlement, Ladoga was empty. Fenris in hand, Oleg walked through the abandoned streets to the northern gate. Already the eight ships of the Finns had set off from the beach below.

"Only one is headed north to the Baltic," Vlad observed.

"It's Anni," Groa said. "She's taking her husband and her son home."

No one asked how Groa could be so sure.

Oleg's gaze turned to the boats rowing south, up the Volkhov River. "Seven ships have slipped past us on their way to Novgorod. Three hundred Finns have chosen to fight another day. They will join the Slavs at Novgorod, hoping to plunder Rurik's hall. That army will not be so easily frightened." He turned, looking for a white beard and black leather armor. And as usual, the Geatish chieftain was not far behind.

"Wiglaf!" Oleg called out. "Are you with us if we row to battle in Novgorod? The odds will be longer."

"It's not the odds, my friend." For once Wiglaf was not laughing. "Rescuing your leader is not our fight. For all we know, Rurik may already be dead. My troops will stay to rebuild Ladoga. We will guard the gap between you and Sweden."

Vlad whispered to Oleg, "That leaves us fifty-five ships. Most of our men are farmers, not warriors. This morning's march was no practice for a real battle. How long can we bluff?"

"As long as they believe." Oleg raised his voice to the troops. "Fighters of the Rus! We sail to Novgorod! We sail to save Russiya. To Rurik!"

The chant echoed back with less conviction. "To Rurik!"

* * *

The Finnish ships ahead of them were not slowed with the cattle and housewares of colonists, so when the Rus fleet finally rowed to the river shallows at Novgorod, the forces of the Finnish-Slavic insurgency had already spent most of a day preparing for the attack. Archers had been hidden in the trees on either shore. That defense could have been devastating, but a single careless arrow splashed into the water beside Oleg's flagship, giving them away. Wearily, Oleg called for the rowers to stow their oars and let the current carry them backwards, out of range.

With his fleet adrift, Oleg put his face in his hands. He twisted the silver ring on his finger. Then he looked to Groa. "I miss Helga. We will have to fight our way through to Holmgard. Helga would have had a plan. She would have known how to reach her brother. Can you see through Helga's eyes?"

"My eyes are different colors," Groa said, "But neither has sight from Niflheim. If you need a spy, look among the living." She glanced to Vlad.

Vlad nodded. "Groa is right. My mother was from Pskov. I can pass as a Slav. If you set up camp downriver, I'll slip into the city tonight. I assume you want me to find out if Rurik is alive?"

Oleg shook his head. "I wish that mattered more."

"Then you want me to determine which tribes are in the city, and their numbers?"

The Viking chieftain sighed, fingering his ring. "Helga would say that's not important either. No, I want you to spread word of the riches our colonists have brought—boatloads of cattle, silver, furs, and amber. Tell them our ragtag army has never been in battle."

"You want me to tell them the truth?" Vlad asked, incredulous.

"Yes. But see to it you come back alive tomorrow night." Oleg looked apologetically to Groa and Hrolf. "My wife was both strict and jealous. As much as I appreciate what you have done for me—you, Groa, in confronting the Swedish king, and you, carpenter, in winching down a fortress—Helga would say that you are not warriors. When the attack comes from Novgorod, my wife would have you standing in the front line."

"What!" Hrolf gasped.

Groa demanded, "Why? Because she would think we are good at dying?"

"No. Because Helga would think you are good at running."

* * *

The Rus colonists were not happy with Oleg's plan. He beached the ships two miles north of Novgorod. There he commanded each of the fourteen captains to separate their battalions by fitness and experience. Strangely, the infirm and the most capable fighters were to be left behind at the ships. All the rest—nearly a thousand, including Groa and Hrolf—were marched a mile toward the city, together with their cattle, and left there to set up a tent camp. Thorkell, the Norwegian jarl who had not been chosen as one of Oleg's captains, was put in charge of this frightened vanguard. Within sight of the city's outlying huts they set up their shields and built campfires. They marched patrols nervously back and forth in front of the tents. Even the cattle were scared, bellowing so loudly that they could certainly be heard in the town.

On the morning of the second day Groa awoke to a chilling battle cry. She quickly put on a helmet and a leather tunic—the only armor she had been given—and hurried outside to grab her spear and shield. Marching toward the encampment from the city was a line of more than a thousand shields. It was the nightmare from Ladoga, except that this time the Rus were on the wrong side.

Thorkell raised his sword, shouting, "Form a wall! Shield to shield. Weapons up!"

At that moment a volley of arrows sailed up from behind the advancing line. Terrified, the Rus colonists cowered behind their round, wooden shields. Feathered shafts thunked into the wood—and the grass, and the tents, and the colonists themselves. Aghast, Groa watched as dozens of people fell. She had never been in a battle. She had never imagined herself a warrior. Why on earth had Oleg—?

And then she remembered the Viking chieftain's words.

"Run!" Groa shouted. "Run for the ships! Take your shields and weapons, but run!"

The Rus had already been faltering. With Groa's cry more than a hundred of the colonists turned and ran. Thorkell's flank held for a few more moments, but then it too fled in retreat.

The battle cry of the Slavs and Finns turned into a victorious howl. They too broke into a run, ready to drive down the retreating Rus with swords and spears.

But the colonists who had been chosen for the vanguard troop were in good form. They might have no great skill with weapons, but as runners they were hard to catch. The race course before them was a mile-long field—a strip of the Volkhov's flood plain. To the right stood a row of riverside willows. To the left was a bluff at the edge of high ground.

The ships ahead were already in sight when three hundred Rus archers, hidden in the willows, unleashed a stinging volley of arrows into the flank of the attacking Finns and Slavs. At the same time a thousand Rus charged down from the bluff with spears and axes, slamming into the back of the pursuing army and cutting off its route of retreat. Meanwhile, the archers emerged from the riverside brush, many of them now armed with swords.

The colonists at the front of the retreat paused to catch their breath.

"Turn and fight!" Thorkell cried. "Form a line!"

Surrounded on all sides, the army of Slavs and Finns backed together, turning and bumping into each other in confusion.

"Kill as few as you can!" Oleg shouted, standing with his arms akimbo atop the bluff. "Those who lay down their weapons will be spared." Beside him, Vlad repeated the order in Slavic.

The spear-men of the Rus held their weapons at the ready. The archers along the riverbank notched their arrows.

Groa wiped sweat from her brow, her heart pounding. The unruly mass of colonists was obviously the weakest side of this cage. If the Slavs and Finns attempted to charge through them, hundreds of colonists would be slaughtered. But even that would slow the charge, leaving the Slavs and Finns exposed to attack on three other sides.

A man in a gilt helmet called out something in Slavic from the midst of the encircled army.

Vlad responded with a single word.

One of the Slavic swordsmen howled in rage, running toward the line of colonists with his blade raised. His cry died when three arrows brought him to his knees. Both armies watched silently as he slowly tipped forward into the grass.

The man with the gilt helmet was the first to throw down his shield in defeat. The army of Slavs and Finns had been led into a cage with no door.

CHAPTER 8
STOCKHOLM, 1961

The ancient wolf sniffed the air, sensing a change. Gods had always been invisible to men, manifesting themselves in other ways. But now, after a thousand years of decline, Fenris smelled the thrilling, acrid scent of opportunity. There was something new in the ether surrounding the world ocean—a strange, tingling fear.

Great armies were gathering. That was not new. This time, however, they had built weapons that shivered atoms. That scale of destruction left an irresistible odor.

Fenris whined, sensing his old strength returning. For ages he had been banished to the dream-world. Now at last, as his power grew, he might once again stalk waking minds.

He had already chosen his favorites: the insecure, the hateful, the weak. The wolf-god's eyes glowed red as he searched for hearts he might sway.

Enemies would try to thwart him, of course. Other gods had drawn up battle lines against him long ago. To succeed, Fenris knew he must win a few strong mortal hearts as well. Not merely the generals and presidents, but a few that neither Odin nor Thor would suspect. A disgraced archeologist in Estonia. A treasonous Marine in Minsk. And a foolish sixteen-year-old girl in Stockholm.

Fenris bared his fangs and snarled.

* * *

"Helen?" Mette tapped cautiously on her daughter's bedroom door. A strange male voice sang inside, presumably from a record. Why, she wondered, was she afraid? You shouldn't barge into a teenager's room, of course, but if this had been a colleague's office she would have knocked instead of merely tapping.

The difference, Mette realized, was that she still considered her daughter a fragile gift. Julius had nearly died in the final days of World War II, when Nazi leaders had used her excavation in Hedeby as a cover for their escape. Helen's birth had seemed all the more miraculous as the years went by and no other children appeared. The beautiful little girl had been their treasure. You do not bang your knuckles on a darling bunny's hutch.

And yet Mette had been troubled by what she had learned at Birka. Had Helen really been slipping off to the university, pretending she was old enough to be a student there? A less partial observer might find Helen's bold behaviors insolent instead of cute.

Perhaps, Mette thought, she herself was the one who needed to grow up—to admit that her daughter had never been a pet. It was a good thing that Helen did not have the soul of a rabbit. But was there a different animal inside, emerging as the girl aged?

Mette knocked more firmly. "Helen!"

"Coming." The music stopped. The door opened to reveal a cheerful young face that eased Mette's fears. "Sorry. I was playing my records."

Mette glanced at the album cover on the floor beside a pink plastic record player. Who was Buddy Holly?

"Mom?" Helen asked. "I know you're busy with the *Vasa*. If there's anything I can do—"

"No, that's not it. We need to talk." Mette looked for a place to sit down. Someday they would need to have a different talk about the room's clutter. For now she lifted a pile of rumpled clothes from a chair and sat down.

Meanwhile, Helen's mind was racing. Her mother's lecture was evidently not about the loudness of her music nor the clutter in her room. That left more dangerous topics. She hopped onto her bed, sat cross-legged, and grinned as innocently as she could.

"OK, Mom. What's up?"

Mette sat with her hands folded on her lap. "Yesterday I went to see Per Gertula's excavation at Birka. He said he'd seen you at the university. He thought you were a student there. He said you'd been singing English pop songs and sharing Russian articles from your Aunt Sasha. Is any of this true?"

Helen knew she could look surprised for no more than five seconds before she had to answer. Under no circumstances could her reply lead to her boyfriend Lennart or to their meeting place, the Hammer and Sickle. Fortunately she had a gift for storytelling. By the count of three Helen had hit on a tale that wasn't entirely untrue.

"But Mom! I've already told you about Culture Club."

"Culture Club?"

Helen rolled her eyes. "You were the one who recommended it."

"I was?"

"Or maybe someone else at the *Vasa* office. Anyway, the after-school programs at the gymnasium are lame, so I've been going to Culture Club at the university instead. It's pretty funny that Per thinks I'm a student."

"Per didn't mention a club."

"Oh, he's just a visitor, not a regular."

Mette unclasped her hands and smoothed the wrinkles in her skirt, as if she were ironing out her daughter's words. "What do regular members of Culture Club do?"

"Cultural stuff." Helen bounced a little to display her enthusiasm. "Language, customs, genealogy. I'm good at English so my project has been to learn some English songs. It was Culture Club that suggested we get pen pals. See? I've been writing to Celeste in Sicily." She scooped a sheet of blue aerogram paper off the bed and held it up to show that she had been writing. Helen didn't say that the pen pals were supposed to be members of the Young Communist Internationale, nor that she had abandoned the idea in favor of using aerogram paper for a diary.

"Pen pals are fun. But you should never invent stories about our family."

Helen widened her eyes. "You think I'd tell them Aunt Sasha's a spy?"

"Your aunt is a tourist agent. An ordinary tourist agent."

"I know, I guess. But what was I supposed to do with the newspaper she gave me for Christmas? I don't read Russian, and some of the others at Culture Club do. We were all excited to find out how the Russian Navy is locating old shipwrecks."

Mette nodded, relieved. She was a little embarrassed to have doubted her daughter, jumping to conclusions. And she really didn't have time for a family crisis now, with the raising of the *Vasa* less than a week away. Still, it was good that they had had this talk, to clear the air. She would need to make sure she followed up on what she had learned.

"I'd like to meet some of your new friends in Culture Club. Maybe I could drop by some afternoon, or you could invite them here for dinner?"

Helen stopped bouncing, suddenly struck with panic. If her mother walked through the basement door of the Hammer and Sickle she would flip out. If Lennart came home for dinner, both her parents would flip out. She would have to invite someone else. Someone discreet.

Five seconds had passed, and Mette was beginning to worry that her daughter's expression had frozen.

"Helen? Don't you want me to meet your new friends?"

The girl came out of her trance with a light laugh. "Of course I do. You'll love Urmas. She's from Estonia and is really interested in genealogy. She's already been in touch with Gramma Kirstin."

"With my mother? Really?"

"Uh huh. You know how Gramma always said we may be related to the old Viking kings of Norway?"

"Yes—" Mette drew out the word uncertainly. Her mother had established her archeological credentials by connecting old Norse sagas with the Oseberg ship excavation in Norway. In her old age Grandma Kirstin had begun to fantasize about a distant familial connection to King Harald Fairhair himself.

"Well, Urmas thinks it's true!"

CHAPTER 9
NOVGOROD, 882

The warrior who had thrown down his gilt helmet turned out to be Miloslav, the chief of a Slavic tribe on the Dnieper River at a place called Kiev. Using Vlad as translator, Miloslav explained that he had joined the uprising against the Rus in the hopes of expanding his realm to the north. With news that Rurik lay ill in bed, people had doubted the legends that Swedish Varangians were invincible gods.

But then the Holmgard fortress outside Novgorod really had refused to fall, despite all their efforts. And then Oleg had appeared out of nowhere with a force of three thousand and had crushed the rebellion with a single brilliant military trap.

"Do you now believe Varangians are gods?" Oleg asked. From their vantage point on the bluff above the river plain they could see the crowds of defeated Slavs and Finns, their hands bound with rope, being herded toward the city like cattle. The pile of confiscated weapons in the field below could have been a silver haystack.

Vlad translated Miloslav's reply: "No, the ones we killed bled like men. But you are worthy leaders." Miloslav lowered his head. His matted black hair hung in strings across his forehead to his brown eyes and a strangely crooked nose. "For generations our people have fought each other. Rurik's illness briefly united us against you. Now it seems that we have no choice but to unite again, beneath you."

"Yes, but beneath which one of us?" Oleg mused aloud, knowing that this would not be translated. He turned to Vlad. "It's time we found Rurik, to see for ourselves how ill he is. Send this chief back to the rest of the Slavic prisoners. I want all twelve of my captains to secure Novgorod and make sure none of the captured fighters escapes. As for my own ship's crew, we'll go to Rurik in Holmgard, bringing word of our victory."

* * *

Groa found herself in a troop of forty-five, marching beside Hrolf toward Rurik's stronghold. The rebels had occupied Novgorod for only a few weeks, but they had managed to wreck the place. Obviously they had come to plunder, and not to rule. Broken pottery and bed-straw littered the muddy streets. Walkway planks and sections of wattle walls had been torn loose. Most of the huts, however, were built of logs less prone to vandalism. And the roofs, made of split wooden shakes instead of thatch, had been out of reach. Groa wondered what had become of the town's inhabitants. Presumably the craftsmen and merchants had fled to the forest, carrying what they could.

The town ended at a reedy swamp where the Volkhov River must once have looped. Now the abandoned channel formed a marshy moat around Holmgard's island-like riverbend. The only dry access to the fortress was a causeway dug from the muck. The path was so narrow that they had to walk single file. At the center of the swamp the route crossed a wobbly single-plank bridge.

Even from a distance Groa could see ropes hanging from the sharp-ened logs of the stockade. Evidently Miloslav's men had tried the Vikings' trick at Ladoga—winching down the walls. But this palisade was not rotten, and the swamp must have been poor ground for the attack. A flock of crows flew up from the reeds. With a start, Groa recognized the half-submerged bodies of men, sprouting arrows like crooked grass.

"Hail Rus!" Oleg held up his round wooden shield, painted yellow and white with a spread eagle. "I am Oleg, returned from Sweden." In a lower voice he added, "I bring news both good and bad."

The watchmen behind the wall conferred skeptically. After two weeks of assault hardly a hundred Norse had survived to defend Holmgard. How could Oleg, with what appeared to be a single ship-load of motley recruits, have dispersed the vast Finno-Slavic army? Still, the motif on Oleg's shield was unmistakable. The gate opened a crack.

"Hail Oleg." A captain of the guard stood in the gate's gap with his sword drawn. "How did you get through Novgorod? Did you bring sorcerers?"

Oleg pointed to Groa with his thumb. "Just the one."

The guardsman fell back, eyeing the young woman with alarm.

"Does Rurik live?" Oleg asked.

The captain tipped his hand uncertainly. "Half and half. Even the living part is possessed."

Hrolf said, "Maybe a sorceress would help."

Groa held up her palms in dismay. Her luck with magic had rarely been good. If expectations were high, she was likely to disappoint.

The captain waved the group to follow him across a courtyard. On the way he confided to Oleg, "We would welcome you with a feast, but all we have left is foul water and rotten fish. We could not have held out much longer."

The captain showed them to a stave hall that was twice the height of the compound's log huts, its curving sides reminiscent of a boat shed. Peculiar twanging wails emanated from the entry, as if cats were inside fighting.

Oleg shared a worried glance with Vlad before venturing into the murk. When Groa followed she traced the noise to a cluster of dimly lit figures beside a smoldering central hearth. A young child was crying, a woman was singing badly, and two men were jangling string instruments made from gourds. There was no sign of the famed Varangian leader.

"Danuta?" Oleg asked. "Where is your husband?"

The woman stopped singing. "Oleg! Just look how my little Igor has grown. But oh, he is fussy today, aren't you, my little sweet?" The woman's light brown hair had been tied up with straps and rings—a device that reminded Groa of a horse's halter. The queen unpinned a strap of her long blue dress to offer a breast to the angry child, speaking to him in a language Groa did not recognize. Perhaps Pomeranian? The boy looked to be at least three winters old— too old to be suckling, Groa thought.

"Rurik," Oleg repeated. "Where is he?"

"Did you bring cows?" Danuta shook her head. She seemed to be speaking to her son instead of to Oleg. "We have missed our cheese curds, haven't we?"

"Danuta!" Oleg commanded. "Where is Rurik?"

She raised her chin. "No one shouts at us." To the screaming child she added, "Do they, my sweet?"

Oleg slowly clenched and unclenched his fists. His red beard seemed to bristle. But by then Groa's sharp young ears had detected a faint gurgle in the shadows beyond the hearth. She pulled aside a hanging mat to reveal a bed with a withered, white-bearded man. He wore a necklace of silver coins.

Without a word Oleg strode past Danuta to Rurik's side.

At first the old Viking really did seem dead, his hollowed face frozen in a scowl, his blank eyes staring up. But then his left eye—and only his left eye—swiveled to confront the newcomers.

"Glerg." The sound bubbled up from Rurik's throat. The left side of his face twitched, lifting one corner of his mouth into a lopsided grin. His chest rose and fell, obviously with an effort.

"Olerg," he said.

"Yes, Rurik, it's me." Oleg clutched the old chieftain's hand in his. "What has happened to you? Were you in a battle?"

"Og." Rurik's left eyebrow lowered and his head tilted slightly to one side.

By now the rest of the crew was gathering around the sick bed. Vlad suggested, "I think he's saying no. This is no battle wound."

Oleg looked to Groa. "Have you seen such an illness before?"

"I'm afraid so." As an old woman in Norway she had lost many a friend to lingering half-deaths. "It is as I thought, a sickness of the heart, the organ that controls thought. One side of his body has failed."

"Will he get better?"

"Possibly a little." She hesitated. "More often, though, a second attack takes the other side too."

"Gow?" Rurik said. He swallowed and tried again, speaking more clearly now. "How break siege?"

Oleg squeezed his hand. "We lured the Slavs into a pretty little box by the river. I've brought the army you wanted—three thousand strong. The realm of Russiya you dreamed of will be yours."

"Not mine." Rurik's one movable eye wandered, searching. "Son."

"Your son Igor?" Oleg shook his head. "The boy won't be ready to rule for at least a dozen winters. You have to get well. Russiya needs you to rule until Igor is grown."

"No. Someone else." Rurik's eye wandered again. "Not Danuta."

Oleg tightened his lips and gave a single nod. If Rurik died his wife would normally be expected to serve as regent for his young son. Although Danuta was a doting mother, she was obviously ill prepared for the task of ruling a Viking realm.

Meanwhile, the fingers of Rurik's one live hand had found Oleg's silver ring. The old man turned the ring slowly on Oleg's fourth finger, feeling the pattern. The right side of Rurik's face smiled. "You married my sister?"

"Yes." Oleg's eyes glistened damply. "Helga and I married."

"Good." Rurik took a deeper breath. Summoning what remained of his strength he raised his voice. "Igor! Danuta! Come here!"

Rurik's wife and son approached from the hearth, clearly amazed at the forcefulness of Rurik's command. Danuta gasped to see her husband lifting himself onto one elbow, dragging the unresponsive half of his body up from the bedstraw.

"Glerg!" Rurik roared, clearing his throat. The little boy cowered wide-eyed behind his mother's draping shawls.

"Hear me!" The old Viking wrenched his mouth to form the words. "When I die—" he gasped to draw in more breath—" Russiya will be ruled—by regents—my sister Helga—and her man Oleg—until my son is older."

After this effort he fell back onto the bed, jangling his necklace. He rolled his withered head toward Oleg. "You swear—to cede power—to Igor?"

Tears were running down Oleg's face into his red beard. "Yes. I do."

"Then it is done. Take my necklace, regent." Rurik's right eye closed. He gurgled, breathing heavily after his exertion.

Oleg's tears fell into the straw as he carefully lifted the old man's head and removed the chain of silver medallions.

When at length Rurik reopened his right eye he noticed that Oleg was weeping.

"Where—" Rurik asked, "is—Helga?"

Oleg wiped his face with the back of his hand, but his lips still trembled. "My wife is at Birka. She and her horse were hit by arrows from Eirik. In return we killed the Swedish king. I had the help of a silversmith with a well-thrown knife." He pointed to Groa.

Rurk's eye wandered to Groa and back. "My sister—stayed in Sweden—to recover?"

Oleg swallowed hard. "Helga lies with the ring that matches mine. She was laid to rest with the honors of a queen."

"My sister—dead?" The right side of Rurik's face distorted with a cramp. He arched his back as if wrestling an unseen demon. Half his mouth opened with a strangled cry of anger. Then he sank back in defeat. His chest no longer rose. His right eye stared up as blankly as his left.

Oleg and the others stepped back, afraid.

Danuta, however, leapt forward. She pounded her husband's chest. She shook his shoulders. For a moment she buried her face beside his. Then she stood back, cursing the corpse with an angry mixture of Norse and foreign obscenities.

"Danuta—" Oleg began.

She turned on him fiercely. "Get out, thief! You can start usurping my rights tomorrow. My husband may have thrown away our realm on the man who killed his sister, but for this one day I will remain in charge. And as soon as my Igor becomes a man, we will make you pay for your treachery."

"Surely you can't think that I—"

"Out!" Danuta pointed to the entryway.

Oleg's hands clenched again—clutching the silver necklace in his left and the hilt of Fenris in his right.

"Out!" Danuta repeated.

Without another word, Oleg turned and left the hall.

* * *

Rurik's widow used the following day with surprising efficiency. When Oleg returned, bringing a much larger contingent that included all twelve of his captains, he discovered that Danuta had converted the stave hall into a fortress within a fortress. Many of Holmgard's Norse defenders apparently felt more allegiance to Danuta than to Oleg. They had stripped everything of value from the rest of the fortress and had stockpiled it in the central hall, which they now defended as if it were an independent palace.

Vlad stroked his carefully shaved chin, summing up the situation. "It looks like Danuta only cares about ruling her own little household. She isn't interested in the responsibility of a queen. All she wants is the luxury."

"Then she shall have it," Oleg said. He too had spent the past twenty-four hours in feverish preparation. He had assigned several metalworkers to Groa, with orders to commandeer a blacksmith shop and rework Rurik's silver necklace. Fifty men with woodworking skills had been delegated to help Hrolf. And each of Oleg's twelve captains had been ordered to drill their best troops, practicing weapons and formations with the rigor they had learned from the Geats.

If Oleg hoped to take command of Rurik's struggling empire, even as regent, he knew he would have to make a stronger showing than he had on the beach in Tunsberg at the start of summer. Had it really been only a month ago that he had sailed back from Norway with a fledgling fleet of just three ships, their prows audaciously tipped with the rune of Tyr?

It took most of an hour for Oleg's troops to thread their way single-file across the marsh's narrow causeway to Holmgard. Queen Danuta and her followers watched from the breezeway of the central stave hall. More than four hundred of Oleg's warriors packed into the fortress' courtyard—twelve battalions, each precisely arrayed in columns of two by twenty. Workmen assembled a stage with steps and a high seat. Poles on either hand flew banners with the yellow-and-white stripes of Oleg's shield, emblazoned with spread eagles. Two trumpeters lifted the snake-like tubes of lur-horns above the crowd and blew a fanfare.

Oleg strode out before the troops. A blue cloak bulged over his armor, making his shoulders seem even broader and his red beard even more fiery. Around Oleg's neck hung the chain of silver medallions, his badge of office. Unprompted, the men broke into the battle cry of the Vikings—a howl that sent a chill down Groa's spine.

Oleg walked past the stage to the central hall. The roar of the crowd prevented Groa from hearing what the Viking chieftain said there, but she could see Rurik's three-year-old son, Prince Igor, cowering in his mother's skirts, crying. Danuta shook her head at whatever Oleg had said. Then she retreated with the boy into the shadows. Oleg nodded, walked back to the stage alone, climbed the steps, and held up his hands for silence.

"Hail Rus!" Oleg called out.

"Hail Rus!" the crowd roared back.

When quiet returned, Oleg spoke more quietly as well. "Rurik, the leader who founded Russiya, is dead. But his goal, to end the fighting in this land and bring prosperity with trade—that goal lives on."

Cheers interrupted him. Once again Oleg held up his hands. "Yesterday, when Rurik lay dying, he named his son Igor as the next ruler of Russiya."

Voices in the crowd began to grumble. Oleg shook his head and continued, "Rurik was wise enough to know that the boy is too young. So he chose his sister and me to serve as regents in the interim."

Oleg's voice caught. He held his right hand before his face, as if to show the crowd the silver ring on his finger. But even Groa could see he was actually wiping a tear from his eye. "My wife Helga died in Sweden, felled by an arrow from King Eirik. That king is dead. I vow before you now to honor Helga's memory and Rurik's wishes by fulfilling their dreams here in Russiya. On this day, twelve years from now, I promise to declare Prince Igor sole ruler of the Rus."

A few of the men—mostly those from the garrison itself—thumped their shields in approval. Oleg's vow was honorable, but was it wise? No one knew what kind of leader a whimpering child might grow up to become.

Oleg held out his hand toward the row of Danuta's soldiers. The guardsmen flanked the central hall like an extra set of staves.

"For my first act as regent, I choose to honor the defenders of Holmgard. These soldiers kept the flame of Russiya burning on a hearth within these walls, although an army thirty times their number stood outside. To them I say, Hail Rus!"

"Hail Rus!" Oleg's troops echoed his call. Danuta's guardsmen, however, did not flinch. They stood as solemnly as if they really were wooden posts.

Oleg surveyed the row of guards. "You are the most loyal and experienced of the Rus warriors. I can sense that Rurik's death has left your hearts uncertain. Some of you may see your duty as the defense of a three-year-old prince and a dowager queen. I respect that choice. But others among you may feel bound to a greater vision—Rurik's quest for a united Russiya. I call upon you now to declare your loyalty. Stand your ground if you would serve only Queen Danuta and her child for the next twelve winters. If, however, you would choose to leave the walls of Holmgard and join us in ruling Russiya, step forward."

The line of guardsmen held firm a moment as the men weighed these options. If they stood their ground they would become the housebound servants of a frivolous queen and her demanding toddler. If they stepped forward they would be thrust into unknown battles under the rule of this red-bearded regent.

The guardsmen began glancing left and right.

Groa closed her eyes and whispered silently, "I will go."

A tall, bushy-bearded guardsman took a step forward. He planted his spear and announced, "I will go."

Groa caught her breath. Had the man heard her thought? Or had she heard his? As a crone in Tunsberg her cry of "I will go" had inspired only mockery.

Soon a second man, and a third, stepped forward, muttering, "Hail Rus." Before long more than half of the guards had advanced a step.

Oleg counted them with his eyes. Then he crossed his arms. "Sixty-four men. You shall be the Jarls of Novgorod, free to trade, settle, or join in our campaigns as you wish."

Groa marveled. Jarls! With a word Oleg had ennobled an entire troop, granting them privileges that could earn them wealth, power, and saga fame. The forty guards who had stayed behind to serve the queen might as well have been slaves in comparison.

The tall guard who had stepped out first asked warily, "And what are these campaigns you would undertake, Oleg the Regent?"

"We have much to do," Oleg replied. He climbed the steps to the stage, but instead of sitting in the throne-like wooden chair he stood to one side with his hand on its arm. It was a gesture that Groa immediately recognized as a stroke of genius. Oleg was demonstrating that he was not a king. As regent his authority relied on the throne of a ghost.

Surely, Groa thought, everyone was picturing Rurik in that high seat, with Oleg's hand resting on the old Viking's arm.

"Yesterday at dawn," Oleg said, "We defeated the army of a dozen tribes. From all across Russiya the Slavs, Finns, Huns, and Bulgars had sent their best fighters to plunder Novgorod. Now we will reverse their campaign—not to plunder, but to rule. I have divided the Rus into twelve battalions under the command of twelve captains. Each captain will choose a tribe and learn what he can from our prisoners about their homelands. The wealthiest men will be returned as hostages, ransomed, and allowed to serve as vassals of the Rus. The remaining prisoners will either be sold to the Geats as slaves or put to work on a special project here in Novgorod. Their properties, of course, will be forfeit. Together with the lands of those who died in battle, these will become the new home estates of the Rus colonists. From Smolensk to Kiev, from Ladoga to Pskov, all of Russiya will be united under the Rus before the first snows of winter fall."

Murmurs ran through the crowd. Could they reconquer all of Russiya in a single autumn? The sheer scale of the enterprise was breathtaking.

The lanky guardsman remained skeptical. "Twelve campaigns at once? That would be the stuff of sagas indeed. But what of us, your newly named 'Jarls of Novgorod'? Many of us have families hiding in the forest, waiting for the siege to end. They may not want to colonize distant estates. What is this 'project' you propose for those who remain in Novgorod?"

Oleg smiled. "This too may be the stuff of sagas." He waved for Vlad to join him on stage. "Let us see if my purser, Vlad, has a clue to offer in verse."

Again Groa marveled at Oleg's mastery of the moment. Inviting a skald to respond was more than an act of showmanship. It was a uniquely Viking way to assert authority over a doubting dullard.

The move also put Vlad on the spot. That morning he had slicked his black hair, shaved fastidiously, and put on a dashing crimson cloak, but he had obviously not been warned to prepare a poem. His handsome smile carried him as far the stage. Then he motioned for the lur-horn musicians to blow an introductory chord, which gave him a few more moments to think. Among the audience he caught Groa's mismatched eyes—green and blue. She nodded encouragingly.

Finally Vlad cleared his throat and asked loudly,

Who wants to walk?

Half of the men in the courtyard froze in place, afraid that Oleg's right-hand man was searching their souls for potential deserters. But others began to smile. This was a verse! The rhythm of Vlad's question and the alliterative W sounds showed that the sly skald had already begun his poem. Vlad raised his eyebrows and continued,

> Wouldn't the Rus rather row?
> Yet the sea-steeds of Sweden
> Are heavy to haul
> Through the forests of Russiya.

Now the audience was with him. Every man who had portaged a Swedish longship from one Russian river to another understood what a chore it was.

> If Tyr were a trader,
> A true Varangian voyager,
> He'd build us a better boat.

Laughter and nods of agreement gave Vlad a moment to prepare his final lines.

> We'd like something lighter.
> A swift, sure sailer,
> Easier on weary shoulders.
> We need a 'Ship in the Woods.'

Oleg laid a congratulatory hand on the purser's shoulder. "Well spoken, skald."

Then he turned to the guardsman. "This will be the project for those who stay in Novgorod—to build a ship suited to the rivers of Russiya. Prosperity depends on trade. Our jarls will become wealthy by bartering the amber of the Baltic and the furs of the Arctic for the treasures to the south. But first we need nimbler dragons that can fly through the river rapids to Miklagard—Constantinople."

The tall guardsman held up his hands. "We are axe men, Regent, not shipwrights. Our carpentry is limited to stockades and stave walls."

"Then let us ask the advice of a master." Oleg motioned for Hrolf to join him on stage. The homely woodworker cringed, ducking his head so that he appeared to have no neck at all. He climbed the stairs as if to a gallows.

"I give you Hrolf of Tunsberg," Oleg announced. "Though he claims to be nothing more than a carpenter, his wiles brought down the walls of Ladoga. For the past day I have assigned him fifty men to plan the ship we need. What have you learned, Hrolf?"

"I—" Hrolf mumbled. "I have never built a ship."

A voice from the crowd shouted, "Speak up, man!"

The carpenter flushed red. He raised his head and bellowed, "I have never built a ship!" He stared down the crowd. "But I spent the past day with fifty men who have. They told me that Russiya does not have the oak we need to build Swedish ships."

Hrolf frowned before continuing. "This may be a good thing. Oak is strong, but it's as heavy as iron. The forests surrounding Novgorod are full of spruce—stringy, light wood. It splits lengthwise into planks that bend but rarely break."

Oleg asked, "How much lighter would a ship of spruce be?"

"Perhaps a third?" Hrolf shrugged. "The 'Ship in the Woods' we could build here would not survive a winter storm on the Baltic. But she could handily carry cargo to the sun-lands."

"Good," Oleg announced. "Build me two a month."

Hrolf nearly choked. "I thought you wanted just one!"

"My plans for Russiya require an additional ship every fourteen days."

"But—but that would mean building two dozen ships in a year!"

Oleg nodded. "Vlad will give you what you need. I'm appointing him Governor of Novgorod. He'll supply men for you to train.

The forests here have plenty of trees, and the bogs have enough iron. Twenty-four ships will be your goal for the first year. In future years I may need more."

"More?" Hrolf croaked the word.

"If you think the task requires magic, I'll loan you a sorceress." Oleg motioned with his fingers for Groa to step forward. "But first I need her for a different purpose."

Hrolf returned to the crowd in a daze. When he stumbled while descending the steps Groa caught his arm. "I'll do whatever I can to help," she whispered. The ugly woodworker was becoming more attractive every day.

As Groa stepped up onto the stage Oleg had the trumpeters blow a flourish. "Warriors of the Rus! This is Groa."

A heckler called out, "Another wife? So soon after Helga?"

"No." Oleg lowered his bushy red eyebrows. "Groa is a silversmith. She has the power to bring down kings. It was her knife, and not mine, that killed Eirik of Sweden."

The soldiers in the courtyard eyed the young woman with new caution.

"I have brought Groa before you," Oleg continued, "Because I suspect she fears—as do some of you—that I might abuse my regency. You think I wish to rule alone. You worry that I might rule by my sword."

He paused, his hand above the hilt of Fenris. Groa could feel the blade's magnetism, tempting him. But then Oleg raised his hands and lifted the necklace of silver medallions carefully off his shoulders.

"Unlike the emperor in Miklagard, Rurik had no crown. Instead he had his smiths fashion this silver chain. The fourteen coins, he said, represent the tribes of Russiya he wished to unite. The front of each coin has the image of two Norse dragons, gripped together, biting each other's tails."

Oleg frowned. "I'm not exactly sure what he meant the dragons to represent. It is an old motif. For me and Helga, it symbolized faithfulness. I will never betray my vow to my wife." He cleared his throat. "But with Rurik's death we have seen that a realm is the work of many people, and not just one. I wonder if this sorceress could demonstrate that truth, if she mistrusts me so much?"

Oleg held out the necklace to Groa.

The crowd hushed. Was Oleg offering to share his rule with a girl?

Groa waved her hand slowly around the necklace. Half of the art of sorcery was distraction. People wanted to believe. As if in a trance she recited the names of the sixteen runes of Futhark:

Fe, Ur, Thorn,
As, Rad, Korn,
Hail, Need, Ice,
Auer, Sol, Tyr,
Birch, Man, Lake,
Yggdrasil.

Then she shook the necklace. At once it opened, dangling free as a single string of coins. This did not surprise the audience—a necklace might have a hidden clasp. But then she detached one coin after the other, revealing that each medallion now hung by its own separate, smaller chain. One by one she draped the fourteen necklaces over Oleg's outstretched hand.

To work this magic Groa had spent the past day piecing together fourteen chains from the tiny steel links of a mail shirt. She had coiled the little chains out of sight behind the coins and tied them together with grass so they would come apart when the time was right.

Oleg held up the chains to the audience, seemingly as astonished as anyone. "Out of one, sorcery has made many. And now, out of many we will make one. Come, my captains! You too, Vlad. Join me in a circle around Rurik's high seat. Let us redistribute his inheritance."

The twelve captains climbed to the stage, completing a circle with Vlad around the empty wooden throne. Oleg slowly walked the circuit, hanging a medallion around each man's neck.

Oleg put the fourteenth necklace over his own head. Then he lifted the coin from his chest. "What is this inscribed on the back? More sorcery, Groa?"

Groa came closer, making a show of squinting at his medallion. "There are runes. The first three are the T-runes of Tyr."

"The same arrows that tipped the prows of the first three ships in my fleet," Oleg commented. "And the final rune?"

"It is Fe, the F-rune. Its twin forks stand for cattle, wealth, and—" Groa paused. This part of the show struck her with an ancient dread. "And Fenris, the name etched on your sword."

114

Oleg unsheathed the sword. He held up its damascened blade. "A sword to unite Russiya. A sword to bind the fourteen bearers of Rurik's legacy." He stabbed the blade into the wooden throne so the steel shaft stood upright.

With this act, Groa realized, Oleg had banished the ghost of Rurik. Fenris now reigned in the high seat. Wasn't this what Groa had feared? Shouldn't she have demanded that Oleg trade his sword for her knife, as he had once promised? Why had she decided to wait?

Oleg walked around the circle of men, tapping his medallion against the medallions on their chests. "We fourteen shall forever be bound to Rurik's quest. Henceforth we and our descendants shall be known as the Order of Varangian Knights."

"With our might," Oleg said, lowering his voice, "the Rus shall rule till Ragnarök."

CHAPTER 10
STOCKHOLM, 1961

On the morning of April 24 all of Sweden watched—anxious, proud, uncertain—as pumps on concrete pontoons gushed water for the final lift of the *Vasa*. Television cameras stared into the empty bay, as ungainly as rhinoceroses at a watering hole. Reporters and dignitaries from around the world filled makeshift grandstands on the island of Skellholm. Something ancient was about to emerge from the dark waters of Stockholm's harbor, a weapon of war that had lain hidden for centuries.

Helen was dizzy with excitement—not so much because of the ship, but because she had been chosen as a hospitality escort for Mr. and Mrs. Jay Bonworthy, the American diplomats who were personal friends of the Kennedys. The Texas oil derrick tycoon had been so impressed with Helen during his December visit that he had asked about her personally. Helen's mother had reluctantly agreed, knowing she would be busy elsewhere and that the Ministry of Foreign Affairs would assign their own attache as well.

Bonworthy and his wife ignored the attache—a dour, chain-smoking man in a black suit—and instead focused on this charming sixteen-year-old Swedish girl, who seemed to know the lyrics of even the most obscure American rock-and-roll songs.

The ambassador's wife asked, "Did you know that Ritchie Valens studied Chopin at the Sorbonne?" She wore a blue wool skirt suit with a matching pillbox hat, cocked at an angle exactly like the photographs of Jacqueline Kennedy. Slowly she smiled, a wide mouth with red lipstick.

Helen laughed. "Mrs. Bonworthy! I didn't know ambassadors were allowed to joke about their citizens."

"Oh, please, call me Estelle." She sighed. "I had so wanted Jay to be stationed in Paris. But I'm finding the Swedes actually understand us better. How did a girl like you learn so much so fast?"

"I told you," Jay lowered his voice. "She imagines that her uncle is with the CIA."

"Oh, then we can speak freely." Estelle rolled her white-gloved hand toward the gray silhouette of the city beyond the bay. "Instead of watching an opera in Paris we're waiting for a muddy old boat."

"This could be important," Jay countered. "We need to keep our eyes open."

Estelle widened her eyes melodramatically. "To watch for a leak!"

"Hush now."

"Don't hush me."

Helen suddenly realized that the ambassador's wife had been drinking. She must have stiffened her tolerance for the event by break-fasting on martinis.

"I have a sense for these things," Estelle told her husband. "A girl like Helen could help us more than you think."

"I could?" Helen asked.

Estelle held up her finger and leaned close. "There really is a leak, and it's not just in the boat. We think there's a spy in Sweden. Someone at the highest levels. Probably here today."

Helen opened her mouth. Then she closed it again, her throat dry. "What makes you think that?"

The ambassador's wife responded by mouthing a single word: "Cuba."

Jay Bonworthy had been gritting his teeth at his wife's whisperings. Now he grumbled, "That much is common knowledge. Somebody must have leaked word that we were arming Cuban exiles for an in-vasion. When our boys landed in the Bay of Pigs, the Commies were ready. Kennedy wound up starting his term with a full-scale disaster."

The Bay of Pigs fiasco had been a hot topic among Helen's friends at the university coffee shop—which they now liked to call "Culture Club," rather than the Hammer and Sickle. For them, Fidel Castro and his colleague Che Guevarra were larger-than-life heroes, daring young men who won the hearts of villagers, smoked big cigars, and wore combat fatigues. When Cuba's bourgeois dictator sent a trainload of federal troops to snuff out the rebellion, Che had borrowed a farmer's tractor and torn up the rails. In the ambush that followed, Che's guerrillas had routed the troops, captured boxcars full of weapons, and turned the tide of the revolution. Then—what bravado!—Che had rid-

den his motorcycle five thousand kilometers across South America, just for kicks. This was the sort of adventure that never seemed to happen to Swedish teenagers.

But now Helen had to think back. What exactly had she reported overhearing from Uncle Lars at Christmas? Certainly nothing specific enough that it qualified as a "leak"? And Lars himself wasn't among the American casualties in Cuba. Mette had gotten a card from him just last week, postmarked in Berlin.

Loudspeakers interrupted her thoughts with an unintelligible echoing bleat. Everyone craned their necks toward the harbor. The rounded stump of a blackened board was emerging from the choppy gray water.

The crowd cheered. The loudspeaker bleated again, this time at a higher pitch. A band began playing Sweden's national anthem. People sang along for the first verse:

> Du tronar på minnen från fornstora dar
> Då ärat Ditt namn flög øver Jorden

> You reign atop memories of ancient greatness,
> When your honored name flew over the world.

When the anthem finished Estelle Bonworthy said, "I thought a Viking ship would be bigger."

"The *Vasa* isn't from the Viking Age," her husband replied. He held up a hand, listening. A new, clearer voice was coming from the loudspeakers. "Who is that, and what's he saying?"

Helen strained to make out the words. A man in a blue military uniform was clutching a podium at the water's edge as if he were afraid that the hulking television cameras might charge, ramming him into the bay.

"It's Holger Henning, the Minister of Defense," Helen explained. "I think he wants money to build an aircraft carrier or something. He's saying Sweden needs to be a world power again."

"Again?" Mrs. Bonworthy scoffed. "When was this place ever a world power?"

"At least twice, actually."

By now enough broken timbers had surfaced between the pontoons that the outline of the rising wreck had become clear—two curving parentheses of ancient beams, nearly as long as a city block. Helen marveled that the ship was real after all. Her mother had been working for so many years on an invisible project that Helen had begun to think of it as a phantom.

"Does this general really think Sweden can compete with NATO and the Warsaw Pact?"" Jay Bonworthy asked.

The question seemed rhetorical, and Helen was distracted enough by the scale of the rising ship, that she said the first thing that came into her head. "At least the Russians are using their Navy for archeology."

"What?"

"Their nuclear submarines have located the wreck of a German submarine from World War II."

The ambassador tipped back his cowboy hat and scratched his head. "Where did you hear something like that?"

"In the newspapers." She didn't dare admit that the newspaper had been *Pravda*.

"That's propaganda. No one's sure what the Russkie subs are up to. For all we know they've been setting up listening stations around the coast of Scandinavia. The Brits just broke up a big Soviet spy ring in London. But we still haven't found the leak on NATO's northern flank."

After a few other speakers droned on, the pumps on the pontoons shut down. Apparently an outline of timbers was all of the *Vasa* that would be exposed today. A man in an old-fashioned top hat said a few final words. Then the band played a march and the crowd began to disperse.

Estelle Bonworthy looked sleepy. "Can we go home now, Jay?"

The silent attache from the Foreign Office finally cleared his throat. "Ambassador? I think you're expected for a photo opportunity with the other VIPs."

Helen could see her mother waving them toward a cluster of dignitaries on a temporary wooden platform beside the podium. Aides and television directors were arguing about who should stand where, and for which photos. As the politicians rearranged themselves, exchanging deferential courtesies, Helen saw a face among the crowd that stopped her cold.

Lenny?

Impossible! And yet there he was, her boyfriend, the skateboarding guitarist from the Hammer and Sickle, wearing a suit in the midst of the VIPs. She wanted to turn and run, but Mrs. Bonworthy was clutching Helen's arm to steady herself as they descended the wooden steps to the platform.

Helen's lips trembled. She flushed hot and then cold. This was precisely the nightmare she had feared—having her mother meet her "imaginary" friend. What could Lenny possibly be doing here anyway?

As soon as Helen had deposited the Bonworthys on the stage she tried to slink away. But her mother stopped her.

"Helen? I want you to meet a family friend." Mette tugged her reluctant daughter to a tall, middle-aged man with handsome dark eyes, a square jaw, and a sleek tailored suit. "This is Colonel Stig Wennerström, stationed with the Ministry of Foreign Affairs in Washington. He's known your Uncle Lars since they were officers at the end of the war."

At that moment Lennart emerged from behind Wennerström's shoulder. The boy lifted one eyebrow just slightly—a gesture that Helen couldn't decipher. Was he apologetic or mischievous?

Mette added, "And this is Stig's protégé Lennart Bronsson, an intern, I believe? Lennart, allow me to introduce my daughter Helen Gustmeyer."

Rather than hold out his hand, Lennart bowed from the waist. "A pleasure."

Helen flushed bright red.

"Too charming," Colonel Wennerström chuckled. "Your daughter is blushing."

"Helen," Mette said with some exasperation. "Lennart is a student at the university. He's studying political science." What she didn't say, but apparently meant, was, "This is the kind of boy I've been wanting you to meet."

Helen had known that Lenny was a political science major. But she had always thought of her boyfriend as a Communist rebel. Now she wondered if he was actually a double agent, leaking word about student activists to the establishment.

A man with a large flash camera shouted, "One more picture with everyone! A cover shot, to show the world that everyone was here when Sweden's flagship sailed again."

"Closer together, please," a woman photographer called out. "And this time, let's put the young people in front."

"Yes!" Several voices among the politicians agreed good-naturedly. The general who had orated earlier added, "Sweden's heritage belongs to her youth."

Helen found herself jostled forward until she stood shoulder to shoulder with Lennart. The flashes of cameras whoomfed before her, blinding her with a startled expression that magazine readers would later misinterpret as joy.

Afterwards Lennart managed to squeeze her hand. "See you at Culture Club," he whispered. "I have a surprise for you."

"Another?" she asked.

"Oh, and you know what? Your mother's even cooler than you said." Then Lennart walked away. He still had the confident, sassy gait of a skateboarding guitarist, even now that he was wearing a black suit with a tie. Who was he really, a rebel or a spy? Helen felt confused and a little bit thrilled.

"Before y'all head home," an American voice drawled, "Estelle and me wanted to thank you for translating." Jay Bonworthy was holding his white cowboy hat in his hands. Beside him his wife smiled, her red lipstick still carefully intact.

"You're welcome," Helen said. "Say hi to Jack and Jackie for me."

"Sure." The ambassador paused. "I just had one last question about the ship."

"What?"

"Well, I was curious if you'd solved that puzzle about the graffiti. I remember somebody had spray-painted three arrows. They looked like the arrows you'd found on a necklace-coin-thing in the ship. Have you figured out who's doing that?"

Helen hesitated. "I don't think they've found any more graffiti."

"Then what's this here?" The ambassador pointed to the side of the podium. There, below the cluster of microphones for the BBC, SR, and CBS someone had drawn three upward-pointing arrows in dark blue crayon. The runes would have been visible in television images around the world.

The ambassador mused, "I thought you said it was the mark of the god of war."

"It is." Helen nodded, her skin prickling with fear. "It's Tyr."

CHAPTER 11
NOVGOROD, 897

Groa suspected that the Arab doctor sent by Oleg was a spy. But for whom?

Fifteen years had passed since Oleg had become regent of Russiya. In the autumn of the very first year he had moved his capital south to Kiev, closer not only to the most rebellious tribes, but also to the trading centers of the Byzantine Empire and the Abbasid Caliphate. This twelfth year was supposed to be when Oleg would relinquish power to Rurik's heir. But few thought young Prince Igor was mature enough to rule, especially in such troubled times. A new disease had spread through Russiya—a powerful ague that weakened the young and killed the old. Oleg had sent the Arab medicinalist to make sure Igor and his mother, the aging Queen Danuta, stayed safe. At least that's what the Arab had been telling people. Why was he snooping around the shipyards?

For her own part, Groa had spent the past twelve years helping Hrolf with the task of building twenty-four ships a year. She and Hrolf had been too busy to actually celebrate a marriage, but they had started living together and, according to Viking tradition, this had eventually declared them man and wife. She had learned to love her unhandsome husband, despite his square head and blocky nose. Hrolf was strong and honest. Unfortunately, the humble woodworker was also gullible. Without her, Hrolf would have been an easy mark for the hucksters, thieves, and shirkers among the shipbuilding project's four hundred laborers. Even now he was proudly explaining the secrets of Viking hull construction to the Arab.

When Hrolf looked up at her, a smile whittled his wooden features. "Groa, my lovely wife. Have you met our visitor? Ali—I'm sorry, what was your full name?"

"Ali Ibn al-Namid," the man said, bowing slightly. His brown, beardless face was as smooth as an egg. He wore a robe with voluminous sleeves, a red sash, and pointed boots.

Groa did not return the bow. "I understood that you came to help at the Holmgard palace. Why are you so interested in our ships?"

"I am interested in everything," Ali replied. His Norse was accented, but grammatically precise. "The more one understands about the entirety of the world, the easier it is to cure a part that is broken."

"That's just what Groa says," Hrolf exclaimed. "You see, my wife is interested in healing too. She's been studying with an old Slavic witch."

Groa was glad her husband no longer introduced her to strangers as a sorceress. Calling her the student of a Slavic witch, however, wasn't much of an improvement. "Mostly I help Hrolf with the ships. But yes, I've also been collecting herbal remedies from local women."

"Excellent." Ali placed his hands together. "The Greeks claim that the herbs of each region hold the salves for that area's wounds. And the Prophet himself said that all disease can be traced to digestion. Tomorrow, would you join me at Holmgard to share your thoughts on medicine?"

"I suppose." Groa still didn't trust this foreign envoy.

"I will look forward to it." Ali swung his drooping sleeve in a theatrical arc. "For today, however, I want to learn how you build these 'Ships in the Woods' so quickly.'"

"Why?" Groa asked.

Ali looked nonplussed.

Hrolf sighed. "My wife is a voice of caution. I think she worries that outsiders will try building ships like ours."

The Arab laughed, exposing surprisingly yellow teeth. "The Caliphate builds much larger and more powerful ships than these. Our caravels have two or even three decks of oarsman. They are able to incinerate enemies with Greek fire. Their prows are fitted with iron rams. Still, your boats are works of beauty. And we agreed to a trade. One piece of your knowledge for two of mine."

Groa turned to her husband reproachfully. "Did you agree to this exchange?"

He nodded.

"What will you get in return?" she demanded.

"Something we both want, I think." Hrolf didn't meet her eyes. They rarely argued. He usually submitted to her advice. But once he had made a decision on his own, she could hardly oppose it outright. Viking men were supposed to have the final word. Groa knew that Viking women had subtler ways of getting their way. She would wait, and not forget.

Ali ran his hand along the prow of a skeletal ship. "The keel, you say, is made of Danish oak. But the rest of the wood is something else?"

"Spruce. It grows only in the north of Russiya." Hrolf glanced to Groa. "That is why Arabs can't build our longships."

She didn't reply.

"You must employ an entire army of sawyers."

"We have three forest troops." Hrolf led the way to the Volkhov River's bank, where men were unloading L-shaped beams from a beached ship. "Each troop is given six weeks to hew the rough wood for one ship. The struts you see here will be used for ribs. We search out roots and branches that curve naturally, so they will be strong. Some of the best struts come from trees that were bent by snow as saplings and grew crooked."

"Ingenious."

They walked along the bank to a row of fifteen unfinished ship frames. The white curls of spruce chips crunched beneath their feet. Groa loved the scent of fresh shavings, rich with the tang of pitch and apples. Amid the chips the bony ships looked as if they were already sailing on a foamy sea.

Hrolf said, "Workers with broad-axes finish the planks, matching each to a template. Then we assemble the planks with iron rivets."

"But you have no iron mines," Ali objected. "I have often wondered where the Norse obtain their steel."

Groa said, "Our iron is forged from water." She felt this was the kind of mystery only the Norse should be allowed to understand.

"From water? How is this possible?"

"Sorcery," Groa replied.

But Hrolf was shaking his head. "Bog water provides the ore. I'll show you." Before Groa could stop him he had walked to a pile of rust-colored clods. "The bogs in the north run red with iron mud. We dry it out and fire the residue in clay ovens to extract the metal."

"Hrolf!" Groa objected.

"This knowledge is of no use to Arabs. They have no bogs."

"It's true, we get the iron we need from rock, instead of water." Ali stroked his wrinkled chin. "Still, it is an interesting technology." His dark eyes surveyed the bog ore, the cylindrical kilns, and a row of forges where men were hammering iron rods for rivets.

"Most interesting," Ali repeated. Then he looked beyond the forges to a stack of large poles. "Next I would be curious to learn how your sailors raise and lower masts so quickly."

Groa held up her hands. "Enough. You've already learned too much from my husband. He has work to do, I have patients to see, and you are supposed to be taking care of Prince Igor. But before you leave our shipyard, what two pieces of knowledge have you agreed to give Hrolf?"

"Whatever he wishes." Ali waved his sleeves grandly. "The wisdom of the Caliphate runs deep. Its doctors are scholars."

Hrolf frowned in concentration. He had been given two wishes, and obviously wanted to make the most of them.

"Inlay," he said suddenly. "One of the jarls of Novgorod showed me a jewel box that had been built at the Caliph's workshop in Damascus. The lid was a marvel of different colored woods, somehow fitted together so precisely that it made a picture of a miraculous flower garden. How is this possible?"

126

Groa nearly groaned aloud. Her husband was a cabinetmaker. He had learned to produce ships. But he had always dreamed of being an artist. They had to turn out ships so quickly that there was little time for more decoration than a simple Tyr-arrow on the prow. Hrolf had traded genuine military secrets for a whim.

"The art of inlay is a rare skill," Ali said. "It requires exotic woods—ebony from Africa, teak from China, and birch from Russiya."

"From Russiya?" Hrolf asked, amazed.

Ali smiled, baring his yellow teeth. "Yes, the Caliphate trades with the Rus for many things. But the inlay artist also requires two tools—a saw and a knife."

"I have those."

The Arab shook his head. "The tools in your shipyard are for hacking. An inlay saw is as thin as beaten gold, with teeth so small they are all but invisible. It takes a steady hand to slice wood with such a saw. Then the inlay knife, a tiny razor, is used to cut precise curves—two sheets of veneer at once. The resulting pieces are fixed in place with glue made from the hooves of mountain goats."

Hrolf gave a sigh that almost broke Groa's heart. He did want to be an artist, and not merely a hewer. He felt that he lacked the means to make that dream come true.

Ali folded his hands. "What else do you wish to ask?"

Hrolf swallowed hard. He looked down and blinked as if his eyes were damp. Was he embarrassed, Groa wondered, or perhaps even ashamed?

"There is a—" he faltered. "There is a problem. I've heard—well no, I haven't heard—but I've been thinking that perhaps this is a problem Arab medicine might cure."

"Yes? What is this problem?"

"My wife and I—" Hrolf cleared his throat. Then he looked up at the Arab doctor and spoke clearly. "Groa and I have been married a dozen winters. We would like a child."

Now Groa was sure her heart would break. "Oh, Hrolf."

"I understand," Ali said, nodding somberly. "In the Arab world, men sometimes take many wives before they are able to produce an heir."

"We don't take multiple wives here," Hrolf objected, an edge of anger in his voice.

"Even in the Caliphate, those who cannot afford a harem ask me for advice. I offer two remedies to acquire an heir. First, burn incense during intercourse. This improves the chances that the child is a boy. Then, during pregnancy, the woman should eat dates. The dried fruit of date palms has a medical quality that changes the sex of an unborn child from female to male."

Hrolf balled his fists, now obviously angry. "I didn't ask about getting a male child. I asked if we could have a baby. Any baby at all."

Ali shook his head. "That is beyond my knowledge. I'm told there are fertility potions, but they are guarded by wizards in the great centers of learning—Alexandria and Constantinople."

Hrolf shook his fist at the man. "You have given me nothing in exchange for my tour of the shipyard—no special tools and no secret potions."

"Neither did you give me a ship." The Arab doctor shrugged.

In that moment Groa realized how much Ali's smooth head resembled a brown egg. How easily it might crack if Hrolf swung his balled fist!

"Let's say good-bye for today," Groa suggested.

The bald Arab doctor looked to Groa. "Very well. I anticipate discussing medicine with you tomorrow at the palace." He turned and walked away.

Hrolf clenched and unclenched his fingers, growling at the retreating figure of the doctor.

Groa put her hand on the tensed muscles of his shoulder. The revenge she had planned melted away. Hrolf had learned more than enough of a lesson on his own. "Oh my love, my love. Have you really been wishing so hard for us to have a child?"

His growl dropped a note. "I thought it would make you happy."

She kneaded his shoulders with both hands. "I am happy just as we are."

How could she tell him that she had lived an entire life with a previous husband, and that they had been childless too? Whatever gods had made her young again had not added the gift of motherhood. Instead she had been given a purpose—yes, sometimes she forgot. There were so many distractions, and a child would be another. She was supposed to undo the evil she had conjured in Fenris. Why did she keep delaying her demand that Oleg yield his old sword?

Hrolf's shoulders sagged. "Vlad says it is my fault."

"Vlad? What on earth has he been telling you?" There had been a time when Groa had desired Oleg's handsome purser, with his slick black hair and his clever verses. After Oleg had appointed him governor of Novgorod Vlad apparently thought he could extend his rule to any woman he fancied. He had married an influential widow, but remained notoriously faithless.

"Vlad says I am inadequate. He says the fact that he has fathered so many children is proof that he would make you happier."

"Hrolf, that's not true." She hugged him, pressing her head against his chest. His heart thumped strong and fast beneath bands of wonderfully taut muscles. Her husband was not much to kiss, but he was a joy to hug. "You are not at fault for our lack of children. It's me, I'm sure of it."

"I am less sure, Groa."

"I don't need a child to be happy. I just need you." She kissed him. His tensed lips seemed wooden, surrounded by bristles.

He tried to smile, but it wasn't very convincing. "It's just—I don't know. You spend so much time with other people's children."

It was true that she had begun a sort of school, teaching the children of Slavic slaves to speak Norse and make jewelry. Gradually she had added other subjects, intending to prepare the slave children for the possibility of freedom. But was she also compensating for her own empty home?

They hugged for a while in silence. Hrolf was not prone to speeches. He had already used up his supply of words for the day. Groa had learned how well the stoic woodworker could communicate with an embrace.

* * *

Groa spent most of the next day with Nadya, the herbal healer Hrolf had referred to as an "old Slavic witch." In fact, his description was about right. Nadya's face was as wrinkled as a dried fruit, overhung with careless strands of gray and white hair. She wore a long black dress with a cowl and countless hidden pockets. Her Norse was terrible, but this did not stop her from rattling on in a jumbled pidgin, stirring in Slavic and Finnish words with abandon. Novgorod was a polyglot settlement, especially in the ship laborers' district. Because the families there relied on Nadya to treat ailments, they had learned to keep listening to her until they eventually understood what she meant.

"Need lick not, but willow bark and old man's beard," Nadya had told Groa that morning. On their tour of the town they had found house after house where people were lying in straw bunks with the ague, alternately feverish and shaken with chills. The disease had spread through the city with amazing speed in the past few nights.

"Old man's beard?" Groa knew willow bark helped with fever. She was less sure how facial hair might slow an epidemic.

Nadya uttered a string of what sounded like nonsense words. Was it an incantation? Then she pushed Groa outside. "Get willow. Hurry! I get beard. Stomach my house."

These instructions were just clear enough that Groa grabbed a basket and hurried to the riverbank. She took out the knife that she kept hidden under her shift. She cut long strips from the willow saplings along the bank. When she had filled the basket she stowed the knife and dashed back into the city.

Novgorod's planked streets were more orderly than the alleyways of Birka or Tunsberg. A rough grid of streets overlay the avenues radiating from the harbor all the way to the outer stave wall that Vlad had ordered built—a palisade the Slavic workers called the "kremlin." The Jarls of Novgorod lived in halls along the harbor. The rest of the Norse-speaking Rus were mostly in the southern half of the city.

The largest of their log homes stood near the causeway that led across the marsh to Holmgard. To the east, the wattle huts of Slavic slaves crowded against the kremlin wall, while the Finnish quarter lay near the shipyards to the north.

Nadya's ancient log hut sagged in a copse of birches just outside the city walls. When Groa arrived, the old woman was boiling something in an iron cup over the hearth fire. "I brought the willow bark you wanted," Groa said, out of breath.

"Hot nerves," Nadya said. She added some of Groa's willow bark to the pot. "My beard man mix sooner."

Groa looked closer at the boiling brew. Gray-green fibers were floating in it. "What did you put in there? Don't tell me it's really an old man's beard."

"Not so old. Greens fight cold, trees fight mold."

The old woman reached into a large linen bag and withdrew a shaggy gray clump of something that did at first resemble a moldy beard. When Groa examined it, however, she recognized it as lichen. She had seen similar fibrous growths hanging from the branches of fir trees in the woods.

"So old man's beard is a type of lichen," Groa said. "How will that help against the ague?"

"Hot beard fight chills with sunshine. Needle three or not, when sick ones need water, no pain. Try it!" She took a horn spoon out of a hidden pocket.

Groa dipped up a spoonful, blew on it a moment, and then hazarded a sip. It was an herbal tea. Unlike the sweet brews Nadya prescribed for hangovers, this was bitter and musty. It was pretty much what Groa had expected from a mixture of mushrooms and bark.

"Beard tea bring everywhere," Nadya said with a commanding tone. "Hurry take willow and beard greedy feeling. You take Rus, I take underneath backwater plan. Tell make beard tea easy seven help, right?"

"All right," Groa replied, hoping she had understood. "I'll take some of the beard lichen and willow bark to people who are sick in the Rus quarters of the city. You'll take some to the Finns and Slavs. We'll both explain that people need to make tea and drink it. The willow will help fight the fever and the lichen will help against chills. Is that right?"

"Right!" Nadya slapped both of her knees. She stood up and dumped the rest of Groa's willow bark strips into the linen bag. She shook the bag to mix things up and then put half of the mixture back into Groa's basket. As she handed it to Groa she said, "Hurry."

"Wait." Groa remembered her promise to Ali from the day before. "After we're done delivering the tea, I want you to come with me to Holmgard."

"Holmgard? Igor not green sick or?"

"No, at least I don't think Prince Igor is sick. But there's an Arab doctor named Ali I'd like you to meet. He's been sent by Oleg to make sure everyone in the palace stays well. He's studied medicine in the cities of the Caliphate. Maybe we can learn from him."

"Maybe." Nadya shouldered her bag of lichen and willow. "Or maybe green sick nerves."

* * *

Groa spent most of the rest of that day delivering tea. By late afternoon she was so tired that she hoped Nadya had forgotten about the Arab doctor at Holmgard. But when Groa arrived at the entrance to the causeway the old Slavic woman was waiting, washing her hands in the marsh.

"Clean city sick seven times before," Nadya said earnestly.

Groa stooped to wash her hands. She didn't want to be accused of bringing contagion to the palace.

"Igor green or big yet?" Nadya's uncertain tone, and the way she eyed the island fortress, made Groa realize that she had probably never been inside the palace. Slavic men generally weren't allowed across the causeway, and women still less often. Perhaps Nadya had never seen the young prince at all.

The narrow path through the marsh had been widened in the years since Rurik's death, but the palisade and gate were as forbidding as ever. When they approached, an unseen guard called out, "Stop, and state your business!"

"I'm Groa, called here by the doctor Ali. This is Nadya, a healer."

A moment later the portal opened and a thin, older guardsman waved them in. "Follow me. The queen is ill. Everyone is coming down sick except the children."

Groa had not been to the fortress for several years and was surprised to see how tired it looked. The log buildings had darkened and the shake roofs sagged. Only the inner courtyard seemed alive. Children shouted, running about as they played a game of chase. There must have been twenty of them, mostly preteens.

"Children sick too," Nadya said, shaking her head. "Healthy sick."

"What does that mean?" the guardsman asked.

Groa shrugged. "Sometimes it's hard to know what she's saying."

The Slavic woman pointed a crooked finger toward an older boy, a strapping lad who was showing off by shinnying up a pole to escape the chase. "Igor?"

"No, that's Voris," the guardsman said. "He's Vlad's stepson from Ingrid's first marriage. Most of these kids are Vlad's in one way or another. But the prince? He's the quiet one there in the middle."

It was hard to believe that Prince Igor was fifteen years old. He looked ten, standing there in the midst of the game with a dazed, hopeful expression that suggested he wanted to be chased, but was glad he didn't have to run. This was clearly not a boy who was ready to lead Vikings into battle.

"Don't the children study skills?" Groa asked. "I'd have thought they'd be in training."

"That's as may be," the guardsman grumbled. "The queen won't let anyone give them orders. Come on, she's not well."

The outside of the central stave hall was as solemn as ever, but the interior had been transformed into a celebration of color and light. Dozens of small glass windows had been mounted into the roof, spreading rays of blue and gold through the smoky hall. Tapestries of wildflowers and deer hid the staves of the wall. Even the wooden pillars were unrecognizable, entirely wrapped in silver, with candles flickering in mirrored sconces. Yet more candles burned in candelabras atop banquet tables.

All that remained of Rurik's dark Viking hall was his massive, four-posted bed. The woman who lay there now wheezed, struggling for each breath. "Who—" she began. She turned her head, tilting her carved ivory crown precariously. Then she coughed so hard that the headdress rolled loose.

The Arab doctor caught the crown and replaced it gently. "Yesterday I met some local healers in town, Queen. This is Gloria."

"Groa," Groa corrected. "And my teacher, Nadya."

Queen Danuta narrowed her eyes, wheezing. "I know—of you."

Groa wasn't sure if this was good or bad, but she said, "Illness has been spreading through the town. Nadya and I have been treating people with a tea made from lichen and willow bark. We've brought the ingredients, if you'd like."

Nadya withdrew a handful of the gray-green mixture from a hidden pocket of her dress. "Green nerves, yes?"

Ali Ibn-al-Namid laughed lightly. "Tea is good, but it should not, I think, be brewed from forest debris."

Groa confronted him. "I thought you said local herbs have the power to cure local ills."

"That is true." For some reason Ali touched a finger to the tip of his own nose. "But is this illness local? No, it has arrived from the far east, after your Varangians opened a trade route from Lake Ladoga to the Volga River. Because the malady is Chinese, the cure must come from far away as well."

Ali walked to the open hearth where a pot hung on a chain from a tripod. "True Chinese tea is a rare and expensive medicine—the drink of empresses." He dipped a silver cup half full of steaming liquid, carried it cautiously to the bed, and helped Danuta to take a few sips. The queen seemed to breathe easier. She closed her eyes without coughing.

"You see?" The Arab waved his free hand with a flourish, sweeping the air with his voluminous sleeve. "I think there may be enough left that you too could taste, and learn."

He held the cup to Nadya. She sniffed it and shook her head. Groa, however, took a sip. Like Nadya's concoction it was bitter and had specks of floating material.

Groa admitted, "I suppose drinking hot water is always helpful."

"Especially for women," Ali said. "You see, the scholars of Arabia have learned that the womb is actually a separate animal within a woman's body. It craves moisture, so if the woman becomes dehydrated the womb begins feeding on the liver, stomach, or even the brain. This is the source of female hysteria."

"Wow," Groa said. "Nadya, what do you think?"

"I think Arab girl sick cucumber brain."

Ali frowned. "What?"

Groa was fairly sure that she had understood Nadya's statement, but decided to translate it incorrectly. "She said the Arab understanding of female anatomy is astonishing."

Ali's broad grin exposed a band of yellow teeth all the way across his smooth brown face. "These exchanges of knowledge are so important. Now I'm sure you will also agree that we need to remove the queen's blood."

"Remove her blood?" Groa asked.

"Yes. How else can we get the disease out of her body? Infections like this settle in the blood. Draining the correct amount, however, is an exceedingly dangerous operation."

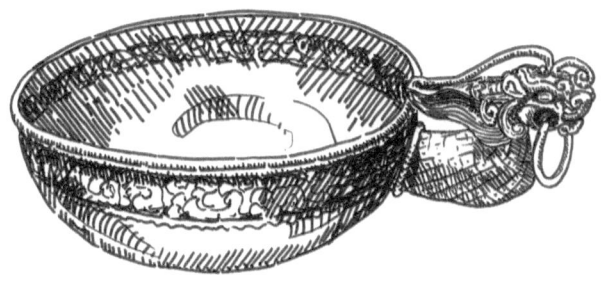

"For the patient?"

Ali laughed again. "No, for the doctor, of course. The diseased blood is so polluted, so vile, that touching it is nearly as dangerous as coming into contact with menstrual blood."

"But women do that all the time."

For a moment the Arab doctor just looked at Groa blankly. Then he shook his head. "This is why the Prophet has laid out such strict rules about isolating women during certain times of the month, and during times of critical decision."

Ali took the tea cup back. "I have appreciated your admiration and your homegrown instincts, Gloria, but now I face a task that requires expert concentration."

Groa sighed. "We'll leave you to it, then. Good luck."

Nadya silently squeezed the queen's hand before following Groa out of the hall. Outside, the dark blue of the evening sky was striped with beautiful red clouds. Groa thought the sunset's colors made the hall's silver seem like tinsel, and its tapestries like rags.

"Seven blue miracles, all lost," Nadya said.

Groa tightened her lips. When she understood Nadya the least, she suspected there was the most to learn.

* * *

Queen Danuta lived for another four days. Ali Ibn-al-Namid left that same afternoon, hurrying to bring word to Oleg in Kiev. Groa suspected that the Arab doctor was also hurrying to escape responsibility for the death.

Two weeks later Oleg came to Novgorod to pay his last respects to the queen. The regent sailed down the Volkhov River with a flotilla of four ships. Three were the new, lighter "Ships in the Woods" with Tyr-rune prows. One was a heavier, older model.

By the time Oleg arrived Vlad had already ordered Danuta's body burned in the manner of her Pomeranian ancestors. But he had kept the ashes in an inlaid box with her ivory crown on top, so that Oleg could hold a Viking ceremony as well.

Shortly after the queen died, Vlad had moved his extended family into her elaborately decorated stave hall, declaring that Holmgard was now the palace of the governor. Prince Igor had moped for a few days, but otherwise seemed to like the new arrangement. Vlad had long served as a kind of foster father for the boy. Now Igor's lonely hall teemed with the children he had grown up with as playmates.

Oleg, always the showman, had outfitted his ships with banners and lur-horns to announce his arrival at Novgorod's beach. But he needn't have worried. As soon as word spread that his yellow-striped sails had been sighted, nearly a thousand jubilant Novgorodans gathered to welcome the regent back to Russiya's former capital.

Oleg had promised the Rus peace and prosperity—and he had delivered. After a few initial campaigns to put down rebellions, all of Russiya paid tribute to the regent in Kiev. The Jarls of Novgorod had grown wealthy with trade. Rus colonists had sired large families on their new estates. The Varangian Knights had undertaken lucrative raids further afield, to the Black Sea and across the steppes of the Volga.

"Hail Rus!" Oleg shouted from the ship's prow. His red hair and beard were flecked with gray, but he was still a giant of a man.

The crowd roared back, "Hail Rus!"

Oleg jumped down onto the sand, embraced friends at the front of the crowd, gave a few orders, and set off with a dozen men toward the Holmgard causeway.

Groa and Hrolf watched from Rurik's mound at the highest point of the city's riverside bluff. The grave hill stood atop a grassy plain that had been left open for festivals, tradesmen's booths, food sellers, lovers, and mourners.

"He can't have forgotten about Fenris," Groa said, fingering the dagger beneath her shift.

"No," Hrolf agreed. "But it's funny how memories change."

* * *

The next day Oleg and a troop of forty men walked through the city, chatting with the locals, admiring their homes, and spreading word that everyone would be welcome that evening, when the ashes of Queen Danuta would be interred in her husband's grave mound. By noon the entourage reached the shipyards at the northern edge of the kremlin wall.

Oleg spread out his arms to greet Groa and Hrolf. "My carpenter! My silversmith! I have missed seeing you, my old friends. I praise your work with each ship that sails from these woods."

"Two hundred and fifty-seven so far," Hrolf replied.

"A lot of praise for a lot of ships." Oleg clapped him on the shoulder, laughing. "The sons of the colonists will be coming of age soon. They will need ships of their own. Tell me, do you think you could push your men to build forty ships a year instead of twenty-four?"

Groa and Hrolf exchanged a glance. She said, "My husband is a tireless worker, but we are not as young as when we began here."

"You've earned noble rewards for your achievements to date. I'll offer a bonus for the extra ships. What reward would you wish?"

Hrolf humphed "What I wish for most can only be granted by a wizard."

"I've given you one of those already," Oleg said, pointing his thumb at Groa. "Aren't you satisfied with your sorceress?"

Hrolf nodded somberly. "I only wish my magic were as strong as hers."

"Forty ships, then?"

Groa eyed the Viking evenly. "Why so many, really? Aren't you about to step down as regent? What campaigns remain, now that you've united Russiya? You swore that you would stop your wars and trade my dagger for your sword when I asked."

Oleg knit his eyebrows. "Our agreement was that I would yield Fenris when Prince Igor rules."

Hrolf cast his wife a glance that said: I told you. Memories are flexible contracts.

Groa crossed her arms. "That was not the promise I remember you making at Birka. Nonetheless, this is the twelfth year of your regency. Everyone know that this is when you agreed to let Igor rule."

Oleg's hand rested on the hilt of the sword at his side. "Very well. We'll let the boy decide. Tonight, in front of everyone, I will ask him. If Igor takes the throne, you can have your sword."

Oleg turned away gruffly. But after a few paces he stopped. "Forty ships," he told Hrolf, and then walked on.

* * *

By that evening Oleg's men had dragged the oldest of their four ships across the beach and up the bluff to the top of Rurik's mound. The upturned prows stuck out on either side of the hill, arching improbably against the sky. With a tattered sail luffing from the mast spar, the ship really did seem about to launch itself from its precarious perch toward the first hesitant stars. A circle of a hundred torches kept the curious crowd back from the base of the mound, where men with wooden spades had spent the afternoon digging a tunnel for Danuta's remains.

When Groa and her husband arrived, Hrolf humphed, "Swedish."

"What?" Groa had been watching the crowd. The people had

divided themselves into groups—Slavs, Finns, jarls, and colonists. "There aren't any Swedes."

"The ship," Hrolf said. "It's one of the old clunkers from Sweden. No wonder they're willing to burn it."

"At least it's not one we built."

Hrolf humphed again—something he did more often as he aged. "That thing weighs as much as a stave hall. You can see where the planks have been patched. Good firewood, though."

Groa and Hrolf were far enough back in the crowd that they missed some of the speeches. After the initial trumpeting of the lur-horns Oleg said something about Danuta and Rurik sailing together on smoke to Valhalla. Then Vlad had recited a poem—disappointingly, a variation of the Norse verse retold at so many funerals.

> Kinsmen die and cattle die,
> But saga-fame will never fade
> For ones who win it well.

At a signal from Oleg men plucked the torches from the ground and began carrying them up the hill. In the deepening twilight the ring of flickering fire slowly narrowed toward the ship, casting the hull in the weird orange glow of an eclipsed moon.

"Hail Rus!" Oleg called out.

"Hail Rus!" the crowd roared back as one.

And the ship erupted in flames. Oiled tinder must have been packed along its flanks, ready for the tossed torches. Within seconds the sail blazed up, billowing as if in a fiery spirit gale. The crowd shielded their eyes against the hot light. When the ropes burned through, the mast tilted backwards, smashing the stern in a shower of sparks. The rudder flipped loose, vaulting down the hill. People screamed. But the tiller stuck in the dirt just short of the crowd.

Vlad ordered the Holmgard guardsmen to open a dozen barrels of mead. Even this huge amount of honey grog did not go far amid such a large crowd. Soon, accompanied by the crackling roar of the burning ship, voices began to sing. At first the songs were somber, praising the gods, the Rus, and the dead. Then someone struck up the Swedish maypole dancing tune and half the crowd joined in. Finally, as the ship on the hill collapsed onto the embers of its oaken keel, a sailor got the crowd started on the mindless rowing ditty that Groa had hated ever since she first blistered her hands on an oar.

"Stop!" Groa shouted, wading through the crowd with her hands in the air. "Stop it, all of you! Have you forgotten this is a funeral?"

A drunk groped for her breasts. "It's a festival, my pretty."

She slapped the man's face and marched on to confront Oleg. "How many oaths can you break in a single day?"

"None yet, I think." The big Viking wobbled as if he too had over-indulged in mead—but a glint in his gray eyes made Groa suspect he was sober.

Oleg clapped his hands. "Blow some more horns and clear out a space to hear what our silver-tongued sorceress has to say. Quick, before the children are all sent to bed."

The lur-horns bleated unmusically. The crowd opened a circle around Groa. Oleg's troops flanked one side of the ring, while the residents of Holmgard stood on the other. To her left Oleg's brawny warriors formed a wall of chain mail and scars. To her right, Vlad's brood of children watched uncertainly beside Prince Igor and the palace guardsmen.

"Well?" Oleg asked.

Groa raised her voice so that all could hear. "Twelve winters ago, Regent, you asked me to speak in front of a different gathering in Novgorod. You asked me to reassure doubters that you would never be king of the Rus. You swore to yield your rule to Rurik's son. Many who are here tonight heard your oath. I call on you now to prove your honor."

Backlit by the last flames of the burning ship, Oleg cast a giant shadow.

"The Rus have lost a queen, but we have never had a king. We left Sweden to escape tyranny. Our founder, Rurik, took no title. I have been nothing more than regent for his son. Prince Igor, my nephew—I call on you now to come forward and choose your path."

Groa thought: Choose a path? Suddenly she realized what Oleg must have planned. The man was a genius at showmanship—and at entrapment. Twelve years ago he had divided the Holmgard defenders into jarls and servants, winners and losers, by letting them make their own choice. Now he was doing the same thing with a child. What chance did Igor have against such a master of strategy?

Igor was pale and small for his age, but he strode forward without the shyness Groa had expected. He had dark brown hair, ethereal blue eyes, and a narrow face. The blue tunic he wore had been interwoven with silver threads, so it shimmered on the boy's small frame.

"You say I have a choice, Uncle?" he asked Oleg, his high voice cracking awkwardly on the word "uncle."

"Ruling is about making decisions. Let me show you your options." Oleg unsheathed Fenris. He used the tip to draw a line in the dirt between him and the boy. Then he laid the sword on the ground to the right, toward the warriors he had brought from Kiev.

"If you choose to become ruler of all Russiya tonight, you will sail with these men back to Kiev. There is no palace in that capital, only a barracks in a fortress without women or children. Your immediate task will be to defend the realm against the Bulgars. They have overrun our settlement at the mouth of the Dnieper, blocking our ships from the Black Sea. Without the ability to trade, your people will revolt. The ruler of the Rus will be expected to pick up a sword and lead a campaign to clear the river."

Oleg motioned toward the sword on the ground. "Go ahead, try your hand with my blade."

The boy picked up the hilt. Only by using both hands was he able to swing the sword, and then only in a wobbly arc. A voice among the warriors chuckled. Igor glared toward the dark faces until silence returned. Then he laid the sword back on the ground and turned to Oleg.

"What is on the other side of this line you have drawn, Uncle?"

"Whatever you wish, here in Novgorod."

Groa knew enough about sorcery that she kept an eye on Oleg. While everyone else had been watching the boy fumble with Fenris, the regent had hidden something under his cloak. Now he threw back the cloth dramatically, revealing what looked like an extremely beautiful bucket. But no bucket would be wrapped in shiny blue silk and festooned with gold filigree. When Oleg turned it over and set it on the ground on the opposite side of the line from the sword, Groa realized it was actually a hat—a strange, fanciful thing halfway between a crown and a turban.

"What is this?" Igor asked, picking it up.

Oleg answered indirectly, drawing out the suspense. "If you decide to stay in Novgorod, you could choose your duties. You could continue living in the Holmgard palace with your friends. You could rule the city while Vlad continues taking care of the details. You could wear this crown as Sultan of Novgorod, with Vlad as your Grand Vizier."

Igor turned the turban in his hands. Then he looked at the Viking sword on the other side of the line.

Groa had to bite her tongue to keep from speaking. It seemed cruel to tempt a child with a pretty toy. And yet Oleg might be right to test the young prince so brazenly.

"Which do you choose?" Oleg asked. "The sword or the turban? To go to Kiev, or to stay in Novgorod?"

Groa closed her eyes, projecting the thought: *I will go.* More than once it had seemed that she could sway minds.

"I will stay." Prince Igor's voice was firm.

When Groa opened her eyes the boy had set down the turban. He was standing astride the line, directly in front of Oleg. "For now I will stay in Novgorod, Uncle. But that does not mean I accept either of your choices."

Oleg frowned. "Ruling is about making choices."

"I choose to wait. I do not yet feel ready to take your place, Uncle."

Groa caught her breath. Had the boy seen the trap and dodged it?

The prince crossed his arms like a man, although the gesture still made him look small. "You have done well as regent. You may continue to serve for a few years. In the meantime, tell me this: Who is your best swordsman?"

"The Rus have many able swordsmen. I am not unskilled myself."

"Who is the best, of all your troops?"

Oleg hesitated. "Perhaps Milovic, a Kievan vassal."

"I want him in Novgorod as my trainer."

"I suppose—" Oleg began, but Igor cut him short.

"The ruler of the Rus needs to know many things, and not merely how to wield a sword. I will want other teachers."

Oleg opened his palms. "There's Ali, the medicinalist. He is a scholar."

The young prince shook his head. "I don't know if your Arab doctor killed my mother, but he certainly didn't cure her. What about the sorceress you seem to keep trusting? The one who reads runes. I hear she started a school."

Igor glanced about the circle of faces until he found Groa. "You, with the eyes of different colors. You will start a school for me in

Holmgard."

Groa swallowed. "If you wish, Prince." Against all odds the boy was behaving like a king.

"Don't call me Prince," Igor said. "I'm not a prince anymore. And I'm not a king either, if that's what you are thinking. Certainly not a sultan." He tossed the turban aside to Vlad.

Groa asked, "Will you have no title then, like your father?"

The boy tilted his head, thinking. "I will use the local word for a realm's leader, a tsar."

"A tsar?" Oleg scoffed at the foreign title. "And what would you call me?"

"My regent, as before." Igor picked up Fenris and handed it to him hilt first. "Defeat the Bulgars. Make Russiya proud. Remember my parents, Rurik and Danuta, now that they have sailed beyond the living. I will let you know, Uncle, when I am ready to rule."

CHAPTER 12
NOVGOROD, 1961

At the midsummer bonfire by the Volkhov River a dozen men in Viking battle gear raised their swords toward the stars and roared in Russian, "Hail Rus! We shall rule till Ragnarök!"

A crowd seated on blankets on a riverside lawn applauded politely. Professor Henrik Talin, however, shook his bald head. "This is pathetic. They're waving wooden swords from a toy shop. And they've put horns on their helmets as if they were cows, not Vikings."

The professor's assistant, Urmas Byelokov, cocked her head, tilting her blond hair over one shoulder. "I think I've seen a helmet with horns in Stockholm's Historiska Museet."

"Antlers, Urmas," Henrik replied wearily. "You saw antlers on a shaman's headdress. Such things were used in Odin rituals. No fighter would mount projections on a helmet. That would funnel sword blows directly onto his head. The reenactments at these medieval festivals are an incompetent waste of time." He stood and straightened his back, grimacing as he worked out the kinks from sitting on the ground for an hour.

Urmas folded their blanket. She was used to the professor's put-downs, but they still hurt. Was it better than being ignored? With a too-large nose and a too-small mouth Urmas knew she turned no heads. Swarovsky of the KGB told her that obscurity was her secret power. Someday she promised herself she would stand out.

"Perhaps tomorrow," Urmas said.

"What?" Henrik's Russian was good, but it was his fourth language, so he sometimes misunderstood a hastily spoken phrase.

"Perhaps tomorrow when you lead your walking tour of Novgorod's kremlin you can set the record straight about helmets."

"Yes. By then a few genuine Varangians should be on hand." He lowered his voice, glancing about at the dark figures leaving the lawn after the performance. "Word of our work is spreading. It will be interesting to see which contingent is the largest tomorrow—patriots, impostors, or spies."

* * *

Sasha arrived on the train from Minsk the next morning, shadowing Vasiliy Swarovsky. Why had the KGB sent an operative to meet with Lee Harvey Oswald again? They had already interrogated the ex-Marine countless times. A year ago the defector had showed up on a train from Finland and had overstayed his tourist visa in Leningrad. When authorities refused him political asylum he slashed his wrists. The Soviets decided the man was a nut case with no useful information. But it seemed wrong to drive a Communist sympathizer to suicide. So they gave him a factory job and an apartment in Minsk.

Keeping an eye on Oswald was the least important of Sasha's many CIA assignments. But Swarovsky's visit had set off alarm bells in her head. The young KGB agent was a recruiter and a trainer. What was he up to? And why, immediately after meeting with Oswald, had he bought a ticket to Veliky Novgorod?

Sasha followed Swarovsky discretely a dozen blocks from the train station to the Volkhov Hotel. She waited a while on a park bench across the street before checking in herself. All of this fit in nicely with her cover as an Intourist travel agent. Already at the train station she had discovered that this was the weekend of a Viking reenactment festival. Intourist really might send an agent to such an event. The KGB, probably not. Whatever Swarovsky had planned, she hoped it would wait until after a shower and lunch.

Sasha washed up, changed her makeup and outfit, bought a newspaper in the lobby, and established a lookout post at a corner table of the hotel restaurant, where she ordered coffee and a brioche. Now, instead of a nondescript traveler with a checkered gray frock and a blond bun she was a nondescript businesswoman with a gray skirt suit and a small round hat.

Sasha loved to wear furs—she had almost chosen a suit jacket with a fur collar—but fur attracted too much attention, especially in summer. Furs had been an unattainable elegance for her Jewish parents. They had been forced by Stalin's pogroms to flee to the US in 1935.

No one wore furs in the wet winters of Eugene, Oregon. She had met Lars Andersen there while teaching Russian to ROTC cadets at the University of Oregon in 1942. Now it seemed that the only time Sasha could indulge her fur obsession was when visiting Lars' mother in Denmark or his sister in Sweden. Furs were always in style in Sweden.

A full hour passed before Vasiliy Swarovsky came down the stairs to the hotel lobby. He looked hurried and a little groggy, as if he had napped in his clothes. Sasha surmised that he had not slept well on the night train, and that he didn't have another suit. The brown one he was wearing was rumpled and remarkably ugly, considering that Swarovsky himself was otherwise attractive, with the physique of a gymnast. The suit stretched in weird ways, attempting to span the muscles of his shoulders, arms, and chest. He slapped a palm on the reception counter for attention and demanded, "Where does the history walk start?"

Sasha had a hard time overhearing the clerk's reply, but the intonation suggested something like, "I beg your pardon, sir?"

"The walking tour of Old Town. Where do we meet the professor?"

Pretending to adjust an earring, Sasha cupped a hand behind her ear to catch the clerk's reply.

"In the middle of the kremlin, sir. At the Millennium monument. You should be able to walk there in time."

Swarovsky grunted and turned to go. But first he scanned the lobby and the restaurant—something he trained all of his recruits to do when leaving or entering a space. He half expected to see the blond, middle-aged woman from the train. If that was her behind the newspaper in the corner, she knew her business. Was it possible that she too had come for the annual gathering of the Order?

* * *

The sunshine was bright enough on the wide streets of Novgorod that Sasha wasn't the only one wearing dark glasses. She worried that the KGB man had seen her too often lately. She knew where he was going so she took a less direct route, past gray stone buildings with government offices. Women dressed like her carried shopping bags or pushed baby buggies. Park-like boulevards converged toward an arched portal in an ancient red-brick wall. Square, pointy-topped watchtowers punctuated the kremlin wall every few hundred yards in either direction. Vendors with pushcarts were selling balloons, flowers, and *shashlik*—fried meat on a stick. Inside the kremlin gate a wide, graveled walkway had been neatly raked, but cigarette butts and food wrappers littered the grass behind park benches. The promenade's cast iron lamp posts would have been more impressive if their glass lanterns had not been broken.

Two blocks inside the wall the walkway opened onto a central circular plaza where one might otherwise expect a fountain. Here, however, there was a fifty-foot-tall bronze sculpture with a bas-relief frieze around the bottom and a gigantic ball on top. Two dozen larger-than-life bronze figures struck heroic poses around the ball—which Sasha first thought must be a model of the Earth. But it was just a giant ball, with an angel and a robed woman clinging to a Russian Orthodox cross at the top.

Sasha merged with a crowd of fifty that had gathered at the base of the monument for the history tour. Swarovsky stood apart from the group, talking with a young woman and a short, older man—almost certainly the professor Swarovsky had mentioned. Not only was the man completely bald, but he wore a stodgy bow tie that practically shouted academia. When Sasha edged closer she noticed that the right side of the professor's face was disfigured by a scaly red skin condition. The young woman—in her mid-twenties, about Swarovsky's age—smiled admiringly while the two men talked. Her blond page boy haircut had a stripe of black roots along the part. Blond hair was immensely popular among Russian women, perhaps because of the Scandinavian influence, but dye was too expensive and unpleasant to use more than once a month. Sasha, too, bleached her naturally black hair. She left the roots dark on purpose to fit in.

"No, I can handle things alone," the professor said. Sasha noticed his accent. Not quite German. Dutch?

"Are you sure?" the young woman asked.

"You two go have fun." The professor lowered his voice so that Sasha could barely hear. "We will all meet again tonight."

Swarovsky glared at him, tight-lipped. Then he took the girl by the arm and walked her away.

Sasha puzzled over what this might mean. The simplest explanation was that the young KGB agent had hurried to Novgorod to meet his girlfriend. But then why were they meeting the professor again that night—apparently in secret? Something was wrong here, and

Sasha could not find out by continuing to follow Swarovsky. She had already pushed her luck, shadowing him so long. At this point her safest move was to follow the professor.

"Welcome to the history walk," the professor announced, raising his voice. "I'm Henrik Talin—that's right, Stalin without the S. I'm a professor at the Institute of History in Estonia. Our institute is helping to raise a sunken German submarine in the Baltic. But I've also led Viking Age excavations at Old Ladoga and here in Novgorod. This afternoon we'll spend an hour trying to straighten out some of the misconceptions about Vikings that you're likely to encounter at this weekend's amateur fair. Are there any questions before we begin?"

Sasha had a number of questions she couldn't ask aloud. For one thing, the professor's name sounded fake. Both Lenin and Stalin had invented their iconic last names. But Talin? Only a foreigner would choose a name so close to Stalin—and to the name of the Estonian capital, Tallinn. "Henrik" was definitely foreign. Most Russians couldn't pronounce an initial H at all, turning "hotel" into "otel" or even "gotel." Henrik sounded Danish—but then why had his name never been mentioned by the Danish archeologists in Lars' family? Was he really involved with the Red Navy's effort to raise a sunken German submarine? And why was he meeting secretly with the KGB, perhaps to discuss an American defector?

"No questions? Good." Henrik held his hand out to the monument behind him. "There is no better place to begin our tour than here at the Millennium of Russia, one of the largest bronze sculptures in the world, built in 1862 to celebrate the thousandth anniversary of the founding of Novgorod—and thus, the seed of the modern Soviet Union. The globe at the top is a *reichsapfel*—the orb of empire, guarded by the personification of Mother Russia. Front and center we have Rurik with his sword, shield, and of course a hornless helmet. Rurik was one of the Swedish Vikings, or Varangians, whom the Slavs invited to unite their land. He built the Holmgard fortress two kilometers south of Novgorod in about 862 and gave his name to Russia. Among the other figures here are Rurik's successors, Oleg, Prince Igor, Yaroslav the Wise, and other tsars."

A man with a black leather jacket raised his hand. "Is it true the Nazis stole this monument? How did they move something so big?"

The professor's bald head nodded. "It doesn't look like it comes apart, but it does. When German troops advanced beyond Novgorod in 1942 they claimed the Millennium of Russia as a war trophy—or possibly for scrap metal. After the war Soviet authorities assigned me to track down lost treasures. I found five flatcars with the monument in a freight yard at Dessau and brought them back."

The crowd applauded. The professor's scaly cheek glowed an even brighter red. He fumbled with his bow tie as if to straighten it.

A woman's voice asked, "Did you find the Amber Room?"

The professor pretended not to have heard. "We'll move on now to the cathedral. This way, please."

Sasha knew about the Amber Room. She wondered if it was one of the professor's failures. Built in Prussia and gifted to Tsar Peter the Great in the early 1700s, the room's ornate wall panels had used tons of amber to create elaborate Rococco patterns over gold leaf and mirrors. When German soldiers captured the tsar's palace outside Leningrad in World War II they had discovered the priceless panels hastily hidden behind ordinary wallpaper. The panels had been shipped to Germany. But then they had disappeared, perhaps forever.

The tour group headed north through the kremlin grounds toward a square white church topped with onion-shaped domes—four of them silver and a central one of gold.

"Behold the first church in Russia," Henrik said, walking backwards so he could face the group. "Saint Sophia was built in 1050 as a smaller version of Constantinople's Saint Sophia, which was the largest building in the world at that time. Sophia means knowledge in Greek, so these churches were not dedicated to a specific saint, but rather to the concept of wisdom. The Varangians in Russia knew Constantinople as Miklagard, or 'great fortress.' They envied that city's wealth, and more than once tried to conquer it. When Constantinople finally fell to the Ottoman Turks in 1453, the Saint Sophia there became a mosque. The smaller Saint Sophia here has been preserved by our socialist society as a museum."

The professor held open a huge bronze door covered with images of saints and beasts. "Silence is required inside, I'm afraid."

Sasha wandered among the gigantic square columns of the dark, smoky nave as if she were groping her way through the mysteries the CIA had tasked her to solve. If churches were supposed to be calming, this ancient tomb-like hall was definitely not. Crooked rows of tiny candles burned beneath smoke-darkened paintings of flat-faced saints, many of them weeping or bleeding. There were no chairs, so the few

old women and monks who had come to pray in the "museum" had to stand, looking weary in their black mourning attire. Tombstones tiled the floor, too worn with age to decipher.

When the group was outside again the man in a black leather jacket asked about the graves. "It looks like a lot of princes were buried in there. What about Rurik? Where's he?"

"Good question," Henrik replied. "Oleg is said to have a burial mound at Ladoga, but not Rurik. Personally, I think he's here."

"Reburied inside the church when Christianity arrived?" the man asked.

"There's no record of a reburial. But the church was built on the highest part of the riverside bluff. If you think like a Varangian, that's exactly where you would have put Rurik's grave mound. Later, the church might have been built on top of him."

Henrik waved to the last stragglers of the group, just leaving the cathedral doors. "This way. We'll end our tour by walking through the kremlin gate to the river bridge."

The group followed a wide gravel path down through another arched portal in the brick fortress wall, this time leading to a long footbridge that arched across the wide, murky Volkhov River.

The woman who had asked about the Amber Room asked if Novgorod's kremlin was named after Moscow's.

This time the professor apparently heard her question just fine. "Actually, it's the other way around. *Kremlin* is the old Slavic word for a walled fortification. The first kremlin we know of was here, centuries before Moscow was founded."

In the middle of the bridge Henrik stopped, turned around, and pointed to the sweep of Novgorod's riverbank. "Imagine the view

here a thousand years ago, in the time of Oleg and Igor. Planked streets would have led through a maze of log huts. Smoke would have drifted from holes in the wooden roofs. Instead of a brick kremlin, a palisade of pointed staves would have ringed the town. And on the beach, Varangian longships would have been pulled up on the sand to unload treasures from Byzantium and the Orient."

The professor turned and frowned at the festival tents on the far shore. "Instead, today we have a fake Viking camp with jousting matches and other inappropriate nonsense. Still, there are those who value the true Varangian spirit. The festival's blacksmith, for example, does authentic work. I leave you with that request—to honor the few who cherish our heritage. This concludes our tour."

Almost everyone in the group, including the professor, continued across the bridge to the festival grounds—a field of tents and booths bordered by a stone wall of white arches. Sasha had assumed it would be easy to follow the bald professor, but he was so short that he soon disappeared into the crowd. Now what? She decided instead to look for the blacksmith he had mentioned. A plume of smoke from the forge made that task easy.

The blacksmith's booth had a canopy on one side with tables of wrought-iron candleholders, coat hooks, and fireplace pokers for sale. On the other side, a helper pumped a bellows to keep the forge's red coals glowing. The smith himself looked like he really had just stepped out of the Viking Age, with a big black beard and a leather tunic. He swung a hammer, clanging a red rod flat on a small anvil. Sparks flew each time the hammer bounced. Sweat and grime glistened on his muscled arms.

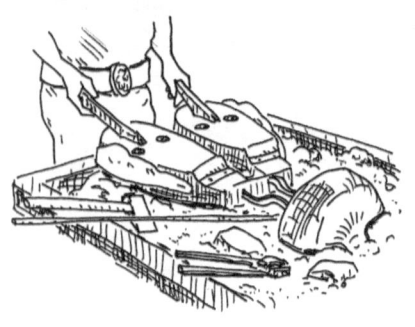

"I'm looking for Professor Talin," Sasha said between hammer blows.

Clang! The smith didn't look up.

"I'm supposed to meet him tonight, but I've forgotten where." Sasha added, "I'd like to buy him a gift, if you have a suggestion."

The smith paused, studying her with deep brown eyes. "A gift?"

"Yes. The professor admires your work. What would he like?"

The smith took a chain from around his neck and held it out. Dangling from the chain was an iron medallion. Hammer blows had pocked the metal disk. On one side, a chisel had gouged three vertical lines. Or no—when Sasha looked closer she saw that the lines were actually three arrows, pointing up.

"Three hundred rubles," the smith said. "To the right buyer."

It was several times more than Sasha thought the necklace was worth, but she took out her purse. "Will you be there tonight too?"

The smith's head gave the slightest nod.

Sasha handed him the money. "Remind me again, where?"

"Same as every year," the smith replied, his voice little more than a growl. "In the kremlin dungeon."

"Of course. Thanks." Sasha smiled as she took the necklace. She wouldn't dare attend the meeting in person, but she would set up a remote camera at the door to photograph the people who entered. It would be interesting to see who else might join a blacksmith, a professor, and a KGB recruiter in a Novgorod dungeon.

CHAPTER 13
NOVGOROD, 907

Groa did her best to teach Igor, the young, self-proclaimed "tsar" of Russiya. Nonetheless, ten years passed before Igor decided he was ready to rule—and even then it was only a result of Oleg's mysterious plan to sell ladders to the Byzantine Empire.

The regent from Kiev, his fiery red hair and beard now noticeably silvered with age, came to Novgorod in person to present his proposal.

"The empire has been strangling our trade with tariffs and regulations," Oleg told a group of jarls and Varangian Knights at the Holmgard palace. "Furs are no longer selling well in Miklagard. The one trade article they desperately need is ladders."

"Ladders?" Groa asked. Why couldn't Greeks make their own ladders? And why had she and her husband Hrolf been invited to this meeting at all? She was more than a little suspicious.

"Exactly," the young tsar put it. "Uncle has explained it to me. You see, the stone buildings in Miklagard are quite tall, but stone stairs are expensive. They will pay handsomely for ladders made of strong, straight Russiyan spruce."

Oleg said, "We'll want four hundred ladders within ten days. Can you do it?"

Hrolf rubbed his square chin, thinking. Unlike the men of the Rus the Norwegian woodworker had never worn a beard. Instead he shaved each morning with the sharp blade of a plane, as if his head were a block of pine. Now he looked as if he were sanding his chin smooth.

"How long do you want the ladders to be?" Hrolf asked.

"Forty feet. As long as will fit easily on a ship's deck. You can divert all your workers from the shipyard. We have enough ships."

"That's good news, at least," Hrolf grumbled. He had been building ships for twenty-five years and was heartily sick of it. "Ladders, huh? Sure, why not?"

"Good. You and your sorceress can go and get started." Oleg waved them out.

Hrolf left the hall in good spirits. But Groa lingered outside the doorway, listening. The fragments of conversation she managed to overhear left her more troubled than ever.

* * *

Groa had been the first of many teachers Igor employed after his mother's funeral. Most of these mentors came and went, largely because the young tsar tended to blame his instructors for his own failures. Groa stayed on for a decade, but had begun to wonder if Russiya would ever be ready for Igor's leadership.

Igor had first devoted his attention to swordsmanship under the tutelage of Milovic. The Slav from Kiev really had been a master with a blade, but no amount of training could give Igor the strength required to swing a full-sized sword. After a few frustrating months they had switched to archery. Igor did well enough with a bow as long as neither he nor the target were moving. They had gone duck hunting together on nearby Lake Ilmen, and had wasted hundreds of arrows before hitting a single bird. After a year Milovic had declared the boy's instruction was complete. Everyone knew, however, that this was just the Slav's way of resigning his position.

Next Igor had hired Yazdegerd, a Persian bureaucrat who had worked for the Abbasid Caliphate. According to Yazdegerd, the Muslim rulers in Baghdad relied on Persians to organize the day-to-day business of their government. Yazdegerd counseled Igor to set up a hierarchy of ministers to count, tax, and regulate the Rus. New cities should be laid out in rectangles, with canals delivering water. Swamps should be drained for agriculture. Oarsmen should be retrained as cavalry.

Yazdegerd's ambitious plans hit a wall when Igor suggested them to Vlad. Oleg's former purser was the governor of Novgorod, in charge of administration. Vlad liked their current system as it was.

After the Persian had been dismissed, Igor enlisted Yuantzu as a teacher. Varangian traders had come across the Chinese scholar at an outpost along the Silk Road. Yuantzu claimed to be in such a remote spot for purposes of meditative seclusion. The fact that he agreed so readily to travel up the Volga to Russiya, however, suggested to some that he was actually on the run. Only later did news spread that China's Tang dynasty had been collapsing, forcing thousands of scholars to flee.

Yuantzu introduced a number of innovations. He taught the young tsar to cook wood shavings, dry the resulting mush, and roll it flat to produce artificial, rectangular leaves. Apparently people elsewhere used this parchment-like material for writing runes, but it was of no practical use in Russiya. Next Yuantzu mixed flour with water, rolled the dough flat, and hung it to dry. He demonstrated that the resulting dough-staves could later be boiled and eaten, but even Igor couldn't understand why they had not simply used the flour to bake bread.

The Chinese sage was summarily dismissed after he mixed charcoal with a smelly powder and set it on fire, claiming that it would produce a spectacular display. It had, but only because the resulting explosion had burned down a storage hut.

All this time Groa had been teaching history, Norse religion, runes, herbal medicine, silversmithing, and a few spells. Igor liked her lessons—especially the silver work. He would sit for hours, carving decorative goblets from blocks of wax. Groa molded clay around his creations, fired the clay to melt out the wax, and then poured molten silver into the resulting cast. The banquet tables of Holmgard were full of Igor's lumpy, mismatched goblets.

When Igor turned twenty, Groa suggested that he employ the Norwegian captain, Thorkell, to teach him skills that she herself lacked. Long ago in Tunsberg, Thorkell had been the first Norwegian jarl to join Oleg's recruiting expedition. But because Oleg had not chosen him as a Varangian Knight, Thorkell had been left to stay in Novgorod, overseeing the rigging of new ships.

As Igor's mentor, Thorkell taught him to sail. Hrolf provided them with a ship, fresh from the Novgorod yard. Thorkell and Igor named it the *Varangia* and set about choosing a crew. The old captain picked two dozen experienced sailors. Igor picked two dozen of his young friends. Week after week they all sailed together down the Volkhov to Ladoga or around the shore of Lake Ilmen, singing songs as they rowed. Along the way Igor and his friends learned to raise the mast, hold the tiller, follow orders, portage the ship, and make repairs. They stopped at river islands for mock battles with wooden weapons. They camped under the stars. They ate hardtack and dried fish. Igor had never had so much fun. And that, Groa surmised, was why the young tsar felt he was ready for greater adventure.

* * *

"The secret to making a good ladder," Hrolf told his wife as they walked into the shipyard, "Is to drill the rung holes first, through a solid round pole. Then, when you saw the pole in half lengthwise, the holes are perfectly aligned."

Hundreds of poles lay in rows along the riverbank—an entire spruce forest, felled for use as ladders. Everywhere workers were drilling holes with augurs and sawing the poles in half.

"You do realize that Oleg's trip may not really be about selling ladders?" Groa asked. "He's ordered every jarl and knight in Russiya to provide a shipload of men. You don't need thousands of warriors for a trading expedition."

"Why not? Everyone wants to see Miklagard, even Igor. They say it's the city of wisdom, where you can find whatever you seek." He looked aside. Was he blushing? "That's why I've asked Thorkell if we can go along."

She looked at her husband uncertainly. "You have?"

"Don't you want to come? Oleg says we're done building ships. Now we can travel like everyone else. Thorkell says his crew could use a woodworker and a sorceress, if we're willing to row." He managed a wry smile. "Or are you afraid of blistering your hands on an oar again?"

Groa wasn't particularly keen on travel, but this expedition hid too many mysteries. Oleg, who still hadn't relinquished his sword Fenris, was up to something with all his ladders. Igor, whom she had taught for years, seemed to think this voyage might prove him worthy of ruling the realm. Even her husband Hrolf was hiding something.

The answers all lay in the Byzantine capital of Constantinople.

"All right," she said. "I will go."

CHAPTER 14
STOCKHOLM, 1961

"You're going too?" Helen asked, astonished.

Lennart shrugged. "I told you I had a surprise."

"But how—I mean why—?" She had been avoiding her secret boyfriend ever since he'd shown up in the VIP section for the raising of the *Vasa*. Was he a renegade or not? Now for some reason he was getting on the bus with the eleventh-year students of her school class for their week-long field trip to Berlin.

"Your teachers were looking for chaperones who can teach you kids a thing or two," Lennart said, stowing his guitar case in the bus's lower compartment. "Your mother agreed to come along as the museum expert. I volunteered to be the political science guide. Berlin's the center of Communism's struggle against the capitalists. The place is crawling with spies. I get university credit and you get a chaperone who knows the city's nightlife. Cool, huh?"

"And you just happened to pick my class?" What Lenny had said about spies made her suspicious. Her Uncle Lars really was planning to meet them in Berlin.

He lowered his eyes and his voice. "I've missed you, Helen. I don't know why you're mad at me. Are you still?"

"Yeah," she said, swinging her own duffel bag into the compartment. Without further explanation she climbed the steps onto the bus. She enjoyed having power over Lenny. She hadn't decided yet how much to let him suffer. But the truth was, her class trip to the German Democratic Republic was going to be more interesting with Lenny along.

* * *

As part of the field trip, the students in class 11c of Stockholm's

Bernadottegymnasiet were required to keep journals in regulation green booklets. They had been working on the journals for weeks already. Helen had filled hers with the usual facts, knowing it would be read and graded by her sociology teacher, Herr Lindt. But then she wrote down the really important stuff in English on sheets of thin blue aerogram paper. Rather than keep this secret diary where it might be discovered, perhaps by her increasingly snoopy mother, she folded the pages for her imaginary Sicilian pen pal Celeste, sealed them, and hid them under a book on a shelf.

For the first hour of the trip, as their bus drove south on the E4 through Södertälje and Nyköping, everyone on the bus was talking, too excited even to look out the windows. After they had stopped to eat packed lunches at a rest station, however, Helen had time to write on the blue paper.

> Dear Celeste:
> Tomorrow I get to see the socialist world first-hand.
> Amazingly, Lennart is with us on the bus as a chaperone.
> Yes, Lenny from "Culture Club." He's sitting with Herr Lindt
> and my mother in the front row, chatting with them as if he
> were a teacher instead of a revolutionary. All the girls are
> eyeing him. This summer they've all done their hair with the
> same "flip" as mine—curling it out at the bottom and holding
> it with hair spray. But most aren't as blond and half of them
> flip at the ears instead of all the way down around the shoul-
> ders. Does everyone in Italy wear stupid puffy skirts too? It's
> like I'm the only sane girl with pants. The boys are playing
> cards, gambling for *tiöre* coins. Lennart brought a guitar case.
> I wonder—

"Green books, everyone!" Herr Lindt called out. Their teacher had thinning hair, black-framed glasses, and a gray sweater that he never seemed to change. "We'll stop at the Kalmar Castle for an hour before going to the hostel. We're honored to have Helen's mother, Fru Gustmeyer, leading the tour, so take plenty of notes."

The bus parked in a gravel lot with a city harbor on one side and the towers of a fairy-tale castle rising above a grassy dike on the other. Twenty minutes passed while the teacher bought group tickets and everyone else waited in line for restrooms. Lennart's job was to keep the boys from running wild along the dike. Finally Mette led everyone into a crooked tunnel through the dike. On the other side a long wooden bridge crossed a moat to the castle's five-sided island. Rows of black cannons topped an outer wall. Beyond, spires rose above greenish copper cupolas.

"The first fortress here was built at the end of the Viking Age in the twelfth century," Mette announced, corralling the group at a viewpoint just before a drawbridge. "Who lived in this area then?"

"Not me," a boy said. A few students snickered. Herr Lindt put his arm around the boy's shoulder—a comforting gesture that could also be interpreted as a threat.

"Swedes?" a girl suggested.

"Actually, Geats," Mette replied. "The Swedish king in Uppsala controlled Uppsala, Roslagen, and Mora to the north. The Geats were a Gothic tribe in the region here between Gothenburg and Gotland. After Denmark became a world power in the eleventh century, King Canute ruled everything from England to what is now southern Sweden. When the Danes tried to expand to the north Kalmar became a battleground. Then Queen Margareta founded the Kalmar Union here at this castle in 1397, binding together the kingdoms of Denmark, Sweden, and Norway as equals. That brought more than a century of peace to Scandinavia."

Mette paused. Only a few of the students were taking notes. She wasn't sure how much these children would already know about Nordic history. "Any questions before we go inside?"

Helen had lots of questions, but they all dealt with Lennart. Was he a Communist informer? Was he a spy for Colonel Wennerström? And how serious was he about being her boyfriend? She knew she wouldn't get answers as long as her mother was dragging the class through a castle, repeating dates they'd memorized in the ninth grade.

Helen came closer to getting answers that evening at the youth hostel. It was a three-story dormered barracks on Ängö, a little rock island connected to Kalmar's downtown by a bridge. From the yard they could see the car ferry shuttling back and forth from Kalmar's harbor to Öland, a purple line on the horizon where the Baltic Sea should have met the sky. After a dinner of parsley potato stew on metal trays Herr Lindt suggested they could write in their journals or go to bed early to prepare for tomorrow's long drive. Most of the class wound up in the common room, although there was nothing there but out-of-date magazines, jigsaw puzzles, and a deck of playing cards.

Lennart surveyed the room, left for a while, and returned with his guitar case. A crowd gathered around as he tuned up. Helen had never seen him play an old-fashioned acoustic guitar, but then a youth hostel wasn't really a place to plug in an electric amp.

"What a wonderful idea," Mette said, walking into the room to keep an eye on things. "Could you play us a folk song, Lennart?"

Helen groaned at her mother's interference. A folk song?

"Any specific requests?" Lennart asked.

Mette had grown up in Denmark, so the first two tunes she suggested were ones Lennart didn't know. "Just play something Swedish, then. To get everyone ready for bedtime."

Helen suggested sarcastically, "How about 'Troll Mother'?"

The students laughed. But Lennart nodded, "Sure. Everyone knows that one." He strummed a few tentative chords and then set out in D major. Soon everyone except Mette was singing along.

När trollmor har lagt

sin elva små trollen
och bundit fast dom i svansen,
då sjunger hon sakta för elva små trollen
de vackraste ord hon känner:
Ho aj aj aj aj buff,
ho aj aj aj aj buff,
ho aj aj aj aj buff buff!

When Troll Mother has put
Her eleven little ones to bed
And tied down their cute little tails
She softly sings to her baby trolls
The prettiest words she knows:
Ho aj aj aj aj buff,
Ho aj aj aj aj buff.
Ho aj aj aj aj buff buff!

Mette stood up, her face warm. Perhaps it had not been such a good idea to volunteer for this trip.

Herr Lindt leaned in the door. "Quiet by nine-thirty and lights out at ten, Lennart."

"Aye aye, captain."

The sociology teacher adjusted his black-framed glasses. "I like the folk songs, though. Good night, everyone." Herr Lindt left, and Mette decided it was wisest if she headed to bed as well.

When the older generation was out of the room Helen asked, "You aren't really going to play more folk songs, are you?"

Lennart tuned a string. "Actually, I just learned an English one you might like. It's part of a new set being played in Hamburg by the Beatles."

"The Beatles play folk songs?"

"Sometimes." Lennart strummed slow mellow chords and sang in his best choirboy voice,

My Bonnie lies over the ocean,
My Bonnie lies over the sea.
My Bonnie lies over the ocean,
Oh, bring back my Bonnie to me.

Lennart paused a moment. He winked to Helen and suddenly

slammed out a jangling jazzy chord. Then he sang the same verse again in the Beatles' electric, howling, rock-and-roll style.

> My Bonnie!—lies over!—the ocean!
> My Bonnie!—lies over!—the sea!
> My Bonnie!—lies over!—the ocean!
> Oh bring back!—my Bonnie!—to me!

The students had watched this performance in amazement.

"Wow," one of the boys said. "Do that again."

Lennart smiled. "OK. But this time, why don't we let Helen sing?"

That's when she knew Lennart might still be her boyfriend.

* * *

The next day really was long, with four hours on the bus to the ferry landing at Trelleborg, another four hours on the ship to Sassnitz, and three more hours over potholed East German roads to Neubrandenburg. The highlight for most students was the ferry's on-board buffet, with all the pickled herring, fried sole, and Havarti cheese you could eat. Helen sat at one of the cafeteria's oblong, stainless steel tables—a supermodern Space Age design—watching the green stripe of East Germany approach. Disappointingly, the socialist world ahead looked even flatter than the choppy Baltic. Herr Lindt and some of the others who were writing in their journals began to pale with seasickness. Several vanished into the bathrooms, regretting the fishy lunch.

When loudspeakers blared unintelligible announcements in German everyone headed down the stairs to the car deck, a steel cave that stank of diesel and fish. Saabs, Volvos, and Volkswagens packed the front of the echoing hall. An entire train, complete with diesel locomotive and sleeper cars, idled on rails to one side. The school bus was in the back among Scania trucks with tarped loads.

When everyone was on the bus, sitting in the dark, waiting for the ship's engines to stop, the bus driver handed Herr Lindt a microphone on a coiled cord. The seasick teacher passed the mic to Lennart. A moment later Lenny's voice loomed out of the darkness.

"*Willkommen in die Deutsche Demokratische Republik.*" He stood at the front, a faceless silhouette. His voice seemed less ominous when he switched to Swedish. "After the Allied powers liberated Germany from Nazi fascism, they divided the country into zones of occupation. Only the Soviet sector, here in the east, chose the path of socialism.

They call their state a workers' paradise. The West claims it is a land without freedom. Which is true? We're about to see for ourselves."

Light broke in from the front as the ship's prow opened, its nose hoisted by giant hydraulic pistons. Truck engines rumbled to life. Taillights blinked red as the first cars began to clatter down a metal ramp.

"What is freedom?" Lennart's voice asked. "Are you free if you are unemployed, sick, or homeless? Are you free if you can't afford schooling or child care? That's what millions in the West face every day. But not in the East. All the people of the German Democratic Republic are guaranteed education, a job, a home, child support, and health care. The freedoms of socialism are different, and come with a different cost. You have to work together, contributing what you can and taking only what you need. As it turns out, some people aren't willing to pay that price. Keep your eyes open. Write in your journals what you see. Each evening, let's compare notes."

Invisible near the back of the bus, Helen began to applaud. A few other students started clapping too, but then the bus jerked into gear, growling toward the light.

After Lennart's pep talk about the marvels of East Germany, Helen was surprised that the country itself seemed bureaucratic and backward, at least on first acquaintance. The ferry landing was a harbor without a city—just a huge parking lot surrounded by farm fields. Policemen in green uniforms waved the bus over to a concrete shed. There the students got out, fetched their luggage, and waited under a hot metal awning until it was their turn. Inside the shed an official slowly pasted what looked like postage stamps into their passports, inked the page with two different rubber stamps, and scribbled a signature on top.

Back on the bus, they drove through a landscape that seemed to be just emerging from the Middle Ages. Ancient tractors and even horses worked in weedy fields. The dingy villages were full of war-damaged houses and empty buildings. People stood in lines outside the few shops. The only cars were Trabants, boxy little putt-putts that coughed black smoke. Children pointed at the big Swedish bus with delight, running after it down the street.

When they reached the day's destination, the provincial city of Neubrandenburg, the students were so tired of sitting that Lennart led

them on a two-kilometer jog around the top of the ancient city walls—
a circular dike with fancy brick portals. Either East Germany didn't
have youth hostels, or else they weren't open to outsiders, because
the class had to spread out their sheet sacks on wrestling mats in a
school gymnasium. Dinner was at the largest restaurant on the town's
main square. With prices three times lower than in Sweden, the students were allowed to order whatever they wanted. Their excitement
dimmed when everything turned out to be variations of sauerkraut
soup, indistinguishable meat in gravy, and pickled vegetables.

That evening, as the class sat cross-legged on mats, Lennart had
them compare journal entries.

A girl asked, "Why does everything in East Germany look so shabby?"

Lennart slowly plucked a minor chord on his guitar. "The Soviet
Union paid a higher price in World War II than the other Allies. They
lost eight million soldiers and twelve million civilians. After the war,
Germany paid reparations to all the Allies, but especially to the Soviet
Union. In their zone of occupation, the Russians dismantled entire fac-
tories and sent them home."

A boy suggested, "After two wars, they wanted to keep Germany
down."

Lennart put away his guitar. "The West took the opposite approach.
The United States started sending money to build Germany back up.
Arguably, it's not socialism that makes East Germany look shabby. It's
the capitalists propping up their puppet state in the West."

Heads nodded slowly, but Helen could sense the students were
having trouble embracing a system that guaranteed everyone sauerkraut soup.

At this point Herr Lindt began turning out the gymnasium's lights
one row at a time. "Tomorrow we'll be in Berlin. We'll have lots more
to talk about then."

In the dark there was little choice but to go to sleep.

CHAPTER 15
CONSTANTINOPLE, 907

Ali Ibn al-Namid was one of thirteen consulting personal physicians to Emperor Leo VI in Constantinople. None of the doctors was able to do much about the emperor's chronic indigestion, nor the fact that his wives kept mysteriously dying. As an Arab, Ali aroused widespread suspicion at the Byzantine court, but Leo the Wise had hired him for two very good reasons: Ali gave a most soothing olive oil massage, and he was a first-rate spy. Ali had traveled through most of the known world ministering to kings and caliphs. Rumors suggested he had once drained the life from a heathen queen in the far north. Most recently he had tended to the elderly al-Muktafi, the ailing ruler of the Abbasid Caliphate in Baghdad.

Emperor Leo emerged naked from the steam of the palace baths. Patterns of gold tiles arched overhead like yellow constellations through the clouds. Stone centaurs held seashells above tiled pools on either hand. Attendant slaves carried white towels by his sides, but Leo waved them away.

The emperor was not a powerful looking man, with a small chest and a beardless chin. He had won his nicknames—the Wise, the Philosopher—because of his bookish ways and his seductively ageless face. Above his boyish lips and his angular nose, clear hazel eyes seemed to be looking straight into the soul of everyone they saw. He ran his fingers through his curly brown hair, shook out the water, and said in Greek, "The shoulders first today, Ali."

The Arab doctor bowed his shiny bald head and held out his hand to a padded table. "Has Your Eminence been hunching over his writing desk again?"

Leo groaned as he laid himself face down on the table. "I'm on the

sixtieth volume."

Ali knew the emperor was working on a compendium of Byzantine law, controversially eliminating the senate and the consuls—Roman traditions that Leo found anachronistic. The man apparently believed that an emperor should be emperor of everything.

Ali began working his lightly oiled palms on the tensed muscles at the nape of Leo's neck. "A man with the weight of the world on his shoulders. I suspect this is why Atlas never married."

Leo chuckled, and the muscles began to relax. "To share the burden, I made my son co-emperor today."

"Zoe's Constantine? But he's hardly two years old."

"Sharing the title will give him a head start."

Ali considered this, working slowly down the emperor's back. The Church's Patriarch had decreed that the emperor's third marriage had been a sin, and that a fourth would be out of the question. Leo had simply replaced the patriarch and taken Zoe as a mistress. When she really did bear a son Leo had married her officially. But the boy's legitimacy remained a subject of dispute.

Ali asked, "Has Your Eminence's stomach been causing more discomfort?"

Leo growled. "Damn these doctors and their green potions."

Ali said nothing. He had diagnosed the emperor's digestive malady long ago. For a man named "the Wise," Leo ate like a fool, partaking of virtually nothing but pistachios, roast goat, and black olives. The only green vegetables he would touch were mint leaves, and the closest thing to fresh fruit was diluted wine. The potions he disdained were his physicians' attempt to administer dietary supplements containing healthy vegetable matter.

"Calves, Ali," the emperor said sharply.

"What?" Ali asked, and then added, "Your Eminence?"

"Massage my lower legs. And tell me more about the illness of the Caliph in Baghdad."

"Al-Muktafi's weakness is his lungs, Your Eminence." Ali began loosening the ball of muscles in the emperor's calves. They felt as tough as pomegranates. "I ascribed the problem to the vapors of the Euphrates, but the prevailing doctors claimed the damage had been caused by a djinn."

"A demon! Do you Moslems really believe in these genies?"

"As much as in angels, Your Eminence. According to the Quran, angels were created on Wednesday, the djinn on Thursday, and men on Friday."

"Do djinn grant wishes?"

Ali shook his head. "Hardly, Your Eminence. The djinn follow their own whims, for good or ill. They are sometimes invisible, but I very much doubt they inhabit the Caliph's lungs."

"How ill is the Caliph?"

"At the rate al-Muktafi is losing breath he will live but a few more months. This much is obvious to everyone, Your Eminence."

"I see."

From the drawn-out tone with which Leo had pronounced these two words, Ali could tell that he had successfully planted the seed of an idea. The trick now would be to nurture its growth in the right direction.

"If I am not mistaken," Leo mused, "The Caliph also has had trouble producing an unchallenged heir. Would his successor be his cousin Abdallah? I've heard he is a dangerously competent man."

"Abdallah would be the stronger choice," Ali agreed, refreshing his olive oil from a vial. "But the Caliph's vizier has instead been promoting the selection of a thirteen-year-old half brother, Ja'far al-Muqtadir. Most government officials also support the boy, imagining that a weak ruler will be easier to influence. And of course the boy's powerful mother, Shaghab, has united the palace behind him. As I left, troops and ships from across the Caliphate were being called home for a succession struggle in Baghdad this summer."

Ali worried: Was this bait too obvious?

Leo slapped the table with the flat of his hand. "Then we've got them."

"Your Eminence?"

The emperor swung his legs to the floor. "For years our Byzantine forces have retreated. We sat by while the Caliphate took Taormina, our last outpost on Sicily. We could do nothing when their pirates sacked Thessalonika. Their troops in Asia Minor marched from Aleppo to Pergamon. Their navy captured Crete. But now—" His fingers gripped the table's edge as if he were strangling it.

"If Your Eminence does not relax, I will have to start again with the shoulders." Ali prided himself in this choice of words. It was just the sort of vapid thing a harmless masseur might say.

"Another day," the emperor said dismissively. He wrapped a towel around his waist and strode off through the steam-shrouded hall. "I have work to do."

When Leo was gone, Ali smiled. "And so do I."

He traded his white massage tunic for his favorite red jacket, the one with brass buttons and voluminous sleeves. Then he made his way to the back of the hall, down the stairs, and out past the palace guards at the servants' entrance. Once on the street he began to hurry, nearly jogging past the marble arches of the Hippodrome. It was market day in the forum, so he had to navigate around carts, shoppers, and tables piled with fruit. He hurried on around the great dome of Hagia Sophia—and as always when he saw this magnificent hemisphere of stone, he imagined it surrounded by minarets, with muezzins singing out praise for Muhammad. The Voice claimed to have seen it in his dreams!

Beyond the cathedral, on First Hill's Acropolis, the temples of the old gods lay in ruins, overlooking the original city. Long ago, a little Greek settlement named Byzantium had clustered atop this peninsular hill. Then Constantine I had moved his capital here, and the city had grown. Water remained the dominant feature on all sides. To the south, the Sea of Marmara widened toward the Mediterranean. To the

east, the mile-wide Bosporus separated the city from the brown hills of Asia. To the west, an artificial moat had been dug through the hills of Europe. And to the north was a sinuous harbor inlet, the Golden Horn, protected at its mouth by a gigantic iron chain. No Arab warship could cross that barrier.

Ali paused to survey the wall that ringed the shore—a ten-mile curtain of brick and stone, studded with towers at each of its thirty gates. The world's richest city was the world's largest fortress.

Ladders, Ali thought.

Mindful of a sore knee that tended to twinge downhill, Ali descended more slowly to the alleyways of the Arab quarter. Muslims were not generally welcome in the Christian capital, but a small colony of doctors, artists, and smiths were tolerated for their skills. Stone steps twisted down between crooked whitewashed buildings. Red geraniums brightened windowsills. The air smelled of fish, smoke, and thyme.

Ali looked around to make sure he was unwatched before he tapped on a low wooden door—three times, then twice, then once.

The door opened just wide enough for Ali to slip inside. He closed it behind him quickly. As always, the sooty darkness made him afraid.

"You are early, doctor." The blacksmith was little more than a gleam of sweaty muscles in the murk.

"I have news from the emperor."

"The Voice is meditating in his library."

"He will want to hear this news."

The shadowy smith uncrossed his arms. "Very well." He led the way to an inner courtyard where a smoldering forge sent a spiral of bluish smoke up past three stories of colonnaded galleries to a small square sky. Hanging on all sides were chains, curlicued hinges, intricate locks, shiny scissors, and scrap iron. Ali climbed a wooden staircase that wound about the courtyard to the topmost floor. He hesitated at a door that was covered with an intricate geometric pattern of inlaid wood. His heart thumped from the climb and the aura of the one behind the elegant door. He rapped—once, then twice, then three times.

Minutes passed before the Voice said, "Enter."

Although Ali had never seen the Voice, he knew the accent well—a deep, melodious Arabic that glossed the harsher gutturals of Baghdad and gave the vowels a milky twang. It was the lovely song of the Moorish west, of Cordoba, of distant Iberia.

Ali lifted the silver latch and ventured into the hallowed library. A dozen leaded glass windows spilled shafts of light across shelves of enormous gold and red leather-bound books, some decorated with jewels. An atlas on the central table lay open to a map of the world, with Africa at the top and beasts of the Arctic writhing across the bottom. Only Christian maps pictured the world upside down, with Arabia near the bottom. The library's ceiling was a vault of dark wood, carved into a pattern of down-turned spires—a fantastical representation of the Cave of Hira, where the Prophet had once retreated for an entire month and had received his first words of divine inspiration.

"Leo is not the fool you think." The disembodied Voice might have come from any of the books. Ali knew that one—or perhaps several—of the bookshelves must swivel to reveal the entrance to the Voice's secret quarters. At times a draft rippled the dark walls behind the bookcases, suggesting that they hid draperies of black velvet. Perfumes hinted at a hidden harem.

Ali responded to the empty room, "The emperor swallowed my story like a greedy fish, my lord."

"Did you lie?"

"Not exactly. There will certainly be a fight over the Abbasid succession. Everyone knows Ja'far is a useless child. I am less sure that the Caliphate's forces have all been called back to Baghdad. But Leo—he jumped at the chance to win back territory while the Arab world is in disarray."

"Did he say where he might attack?"

"He mentioned several places, my lord." Ali ran a finger around the Mediterranean on the atlas page before him. "The loss of Taormina hurt him, but Sicily is too far away. Thessalonika was an embarrassment, but it has been refortified, and he has built up the fleet. That leaves Asia Minor. My guess is that he will send the fleet to retake Crete. Simultaneously he will march the army overland to Pergamon. The Arab raid there was dangerously close to Constantinople."

"Yes." The Voice spoke with uncanny assurance. "From those bases he dreams of controlling the entire eastern Mediterranean once more."

Ali swallowed. The Voice sometimes foretold events that should not yet be known. "Will the emperor succeed?"

"In part, yes. If Leo empties Constantinople of troops his forces will have the advantage of numbers against the Caliphate. This is why our strategy must be to press the Christian armies from a second front—from a direction they do not anticipate. Our secret weapon lurks in a wasteland of mythical monsters. It is right beside your finger, doctor."

Ali looked down at his hand in surprise. His finger had in fact drifted to the dragons and giants among the ice floes at the northern edge of the atlas page. He swallowed nervously again. "Shall I go back to Oleg, the ruler of the Varangian Rus?"

"No. I will send a swifter, more convincing messenger." The Voice paused, and then asked, "You say there are djinn among these wayrangers?"

"They believe in countless spirits, my lord. Many of their demons are vengeful and evil. One of the most feared seems to live inside Oleg's sword. Of course these are all imaginary, false gods."

"Not at all," the Voice replied. "They are the same as our djinn, merely with different names."

Ali took a step back toward the inlaid wooden door. Was this heresy or wisdom?

"Go, Ali Ibn al-Namid," the Voice said. "And bring me this sword."

CHAPTER 16
BERLIN, 1961

Lars Gustmeyer waited nervously by the Brandenburg Gate, watching the *Vopos*—the East German police—milling about the sidewalks of *Unter den Linden* in the Soviet sector. They weren't stopping traffic, but they were up to something. He had agreed to spend half a day showing his niece's school class a few of Berlin's sights. There was a tension in the hot August air that made him wish the Swedish bus weren't coming now, just as he was about to pick up a communique from Sasha about her work in Russia.

The bus itself was easy to spot—newer and larger than the Berlin buses, with his sister Mette waving in the front window. When the door opened she stepped out to hug him where they wouldn't be overheard.

"I've been worried about you," she whispered as they embraced. "Since Castro, you know, I've been afraid you'd lose your Cuban accounts."

"I've got other irons in the fire, Sis."

"Careful what you tell Helen's class. We've got a card-carrying Communist on board."

"Who? Your daughter?"

"No, silly. A very nice young man. I think you might know him." She led Lars up the bus steps. "This is Björn Lindt, the sociology teacher who is leading our field trip."

Lars shook the hand of the balding, gray-sweatered instructor, searching his features for familiarity or Communism. "Have we met?"

"No, but your sister tells me you may have met our political science specialist, Lennart Bronsson." He tilted his head toward the gangly young man beside him. "He's been interning part-time with Colonel

Wennerström."

Lars didn't offer his hand, and neither did the boy. "So you're the one working with Stig," Lars said. "He's mentioned you. What brings you on a field trip to Berlin?"

"Doctor Gustmeyer suggested it, and I need the credit for my poli sci major." Lennart shrugged. "The class could use different viewpoints. Mind if I chip in during your tour?"

"I'd rather you didn't. But let's get started."

"Excellent." Herr Lindt turned on the microphone. His cracking voice filled the bus. "Class? I'd like to introduce Lars Gustmeyer, Helen's uncle. You'll hear from his accent that he's originally from Denmark, but now he's stationed here in the American sector of Berlin. I believe he's a consultant for an export firm."

Herr Lindt gave Lars a questioning look and offered him the microphone, whispering, "Press the button to speak."

Lars pressed the button. "Hello everyone. Hi, Helen, there in the back. As my niece has probably told you I work for LogistEx Incorporated. I've had an office here in Berlin for a few years, and now I've been roped in to tell you about the place. You can start by looking out the window to my left—your right."

He stooped to point. "That's the Brandenburg Gate, with Roman pillars and a four-horse Roman chariot on top. The Prussians were already dreaming of empire a hundred years ago when they built it as the entrance to the city. I've always thought it looked like the porch for a library that isn't there.

Now it's the entrance to the Soviet sector. Quick question: Who can tell me why, if the Allies divided the city four ways after World War II, the Russians got a bigger share that included all of downtown?"

Only Lennart raised his hand. Reluctantly, Lars gave him the microphone.

"The city was originally divided into thirds, not fourths," Lennart explained. "France wasn't part of the Big Three. Later the Brits and Americans decided to carve up their sectors to make room for the French. As for downtown, whose army liberated Berlin? The Soviets, right?"

"Right." Lars repeated the word quietly. He hadn't envisioned this tour as a debate. He told the driver, "Let's move on."

"The next big building on your right," Lars announced, pointing to a huge crumbling shell of black stones, "Is the Reichstag, the German parliament. It looks like a war ruin, but it isn't. The building burned in 1933. Shortly after Adolf Hitler was sworn in as chancellor a Communist student set a fire that burned it down." He lifted an eyebrow at Lennart challengingly.

"Do you believe that story?" Lennart asked, hands on his hips.

"Not very much," Lars said in the microphone. "The kid was probably framed. Hitler wanted an excuse to get rid of parliament. But they guillotined the Communist student anyway. Driver, make a U-turn here. We'll head for the old Tempelhof Airport next."

The airport was practically downtown, just one kilometer inside the American sector. On the way Lars described the Berlin Airlift of 1948-1949, when the Soviets attempted to annex West Berlin by starving it into submission. At the start of a post-war 'hunger winter' they closed all land routes from West Germany to the city, cutting off supplies of food and fuel.

Lars pointed to a traffic circle ahead and told the driver, "Just circle there for a few minutes."

"Just circle?"

"The airport's not as interesting as the roundabout in front." Lars pressed the mic's button again. "See that claw-shaped statue sticking out of the traffic circle? That's what Berliners call the *Hungerharke*, the 'hunger rake.' It commemorates the Allies' response to the land blockade. They flew in potatoes, coal, and medicine to keep West Berlin alive. Freighters landed at this little airport every thirty seconds. The planes were unloaded and refueled in three minutes, and then were back in the air. After eleven months the Russians caved. They reopened truck and rail routes to West Germany."

Lars told the driver, "Now take that street there to *Wittembergplatz.*" He glanced to Lennart and said over the loudspeaker, "It's not so easy to break the will of a free people."

Lenny silently held out his hand for the microphone. Lars hesitated, but gave it to him.

"Who really started the Berlin blockade?" Lennart asked. "After the war all of Germany used the same money, the Reichsmark. In 1948 the three Western Allies decided, without consultation, to replace it with a new currency in their sectors. They declared the old Reichsmark worthless—but of course the old bills could still be spent in East Berlin. Paper money flooded in. The whole scheme was a capitalist plot to destroy the economy of the socialist state. The West forced East Germany to defend itself with a blockade until they could introduce their own new currency."

"Stop right there!"

"What?" Lennart asked.

"I'm talking to the driver." Lars took back the microphone. He held out a hand toward a seven-story department store that filled an entire block, its picture windows fronting a busy square. "The most popular store in all of East Germany isn't in the East at all—it's the KaDeWe, here in West Berlin. KaDeWe is short for *Kaufhof des Westens*, the department store of the West. It opened in 1907, the grandest emporium in the world. Nazis dispossessed the Jewish owners in 1933. An airplane fell through the roof and burned out the place in 1943, but now it's reopened in its full glory. More than half the customers and staff come from the Russian sector. They may not be able to vote in real elections, but they can vote with their feet. The rest of the Iron Curtain pens up its citizens pretty well. Because Berlin is an open city, however, there's nothing stopping comrades from riding the subway to the KaDeWe for the day. So far about three million have decided to stay. That's right—almost ten percent of East Germany's population has fled their workers' paradise. I guess they like it better in the West."

Lars released the microphone button and asked Lennart, "What does our political science commentator say to that?"

Lars had expected the boy to say that the East Germans who fled were traitors, or that they were thieves because they had accepted a free education in the East and had left without paying it back.

Instead the young man shook his head. "It worries me. There will be trouble."

For the first time Lars began to see why his friend Colonel Wenneström had taken on this student as a protégé.

"I think you're right."

Herr Lindt leaned forward from his seat. "Are we still planning to have dinner in the store cafeteria?"

"Without me, I'm afraid," Lars replied.

Mette looked worried. "You're leaving already?"

"I need to get back to the office." Lars frowned. "The LogistEx business has been picking up these past few days. I have an important meeting tomorrow in the Russian sector."

"And so do we," Herr Lindt said brightly, adjusting his glasses. "Your erudite sister has agreed to show us the Pergamon and Bode museums."

Lars squeezed Mette's hand. "Maybe I'll run into you over there." Then he opened the bus door and walked across *Wittembergplatz* to the U-Bahn subway stairs.

* * *

Helen's class was allowed one hour to explore what Lennart downplayed as KaDeWe's "decadent bourgeois excess." They rode escalators past displays of slitted Italian evening gowns. They floated amid the seductive scent of French perfumes. They found American electric guitars, Danish plastic toys, Belgian diamond jewelry, and a basement supermarket with a pyramid of pineapples. But everything was so expensive that they wound up in the cafeteria ordering little more than *bratwurst* and big puffy pretzels with mustard.

The Berlin youth hostel, a few blocks closer to the Brandenburg Gate, was a repurposed brick warehouse with four hundred kids from all over the world. The furniture and most of the regimented atmosphere seemed to have been left over from the *Wehrmacht*. The girls' hall where Helen stayed had endless rows of metal cots with squeaky iron springs, thin mattresses, and woolen blankets. The blankets were all neatly folded up at the foot end of the bed to expose the woven word, *Fussende*, which Helen eventually realized simply meant "Foot End." The only storage was in rows of green metal lockers.

Helen had hinted to the class that they could slip out with Lennart to find a beer hall with live music that night, but by the time everyone had checked into the hostel there was only an hour before curfew. They walked as far as the *Tiergarten*, a park with a shuttered cabaret, before turning back. The muggy night air was full of sirens and shadows. Helen paused in one of the darkest spots, just before the door, her heart pounding. After the other students had gone inside Lennart came back to find her. She put her palms on his chest to push him away, but then just held them there, feeling his heart beat through the muscles. Why was his musky scent so exciting? He kissed her lightly on the lips. When he reached out to kiss her harder, however, she really did push him away and run inside.

At exactly 6:30 the next morning all the lights in the youth hostel glared to life. Loudspeakers squawked German commands. Groggily, Helen learned from the other girls that this was the hostel's normal wake-up call. The loudspeakers were instructing everyone to fold up the woolen blankets at the foot end of their cots so that the word *Fussende* was visible right-side-up. Breakfast would be at 7am sharp and everyone must be out of the hostel by 9am.

"*Zack zack*," a girl told Helen.

"What's that?" Helen asked.

She clicked her heels. "The sound of German efficiency."

In the breakfast room the loudspeakers were blaring a German newscast, which didn't set a relaxing mood either. Stranger still, everyone was listening. Helen didn't speak enough German to pick up much, so she got a tray, took three bread rolls from a big basket, and grabbed some prepackaged portions of jam, honey, and butter. Then she plunked the tray down at her mother's table. "What's going on, Mom?"

"Shh!" Herr Lindt held up a finger, frowning.

Mette whispered, "It's East Berlin. The police there have put up barbed wire along the border."

"Barbed wire? To keep people out?" Helen had been looking forward to this day. She had helped her mother make lists of all the things they wanted to see at the East Berlin museums.

"No," Mette replied. "Apparently they're building a wall to keep their own people in."

The newscast ended with three chimes. After a few more German words the loudspeakers switched to Dean Martin's boozy voice crooning about *amore*.

Herr Lindt groaned. "We've got a ten o'clock appointment at the Pergamon. I confirmed it just yesterday. What are we supposed to do all day with twenty-three students if we can't walk to the museum island?"

At that point Lennart slouched in from the reception hall, looking unhappy. He ignored Helen, as if their kiss the night before had never happened. He sat heavily on a chair opposite Mette. "Your brother's outside, Doctor Gustmeyer."

"Lars? What does he want?"

"To talk to you alone. I guess it's all too hush-hush for the likes of me." Lenny reached for one of Helen's rolls. "Can I borrow a bun?"

"Get your own!" She swatted his hand away. He moped off toward the breakfast counter.

Mette was gone for fifteen minutes, time enough for Helen to finish her rolls, get a cup of coffee with milk, and start to worry. When her mother finally came back she had a shell-shocked look on her face and a newspaper in her hand.

"What's the news?" Lennart asked.

"We're all set to go," Mette said matter-of-factly, sitting down.

"Really?" Herr Lindt adjusted his glasses. "Despite the barbed wire?"

"Yes. Lars has straightened everything out. There's a checkpoint with a gate on *Friedrichstrasse*. They'll be expecting our Swedish school class at 9:30."

"Wow," Lennart said, a touch of satire in his voice. "That export company of his really must have connections."

Mette met his gaze sternly. "Walking to the Russian sector today should give the class a chance to ask you all kinds of political questions, Lennart."

Helen knew at once from her mother's tone that there was more at stake here than merely a museum visit. But what was it? Asking her in front of everyone wasn't going to work.

Herr Lindt, for his part, beamed with relief. "Excellent. I'll tell the class to get ready."

"Make sure they have their passports," Mette put in.

"Good idea."

When Herr Lindt was gone Mette opened the newspaper in front of her like a screen.

"Mom?" Helen asked.

"Not now, sweetheart, I'm reading." She turned a page. "But perhaps you could get me a cup of coffee."

* * *

When class 11c of the *Bernadottegymnasium* assembled in the hostel's reception hall Mette explained what was going on—although Helen suspected a lot was still unsaid.

"Last night the East German police surrounded West Berlin with barbed wire. They plan to build a wall, but they say it's not another blockade. People from West Berlin can still drive on three highway corridors to West Germany, and there are checkpoints where tourists from the West can visit East Berlin."

"Then who is the wall for?" a voice asked.

Mette turned to Lennart. "I believe that's a question for you, Herr Bronsson."

Lennart sighed. "It's to stop the brain drain. Remember what I said about everyone in a socialist state taking just what they need? Well, some people want more than their share. The doctors and engineers who got a free ride at East German universities can earn twice as much if they run away to the West. The wall is to make sure they stay home until they've paid off their debt."

"Then their education wasn't really free?"

Lennart sighed again. "Nothing is really free, East or West."

Herr Lindt opened the hostel's front door. "I'm told three main checkpoints are open this morning—Alpha, Bravo, and Charlie. I guess they're named for the letters A, B, and C. We'll be going to Checkpoint Charlie, about six blocks away. Stay close together."

At first it seemed like an ordinary Sunday morning in Berlin, with newspaper kiosks selling cigarettes and hot dog carts selling *currywurst*. *Friedrichstrasse*, however, was a mess. Crowds of people were gawking and shouting. Delivery trucks honked as they tried to make U-turns. The class marched through it all to a flimsy little booth planted in the middle of the street behind sandbags and a sign, "U.S. ARMY CHECKPOINT."

An American officer in a bell-shaped battle helmet grinned when he saw them coming. His accent sounded as broad as the Mississippi.

"Say, there y'all are, a whole damn flock of Swedish ducklings. Are you Mrs. Gustmeyer?"

Mette held out her passport, but he waved her on.

"No problem, ma'am, you're good to go on our side. How many you got here, twenty-four kids and two grown-ups?"

"Twenty-three children and three adults," Lennart corrected.

"Well, good luck with the *Vopos* on the other side. Y'all have a great day now, hear?"

Lennart spoke German better than anyone else in the group, and he was in fact a Communist, so he went first with Herr Lindt. Mette and Helen brought up the rear as the class walked across an impromptu no-man's-land, a hundred-foot-long stretch of bare asphalt between gates. The five-story buildings on either hand looked as though they had been abruptly abandoned—except for soldiers with automatic rifles in the upper windows. Ahead, beyond coils of barbed wire, two armored trucks with red stars on their doors had parked on the sidewalk.

"I'm not sure this is such a good idea, Mom," Helen said.

"It's all part of a modern Swedish education, honey," Mette replied. Ahead of them a green-uniformed *Volkspolizist* raised the gate's boom. A second *Vopo* checked each of the students' blue Swedish passports and nodded. Helen knew she shouldn't be afraid—she had been in East Germany just the day before—but her heart was still in her throat as she held out her passport and said brightly, "*Guten Tag.*"

The soldier waved her past without reply. But the next moment he barked, "*Halt! Das ist kein schwedischer Pass.*"

Helen turned, terrified, to find the policeman examining her mother's passport. Mette began to say something in German, but the *Vopo* shook his head, held out his arm like a bar, and yelled in Russian. A moment later an officer in a brown uniform stepped out of the armored truck. His cap had a shiny black bill and a bright red band. The holster of a pistol was strapped to his belt. He took Mette's red Danish passport and frowned.

Helen looked to Lennart for help, but he and all the rest of the class were already beyond the checkpoint, waiting on a sidewalk. They couldn't return without raising questions. Helen swallowed, standing her ground in limbo just one step inside East Berlin.

"You are Danish citizen," the Russian officer objected in heavily accented English. "Why with Swedish class?"

"I'm a historical advisor for their visit to the Pergamon Museum," Mette replied.

Helen wondered why she hadn't said the obvious, that she was the mother of one of the students. Was her mother trying to protect her?

The Russian flipped through the passport pages, inspecting the many visa stamps. "United States, United Kingdom, Federal Republic—" he stopped, shaking his head. "*Nyet*. We need no historical advisors today."

The *Vopo* held his arm out still further, a gate between Helen and her mother. "*Zurück. Nur die Klasse darf weiter.*"

In desperation Mette reached for Helen. "That's my daughter!"

"Stay back!" the policeman held out his arm between them.

Mette's expression suddenly changed, the terror of a mother yielding to a different, even steelier determination. She held out her clipboard over the policeman's arm. "My museum notes. *Die Notizen für die Klasse.*"

Helen barely managed to take the clipboard—and the folded newspaper underneath—before the soldier's arm pushed Mette back.

Helen was scared and puzzled. Would they release her mother? Would the class have to turn back? And why the newspaper?

Mette stopped in the middle of no-man's-land, turned, and spoke in broad Danish—a secret code that even the Swedes would have trouble understanding. "Trade the newspaper for your aunt's copy at the Pergamon altar."

"Me? You want me to—?" Suddenly Helen realized that Berlin's wall had changed her mother, and the purpose of their visit. That morning Lars must have revealed that he and Sasha were in fact agents of the CIA. Aunt Sasha's report had to be smuggled out of the eastern sector. Did they think no one would suspect a Swedish schoolgirl? But what if she was discovered? And did she want to help the CIA at all?

"See you tonight, honey," her mother said. "Have a nice day at the museum."

Meanwhile the Soviet officer had walked back to his truck. He unhooked a microphone and said quietly in Russian, "Tell Agent Veliky they're here."

CHAPTER 17
VOLKHOV RIVER, 907

Groa had forgotten how much she disliked rowing. She had hated the task long ago in Norway, when she had awakened as a twenty-year-old girl. Then she had escaped Tunsberg on Thorkell's longship. Now, twenty-five years later, pulling an oar was even harder on her hands, her back, and her dignity. For all she knew she was the only woman in the fleet rowing away from Novgorod—against the current, against the wind, and against her own best judgment. This time she was not fleeing a miserable life. She had been happy as a teacher and a healer in Russiya. This time she was flying directly into all manner of unpleasantness. Any idiot could see that this was not a trading expedition to sell ladders in Miklagard. Eighty-four shiploads of fighters? This was an invasion force.

And yet as the walls of Novgorod disappeared behind a river-bend and the fortress of Holmgard slipped past among the willows, the thrill of adventure blew through the army of nearly four thousand Varangian men like a wild ocean breeze.

While Groa rowed beside Hrolf, seated on the same carpenter's chest they had shared years ago, Groa allowed her thoughts to drift into the minds of the men about her. She didn't consider this to be sorcery, although it was an essential tool of that trade. Everyone was able to read other people's emotions if they tried. Women might be more adept at mental trespassing, but only because they cared enough to listen. At least that's what Groa told herself as she eavesdropped on the thoughts of the others aboard her Ship in the Woods that morning.

Thorkell, the white-bearded Norwegian captain in the prow, was dreaming of wealth. He had been a jarl in Norway, and had never understood why Oleg had demoted him to serve as a sail-rigger in the

Novgorod shipyard. Groa's suggestion that he teach sailing to Igor, the young tsar, had reawakened old ambitions. If their expedition to Miklagard was a success, why shouldn't he be declared a jarl once more? Then, instead of captaining Igor's ship he would sail his own, become wealthy through trade, and buy an estate where he could retire in splendor.

Igor, sharing an oar with a friend near the stern, was thinking that he would row for another hour, until they reached Lake Ilmen. Then he would trade places with Gunnar, the helmsman. Igor liked the monotony of rowing. It demonstrated that he was part of the crew, but a tsar deserved a position of command at the tiller. The expedition to Miklagard was his chance to prove himself. Finally the Rus would clamor for him to take the tiller of Russiya away from his uncle Oleg, and he would finally consent.

Voris, the muscular young man rowing beside the tsar, was terrified. Groa turned, studying the oarsman to be sure. Voris had always behaved like an older, protective step-brother to Igor, although they weren't actually related. Voris was the eldest son of Vlad's wife Ingrid. As governor of Novgorod, Vlad has moved his extended family into Igor's palatial hall. Voris had been one of Groa's students at Holmgard. He had always seemed the most warrior-like of her pupils. Even now his stony expression appeared confident. But inside, his heart was a furnace of fear. He knew they were sailing to battle, and he was sure he would die. The Byzantine Empire had bigger ships and better armor. Their soldiers were conscripted from half the world. They were hell hounds, driven by the fury of their Christian god. Attacking Byzantium was a suicide mission. If only he could run away without dying yet a worse death from shame!

And then there was her husband Hrolf, pulling on their oar like a yoked ox. The dear man was compensating for Groa's lesser effort. Physical work did not faze him, regardless of how repetitive it might be. One of the reasons Groa loved her homely husband was his transparency. Yes, his head looked like it had been hewn from a stump, but his mind was usually as clear as glass. Now she paused, bewildered by what she was reading there.

Hrolf didn't want to go on this expedition either. He had persuaded her to come by faking his own enthusiasm.

"Really?" she said out loud between strokes. "You don't like to travel? You're afraid our ship will sink in the rapids?" The hulls they had built were so light that an errant rock really might puncture the flank. "Then why—?"

Between pulls Hrolf gave her a tired smile that merely repeated what she already knew: He loved her. Beyond that, the glass fogged.

The other message Groa understood was that her husband was not turning back.

* * *

The fleet from Novgorod reached Lake Ilmen before noon. There the wind shifted, allowing them to hoist sails for the crossing of the shallow lake, slate-gray all the way to an overcast horizon. Thorkell had a mixed crew—half of them seasoned rivermen and half of them Igor's young friends—but they had trained together well. Raising the mast was no easy feat when the length of the deck was clogged with sixteen ladders and a variety of baled trade goods. Nonetheless, their sail was among the first to rise—blue and white stripes with the young tsar's favorite mascot in the middle, a double-headed eagle.

"Is the eagle's second head for Oleg?" Voris chided.

Igor shrugged evasively. "Two heads are better than one."

Eighty-four winged dragons! The fleet had nearly emptied the Northlands of Rus men, leaving Vlad as governor in Holmgard with little more than his decorative palace guards. Years ago the Slavs and Finns might have revolted, using the unwatched summer to pillage. But time had taught them to respect the Varangians. The Rus women, children, and elders who remained were far from defenseless. And the fleet of four thousand would return in a few months to avenge any lawlessness. The Rus ruled hard, but well.

Sailing across the lake, even Groa began to be caught up in the breeze of adventure. The dragons raced each other across the silent water, leaving great Vs of ripples and long trails of white-bubbled wakes. In their years at the shipyard, Groa had equipped ships with standard yellow-and-white sails to match Oleg's shield. Hrolf had outfitted prows with an arrow shaped like Tyr's rune. But many of the jarls of Novgorod had modified their ships. The various sails billowed a red spiral, a black raven, a brown ox, or a green star. Likewise the prows had become a menagerie of growling beasts and screaming bird-heads. Along the flank of each ship the rows of round shields were a riot of colored wheels. Each man had individualized his own circular shield with patterns and monsters.

Anyone who saw this swift, motley horde of dragonships would understand the message of its onrushing roar: If you do not treat us as honored traders, prepare to surrender, flee, or die.

That evening the fleet beached for the night at a grassy island near the far shore of the lake, where way-rangers had obviously camped before. Thorkell's crew built a fire and boiled a kettleful of barley gruel with dried pork. Then there were songs and saga poems. Inspired by the mood and prodded by her husband, Groa recited three hundred verses of the *Ynglingatal*. She chose the portion she knew best, where an insolent fifteen-year-old princess tells a boy named Harald that she will marry him on the condition that he first conquer all thirty-one kingdoms of Norway. Nine years later, after Harald Fairhair's fleet had defeated the Viking Alliance at Hafrsfjord, the boy-king had reigned unchallenged.

"No," Thorkell said, shaking his grizzled head. "That is not how it was."

Too late, Groa remembered that Thorkell had been one of the beaten jarls. He had sailed to Russiya rather than submit.

"Harald cheated." The old Norwegian was little more than a voice in the shadows. "He stole the Viking sword and invoked the gods of doom for his victory. I do not know how, but I fear our regent Oleg now wields the same charmed sword."

"Then that means we will win in battle?" Voris asked, a note of hope in his words.

Thorkell wagged his gray beard. "In the end, it means we will all lose."

Nothing more was said before the crew dispersed for the night. Most of the men slept on the ship, ostensibly to guard their trade goods, but more likely to escape the imagined vapors and vipers of the island night. Perhaps they thought that the deadly hugorm snake of Scandinavia lived here too. Scoffing at such myths, Voris helped set up an elaborately decorated tent on the island for Igor, the young tsar.

Hrolf pitched a much smaller tent—a sheet of canvas draped over a pole—by the embers of the fire. Inside, rolled in a blanket with Groa, he asked, "Is Oleg's sword really as valuable as they say?"

"It must be destroyed. Oleg has promised me this. That is why we are going to Miklagard."

"Yes," Hrolf said. "That is why."

* * *

In the morning the flotilla rowed up a marshy delta to the Lovat River, a much smaller stream that meandered between farm fields. On either bank Slavic men plowed black earth with teams of cattle. The farmworkers looked up in alarm at the mile-long procession of mastless ships rowing in single file around the fields.

By afternoon the creek's twisting channel had become so narrow that the oars could be used only on one side at a time. Beyond that the oars had to be pulled in altogether for use as poles. Oarsmen walked aft as they pushed, yanking their oars from the mud at the stern and then carrying the oars overhead as they walked back to the prow.

Camp on the second night was at the village of Luki, a cluster of mud-wattle huts. The Slavic villagers there did not farm, but rather depended entirely on ships in need of portage. For a fee they would loan travelers the use of carts and horses to haul their goods six miles to the Dvina River. The villagers helped unload ballast rocks from the ships' holds, pulled the lightened boats through the swampy woods, launched them into the Dvina, and balanced them with ballast from a different pile of stones.

Because the Novgorodans had brought so many ships the entire operation took three days. Groa grumbled, slogging through the mud with a rope at her shoulder. The old-timers on Thorkell's crew warned her that this was the easy portage. The land was virtually flat, strewn with small stagnant ponds. The longer portage through the mountains to the Dnieper, they said, was the one that broke backs.

When at last all eighty-four longships had been refloated in the Dvina it was the evening of the voyagers' fifth day. Without any particular command, most of the crews broke open barrels of ale to celebrate their progress. Wood for bonfires was gathered for the riverside encampment.

The impromptu gaiety ended abruptly when a watchman's lur-horn sounded a long, mournful warning call. There were sails downriver—dozens of ships. And although the armada was still distant, a brisk west wind was speeding it upriver against the current.

"To arms!" Thorkell called out. Thousands of men stumbled chaotically to the ships for their weapons. Why, Groa wondered, had no one practiced this drill? Only the crews of the jarls were quick to ready a defense, and even these lacked a unified plan.

Worse, the approaching sails lacked the stripe of Oleg's shield. The sails were dirty off-white, pink, or tan—the sloppy random rags of pirates. Forty-six sails! Already the roar of the fleet's battle cry carried over the water.

"Hold!" Thorkell raised his hand to stop the crewmen who were notching arrows to their bows.

The first two ships lowered their sails to half mast and steered aside to let a longer ship through. Although its gray sail also lacked blue stripes, it billowed the emblem of three gigantic black arrows pointing skyward.

"Hail Rus!" Thorkell shouted across the water.

"Hail Rus!" a voice replied.

The Novgordans lowered their weapons with relief. But Groa saw at once that this was not a ship Hrolf had built. Instead of a crew of fifty, this dragon had room for seventy or more.

"I am Farlof, a knight of the Varangian Order!" The man in the ship's prow wore a square blond beard, a shiny acorn-shaped helmet, and black chain mail. He scanned the crowds of men along the shore. "Where are you from, and who among you is a knight?"

After an awkward pause Thorkell called back, "We come from Novgorod. We have jarls among us instead of knights. But our leader, and yours, is Tsar Igor."

Farlof signaled his helmsman to steer the ship to shore. With bewildering efficiency the crew lowered their sail, extended a plank to the shore, and secured the beach with a semicircle of swordsmen. Two dozen archers lined the ship's flanks, bows drawn. Farlof descended the gangplank using a battle axe as a staff. The swordsmen formed a protective ring around him, pushing back the crowds as he climbed to the height of the riverside bluff to confront Thorkell.

"We have heard of this boy who calls himself tsar," Farlof said. "But we have never seen him. Where is the child hiding now?"

"I am not hiding," Igor said, stepping forward. "I am Rurik's heir, Tsar of Novgorod and future ruler of Russiya." He wore a fur-lined red cloak, but stood half a head shorter than either Thorkell or Farlof.

Farlof sized up the young tsar with a sigh. "Hail Igor. For now I'm told we have a regent in Kiev. Oleg has called the Rus to join his expedition to Miklagard. As you can see, the men of the Westlands have answered."

"Excellent," Igor said. "Camp with us tonight. Tomorrow we will all sail together. You—" he hesitated. "You seem to know the way."

Farlof chuckled, rubbing his eyes with his hand. "Yes. I do."

* * *

That evening Igor invited Farlof to a conference in his tent. The Varangian knight left his battle axe outside but strode in together with a burly young man whose massive arms could have qualified as weapons. Groa thought the guard looked capable of ripping an opponent limb from limb.

"This is Grim," Farlof announced. "He is my best friend's son, and my helmsman."

Igor, seated on a folding stool beneath a candle lantern, introduced the three people in the shadows behind him. "This is Thorkell, my captain, Voris, my seatmate, and Groa."

Farlof scowled. "You brought a woman on your crew?"

"Groa is a healer," Igor replied evenly. "And a sorceress."

Farlof looked closer at Groa's eyes—one green and one blue. "I remember you. You spoke at Holmgard the day after Rurik died. They say it was your wizardry that allowed our colonists to defeat an army."

Groa shook her head. "My skill in that battle was in knowing when to run away."

The knight viewed her guardedly for a moment, and then turned to Igor. "At Novgorod a retreat was what led to victory. I wonder if our regent has forgotten that lesson?"

"Explain yourself," Igor said.

"Grim and I have been to the Byzantine capital many times on trading expeditions. Miklagard is protected by sea chains, giant warships, and stone walls. Their empire's power is so great they are able to ruin our trading with taxes and rules. Oleg is mistaken if he believes we can force them to our will with ladders."

"Our ladders are trade goods," Igor said—evidently unaware that he was the only one in the tent who still thought the ladders would be for sale.

Farlof rubbed his eyes with his hand, as he had done at their first meeting. "Well, Tsar, I think our expedition could strike a more profitable bargain elsewhere. Instead of battering ourselves against the stone citadel of Byzantium, why not use our forces to help the Rus of the Westlands clear the Dvina River to the Baltic? Then there would be no need for this portage you have just undertaken. Our markets are in Scandinavia and Frankia to the west, not in the Finnish wastes north of Novgorod. Sailing down the Dvina would save three hundred miles and a week's travel on the route to Sweden."

"Why don't you use this shortcut yourself, if it is so convenient?" Igor asked.

Thorkell put in, "I'm told that they try, but only at night, and only with heavily armed flotillas like the one they brought here."

Farlof frowned. "Latvians control the river mouth at Riga. Their defenses are light compared to Miklagard. We are not yet numerous enough to overpower them. With the armada Oleg is gathering we could extend the realm of Russiya all the way to the Baltic shore."

Igor tapped his fingers on his knee, thinking. "Your proposal is interesting, Farlof. We don't yet know Oleg's plans. I suggest you make your case to the regent when we arrive in Kiev."

With a frustrated growl Farlof turned on his heel and stormed out of the tent. Grim inhaled through his nostrils, flexing his massive arms in a show of strength before following.

Groa needed no special powers to read the thoughts of the three remaining men in the tsar's tent.

Igor was embarrassed that he had deferred a decision to his uncle yet again. Farlof's plan for expanding the realm sounded bolder than a mere trade expedition. How were the Rus going to respect him as tsar if he didn't dare to take command?

Thorkell, for his part, hated Farlof's idea. Conquering a few Latvian tribes would bring blood, but no wealth. The source of silver lay in the south, where Oleg was headed. Even if the Rus did succeed in opening a shortcut down the Dvina, all it would accomplish would be to leave Novgorod abandoned as a ghost town on a useless detour. All their years of building the city would be for nothing.

The thoughts of Voris, Igor's silent seatmate, were jumbled by his increasing terror. Voris knew Farlof was a practical strategist who had actually been to Miklagard. The knight's first-hand description of the city's unbreachable defenses confirmed Voris' fears. Oleg was leading them into a death trap. Perhaps it was all a ruse to murder Igor so Oleg could remain in power.

"Let's get some rest," Igor said.

Groa nodded. But she knew the night would bring uneasy dreams to them all.

* * *

The addition of the Westlanders increased the Rus fleet to 124 ships and more than six thousand men. A persistent west wind succeeded in pushing the entire armada sixty miles upriver to the village of Zharkov in a single day. Although the Dvina continued east as a navigable river, Farlof assured Igor that this was the closest point for a portage to the drainage system that would take them south to the Black Sea.

Zharkov itself was mostly a tent city of hides stretched on poles. The inhabitants were Drevlians, a non-Slavic tribe of nomadic herders who ranged their cattle on the mountains that extended southeast to the treeless steppe.

"Mountains?" Groa asked, assessing a brown line of low rolling hills to the south. She remembered genuine mountains from Norway. The cliffs there rose thousands of feet from fjords to a gleaming white cap of glaciers that shrugged loose waterfalls. Frost giants lived in those icy summits, terrifying travelers at night. Russiya was a different kind of land. Here you could sail up a river on tidewater for days and still see nothing but flat, swampy woods in all directions. Zharkov's hills would count as mountains, Groa decided, only if you had seen nothing taller—or if you were ordered to drag ships over them.

Somehow the Drevlians had been alerted to the approaching fleet and had rounded up several thousand head of cattle to help with the portage. The herdsmen had no wagons. Instead they tied each cow to a ladder, lashed trade goods on top of the rungs, and drove the cattle up the mountain road, dragging the ladders behind.

Hrolf objected that this would damage the trailing ends of the ladders, lessening their value for trade.

Thorkell chuckled at the woodworker. "I promise you, the Byzantines will pay exactly the same price for used ladders as for new."

Hrolf shook his head at this nonsense.

Five yokes of cattle pulled heavy ropes at the prow of each ship. Each ship's crew was divided into three teams. Groa and Hrolf had rowed on the starboard side, so they became part of the starboard team, pushing the right-hand side of the boat up the road while the port team pushed on the opposite side. A third team placed log rollers under the front of the prow, ran around to the back of the ship, picked up the loose logs, and lugged them to the front again.

It was hot, sweaty work in the late June sun. There was no shade, Groa was told, because the Drevlian herders had intentionally burned the mountains' pine woods—evidently preferring a grassland of black snags to a forest. The keel rumbled on the rollers, vibrating through the ship like a thunderous drum. Groa feared that a roller might crush her foot, or that the port team would push too hard and tip the boat on top of her. Horseflies bit where she could not slap. The rocky track stank with the piss and dung of countless cattle.

Why had none of the men on her crew thought to bring drinking water? As soon as Groa shared her flask it was empty. Igor and Voris rode past on horses, offering nothing but words of encouragement. When the road traversed a slope with a clear, flowing spring half the crew abandoned the boat to drink. As a result the ship really did tip onto its right flank. Groa and Hrolf barely jumped aside in time. And then the ship began sliding downhill on the rollers.

"Hold the ropes!" Thorkell cried.

Even the yoked cattle were being pulled off their feet. If the ship slipped over the edge it might smash on the rocks below, taking the cattle and perhaps some of the crew with it.

A boulder finally stopped the hull with a sickening crack of broken wood. The crew gathered somberly to survey the damage to the *Varangia*. If the rudder had not been removed for the portage, it would have taken the blow and splintered to kindling. As it was, the rock had punched a hole in the starboard flank large enough for a man to crawl through.

"Carpenter, can you repair it?" Thorkell asked.

Hrolf shook his head. "I would need pitch. I have rivets and wood, but I would need buckets of pitch." Only Groa heard his additional thought: And the ship would never be as strong as before.

"Good. Then we are going to the right place," Thorkell said. "Smolensk was named for pitch. The Slavic word for pitch is *smol*. The rivermen there use pine sap to prepare boats for the Dnieper rapids downstream. We will too."

The old Norwegian captain scanned the road ahead. Two other ship crews were already passing them by, sniggering at their misfortune. "We might as well drink our fill at the spring before righting the ship."

The road summited the mountain in a broad pass of tree stumps. Here the Drevlians unyoked the cattle, untied the ladders, and demanded their pay. They explained that the crew should not need help to pull their ship downhill to Smolensk, even with cargo on board. In fact, they would need help *slowing* the ship on the steepest portions of the road. This was why the previous crews had cut live pine trees, to drag them behind the ship as brakes.

A day later they reached Smolensk—a palisaded settlement nearly as large as Novgorod. The Dnieper River beside the town was wide enough that Groa thought it would be hard to throw a rock across—but it might be possible to walk across on the decks of ships. Even before the armada from Novgorod arrived, seventy-one dragons already crowded the river. Seven of them bore the black Tyr-arrows of Varangian knights. Smolensk's position at a strategic portage, and its rich hinterland of farm fields, had attracted the wealthy warrior-traders to establish bases here.

The town did have a good supply of pitch. Hrolf also quickly found shipwrights who knew all about patching hulls. What he didn't find were carpenters who understood ladders. Sixty of the fleet's ladders had been so badly damaged on the portage over the mountain that they would be useless without repair. Short on time and short on labor, Hrolf banged the ladders apart, salvaged what he could, and reassembled thirty from the parts. No one, he thought, would pay full price for such wares. And he would need money for his secret plan to succeed in Miklagard. Where would he get it?

Meanwhile, no one seemed to be in charge of the fleet. The expedition now had 195 ships and nearly ten thousand men, but the eight Varangian knights and twenty-six jarls each saw themselves as equally deserving of command. Igor, for his part, wasn't sure what orders to give. One thing was obvious: If such a large army stayed in Smolensk very long the idle Rus crews would eat up the town's food supply, drink its ale dry, and then probably tear the place to pieces.

The Smolensk knights were the first to set out downriver, followed soon by Igor, Farlof, and the other crews. Rowing beside Hrolf, Groa noticed that her husband had once again lost himself among opaque thoughts.

"Are you worried that your patch might not hold in the rapids?" Groa asked.

"No," he said. " I mean, yes." This had not been his foremost worry, but now that she had brought it up, it was. "It bothers me that neither our captain nor our tsar seem familiar with the Dnieper. Thorkell has been asking advice from the older hands on our crew."

"And what do they say?"

"They say that the river descends through a gorge. There are seven named rapids. The last two are easy to navigate—Hlæjandi and Strukum."

"The final rapids are called 'Laughing' and 'Swift Current'?"

Hrolf nodded, pulling on their oar. After a few more strokes he said, "The first five rapids increase in difficulty to Barafoss."

"'Barren Falls,'" Groa said. The name suggested a waterfall over a bedrock cliff.

Hrolf said, "I've asked Thorkell to call out their names as we approach."

Creak, splash. Creak, splash.

And then Groa began to hear a distant gulping roar.

"Grip your oars," Thorkell ordered. "Supandi ahead!"

Groa thought: The first rapids is 'Slurping.' She sat taller to peer past the prow. There were no rocks or obstructions, just a glassy curve where the river slid a few feet downhill. It looked as though the thunder god, Thor, had tipped the river and was draining it as he had once drunk the ocean.

The gulping sound grew louder. Then the ship's prow tipped forward and Groa's oar paddled nothing but air. Over the gunwale she saw a suckhole where the river arched over an unseen ledge and curled back upon itself, gulping.

Whitewater sprayed as the prow bobbed up, but the ship was long enough that it easily bridged the suckhole and glided free.

"That was fun!" Groa exclaimed. When she turned to her husband she saw he wasn't smiling. The beads of moisture on his brow were not river spray.

Beyond Supandi the Dnieper drifted lazily into a long sinuous pool. They rowed for a dozen miles until the current grew swifter at the start of a large island of willow brush.

"Holmfoss!" Thorkell called out. *Island Falls.*

"The trick here," the helmsman Gunnar explained to Igor, "Is that the broader part of the river on the left of the island looks like it's the easy passage. But that route spreads out into shallows full of cobbles. Instead we need to steer through the swift, narrow chute to the right."

"Yes, I see," Igor replied, scanning the river ahead.

"Here, Tsar," Gunnar said, offering him the tiller. "Why don't you try steering us through?"

"All right." The young tsar eyed the channel and edged the ship to the right.

"Oars up!" Thorkell shouted from the prow. The chute ahead was hardly wider than the ship itself. Voris just managed to lift his oar in time. A mossy rock wall shot past on the right, inches from the gunwale. Willow branches from the island whipped the crew on the port side.

When the ship bobbed out into a pool below, Igor laughed out loud. He held his fist victoriously in the air. Behind them, ship after ship ran the chute, bobbing free into the broader river below the island.

That evening the fleet camped in a plain at the mouth of the Dnieper Gorge, where the river disappeared into a noisy ravine.

"The roar you hear is Gellandi," Gunnar said at the campfire that night. "'Yelling,' the third rapids, is like a warrior with a big voice and a short sword. It's a series of a dozen standing waves. Each of them has a whitewater crest, so they make a lot of racket, but the boulders beneath are too deep to hit our keels."

"Will our tsar be taking the tiller again?" Thorkell asked, winking to Igor. "You got us through Holmfoss well enough."

Igor puffed his chest at this praise. Most of the crew offered their encouragement. But Groa noticed that two of them were silent: her husband Hrolf and Igor's seatmate Voris.

In the morning nearly a thousand men walked from camp to the edge of the gorge to watch the first of the flotilla's ships run the Gellandi waves. There were cheers for the helmsmen who shot through the middle of the steepest waves. There were hoots for the cowardly boatsmen who tried to skirt to one side or the other. One showoff ran the rapids sideways. He paid for his stunt, however, when his ship rocked so violently that a dozen crewmen wound up swimming. The men were fished out of the calmer waters below, but the crowd on the shore was somber. They walked back to their ships, thinking: Only a fool plays games with the Dnieper rapids.

As it turned out, Igor had no trouble steering their ship through Gellandi. The success inspired the young tsar to tackle the fourth rapids as well, Eyforr, 'Ever Fierce.' In the deepest part of the gorge the river hit a rock wall and turned sharply left. Gunnar explained that the strategy here was to pull in the starboard oars and steer hard to port.

Once again the young tsar handled the rapids smoothly, missing Eyforr's cliff by a full oar's length. Disturbingly, however, the wreckage of older ships littered the banks downstream.

"What's next?" Igor asked.

"Let me take it from here, Tsar," Gunnar replied.

Igor tightened his grip on the tiller. "I asked, what is next?"

"Barafoss," the helmsman said.

The name of *Barren Falls* made Groa shiver. Beside her Hrolf tensed.

Ahead of them Voris called out, "Hey, Igor. Help me row for a while." Igor's companion was strong, but he had been left to pull an oar by himself all day. Groa realized that he was tired as well as frightened.

"Tell me about this barren waterfall," Igor commanded.

The helmsman held up his hands, trying in vain to draw a picture in the air. "It's not a waterfall, Tsar. Barafoss is a maze of giant boulders. The current is swift among them, but there is no straight path through, and there is no time to steer forwards."

"Then how do you maneuver?"

"Backwards, Tsar."

"Backwards?"

"It's the only way. The crew has to row against the current to slow the ship down. Then it is possible to steer around the boulders. But because the ship is sailing backwards the rudder is reversed. Every movement of the tiller has the opposite effect."

Igor thought about this a moment. "Normally if you push the tiller to the left the ship turns to the right."

"That is true, Tsar."

"Then if we're sailing backwards, pushing the tiller to the left will make the ship turn to the left. It's actually simpler than sailing forwards. You just point the tiller the direction you want to go."

The helmsman exchanged a worried glance with Thorkell.

The captain said, "Let Gunnar get us through Barafoss, Tsar."

Igor straightened, obviously displeased by this challenge to his authority. "Gunnar and I will steer together." He turned to the helmsman. "What is our first maneuver?"

Gunnar scanned downriver. "A dozen ships are ahead of us. The current is picking up. We should turn around and row in place to see how the other ships make it through the boulders."

Igor pushed the tiller to the left. "Prepare to come about."

"Port rowers only!" Thorkell called. Groa and Hrolf held up their oar as the ship swung about in a broad arc.

"Everyone, row at half speed," Thorkell commanded.

The current was swift enough that they were still slowly drifting downstream. For the first time on the voyage Groa was facing forward, able to watch the ships ahead of them. It seemed strange to see the rudder at the front of the ship, and stranger still to watch the riverbank slip by in the opposite direction they were rowing.

One of the ships ahead disappeared behind a boulder, starting its run through Barafoss.

Igor asked, "If it's this hard to get ships down the rapids, how do you get them back upstream?"

"We line them," Gunnar replied. Another ship disappeared behind a boulder. The channel was studded with rocks the size of haystacks.

"You line them? Explain."

The helmsman held out his hands again as if to demonstrate,

although this did nothing to help. "We pull the ships with ropes from a tow path on the bank. It's dangerous because that's when Pechenegs tend to attack."

"Pechenegs are horsemen," Igor said.

"Yes, Tsar. They ride up, knock the rope loose, and let the ship drift into the boulders. Then their confederates downstream salvage the flotsam." The helmsman paused. "We could line the *Varangia* downstream through Barafoss. It might be safer."

"No."

Gunnar drew a steadying breath. "Very well, Tsar. Then we must steer near the boulders if we are to make turns in time. The best route is left of the first rock, then right, and finally left again."

"Left of the first rock," Igor repeated. Both his hand and Gunnar's held the tiller as the ship slipped ever closer to the first boulder, where the river heaved up a collar of whitewater.

"Port oars up!" Thorkell called.

The crew hesitated. With the ship sailing backwards, the port rowers were now on the starboard side. Which were the port oars? It soon became obvious that the oars on the right-hand side would have to lift to avoid the rock ahead.

The *Varangia* dipped into the trough of the boulder's wake, tilting the stern in a sliding dance step that threw the two tillermen off balance. A sheet of spray momentarily obscured the river ahead. When the view cleared, Groa gasped to see the next boulder looming directly in their path, as large as a house.

"To the right! The right!" Gunnar cried, wrestling with Igor over the tiller.

"Starboard oars up!" Thorkell called. "All the way up!"

With the rudder turned hard to the right the front of the ship managed to nose around the right-hand side of the boulder, but the flank passed so close that several shields smashed loose. Worse, because Voris was rowing alone, he had been unable to lift his oar upright in time. The blade caught on the passing rock and pivoted in its oarlock, jerking the handle forward out of Voris' hands. With tremendous leverage, the oar handle caught the back of the man in front of Voris, lifted him like a wet rag, and flung him screaming over the gunwale. In an instant, both the oar and the man had disappeared into the raging foam between the ship and the boulder.

Slowing the passage of time is another skill of a sorceress—or perhaps of any quick thinker. In those seconds of terror, Groa saw the spray suddenly turn into lazily drifting drops of water. Voris stood frozen, half pulled from his seat by the vanished oar. At the front of the ship Igor's mouth was stuck wide open in the midst of a howl. But the thoughts Groa read in that moment were racing even faster than the river.

Voris was thinking: Was the crack I heard the sound of a snapping oar or a man's back? This is my fault, for not lifting the oar in time. I should have been tossed overboard, and not the old riverman in front of me.

Groa marveled that Igor, standing by the rudder, did not blame himself. Protected all these years in the Novgorod palace he had never seen a man killed. Now he did not want to believe it had happened, and could not comprehend that he might be at fault. His strongest thought was a mental command: One of you on the crew must jump overboard to bring that man back.

When time sped up again the current swirled the ship sideways beyond the rock. Voris stood up—without his oar, swaying precariously, watching the water. When a dark tunic surfaced briefly amid the foam, Voris took a step and vaulted over the gunwale.

"No!" Groa cried.

"Row to port!" Thorkell called out. "Hard to port!"

In the few seconds that the crew watched Voris swim toward the shape, and while Igor stood frozen at the tiller, the ship drifted sideways toward the third boulder. Voris vanished around the boulder to the left. But the river smashed the boat amidships against the rock, snapping oars and tilting the deck so violently that half a dozen men on the port side were flung loose. Sea chests and bundles of trade goods tumbled overboard. With the starboard side tilted uphill, Groa and Hrolf found themselves sprawled on the ladders in the middle of the deck. As they clung to the rungs, the roar of the river all but overwhelmed the cries of the men and the creak of the bending hull. The current held the ship pinned against the rock, threatening to snap it in half. Hrolf clutched Groa, his powerful arms trembling. She realized that this had been the woodworker's greatest fear—not that the light planks of his ship would crack in the rapids, but that he would lose her—that he would disappoint her. He had always been afraid that she was too beautiful and too talented for him to deserve.

At that moment a snarling dragon rose from the waves. The toothed monster reared out of the whitewater with a roar of Rus voices. The prow of Farlof's ship! The Westland knight stood behind the carved dragon, shouting, "Rope the Tyr-rune!"

Farlof's ship slid past with its crew rowing forward at full speed. Meanwhile the helmsman Grim threw a heavy loop of rope over the arrow-shaped prow of the *Varangia*. A moment later the rope sang taut. The pinned ship groaned like a wounded animal, flexing as its prow dragged across the rock face.

"The patch!" a voice cried. Water poured into the hull through a ragged hole, but the keel held. When the prow had pivoted partway around the boulder the current caught the flank and sent the ship wobbling downstream. The *Varangia* rode so low in the water that she could not be steered. Farlof's ship dragged the wreck to a beach below the rapids. Several dozen ships had already beached on the cobbles where the river idled, swirling detritus among the foam of Barafoss. The crews waiting there began fishing up men, oars, and sea chests from the water.

"Is there a healer among us?" a voice called out.

Dripping wet, Groa stumbled across the cobbles to the limp forms of two men dragged from the waves. She recognized Voris first, although her former student's fish-eyed stare struck her with fear. She rolled him on his back and pumped his chest with her knee. When this had no effect she put her mouth over his and blew in all the breath she had. His leg flopped, but the eyes still stared. She blew in a second breath and was rewarded with a convulsion that vomited a watery stream across her face. Voris gagged and his eyes finally blinked.

Groa paused only to wipe her face with her sleeve before turning to the second man. The dark tunic and the grizzled face told her that this was the oarsman Voris had jumped overboard to save. But she saw at once that the gaze in these frozen eyes was not coming back from Niflheim. The man was bent at an impossible angle, like a snapped fish. When she rolled his shoulders over the hips did not follow. The oar had severed his spine. He had been dead before he hit the water.

* * *

The Rus tallied their losses at a camp that night on the grasslands beyond the beach. Barafoss had destroyed two ships in addition to the

Varangia. Seventeen men had drowned, three of them from Thorkell's crew. Groa had not known them well.

The young tsar's tent had been among the salvaged gear, but the poles were missing. While Hrolf fashioned new ones Igor held a council around a bonfire. Groa could hear the silent reproachful grumblings of the crew, blaming Igor for the wreck of the *Varangia.* Igor obviously could not.

"I want a stouter ship for the remainder of the journey," the tsar announced.

Around the circle of faces, men lowered their eyes. Eventually Farlof spoke up.

"You may use my flagship, Tsar, until we reach Kiev. We have a day and half of sailing left before we meet with Oleg's forces. The last two rapids after Barafoss are easy, and then the river flattens out for good."

"What will your crew do without a ship?" Igor asked.

"I have five other ships, Tsar. There is room."

Igor nodded. "Your generosity will be remembered, Knight."

Farlof nodded in return. Groa could hear him thinking, "Yes, Tsar, you will repay my generosity tenfold before this trip is over."

"I see that my tent is ready," Igor said. "I need to rest. But let us all remember in silence tonight the men who have sailed beyond us to Valhalla."

Hrolf held open the tent's flap, an axe at his side. The young tsar paused to run his hand along the rough, crooked pole at the entrance. "As crudely done as your ships, carpenter."

Hrolf's face flushed as red as bog ore.

Groa pulled her husband aside, afraid that he might say something he would regret. He followed her stiffly, like a wooden puppet. In the shadows she embraced him. "It's not your fault, Hrolf. It's Igor. I've taught him many things but I fear he will always be a spoiled child, unable to admit when he is wrong."

"He wasn't wrong."

"What do you mean? The ships you've built are the best in the world."

"They are too light. If I had seen Barafoss before, I would have made them stronger."

Groa had no ready reply.

Hrolf turned aside, his face a single shadow. "It's also true that the tent poles are crude, hewn with a battle ax."

Groa sensed a mystery here. "Why? What has happened?"

"Our sea chest came open when it hit the rock. The tent and your clothes remained inside, but heavier things fell out. Your jewelry."

"That's no great loss. I hardly brought any. I can make more later." Then she stopped. "Your tools. Your woodworking tools."

He hung his head.

"Oh, my dear husband. Your most precious tools are your hands and your heart. You still have those. That's what matters to me."

She hugged him again—a wooden statue, an endlessly talented but insecure man who had just been abased by a tsar.

She tried to reach into his mind to reassure him, and was frightened to discover that she could not. Whatever secret he had brought with him on this voyage still lay mortared behind a mental wall of stone.

CHAPTER 18
BERLIN, 1961

Herr Lindt held a summit with Lennart and Helen on the *Friedrichstrasse* sidewalk. They could see Mette on the other side of Checkpoint Charlie. She waved and turned to go, as if this were a normal thing to do on a day when Berlin had been divided by a wall.

"I am very much surprised," Herr Lindt said.

"Me too," Lennart put in. "Why would anyone turn back a Dane?"

"That I could understand," Herr Lindt replied. "But Doctor Gustmeyer had her heart set on seeing the museums. I suppose now we'll have to go back to the hostel—although the doors there will be locked until three."

Helen held out the clipboard. "I have my mother's notes. I could read them out loud on the tour. We worked out the route together."

"And we still have two adults for supervision." Lennart looked at his watch. "There's fifteen minutes until our appointment at the Pergamon. We can easily walk there in time."

Helen put her hand on Herr Lindt's arm, despite her aversion to his old gray sweater. "Don't worry about Mom. She's got my uncle to help iron things out."

It was an easy decision for Herr Lindt, a man who was not adept at switching plans.

Lennart led the class group from Checkpoint Charlie to *Unter den Linden*, the old downtown's main street. There they turned right and passed Humboldt University.

"Albert Einstein taught here," Lennart noted. "Until he fled the Nazis in 1936."

The wide streets in front of the university were empty except for a few bicyclists and one clattering streetcar. They crossed a bridge over the Spree River to an island dominated by the huge, classical dome of the Berlin cathedral. The church had been badly damaged in the war, he said, and had not yet been fully repaired because the atheist country had other priorities.

The downstream end of the island was crowded with hulking stone museum buildings. "This is where you take over," Lennart told Helen.

She frowned at her notes. "There's an Old Museum, a New Museum, a Pergamon Museum, and a Bode Museum." She looked up at the buildings, all of them surrounded by sooty stone pillars. The tour had been easier to plan in theory. "We want to do this in order, from the oldest to the newest stuff."

"So, the Old Museum first?" a boy asked. His teasing tone was clearly intended to challenge the authority of a girl his own age.

"No, the Pergamon has the oldest collection." She led the way decisively to the newest of the buildings, a squarish narrow-windowed monstrosity that looked like a Nazi mausoleum. At the far end of an austere stone courtyard, large glass doors opened onto an echoing hall. Helen glanced around for her Aunt Sasha, but none of the few visitors resembled her family's blond Russian spy.

Lennart spoke in German to a white-haired man at a ticket counter. Then he told Helen, "They've been expecting you, but they thought Doctor Gustmeyer would be older."

Helen smiled. "Tell him I use a Swedish skin crème that works like magic. I could sell him a jar."

When Lennart translated this the receptionist raised his eyebrows. But he also beckoned an elderly woman from the coat check counter. In English he said, "Your group has been assigned a docent. This is Frau Osterberg. She speaks many languages."

Although the docent looked extremely old, with sparse white hair framing a face as wrinkled as an old apple, she walked with a spry step. Her conservative white blouse and black skirt would have suited a middle-aged nun. Alarmingly, her eyes were different colors—one sapphire blue and the other emerald green.

The old woman sized up Helen and announced in accented Swedish, "You are not Fru Mette Gustmeyer." Her voice was an ancient croak as she added, "But you might be her daughter."

Helen struggled for words. Of course her mother was famous among museum people. It shouldn't be surprising that a docent would know Mette Gustmeyer. But this woman's probing manner was unsettling.

Helen managed to say, "I am in fact her daughter. I have my mother's notes for the tour. We did not ask to be accompanied by a docent."

"It is not optional, Fröken Gustmeyer. Docents are a security measure for groups such as yours. Perhaps I can add a few insights to your visit."

"Excellent," Herr Lindt said. "We could use another pair of eyes to keep the class in line."

Helen wondered if Herr Lindt had also noticed the docent's eyes. The old woman seemed to be scanning them all with X-ray vision. The sociology teacher babbled on, "How did you learn to speak Swedish so well?"

"I grew up in Norway, back when—" The old woman's voice trailed off and her gaze grew distant.

"When Norway was under the Swedish king? That's been almost sixty years." Herr Lindt shook his head. "Well, what's first on our tour?"

"Babylon," Helen said. "I believe the Middle Eastern collection is in the South Wing to the left."

"Yes," the old docent said, pointing a crooked finger in the opposite direction. "It is in the North Wing to the right."

Without missing a beat Helen led the group to the right. But her face was flushed as she read her mother's notes out loud. "After the unification of Germany under Kaiser Wilhelm in 1871, the country's increased prosperity allowed an entire generation of German scholars to set out on archeological expeditions. Some of these adventurers were little more than treasure hunters, like Heinrich Schliemann, who discovered Troy. Their background was Christian and Classical, so they focused on sites from the Bible, the Homeric poems, and the Roman world."

The old docent interrupted, "But some German diggers did go to Scandinavia." Then she slapped a student's hand away from an exhibit of cuneiform tablets. "Don't touch the glass cases. Smudges!"

Helen waved the group onward through a fifty-foot-tall arched portal of blue ceramic tile. Full-size images of lions, unicorns, and gryphons marched stiffly on either hand. Aunt Sasha wasn't in this hall either.

Helen read from her notes, "This is the Ishtar Gate and the processional way of Babylon. Both are described in the Old Testament. Beyond you can see the throne room of the Babylonian king Nebuchadnezzar II. German archeologists crated all of this up and brought it to Berlin, but there was no room to display it. The Old Museum from 1830 was too small and the Bode Museum from 1904 was already full. So they started building the Pergamon Museum in 1910."

Dwarfed by the monumental ancient walls, the students looked up in wonder at the blue-tiled patterns and the crenelated bulwarks atop the gate. Even Helen had trouble imagining how such a massive structure could be transported to Germany and reconstructed indoors. But then she remembered the *Vasa*—an even larger marvel raised from the depths of Stockholm's harbor.

"This is German imperialism at its worst," Lennart said.

When several students looked at him Lennart raised his voice to a lecturing tone. "The German Reich got a later start than England or Spain in the business of collecting colonies, so they set about plundering impoverished countries in a different way. The Germans bought or simply stole things like this. With the Ottoman Empire crumbling, the Middle East was an easy target. The archeologists said they were preserving the world's treasures for science. If that were true, why don't they return them now?"

The old docent lifted her bony chin. "Why don't the Soviets return what they looted? In 1945 they took everything from this museum that wasn't nailed down. Half of it is still in Russia."

Helen interceded. "We don't have much time. Which way is the Pergamon altar?" Her mother hadn't said when Sasha would be at the altar to trade newspapers. Perhaps she was already there. Certainly she wouldn't be expecting Helen instead of her mother.

"The Antiquities Collection is in the other wing. This way." Frau Osterberg crooked her finger back through the Ishtar Gate.

The route to the altar traversed room after room of Greek vases, marble statues, and stone sarcophagi, all of which had accompanying notes from Helen's mother that she felt obliged to read.

"Pergamon is in present-day Turkey," Helen read, "But after Alexander the Great took Asia Minor from the Persians in the fourth century BC the entire coast was settled by Greeks. Two hundred years later, when Greece became a Roman colony, the Romans began re-building Pergamon in their own style. They constructed a Great Altar that became famous throughout the ancient world. By the time Rome's power weakened and this area became part of the Byzantine Empire, Pergamon was in decline. German archeologists who brought frag-ments of a marble frieze to Berlin in 1871 eventually realized that they had actually discovered fragments of the Great Altar."

"The Great Altar in the next room–" Helen began, but immediately broke off. What struck her was not merely the sight of the Pergamon altar—a colonnaded marble temple the size of a national bank—but also the woman sitting on its steps. Half a dozen tourists had stopped to

rest on the broad white staircase leading up between the temple's two wings. Most were looking at maps or their cameras. One, however, peered over the creased V of an upheld newspaper.

Sasha Gustmeyer wore a brown skirt suit that would have been unremarkable except for its fur collar—in August, no less! She had tied up her long blond hair into a frowsy bun. For an instant the look in her dark eyes betrayed recognition. And then, just as suddenly, the look went blank. Helen wondered, what sort of spy would sit in the middle of a museum reading a newspaper? No genuine tourist did that.

"Wow," a girl said. Other voices asked, "Is this the altar?" and "Did they kill people on it?"

Sasha vanished behind the screen of her newspaper. Helen decided it would look less suspicious if she returned to reading her notes aloud. "The Pergamon Altar dates to the second century AD. Some say it was dedicated to Zeus and Athena, but more likely it was a pantheon, serving all the gods."

"How refreshing," Herr Lindt commented. "I wish churches were as open-minded today."

"Not all gods were welcome here," the old docent said darkly. "Yahweh, the Jewish god, allowed no rivals. Egyptian gods and Baal had cult followings among the Romans, but they were exiled to separate, secret temples."

Sasha stood up and folded her paper, her face turned away.

Helen kept reading aloud. "Extending around the base of the temple is a 113-meter-long frieze with oversized sculptures depicting Gigantomachy, the battle between giants and gods when the world was young." She looked up from a sketch in her notes and pointed to a group of large figures struggling in togas. "I think this is Zeus, the thunder-god, with his curly beard. The next would be Hera, and this with the helmet must be Ares, god of war."

"Or are they the Norse gods in disguise?" Frau Osterberg asked. "You from Sweden ought to see the similarity. These figures might just as easily be Thor, the thunder-god, with Freya and Tyr, god of war."

Meanwhile Sasha had walked down the steps and across the room. Before leaving she laid her newspaper on the rim of a wastebasket, as if to offer some future visitor the courtesy of a free read.

Herr Lindt chuckled, "I really don't think the Vikings had much contact with Turkey."

How could Helen get the newspaper unobtrusively? She needed something to throw away. With a flash of inspiration she reached into her purse.

"As for the battle between gods and giants depicted on the altar," the old docent continued, "Is it a struggle at the beginning of time or is it Ragnarök, at the end?"

Helen unwrapped a stick of chewing gum, wadded the wrapper in her hand, and began to chew.

The docent reared back her head, her eyes on fire. "We do not chew gum in a museum!"

"Sorry." Helen headed toward the wastebasket. Meanwhile, half a dozen of the boys in the class had grown bored of all the talk and were running up the stairs.

With a strange growl the old docent grabbed two of the boys by their collars, immobilizing them with improbable strength. "And we do not run!"

Aided by this distraction, Helen spit her chewing gum into the wrapper, dropped it in the trash, and switched newspapers. Sasha's copy was the exact same edition, folded just the same way. The transfer had gone perfectly. Helen felt like a suave courier on a secret mission.

Frau Osterberg released the two boys, but remained in the center of the stairs with her arms crossed, as if she owned the place.

The boys whined a complaint to Herr Lindt. He avoided conflict when he could, so he merely looked at his watch. "Isn't it about time for coffee?"

"There's a café at the Bode Museum next door," Helen said. She waved a farewell to the old docent. "Have to run. We can find our own way out."

"I'm not sure you can." The old woman descended the stairs, her unsettling gaze fixed on Helen.

No one spoke as the group made its way back through the rooms of the Antiquities Collection. But as the docent opened the museum's glass door for Helen she announced, "The world is a more dangerous place than you know, Fröken Gustmeyer."

* * *

Coffee helped lift the somber mood of the old woman's words. That afternoon the class listened as Helen read her mother's notes about the Bode Museum's Byzantine collection. Swedish Vikings, she told them, had indeed traveled to the Byzantine capital of Constantinople. An elite group of Viking warriors, the Varangian Guard, had served as the emperor's bodyguard. They had fought in battles from Sicily to the Holy Land. Ottoman Turks had later conquered Constantinople. Unable or unwilling the pronounce the capital's name, they had shortened Constantinople to Istanbul.

Helen was so pleased with the successes of the day that she boldly tucked Sasha's newspaper under her arm in plain sight as they waited to show their passports to the *Vopos*. She paid little attention to the German women crying behind the barbed wire of Checkpoint Charlie.

Men were shouting that they had been cut off from their families, that they couldn't get to their workplaces, that they were on the wrong side of the border. Meanwhile a construction crew was mortaring concrete blocks across the sidewalk.

"I saw what you did," Lennart said quietly.

"What?" Helen asked.

"You know, trading newspapers."

She stared at him, her mouth suddenly dry. "What do you mean?"

"Oh, come on. What's hidden in the newspaper? Money? A letter?"

An East German policeman took Helen's passport, flipped through it, and handed it back. She and Lennart began walking across the asphalt of the no-man's-land between gates. The newspaper under her arm suddenly felt like a red-hot iron.

"I don't know," she whispered back.

"Don't you want to find out?" he asked.

"No."

But she was in fact curious.

Still, she wouldn't have opened the newspaper if her mother had been waiting for them at the US Army booth on *Friedrichstrasse*. Even at the youth hostel the receptionist handed her a note from her mother saying that everything was fine, that she was with Lars at the Foreign Affairs office, and that they would be back to retrieve any news Helen might have that evening.

"Want to go for a beer?" Lennart asked over her shoulder.

She bit her lip, weighing her allegiances. Lenny was her boyfriend, her secret conspirator. But Sasha Gustmeyer was family, and if her aunt's cover as a CIA agent were revealed, she might be in danger. The newspaper under her arm glowed hotter and hotter. What if it really were full of money? Or if it contained the formula for a new nuclear bomb? As long as she kept Sasha out of it, didn't she deserve to take a look?

"You know a good place?" she asked.

Lenny grinned. "Yeah. But I wouldn't take anyone else from the class there."

The place he took her to was a smoky jazz bar on an alley off the *Kurfürstendamm*. The inside was painted entirely black, with colored bulbs spaced randomly along the walls. They made their way to an empty booth with a bare light bulb sticking out of the middle of the tabletop. A Black saxophonist—one of the first truly dark-skinned men Helen had ever seen up close—was wailing a mournful version of "Old Man River." A pianist fingered chords with his left hand while smoking an unfiltered Gauloise with his right. A waitress with a white apron and a leather money belt took Lenny's order in such quick, dialectal German that Helen had no idea what they were getting.

"How did you know?" Helen asked.

"About the newspaper?" Lenny smiled. "Nobody reads a paper in a museum. And it's not like you to chew gum while leading a tour. I figured it had to be a ploy."

"Aren't you going to ask who she was?"

"Your contact? No, you'd tell me if you thought I should know."

This was the right answer. It lit a warm spark in Helen's chest.

The waitress chipped a couple of cardboard coasters on the table and set down two beers—a big mug for Lenny and a foot-tall goblet for Helen.

"It looks like an overgrown champagne flute," Helen laughed.

"It's Pilsner Urquell."

"Why does it have a paper doily on the base?"

Lenny shrugged. "That's how you serve a *pils*. If they've poured it right the head of foam should last five full minutes."

"Not if we drink it first." She tapped her glass to his "*Skål*."

"*Prosit*."

The foreign beer and the mellow jazz began to melt the tension that had kept her taut all day. She flopped the paper on the table. "Shall we see what's in the news?"

"If you want."

Helen smoothed out the newspaper and began turning pages. The bulb on the tabletop flashed each sheet of newsprint white, simultaneously casting their faces as shadows.

There was no money, and no letter. Helen turned the last page with disappointment. "Nothing."

"Go back to the obituaries."

She turned to a page of black boxes, each of them the size of a business card, with white crosses and somber names.

"That one there." Lenny pointed to a shiny obituary near the fold.

Helen used her fingernail to peel loose a small sheet of black plastic that had been taped to the page. "What is it?"

"Microfilm. Hold it up to the light."

She did. "I still don't see anything."

"That's because the images are so small. A piece of film this size could contain an entire book." Lenny reached into his pocket and took out a fat red Swiss Army knife. He unfolded from its many blades a small but very powerful magnifying glass. "Here, try this."

Helen held the film up to the light bulb and looked at it through the lens. The entire sheet was covered with tiny pictures and text. Equally amazing was Lenny's magnifying glass. She turned the knife over, examining it suspiciously. "They don't make real Swiss Army knives like this."

"Sure they do."

"With a jeweler's loupe?"

"You can get whatever you want in Switzerland." He pointed to the film. "What do you see?"

She looked again. "Lots of text, mostly in Russian and too small to read. Then there's a whole series of photographs."

"Of what?"

"Time machines! Rocket ships!"

"What?" He leaned back, bewildered.

"No, duh, I'm kidding. These are mostly pictures of faces. First there's a castle wall. The turret has a big hammer-and-sickle flag so it's probably somewhere in Russia. Then there's a doorway with a grille and a big lock, like a dungeon. After that, just faces."

"Do you think they're political prisoners?"

"That's what you'd expect in a Russian dungeon, I guess." She looked closer. "The first two guys could be wardens—lots of muscles. Next there's an old bald man with glasses."

"Could be a political prisoner."

"Could be. Except, wait. No way!"

"What is it?"

Helen laughed out loud. "Urmas!"

"What?"

"The next person looks exactly like Urmas."

"From Culture Club? Are you sure?"

She looked again. "I swear it's her. What's Urmas doing in a Russian jail?"

Lenny wasn't laughing. "She went home to Estonia for the summer. She said she was helping with an excavation."

"In a jail?" Helen thought this was hilarious. Why was Lenny acting so grim?

"Anyone else you recognize?"

Still smiling, Helen scanned the column of photos—a motley collection of strangers, like so many clowns. But her smile died when she saw the last face.

"Impossible!"

"What? Who is it?" Lenny asked.

The withered face had a haunted, hunted look. But there could be no mistaking the eyes.

"It's the docent from the Pergamon Museum." Helen shivered, as if an arctic wind had blown the smoke out of the cave-like bar.

Echoing in her head was the old woman's warning: "The world is a more dangerous place than you know, Fröken Gustmeyer."

CHAPTER 19
KIEV, 907

In the Russiyan capital of Kiev, where the Dnieper River meanders among a dozen islands before sallying out across the prairies, the regent Oleg had mustered an additional 122 ships, swelling the Viking armada to 15,000 men.

Unlike Smolensk, Kiev absorbed this army with ease. Immense granaries of tightly notched logs had been collecting wheat, barley, and rye from the outlying farms for two years in anticipation of Oleg's expedition. Barrels of ale and stockyards of cattle stood at the ready. Although it was true that the palisaded fortress grounds on the city's western hill only had room for the retinues of the realm's fourteen Varangian Knights, and it was also true that the streets of the lower town, home to the garrison's wives, had been declared off limits to soldiers, vast tent cities had sprung up in the fields on all sides. From the fortress gate where Groa paused it looked as if the plowed furrows of the surrounding farms had sprouted endless rows of square canvas flowers.

Groa and the other survivors of Thorkell's crew had been permitted inside the stockade as part of Tsar Igor's entourage. She turned to watch the young tsar as the fortress gates creaked slowly outward on massive iron hinges. Igor's friend Voris and the helmsman Gunnar stood on either hand, proudly carrying spears with the tsar's double-headed eagle banner. Behind them the rest of the crew formed a wedge-shaped phalanx of battle axes and swords. Groa and Hrolf followed, carrying two more banners on slightly crooked tent poles.

Igor had obviously intended to make an impressive entrance on the occasion of his first visit to the capital. But just as obviously he was unprepared for the splendor of Oleg's stronghold. Inside the gate hundreds of warriors in identical helmets and chain mail stood at attention alongside a planked street that led up to a central hall. Behind them rose the pillared breezeways of barrack halls topped with yellow-and-white-striped flags. Each of the wooden pillars had been carved and painted, some with bright geometric patterns and others with writhing dragons or red-eyed wolf heads. The central hall itself looked large enough to house several Holmgard palaces. A crown of arrow-shaped Tyr runes topped its gables.

"Hail Tsar!" the soldiers chanted as Igor's ragtag procession made its way up the street. Groa could almost feel the heat of the young tsar's emotions—jealousy, anger, anything but the shame she wished he could know. For a dozen years he had played with his friends in Novgorod, leaving his uncle Oleg the task of ruling Russiya from Kiev. And now—only now—the young tsar was jealous?

When they entered the central hall and Oleg stood up from the regent's high seat, Igor practically exploded, "You have lied to me, Uncle!"

"A strange greeting, Nephew. I think I have served you without deceit." Age had lessened the old Viking's giant stature and grayed the fiery red of his beard, but his eyes were as steely as ever. He held out a hand to the throne. "Here, Tsar, take your proper place and tell me if you have a complaint."

Igor settled into the carved chair, clenching his fingers on the beast-heads of the arms. "You told me that Kiev was a military outpost with simple barracks."

"It was, a dozen years ago. It's still more of a fortress town than your Novgorod."

"My Novgorod," Igor scoffed. "You tried to tempt me once with the title, 'Sultan of Novgorod.' I should have been here all along, ruling the realm. I intend to end your regency and take command."

"As you should, Nephew, once we've completed the expedition to Miklagard."

Igor's fingers tightened on the carved beasts. "I suspect this is another lie, Uncle. At first I believed that we were setting out on a trading expedition. But you do not need 15,000 armed men to sell a few hundred ladders."

For a moment the hall was silent. Then Oleg's whiskers stretched into a grin. Thorkell dared to chuckle. Soon all the men were laughing. Hrolf looked about with sudden insight and began laughing too. He really had thought they were ladder merchants.

Only Igor remained stern. When the laughter died he demanded, "Well, Uncle? Why would you have us attack the Byzantine Empire?"

"Attack is such a harsh word," Oleg replied. "Once we lean our ladders against the walls of Miklagard, we'll sell them for a good profit. The Byzantines have treated our traders unfairly for years. I think it's time we struck a better bargain."

"But Constantinople is the most powerful city on Earth. Even the warships of the Arab Caliphate cannot threaten it. What makes you think the Rus can?"

"But that's just it," Oleg said, spreading his hands. "Our spies tell us that the Abbasid Caliphate is in the midst of a succession struggle—virtually a civil war. Sensing an opportunity, the Byzantine emperor has sent his forces south to regain lost land. Only a minimal garrison remains to defend the capital. They are unaware that the traders of the Russiyan rivers are able to gather so many ships."

"Our ships are light and weak," Igor said, casting a dark look at Hrolf. "I have seen them wreck in the rapids of the Dnieper."

Oleg held up a palm in objection. "Their weakness may be their strength. I have a plan. There is risk, Nephew. But this is your chance to win genuine wealth and saga fame. Do you want to sit in that chair and send your army home empty handed? Or would you sail with me to Miklagard and earn the right to be called a tsar?"

Igor's fingers no longer clenched the throne. Instead they traced the patterns on the dragon heads as he thought. Groa listened in, and was pleased to hear that the angry boy had given way to a calculating adult. If the expedition to Miklagard failed, the blame would be entirely Oleg's. If they succeeded, the rewards would be Igor's. Aloud he asked, "What exactly is your plan?"

Oleg held a finger to his chin. "Some things are best kept quiet. We are not the only ones with spies."

The adult in Igor quickly gave way to an exasperated boy once again. "But will your plan work?"

Oleg drew his sword. He held the blade up before them. The damascened steel flashed, revealing its runic letters. "My sword is its own prophecy. Fenris has never failed to win a battle."

"No!" Hrolf jumped up, daring to speak out. "That sword is trouble. If you want to know the future you'll have to ask a genuine sorceress, like the one at my side."

All eyes turned to Groa. She reached into her tunic and withdrew a small dagger etched with a pattern of biting beasts. "I have seen the past, when tyrants fell." The little blade balanced like a dancer in her hand, a reminder of the time she had thrown it to save Oleg's life. "There was a promise made. In the future, I see a promise kept."

Oleg lowered his sword. His voice was weary. "Let me win this one last campaign."

In reply Groa silently tilted the dagger back and forth.

* * *

With 314 ships, the Varangian fleet took a full week to sail downriver to the Black Sea. Even then Oleg insisted that the armada spend another week on a series of mysterious maneuvers that left Igor grumbling.

The young tsar was already miffed because Oleg had made him return Farlof's sturdy flagship and had instead issued him a standard, lightweight Ship in the Woods. "You will thank me later, Nephew," the regent had said. Worse, although Igor was eager to see the notorious river mouth fortress that the Varangians had twice reconquered from the Bulgars and the Byzantines, Oleg had commanded that the fleet drift by silently on a moonless night. Forbidden to speak, using neither sails nor oars, Thorkell's crew watched moodily as the lazy current carried them past the unseen stockade to the Black Sea. Igor growled like a caged animal. Gunnar touched his arm and silenced him with a single word: "Spies."

Instead of turning right toward Constantinople, Oleg had unexpectedly turned the fleet left across the Black Sea to the east. At an uninhabited bay he announced that they would camp on a barren sandy island to practice.

"Practice what?" Igor demanded that evening. "There are no city walls here. There's nothing tall enough to use a ladder on."

"The ladders will take care of themselves," Oleg replied with a sly smile. "What our troops need to practice is music and art."

At that point Oleg revealed that his flagship had in fact brought a cargo of lur-horns and parchment-like leaves. Groa recognized the sheets as paper, the same material that the disgraced Chinese mentor Yuantzu had attempted to manufacture in Novgorod.

Igor tried one of the long, coiled trumpets, blowing out a squawk. "Are we to serenade Constantinople?"

Oleg winced. "Your music might make them surrender. But no—the horns are for signaling. We need a way to spread commands quickly among the fleet, even when our ships are strung out for miles. I want each crew to designate a hornsman. They will meet here tomorrow to memorize a dozen different signals. Later we'll practice the signals while sailing in the bay."

Igor nodded, reluctantly accepting the practicality of this plan. "And what of the leaves? Do you propose to use them for art as well?"

"Yes. An art that requires sorcery." Oleg turned to Groa. "You know the skill of carving runes. I've seen you do it on the Varangian medallions and on my ring. Can you also write runes on paper, like the Greeks? I'm told they use the feathers of birds."

"Yes, I think so." Groa and her Slavic herbalist Nadya has once cut quills to paint delicate patterns on her door using blood for red ink and soot for black.

"Good. I want you to write down the name of every knight, jarl, captain, and helmsman in the fleet."

"But that would be more than six hundred names!"

"Organize the list by ship and district of origin."

Groa shook her head. "A task like that will take time, Regent."

"You have five days. I'll assign people to help. Train them well enough that they can also make 314 copies of this." Oleg handed her a piece of paper marked with a crooked gray triangle. It looked like a very bad drawing of a dog's head, with a pin sticking out of the nose.

"What is it?" Groa asked.

"A map of Miklagard. The black spots are the thirty gate-towers of the wall. The harbor of the Golden Horn is to the north and the Sea of Marmara to the south. They've dug a moat through the hills to the west, so the walls are surrounded by water on all sides."

"What's this straight line?" She pointed to the pin on the dog's nose.

"A chain sealing off the harbor. No Arab ship can cross it."

"But perhaps ours can?" Igor suggested. "Our ships are so light."

Oleg shook his head. "Even our keels are too deep to pass without sorcery." Then a slow grin stretched his reddish whiskers. "This is why we need a week beyond the reach of spies. To practice magic."

* * *

Emperor Leo the Wise loved taking his family to the Hippodrome when the army and the fleet were out of town. Soldiers wanted to watch battles, the gorier the better. You do not take a delicate young wife and a three-year-old son to see slaves slaughter animals—or each other—with hideous weapons. The naval shows were just as bad, when they flooded the Hippodrome's forecourt, floated ships around, and turned the water red with blood. Instead, with the most bloodthirsty portion of the audience fighting actual battles in Asia Minor, the Hippodrome could be used for its true and original purpose: horse racing. Leo himself was fond of quadrigas, the four-horse chariots that demanded real skill to drive. Leo had ordered his tribunal loge moved to the track's far curve, rather than the finish line, so he could watch the charioteers tilt their wagons precariously as they jockeyed for the lead. His wife Zoe waved a silk scarf to encourage her favorites.

Little Constantine didn't care much about the horses, but he was so delighted by the marble racing machine in the lobby that Leo had the contraption moved to their Imperial loge. A clever craftsman had drilled countless holes into a block of sandstone. For a copper coin he would let you drop four glass marbles into the top—three of them black and one white. The marbles then raced frantically through inner passageways, occasionally appearing at windows or colliding. If the white marble dropped out the bottom first the man would pay you two copper coins. But no matter how you put the marbles in at the top the black ones generally seemed to finish first. The three-year-old co-emperor couldn't get enough of it. By day's end the vendor had harvested a fat bag of copper coins. Leo was just happy to watch his young son attempting to puzzle out the vendor's trick.

After the last race, when a particularly handsome charioteer drove a victory lap with a laurel wreath and Zoe threw him her silk scarf, Leo walked his family back to the Imperial palace as relaxed as if he were returning from an olive oil massage at the baths. As the sun set on a glorious midsummer evening he and Zoe sat amidst the potted date palms of their rooftop garden, drinking chalices of diluted Persian syrah wine. The empress tasted samples from a platter of fruits and cheeses. Leo cracked pistachios as he looked out over the city.

Constantinople had been built on seven hills—not to replicate the squalid decay of old Rome, but rather to mirror the shining City in the Sky. Would even Paradise itself, he wondered, be crowned with a golden dome to match Hagia Sophia, the shrine of Sacred Wisdom? And would Saint Peter's pearly gates be as secure against devils as Constantinople, walled with towers, moated with oceans, and surrounded by a vast, impregnable empire?

"Come, Leo," Zoe said quietly. "You worry too much. Come to bed."

* * *

That night the 15,000 Vikings slept fitfully on the decks of their ships, adrift in the Black Sea, waiting for the lur-horn signal that would send them sailing to glory or death.

"Wait," Oleg told his helmsman. Milovic had lifted the coiled trumpet when he saw the tip of a crescent moon spear up from the dark waters to the east. "Let it rise all the way. Even you cannot sail entirely blind."

Already the fleet had sailed by dead reckoning for three days. Rather than skirt the shore of the Black Sea—the usual, curving route to Constantinople—they had cut directly across the middle of the inland ocean, where no one would see their sails. When Milovic had spotted the lighthouse at the mouth of the Bosporus they had quickly lowered their sails and rowed back out of sight to await the night.

"Now," Oleg said.

Milovic's trumpet sounded a long, owl-like call followed by two higher tones. An unseen ship nearby soon answered: *Ooooo-too-too*. Then another, and then dozens, until the night air seemed full of owls.

On Thorkell's ship the crew cursed as they rolled up their blankets and prepared to hoist the mast. In the dark, with a ladder down the middle of the deck, the men stumbled before securing the mast's stays and raising the sail. By then the long, low moan of Milovic's lur-horn was calling the helmsmen to follow him west, leaving the reflection of the sickle moon a wavy blur in their wake.

Tsar Igor stood with Thorkell in the prow, peering anxiously ahead as the dark shoulders of Asia and Europe emerged, dim phantoms above the predawn fog. The breeze from the Black Sea was just strong enough to fill the sail, creaking the mast and splashing a curl of white before the Tyr-rune prow.

For an hour no one spoke, even when a dozen dolphins arced from the water alongside the ship, eyeing them curiously. Groa wondered if these strange southern fish were a hopeful sign or an omen of doom. In northern waters the seals that watched ships were the spirits of men lost at sea, warning that others may also be steering toward the same fate.

At the tiller, Gunnar squinted through the fog, trying to discern the different sails and keep their ship in formation. Crewmen put on their chain mail tunics, counted their arrows, or adjusted their steel helmets. Even Groa and Hrolf had been assigned armor. Hrolf's helmet fit so tightly that it pinched his ears flat. Groa's metal cap was the smallest available but still wobbled when she turned her head. The protruding rectangular nose piece tilted in front of one eye and then the other, as if trying to disguise the fact that one was green and the other blue.

By the time Thorkell finally raised his hand a dirty, yellowish glow from the east had washed out the stars. He turned to the crew to make sure he had their attention, and then lowered his arm like a falling tree. Without a word the crew set to work lowering the yellow-and-white-striped sail. In the fog to starboard, dozens of other ships were lowering sails and masts. To their left, however, an even larger contingent of the Vikings' ships sailed on as before.

The wisps of fog were thinner to port, over the Sea of Marmara. Groa could see ragged scraps of blue sky above the brightly colored sails—and for a moment she glimpsed the jumbled white buildings and golden domes of Miklagard itself. A brilliant flash of light from the summit of that city in the sky made the entire crew stop short.

"Dawn," Gunnar whispered, breaking the silence.

"In the west?" Igor asked, trembling at the thought of sorcery so powerful that Thor's chariot might be made to ride backwards across the heavens.

The helmsman nodded. "Reflected in the glass windows of Saint Sophia."

Thorkell angrily sliced his hand across his throat to signal silence. Then he rolled his fists in circles. Silently the crew set their oars in the locks. Soon they were rowing into the denser fog, accompanied by the ghost-like shapes of a hundred other mastless ships. Without their sails it was hard to tell one dragon from another. The mist also made it difficult to tell where they were, although Groa had copied enough maps of Miklagard to suspect they were very near the needle at the tip of the dog-shaped peninsula's nose.

Suddenly a clanking thump resounded through the ship, and Thorkell let out a curse.

"The chain!" Igor exclaimed.

Thorkell reversed his rolling fists. "Row backwards."

Groa leaned over the gunwale to look. Water was sloshing on rusty links as thick as a man's arm. Obviously it was true that even the light ships of the Rus could not breach this chain. Already the iron barrier had stopped a dozen ships nearby.

Soon, however, the ships began maneuvering into columns of five, and the crews began lashing the ships together stem to stern. At the tiller Gunnar caught a rope and bound their ship's tail to a Tyr-rune in the mist. Gradually, giant dragons began to assemble—great sea-snakes five ships in length. Each of these multi-bodied beasts would be powered by two hundred and fifty oarsmen. Would those wings be enough to fly them across the chain to the harbor of the Golden Horn?

When all twenty of these elongated dragons were in position facing the chain, a distant roar rose up from across the city. A mile away, on the sunny southern side of Constantinople, the larger portion of the Varangian fleet was awakening the city with the blood-curdling battle cry of the Vikings.

CHAPTER 20
NOVGOROD, 1962

The battle cry of the Vikings echoed across the city in the summer twilight. Groa shivered. She had forgotten much over the years but she would never forget that chilling roar. When the cry subsided, a sound she did not recognize started up. Was it music? A bass was thumping, electric guitars squealed, and an amplified voice wailed about a "Baby, baby."

She walked back partway across the Volkhov River footbridge and squinted. The pseudo-warriors at Novgorod's annual Viking Fest had put down their shields and were gyrating in a field alongside girls with flowers in their hair. Although they didn't actually touch, they appeared to believe that they were dancing together.

Professor Talin might be wrong about many things, but Groa decided he was right about the annual Viking reenactment festival. It was a silly hoax.

Last year she had joined the professor's "Varangian Order" as an infiltrator. Her uncanny ability to guess people's thoughts had revealed that she wasn't the only spy stalking that meeting in Novgorod's kremlin. She had been given an assignment and a name—Agent Veliky, which appropriately meant "ancient," just like Veliky Novgorod. She had actually enjoyed her assignment to a museum in East Berlin. She loved history and was happy enough to keep an eye on the doings of the Gustmeyer family. She went back a long ways with Helen's grandmother Kirstin.

And this was the problem with infiltrating an enemy camp. The longer you lived among them, the more sympathetic you became. The professor was right about the importance of the female line, although Groa sensed that his motives were more tangled than he let on.

Inside the old town wall, as she shuffled in her old black walking shoes past the Millennium of Russia sculpture, streetlights flickered on. So many of the glass globes were broken that the resulting shadows seemed even darker. Was one of those murky corners concealing last year's other spy, the blond businesswoman who liked furs? Or did she mistakenly imagine there was more pressing business in the world by now?

At the dungeon door Groa showed her medallion through the grille and gave the password, "Hail Rus." The muscular man who let her in was still wearing a sooty leather apron from his blacksmithing booth at the festival. Behind him candles in iron chandeliers lit the brick vaults of a dank chamber. Already thirty men and half a dozen women were sitting on benches around four wooden tables that had been pushed together in the middle.

"Veliky," the professor said, ticking the name off a list. Candlelight reflected orange on his shiny bald head. As always, he wore a bow tie. "We have already begun."

When the old professor turned, the light made the scaly skin on the damaged left side of his face glow red. "Swarovsky, please continue."

Groa remembered the KGB recruiter, an otherwise attractive young man who looked like an overbuilt gymnast poorly stuffed into the brown suit coat of an ordinary-sized human.

"I'm afraid our Order's plans need to shift away from Berlin." Swarovsky clenched his hands as if he were squeezing lemons. "Neither superpower would gain by starting a nuclear exchange in Germany. I believe our new focus should be Cuba."

"Why Cuba?" The man who asked spoke Russian with an American accent. "Kennedy's invasion at the Bay of Pigs failed. It was an embarrassment he is unlikely to risk again."

Swarovsky shook his head. "Our Swedish contact says that the American military has already prepared a secret invasion plan, Operation Mongoose, that would build on February's economic embargo."

Groa found herself stuck on the words, "Our Swedish contact." Apparently there really was a Swedish spy, and it was not someone in the room. Did the authorities in Sweden know they had a traitor in their midst? Was it a Gustmeyer?

"According to our source," Swarovsky continued, "CIA operatives will slip into Cuba this summer to sabotage the government and organize opposition. Open revolt would commence in October."

"Is this information reliable?" the American asked.

At the opposite side of the table a round-faced Russian man with a military buzz cut said, "Khrushchev believes it. He thinks the only way to stop the invasion is to build nuclear missile bases in Cuba. This would level the playing field."

"Level the playing field?" the American scoffed. "What about the missile gap?"

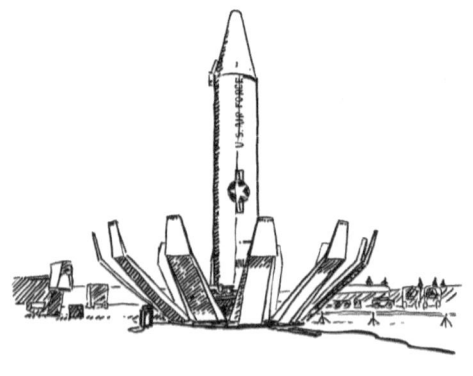

The Russian shook his head. "There is a gap, but it's not the way you suppose. Kennedy won his election by scaring Americans, saying that they were behind in the arms race. He believed Khrushchev's boasts that we are turning out missiles like sausages. In truth, we are at least a year behind. You Americans have nuclear missiles based in Turkey, right on the Soviet border. They can strike Moscow. All we could do in return is threaten Alaska. But a base in Cuba—that could target any city in America."

"Kennedy would never allow a Soviet base so close."

"Are you sure?" the Russian countered. "Kennedy is young, a weak leader."

All around the dungeon table people began arguing. Only Groa sat silent, waiting for the professor to speak his mind. And sure enough, he rapped the table loudly for attention.

"Knight Swarovsky is right. Cuba suits our purpose better than Berlin. This is our chance to help Fenris clear the way for a new world order—the Varangian Order. Fortunately, the raising of the U271 has given us the resources we need to proceed."

"What resources?" Groa asked, her voice little more than a croak in the dark.

The professor turned to a middle-aged man with a protruding clean-shaven jaw and a naval officer's hat. "Captain Savitsky? Some of our knights are new to the Order. Fill them in."

"Well," the captain said, tipping back his cap. "Two years ago I was first mate on a nuclear submarine undergoing sea trials in the Baltic. I helped persuade the Admiralty that it would be good for public relations if we tried Professor Talin's experiment. His idea was to use our sonar to scan the Baltic seafloor for World War II wreckage—specifically, the U271. That's the high-tech Nazi submarine that Heinrich Müller, head of the Gestapo, used for his escape during the final days of the war. From records in the military archives, Talin believed the German U-boat had been targeted by a Soviet bomber with depth charges off the coast of Hiiumaa Island, presumably en route to Helsinki. As usual Talin was right. But because the sub's hull had been damaged it took divers more than a year to seal it up and refloat it. A few months ago we towed it to a dock in Estonia."

The professor took over the narrative. "Now the East Germans want the ship to serve as a floating war cemetery in Rostock. The Russians want it as a victory monument in Leningrad. The Estonians want to keep it as a tourist attraction in Tallinn. While they were arguing I assembled an archeological team of loyal knights to inventory the ship's contents. Urmas?"

The professor tipped his head toward a young woman sitting between him and Swarovsky. Groa remembered her from last year's meeting—a plain, awkward girl with a page boy haircut that apparently had been cut at a slant on purpose. Last year Urmas had spent the entire meeting silently admiring the men beside her, the learned old professor and the handsome young KGB agent. This time Groa sensed a new confidence, as if the woman had grown tired of subservience.

"I am Urmas Byelekov," she announced, as if to make sure that everyone remembered the name. "Because Professor Talin has been assuming an increasingly political role within the Order, I have taken responsibility for our archeological work. As expected, we found that the U271 submarine is both a morgue and a treasure house. The ship contains the remains of 183 individuals. Judging from the uniform insignias, many were high-ranking officers of the German Reich."

The blacksmith cleared his throat. "Warriors who die in battle rise to Valhalla."

Groa thought this was an unusually sympathetic comment, given that twenty-six million Soviets had died at Nazi hands. But the Varangian Knights at the table were nodding in agreement.

"That may be," Urmas said. "But the valuables they brought on board this submarine did not rise with them. We have officially inventoried all of these artifacts except for the two that Professor Talin predicted would be found with General Müller—a twenty-five kilogram box of gold ingots and a rusty Viking Age sword inscribed with the runic name Fenris."

Groa wheezed, her throat so tight she could hardly breathe. Suddenly she had realized who Professor Henrik Talin must actually be. He was the Danish Nazi who had helped Mette Gustmeyer oversee the excavation of a Viking ship in Hedeby during the war. Who else would know where to search for the missing sword? Hitler had funded that excavation because he believed in the power of Germanic legends. When the Reich collapsed, Henrik had not been important enough to warrant a spot on the escaping U-boat. As a Nazi collaborator, he would also have been unwelcome in post-war Denmark. Somehow he had made his way to Estonia and reestablished his career under a new name.

"Where—" Groa asked. "Where is it?"

"The gold has been cashed," the professor said without looking up to see who had asked the question. "The Order is using the money to finance our operations. Swarovsky? Did you manage to buy a passport for the defecting American Marine?"

"Yes, with difficulty," the young KGB agent replied. "The Americans do not bribe easily, and they really did not want Lee Harvey Oswald back. He had turned in his original passport when he defected to Russia. Then he grew tired of working as a lathe operator in the Gorizont electronics factory in Minsk. We also suspect that his new Belarusian wife wanted to experience the decadence of the West. Oswald is now living with her in Texas."

"Our backup plan," the professor said.

"Fenris," Groa breathed the word. "What has become of Fenris?"

This time the professor looked up to meet her eyes—and drew back when he saw they were mismatched, green and blue. "The sword is safe."

"'Fenris vests the Vikings' fate,'" Groa recited, remembering the ancient saga verse. "Where is the sword?"

"Soon Fenris will return to Oleg's hand, ready to summon a new age."

Groa narrowed her eyes. What sorcery was the professor imagining? Oleg, the regent of Russiya, had been dead for a thousand years.

"Knight Sergei?" Professor Talin signaled to the blacksmith, still standing guard by the dungeon door. "Bring the transmitter."

The smith retreated into a side corridor. A moment later he returned, lugging a heavy metal bar that Groa first thought might be some piece of railroad equipment. He hefted it like a weightlifter's barbell. Then, when he clunked it onto the wooden table, the circle of knights drew in their breath.

It was a gigantic sword. At least six feet long, the weapon was far too large to be wielded in battle by a human.

The Russian with a buzz cut marveled. "Is this the wolf-god's weapon?"

"No," the professor replied. "It is merely a shell, waiting for the return of Fenris."

"I'm afraid I don't understand."

"This is the sword from the Millennium of Russia monument in the kremlin square. An oversized bronze statue of Oleg rests his hand on the sword's hilt."

"You've removed the sword from the statue?"

"For restoration." Henrik smiled. "I retrieved the Millennium statue from Germany after the war. I remain responsible for its conservation."

He reached forward, using his finger to trace a narrow slit around the edge of the sword's blade. "Like the rest of the statue, the sword is hollow. But here you can see that the seam has been left open, merely tacked together at a few braze points. This has caused the bronze to weather, justifying its temporary removal for cleaning. That, in turn, serves to disguise our true purpose."

"Which is?"

Groa was glad someone else had asked this question. The answer, however, did not come from the professor, but rather from an old man who had been standing in the shadows along the dungeon's wall all this time.

"Our mission is Ragnarök," the old man said. He wore the black robe and long white beard of an Orthodox cleric, but the old Norse word he had used for 'twilight of the gods' was not a Christian term.

"One hundred years ago, in 1862, Knights of the Varangian Order designed the Millennium statue to honor the thousandth anniversary of the founding of Novgorod. Rurik stands in front. But at his side is the leader who actually united Russia. It was Oleg, aided by his sword Fenris, who conquered the realm between Finland and the Black Sea. It was Oleg who challenged the gates of Constantinople. It was Oleg who founded our Order by carving three runes for Tyr, the god of war, into our medallions."

Groa was about to object that she, and not Oleg, had carved those first runes, but it didn't seem particularly credible, even to her. Instead she asked, "Why was the statue's sword left hollow?"

The old man in priestly robes rolled his eyes back until only the whites showed. Presumably he was blind. "Because our Order has always believed that Oleg's lost sword would one day be found. Returned to Oleg's hand it would be a beacon, a transmitter summoning the wolf-god to the final battle. Only when the Earth is purged can the next cycle begin—the Varangian Age."

Professor Henrik Talin stood up. "Knight Theosophus reminds us of our sacred duty. The end times we have awaited for more than a millennium are at hand. The nuclear age is our gateway to a purer world. Each of us will have a task in the critical months ahead."

He turned to the officer with a naval cap. "Knight Savitsky, I understand you are captaining a nuclear submarine to Cuba."

"The *B-59* employs diesel-electric engines, professor. But she is fresh out of the Admiralty shipyard, equipped with a T-5 nuclear torpedo."

"Excellent. Can you take Knight Swarovsky with you?"

"We've already been assigned a political officer. I suppose I could arrange to have Swarovsky on board as a communications adjutant."

"Do it." The professor turned to the blacksmith. "Sergei, I want you to open the hollow sword, mount Oleg's original sword inside, and seal it up permanently."

The smith nodded.

Groa asked, "Are you sure this is Oleg's original sword?"

Henrik frowned. "Of course. The Fenris runes are still legible. The sword was found at the Hedeby battle site where Harald Bluetooth was mortally wounded." He paused. "There is some uncertainty about where the sword was for the century between Oleg's attack on Constantinople and Harald Bluetooth's battle in Denmark."

"Copies were made," Groa said darkly. "One of them conquered England. It is mounted in a cross atop St. Paul's Cathedral in London."

"An old rumor. How would you even know if such a thing were true?"

"I am old."

The professor ran a hand over his bald head in exasperation. "We need to focus. Once the beacon is installed time may be short. The new world will need pure blood. My assistant Urmas has traced the lineage of the first Viking royalty and has found a direct descendant of Harald Fairhair, the king who united Norway. Knight Urmas, what can you report?"

The young woman tilted her head so the page boy haircut hung nearly level. "The genealogy I have researched traces the female line, starting with Harald's grandmother, Queen Asa. There is a direct descendant who is alive today. She is a seventeen-year-old girl in Stockholm."

Groa clapped her withered hand to her mouth. Helen Gustmeyer! Groa had come to the same conclusion about the lineage years ago. Her suspicions had been aroused when the girl's grandmother, Kirstin, had such unlikely success excavating Queen Asa's burial ship in Norway. Groa had tried to warn the Gustmeyer girl in the Pergamon Museum, but the girl's young blood had made her too arrogant to listen.

Henrik licked his lips, a lascivious gesture that Groa found horrifying. "Do you think you can entice this descendant to join our cause?"

Urmas nodded. "I have a plan, yes."

* * *

"They've found Oleg!" Helen exclaimed, bringing the letter into the kitchen to show her mother.

"Who?" Mette looked up from the cutting board where she had been slicing hard-boiled eggs for smørgås sandwiches.

"Oleg, the Viking king of Russia."

"Oh, that one." Mette was proud of her daughter's knowledge about archeology, but she worried that it would be wasted. Helen was so bright that she had graduated early from the gymnasium. So far the girl had not bothered to apply for admission to a university. "Where has old Oleg been hiding all this time?"

Helen rolled er eyes. "In a burial mound in Russia. You remember Urmas, my friend from Culture Club? She's helping oversee an excavation in Old Ladoga, near Leningrad. It's a burned ship of the right age. She wants me to come help this fall."

Mette wiped her hands on her apron, took the letter, and smoothed the crinkly blue aerogram paper on the counter. "Why is she inviting you and not me?"

"I'm the one she knows. Besides, you're all tied up with the *Vasa*. Everyone knows you're going to be busy cleaning mud for years. This fall I'll have plenty of time."

"You're too young to go to Russia by yourself. And without advanced training you'd merely be a laborer. If you want to be taken seriously you need to study at a university first."

"Mom! This is better. It's the real thing. Urmas is offering to pay my way."

"Seriously?" Mette read through the letter. It was handwritten in English. "Who is this professor she's working for?"

"Some guy at the University of Estonia."

"Professor Talin. Why don't I know that name?" Mette shook her head. It was a shame that the Iron Curtain had left academia so divided. The few archeological papers from the East Bloc that had been translated into English were usually discounted as propaganda. Often as not they were thinly veiled attempts to glorify the Soviet Union by attempting to show the supremacy of Russian ancestors. The Space Race and the Arms Race weren't the only competitions in a dangerously divided world.

Mette handed back the letter. "I don't know, honey."

"Don't call me honey."

Mette closed her eyes and took a breath. The word had slipped out. Did they have to clash over this too? "I'm sorry. It's just—well, something about this sudden offer doesn't seem right."

"I'll get to live in Leningrad, near the Hermitage and all the other museums. Can't I have a little good luck once in a while?"

Mette knew it would be difficult to stop her headstrong daughter. Maybe this was the opportunity she needed, to get her hands dirty with some practical experience. Soon enough she would realize that she could never advance without a university degree. Still, Mette couldn't help throwing in a final barb.

"What about your Communist boyfriend? Would he come along to train as a Russian spy?"

"Lennart's not my boyfriend, and he's not a Communist." Ouch! Two lies! To hide the flush on her cheeks Helen snatched away the letter and stomped out of the kitchen.

The worst thing, Helen thought, was that part of her mother's barb might be true. There had been so many little hints—Lennart's interest in her Aunt Sasha's microfilmed communique, his strange pocket knife, and his work for Colonel Wennerström, a top-level Swedish military attache. Was the guitar-playing skateboarder secretly a spy?

CHAPTER 21
CONSTANTINOPLE, 907

A breathless captain of the Imperial Guard shoved aside servants to burst into the bedroom of Emperor Leo the Wise. "Your Eminence! The city is under attack!"

Leo rolled aside from Zoe and lifted himself onto one elbow. "Oh, really?" He lazily considered exactly how to punish this impudent soldier. Barging into the Imperial bedchamber was the sort of crime that cried out for a revival of the gladiatorial contests. Something with very hungry tigers and a suit made of red meat.

"Yes, Your Eminence!"

Leo sighed. "Have the Bulgars tunneled under the moat? Have Arabs used genies to fly in from Baghdad?"

"Neither of those, Your Eminence," the officer said. "I don't know who they are, but there is a fleet off the Lion's Gate. Don't you hear it?"

What Leo heard sounded like a distant windstorm that had raised the surf. Not for the first time it occurred to him that his Imperial Guardsmen were idiots. They certainly dressed the part, with goofy red plumes waving above little round helmets. The excitable man in his bedroom was identifiable as an officer because his shirt was hung with foppish tassels and his leggings were striped red and green. Who had invented these costumes? His guards looked like the Hippodrome clowns that battle each other with fruit between acts.

But then the great bells of Saint Sophia began ringing—apparently all of them at once. Leo frowned, swung his feet to the floor, and reached for his dressing gown.

"Mmm-hmm?" Zoe mumbled.

"I'll be back, my love." Leo slipped on sandals and waved the guard before him out the door. A dozen soldiers in the hall snapped to attention.

"A fleet, you say?" Leo asked, yawning.

"Yes, Your Eminence. Small ships, but perhaps two hundred."

"Two hundred ships. Of unknown origin. Out of thin air. Well, let's have a look." The emperor began shuffling up a flight of stone stairs toward the rooftop garden terrace. On the way he asked, "What's your name, captain?"

"Claudius Secundus, Your Eminence."

A Roman. Leo paused. "Weren't you in the service of Catullus?"

"Yes, Your Eminence."

This was the other problem with Imperial Guardsmen. Many were secretly loyal to wannabe usurpers. Catullus had been one of the Roman consuls Leo stripped of power. Men like that could threaten the empire from within. Leo could never be sure that his own guard might turn against him. He quickened his pace up the stairs.

Half the palace staff seemed to have already crowded onto the rooftop terrace. They quickly cleared a path for the emperor, but three men remained at the railing—General Petrion and two of his lieutenants from the Imperial Reserves. They were not wearing clown suits, but rather full armor. The general pointed silently toward the sea.

It took Leo a moment to focus on the armada below. There were in fact hundreds of ships, and although they were small by Byzantine standards, each was packed with helmeted men waving weapons and shouting. Half the sails were lowered. The rest billowed with colorful stripes and demonic beasts.

"They're Varangians," Leo marveled.

"Indeed, Your Eminence," General Petrion said. "The barbarian traders of Russiyan rivers."

"But there are so many! And what are they doing here?"

"Two hundred and twelve ships, Your Eminence. Roughly ten thousand men." The general paused. "I don't think they have come to trade."

"What's on their decks?" As the sails went down, poles were going up that stood even taller than the masts.

"Ladders, Your Eminence."

Leo's initial shock had given way to the chill of genuine fear. The seawall by the Lion's Gate was a curtain of stone, but its crenelated top might be within reach of a long ladder.

"Divert our defenses to the Lion's Gate," Leo ordered.

"Already done, Your Eminence."

"How many troops do we have?"

"Most of our forces are in Crete and—"

"I know that!" Leo cut him short. "I asked how many men we can muster."

"Well, Your Eminence," General Petrion touched his fingers as if to tally. "There are four thousand reservists, five hundred men in the Imperial Guard, six hundred gatekeepers—twenty for each gate—and eight hundred other sundry police. About six thousand in all."

"Is that enough to hold the Lion's Gate?"

"Oh, yes. Most certainly, Your Eminence. Our defensive position gives us an overwhelming advantage."

Leo stroked his beardless chin, thinking. "Perhaps Oleg knows this."

"Your Eminence?" The general looked at him uncertainly.

"I've heard about the leader of the Varangians—a man named Oleg. Somehow he managed to subdue the tribes of the north when we could not. He must have discovered that our forces would be busy elsewhere this summer. But then how foolish it would be to wake up the city with a noisy parade at our best defended wall, directly in front of the Imperial palace."

"He is a barbarian, Your Eminence."

"Yes." Leo narrowed his eyes, scanning the morning fog that still lingered along the edges of the Bosporus. "But where is he really, this Oleg?"

* * *

Oleg slowly rolled his fists in the air to signal the assault. Soon five thousand oarsmen were rowing for all they were worth. As the fog began to lift, twenty enormous dragons—each composed of five ships lashed end to end—raced each other toward the great iron chain blocking the harbor of the Golden Horn.

Thorkell's ship was the first to hit, with a lurch that sent Tsar Igor sprawling back into the arms of the oarsmen. The Tyr prow reared up as if its arrow meant to stab the sky. Then the whole ship balanced its keel atop the chain. Groa's oar paddled nothing but air. Lashed ropes creaked as the four ships behind pushed the keel forward, scraping across the iron. Then the stern smacked into the water on the harbor side, and just as quickly the next ship's prow thumped against the chain. Now the oars on Thorkell's ship gripped water once again, pulling the second ship over the barrier.

The dragon beside theirs, however, was not slithering so smoothly. Its first ship had hit the chain at an angle. Pushed from behind, the ship had buckled sideways against the chain and flipped. The second ship had also capsized before the captains in the final three ships realized what was happening and shouted for their oarsmen to stop. The cries of drowning men, weighed down by their armor, haunted the morning air.

In all, nineteen of the linked dragons managed to clear the chain.

The captains cut the ropes holding their ships together. Helmsmen re-attached the rudders that had been removed for the crossing. As the first rays of the sun lit the walls of the Golden Horn's inner harbor, nearly five thousand men of the Rus were sailing where no enemy ship had sailed before.

They knew their target from the maps that Groa's scriveners had copied—the Gate of Eugenios, beside the Prosphorion docks. It might once have been the stoutest tower in the old wall of ancient Byzantium. But when the fishing village became the capital of an empire, other fortifications had seemed more important. After all, the Eugenios Gate was protected by the harbor chain. And the gate merely led to the Arab Quarter, in the shadow of the abandoned heathen acropolis.

That morning, as the great bells of Saint Sophia rang in alarm, six of the Eugenios Gate's usual contingent of twenty soldiers had been summoned to defend the Lion's Gate on the far side of the city. Twelve of the remaining men were cooking flatbread for breakfast in a guard-room fireplace.

The two sentinels on the tower's walkway had spent most of their watch peering down into the city streets, suspecting that Arab sympathizers might emerge to aid in the Lion's Gate assault. They had noticed an irregular thumping sound in the fog, but had assumed it was a heavy cart bumping down a cobblestone alley. One of the watchmen had even imagined he heard an anguished cry. Eventually he glanced the other way, toward the harbor. And he dropped his pike in astonishment.

Sea monsters were rising out of the harbor mist. With horrible heads and slowly beating wings—or no, worse! Less probable and far more terrifying than mere monsters, scores of alien ships were rowing across the bay.

The watchmen tumbled down the stairs to the guardroom, gibbering about an attacking fleet. The tower's sergeant had been sent to the Lion's Gate earlier that morning, leaving the slow but burly Corporal Demetrion in charge.

"Oh, really?" the corporal asked, unintentionally mimicking the words of his emperor. "Let's have a look."

A minute later fourteen soldiers stood on the tower walkway, their hearts thumping as they watched the silent Varangian ships. The first of the long rowboats was nearly at the docks. Already some of the crews were using ropes to raise ladders above their decks.

Corporal Demetrion said nothing while the others ranted: "Who are they?" "Where'd they come from?" "We need to warn the others!" "Could the Castellion have lowered the chain?" "Call the reservists!" "The Lion's Gate must have been a feint." "We've got to send for help." "I'll go!" "Me too!"

Finally the corporal stopped them with a growl. "If all of you cowards run for help there will be no one left to guard the gate."

"Against an army? There must be thousands."

"We guard the gate. That's our job." Demetrion studied his men. His gaze stopped at the smallest, a boy young enough to be his own son. "You're the swiftest runner. Go inform the Imperial palace. Now."

The boy took off at a sprint.

Demetrion clapped his hands onto the shoulders of the next two smallest guardsmen, as if he were arresting them rather than setting them free. "You two will secure the portcullis on the gate. Then run to warn the next watchtowers—you to the Neorion Gate and you to the Gate of Barbara."

Even before the two men were gone Viking arrows had begun to carom off the tower's stonework.

"What about us?" one of the remaining soldiers asked.

"We use our arrows first, then pikes, then swords, like you've been trained. When possible, stay behind the stone risers. You, fetch the bows from the guardroom."

But the man who went to fetch the bows did not come back. And then the rungs of a ladder clunked into the gap between two stone risers.

"Push it away!" the corporal ordered. When his gatekeepers merely cowered, Demetrion grabbed the ladder himself and heaved it aside. It slid across the face of the wall and crashed onto the docks below.

Almost at once a second ladder appeared nearby, this time accompanied by a hail of arrows. Crouching behind a riser, Demetrion used the point of his pike to tip the ladder backwards. A Viking warrior clung to the rungs as the ladder tilted across a ship's deck and splashed into the harbor.

Laughing now, the corporal jogged to a third ladder. He heaved it back with his pike, but the weight of two men near its top kept it from tilting very far. For an instant, as the ladder balanced in mid air,

Corporal Demetrion found himself looking into the eyes of the two foreign fighters. At the top was a man his own age—absolutely fearless, with the look of a sailor who had climbed masts in stormier weather than this, although perhaps not with a battle axe in hand. Below him a terrified younger man clung to the rungs like a spoiled boy, holding a short sword.

As the ladder began tilting back toward the tower Demetrion braced his pike against a chink in the pavement and chose which of the two men would face its razor tip.

* * *

"No!" Tsar Igor shouted. He had wanted to be part of the attack. When Gunnar, the confident helmsman, had climbed up the ladder first, Igor had urged his friend Voris to follow. And now, watching from the deck below, Igor had seen the ladder slam against the tower wall, impaling Voris on a bloody spear.

Groa didn't need to reach inside Igor's mind to see that he had learned the meaning of guilt. Without a word Igor unsheathed his sword and set off up the ladder.

"Tsar, wait!" Thorkell cried.

Igor climbed onward, crawling past the body stuck in the rungs. Gunnar, meanwhile, had sprung to the walkway with his battle ax. But Demetrion had drawn his own sword and was keeping Gunnar so busy dodging blows that the helmsman had no time to get in a proper swing himself. By then half a dozen other ladders had landed against the wall, isolating Demetrion from the other gatekeepers.

Igor reached the top of the ladder, fired by the fury of vengeance. But then he lost his footing and stumbled onto the walkway, banging his helmet against Demetrion's knee.

The corporal staggered back a step, off balance. When Demetrion raised his sword to dispatch the clumsy warrior at his feet, Gunnar finally had the chance to swing his axe two-handed. The heavy blade lopped Demetrion's head just below the chin.

For a moment the torso stood its ground, spouting blood like a grisly wine fountain. Then its sword clattered to the ground beside the Tsar of Russiya, and the headless corporal tipped backwards against the parapet.

Moments later the surviving gatekeepers threw down their weapons. They tried to raise their hands in surrender, but were hacked to death by overeager attackers.

The assault had been swift, deadly, and almost entirely silent. Now, however, a victorious battle cry arose from the Varangians atop the tower.

Thoughout the crooked streets of the Arab Quarter people emerged from doorways and balconies, peering about fearfully for the source of this new alarm. Rumors of a Caliphate attack or a palace coup had been spreading since the cacophonous ringing of the cathedral's bells. Now soldiers were shouting from the battlements of the Eugenios Gate. But who on earth were they, these strange, bearded men waving swords? The only Imperial helmet in that mob had been hoisted atop a bloody pike.

Ali Ibn al-Namid pounded on the wooden door of the fourth-floor library. After a maddening delay the Voice finally responded, "Enter."

When Ali burst inside a globe of the night sky was still slowly spinning in the corner of the room. "They're here!" Ali cried.

"Where?" The word seemed to come from the globe itself.

"At the Eugenios Gate, as you suggested."

"Then Oleg will need a translator who speaks both Greek and Norse."

"You want me to—"

"Go, Ali," The Voice commanded. "Massage the infidels' words as carefully as you would their necks."

* * *

Even when Oleg stood on a stone riser at the top of the tower he had trouble being heard above the jubilant din. Finally he told Milovic to blow a dozen rapid lur-horn notes as a signal for attention. And still other voices were louder: "Miklagard is ours!" "Raid the city!" "Slaves and gold!"

"Stop!" the old Varangian regent bellowed. "If you want plunder, listen to me!"

Gradually the clamor ebbed. Oleg's eyes, the color of sharpened steel beneath his bushy red eyebrows, surveyed the motley army. Hundreds of Rus warriors stood atop the wall. Thousands more were on the ships below, almost beyond the range of his voice.

"If you have captured a cow, do you slaughter it at once?" Oleg asked, shouting the words. "Or would you rather milk it for years? I have a plan that will bring us more silver by trading than by raiding. And do not think, because we have taken one gate, that the city is ours. The emperor has many thousands of troops yet in Miklagard. They know the streets and you do not. Every alley and house would be your death trap."

"Then burn it down!" a voice shouted.

"And achieve what? Nothing! Nor will you find that a city of stone is so easily burned. I call on all of you to keep to my plan. Hold this one gate. Make the emperor come to us."

There were grumbles, but the only outright objection came from a voice with a thick Arabic accent calling up from the street below. "You speak well, Oleg the Regent. However, you do not speak Greek. How will you bargain with Leo?"

Oleg leaned over the edge of the wall to look down at the heckler—a bald brown head with a crimson cloak and pointy shoes.

"Ali! The Arab doctor. What are you doing here?"

"I live in Constantinople, Regent." The Arab's Norse was as grammatically precise as ever. "If you are not going to burn down my neighborhood, perhaps I could take a message for you to the emperor?"

"In fact I have two messages for him," Oleg replied. Then he looked back at the warriors on the walkway. "Who among you is bold enough to accompany this Arab through a hostile city to the Imperial palace?"

To everyone's surprise the young Tsar Igor raised a hand. His tunic was splattered with blood and his face was still pale from the trauma of battle.

"You, Tsar?" Oleg asked.

Igor held out his hand to a nearby captain. "I would just point out that Farlof here, the Westlands knight, says he has been to Constantinople many times. He knows the streets. I believe he even speaks Greek."

Farlof flushed red. "Is this my repayment for loaning you a ship after you wrecked your own in the Dnieper rapids? You would reward me with a suicide mission, Tsar?" He almost spat the final word.

Igor withdrew his hand. "I thought—"

"You did not," Farlof interrupted. "You are as unthinking as a child. We've seen you repay the loyalty of a friend by sending him to his death."

"Voris didn't—" Igor stammered, "I tried to—"

"Enough!" Oleg held up his hands for silence. "Be careful, all of you. Remember that Igor is Rurik's son. He is the Varangians' rightful heir. Soon I will step down. Then Igor, and none other, will command you. Today I am asking for a volunteer. I need someone with the courage to carry a message to Emperor Leo."

The silence that followed was as profound as before the battle had begun.

At length a voice said, "I will go."

Oleg followed the voice to the Norwegian captain he had met in Tønsberg long ago. "Thorkell?"

"Jarl Thorkell, once." The old captain lifted his head. "And perhaps a jarl once more, if I serve you well today?"

"Perhaps."

"What message would you have me take to the emperor?"

"Tell Leo that we need to talk in person. Here at the gate where I've nailed my shield."

Ali called up from the street below, "I thought you said there were two messages."

Oleg smiled. "The second message will be delivered by lur-horn. Leo will receive this message very soon. But I wonder if he is wise enough to understand its meaning."

Oleg nodded to Milovic. The Slavic helmsman lifted his spiral trumpet and blew a long, slow, two-note fanfare—high and then low. Moments later the ninety-five ships in the harbor began repeating the call, a lur-horn message so loud that it would be heard by the rest of the fleet, nearly a mile away.

CHAPTER 22
LADOGA, 1962

Oleg's tomb was a much less interesting archeological site than Helen Gustmeyer had expected. She did, however, enjoy being treated by the Russian excavation team as if she were a visiting princess. Her mother had predicted that she would be dismissed as an uneducated laborer. Wrong! Unlike the Russian women, she was blond without dark roots, and unlike the men, she was tall without platform shoes. Those who could speak English hung on her every word as she strode about the excavation, examining the rows of rust stains left by the burned ship's iron rivets.

Only a few lumps of melted silver remained where the tomb's occupant had been. If it was in fact Oleg, he obviously had been cremated together with some sort of jewelry. Helen presumed the silver came from a handful of rings, but Urmas and others seemed  quite sure it must have been a melted medallion, made from a silver coin. Why a medallion? Then she noticed that one of the Russian men working without a shirt was actually wearing a coin on a chain about his neck. Was she imagining it, or did the pendant really have three upward-pointing arrows carved on one side? If you don't speak Russian it's awkward for a young woman to inspect a coworker's chest.

The medallions were just one of a series of increasingly worrisome developments. Helen sat alone in her room at the huge, concrete Intourist hotel in Leningrad, listing her concerns in a letter to her Italian pen pal Celeste. Of course Helen had invented Celeste three years ago as a way to keep a diary—and to play a little joke on her mother. Mette had believed that Helen's boyfriend Lennart was imaginary and that her pen pal Celeste was real. Ha! And yet now, as the long evening in her hotel grew lonely, Helen would have preferred to be confiding in a real friend.

Dear Celeste,

I wish you were here! My mother had warned me that something didn't feel right about this offer to work on Oleg's excavation in Russia, and now that it's starting to get scary, I'm afraid to tell her that she might have been right. The worst thing isn't the dig itself, which is a bit boring, but rather the political crisis in the Caribbean. Who would think something that far away would make people jittery here? The TASS news reports all say the US is lying about its aerial photographs of long-range nuclear missiles in Cuba. They're supposed to be ordinary short-range missiles. They're supposed to defend Cuba against US planes and ships if Kennedy decides to invade. But no one here seems to believe the Russian news.

Urmas is insisting that we move out of the Intourist hotel this week because Leningrad would be one of the first targets in a nuclear war. Instead we're going to Novgorod, the Vikings' original capital. Now it's a small provincial town with no industry, completely off the US radar. I guess the commute to the Ladoga excavation will be slightly shorter. I won't really miss this hotel either. It's built like a big cement prison, with no movie theaters or coffee shops or nice stores nearby. In Novgorod we'll be staying in a basement bunker in the town's old kremlin. How will that be better?

Amazingly, the rest of the crew all seem excited about the move. They're planning a big celebration at a monument in Novgorod's main square. I'll finally get to meet the mysterious Professor Henrik Talin, the guy who's in charge of everything. They say he'll answer all my questions.

The first question I'll ask is this: What the hell is going on with the medallions? I think most of the excavation team is wearing them on necklaces, although they're usually kept hidden. And here's the creepy thing: They're the same size and shape as the silver pendant we found in the *Vasa*. That was supposed to be from the seventeenth century. I even think they've got the same markings, three arrow-shaped runes, like the graffiti that's been showing up in Stockholm.

On top of all this, I've recognized some of the excavation crew from the microfilm photographs I saw in Berlin. Something really is wrong. I wish you were here. Then we'd figure everything out and I could go home to a safe place where the world isn't burning up.

Your pen pal, Helen

Her hands were shaking as she creased the thin blue paper on the dotted lines that read, "Fold Here." Then she licked the gummed edges and sealed the aerogram, turning the sheet into its own envelope. She was about to shelve it alongside all the other blue envelopes for Celeste when she paused.

Only a coward would whine about something this important to a secret diary.

With sudden determination she took the letter in hand. Then she left her hotel room and marched down the echoing corridor past rows of identical doors. She clopped down four flights of stone terrazzo stairs to the hotel lobby and slapped the letter on the reception counter.

"Can you mail this?"

The receptionist picked up the envelope, batting eyelids heavy with mascara. She wore bright red lipstick, a blond hairdo piled up like an enormous brioche, and a blue woolen suit that might have been tailored for an airline stewardess.

"Foreign aerograms are not valid in the Soviet Union. International airmail would be forty kopeks."

Helen slid a brown one-ruble note across the counter.

The clerk filed the bill in a drawer and took out two coins in change. She tore off a postage stamp with a picture of a spaceship marked "CCCP". With her eyes half closed she licked the stamp. Then she slowly pressed the stamp in place with the heel of her hand. After all of this she still shook her head.

"Your letter needs an address."

Helen wondered what to write. Tyr? Fenris? Certainly not her mother. Perhaps her grandmother Kirstin? Was there an address for her Uncle Lars? He was with the CIA in Berlin, but where? And none of those people were the pen pal she needed now.

Helen took a chained pen from the counter and wrote,

Lennart Bronsson
Universitetsgatan 34c
Stockholm, Sverige

Then she added in large block letters: SWEDEN

* * *

The next morning Helen's uncle Lars Andersen was hurriedly re-called from Berlin for consultations at CIA headquarters. A black limousine with a police escort brought him from Andrews Air Force Base in Maryland across the Potomac River to Langley, where the huge new building rose like a concrete computer punch card from a sea of parking lots amid Virginia's forests. A man in a black suit who introduced himself as Agent David Stern met him at the entrance to help him through security.

"You served six months in Cuba," Stern said. "Did you meet Castro?"

"Yeah, and Guevarra. Several times." Lars looked about the lobby. "What's with all the fish tanks?"

"Morale." Colorful tropical fish idled behind the glass of several dozen aquariums. Stern pressed an elevator button. "Water also absorbs fallout radiation less obtrusively than sandbags."

They rode down two floors to a communications bunker Lars had not known existed. Television monitors and maps lined the walls. Women with headphones typed at rows of desks. Bullet-shaped cylinders zipped through pneumatic plastic tubes, presumably transporting documents from other parts of the building. In a raised glass booth in the middle of the room sat a balding man Lars recognized as CIA deputy director Marshall Carter. Wearing a lieutenant general's uniform, he swiveled in a chair, touching his fingertips together as he talked into a wire that extended from his ear to his mouth. His lips moved soundlessly behind the glass—much like the fish in the aquariums upstairs, Lars thought.

Aloud Lars mused, "You know, if the Russians target this place, fish tanks aren't going to save anybody."

"We didn't think they could target Langley," Stern replied. "We knew they had a dozen ICBMs based in the Soviet Union, but those are as accurate as shotguns. These new intermediate range R-14 missiles in Cuba can pinpoint any target in the US. From our U-2 photos it looks like a few of the sites are already operational."

"Is the naval blockade working?"

"We may be able to stop resupply freighters for a while, but they're accompanied by submarines."

"Why do you need me here at ground zero so urgently?"

"In an hour the President is meeting CIA director McCone, the Joint Chiefs of Staff, and four other top advisors. Carter's our link to that conference. He asked to see you before they start."

Stern pressed a button on a panel beside the glass booth. "Agent Andersen is here from Berlin."

The deputy director inside the cubicle swiveled toward them. A glass panel slid aside with a whir. "Andersen! I remember how badly you beat me at racquetball at Camp David. Come on in."

Lars hadn't played racquetball for ten years, but he had beaten a lot of CIA opponents in his day—apparently even Carter. When Lars stepped inside, the glass door whirred shut behind him. There was no place for him to sit down. He noticed that the arm of Carter's chair was a miniature switchboard of colored lights and buttons.

Carter's friendly manner shifted suddenly to business. "I want your assessment of Castro."

"In what way, sir?"

"We're on the brink of thermonuclear war. Kennedy won't tolerate offensive missiles in Cuba. The Joint Chiefs have unanimously agreed that the only solution is a military invasion of the island."

"That didn't go so well the last time, sir."

Carter waved his hand as if he were dispelling unpleasant cigarette smoke. "The Bay of Pigs was a half-assed banana republic putsch. Kennedy allowed a thousand ragtag Cuban exiles to go in without air or naval support, thinking that's all it would take. He'd only been in office a few weeks and was afraid to risk American lives. This time the chiefs are recommending two carrier groups, landing craft, Marines, air cover, the whole enchilada. The Cuban military would be completely overwhelmed."

Lars held up his index finger. "Isn't that why Castro asked the Soviets to put missiles in Cuba?"

"Yes. The question is, will he use them? We've also heard that Kennedy's not so keen on the invasion idea. He thinks if we take Cuba, Khrushchev will respond by taking West Berlin."

Lars nodded, thinking. "That's probably true. Berlin's a bigger prize. Khrushchev would win."

"Unless we all lose. That's why I want your opinion." The CIA deputy director swiveled, waving a hand toward the maps on the wall. "We're at DEFCON 3, headed for DEFCON 2, the highest military alert status in history. We have 170 ICBM sites on full alert, ready to launch on targets throughout Cuba and Russia. All eight of our nuclear submarines have Polaris nuclear missiles at the ready. The Strategic Air Command has a hundred B-52 bombers in the air, on orbital trajectories that allow them to drop nuclear weapons throughout Russia within hours."

Carter swiveled back to face him. "If the Soviets refuse to remove their missiles from Cuba and we're forced to invade, would Castro ask Khrushchev to push the button?"

Lars sighed. "Yes, sir. I believe he would."

"Even knowing that the resulting nuclear exchange would kill every person in Cuba?"

"Yes."

Carter studied Lars silently for a moment. Then he looked aside. "I understand that your wife is also an agent of ours."

"Yes, sir. Sasha has been stationed in Russia for the past twelve years."

"Have we heard from her lately?"

"Not much, sir. Communication has been difficult since the Berlin wall went up. In her last communiques she has been warning that a white supremacist group may have secretly infiltrated the top levels of government in both Russia and the United States. She says they call themselves the Knights of the Varangian Order."

"Strange name. What's their angle?"

"Nuclear war, sir. She says they plan to survive in bunkers and later repopulate the world with a purer race."

"Crazy." The CIA deputy director shook his head. But he also pushed a button, sliding open the glass door as a signal that their meeting was over. "I hope your wife stays safe, Andersen. Let's just pray she's not in Moscow."

***

When the Intourist travel agency finally promoted Sasha from Minsk to their Moscow headquarters she could hardly believe her luck. Not only would she be closer to the center of Soviet power, but her office space was posh. The four-story neoclassical building on Arbat Street, just six blocks from Red Square, had once been a ducal palace.

Visiting delegations from all over the world called there to arrange accommodations. She spent most of her days helping Nigerians, Chinese, or Bulgarians set up factory tours as part of trade deal negotiations. She also helped a number of top Soviet officials when they needed to travel. And this was how she had met Petra Barents, a secretary for Andrei Gromyko, Khrushchev's minister of foreign affairs.

Like Sasha, Petra had grown up Jewish during Stalin's pogroms in the 1930s. While Sasha's parents had escaped to America, however, Petra's relatives had died in a Kazakhstan work camp. As an attractive young orphan, Petra had been adopted by a childless Moscow couple—physicians who had done their best to erase her past and give her a fresh start. Now in her 30s, Petra had rediscovered the horrors her family had suffered at the hands of Soviet authorities. As retribution, she kept finding excuses to drop by the Intourist office. She claimed to be researching possible Black Sea cruises or skiing vacations in the Caucasus for her superiors. While in the office, Petra shared office gossip about foreign affairs with a sympathetic travel agent. In exchange Sasha gave her complimentary passes to shows and restaurants. Did Petra know that her information was being relayed through the neutral Swedish embassy to the Americans? Petra didn't ask, but yes, she knew.

Although the former palace had been stripped of most of its finery, it still had creaking parquet floors, fourteen-foot ceilings with peeling plaster, and some original gilt woodwork. Only the ground-floor rooms facing Arbat Ulitsa had been fully modernized—with ugly checkerboard tile floors, "decorative" panels of expanded steel, and bare light bulbs.

The chill October wind that blew dead leaves through the streets of Moscow also seemed to leave the city shivering with fear. If TASS, the official news agency, could be believed, the Americans were merely rattling sabers. But then why were Moscow officials telling everyone to stock their basements with food and water? And where were the intercontinental ballistic missiles, really, that had been so proudly paraded through Red Square five months ago for the May Day celebration?

Petra Barents clutched her overcoat together against the wind as she hurried along the sidewalk. Before opening the Intourist door she looked both ways—a guilty gesture she immediately recognized as stupid. How would she know which of the hundreds of passersby might be following her? Inside it was warm enough that she unwrapped her scarf and took off her gloves. The young, doll-faced receptionist greeted her by name—another bad sign—and pressed an intercom button to summon Sasha. "She'll be right down, Miss Barents."

"Actually, I—" Petra began, about to change her mind. But it was too late, and her news was too important. "That's fine. I'll wait."

Sasha sensed her informant's tension as soon as she saw her haunted expression. Sasha countered by being overly cheerful. "Miss Barents! I've had the devil of a time getting your tickets. It seems nobody else takes winter vacations on the Trans-Siberian Railroad. Come back to the samovar and we'll talk about options."

They stopped to get tea from the brass pot in the break room, but then Sasha led the way, as usual, into the old butler's pantry. Sasha had searched the little room to make sure it had no hidden microphones. They sat on wooden lawn chairs with the teacups between them on an empty cooking oil drum.

Petra started to cry.

"What is it, Petra?"

"I'm afraid."

"Of what?" Sasha leaned forward. "Are there really nuclear missiles in Cuba?"

Petra nodded, crying harder. She wiped her eyes with her gloves.

Sasha gave her a handkerchief. "But everyone in the government has denied it, from top to bottom."

"*Maskirovka*," Petra replied through her tears.

Maskirovka—the masking game. Sasha sat back, thinking how much of their miserable Cold War world relied on disguises. She and Petra had grown up running away from religious persecution. Sasha was a few years older but forced herself to look younger. Without her make-up, her bottle-blond hair, and her stylish clothes she could easily pass as Petra's twin—a frightened government secretary. Which version was the disguise, and which was real?

Petra blew her nose. "We've already sent 43,000 troops to Cuba."

"What! How is that possible? The soldiers themselves would have let word leak out."

"They weren't told where they were going. The official code name was Operation Anadyr."

"Anadyr? That's a base in Siberia."

Petra nodded, still holding the handkerchief to her nose. "When technicians started shipping out in July they were outfitted with winter gear—fur parkas and ski boots. In Cuba they were introduced as irrigation specialists and farm machine operators. The missiles themselves were trucked through villages at night and hidden with palm trees."

"Then the American aerial photographs are genuine. All the denials, day after day, have been lies. Why?" Sasha thought for a moment. "Is Khrushchev stalling until the missile bases are operational?"

"But they already are. That's the problem."

"I don't understand."

Petra set the handkerchief on the oil drum. She picked up her cup, blew steam off the tea, and took a sip to steady her nerves. But as she replaced the cup her shaking hand sent rings quivering across the surface of the tea.

"Khrushchev is afraid he's losing control. All it would take to start a nuclear war is a spark. Matches are everywhere. Already an American spy plane was shot down without his permission. How can he communicate orders to our submarines when they are underwater? Khrushchev is even more afraid of backing down. He would lose face."

Sasha sighed. "Kennedy probably feels the same way."

Petra wiped her eyes one more time. Then she stood up and pulled on her gloves. "Men are so stupid. All this hate—all these wars—it would not happen if you and I were in charge."

"Do you want a train ticket to Siberia?" Sasha asked. "Free of charge. You could leave tonight if you like."

The secretary's shoulders sagged, as if she had just put on a very heavy coat to face the world outside. Silently, she shook her head and turned to go.

* * *

Vasiliy Swarovsky had suspected that living on a submarine would be unpleasant, but he had not anticipated just how bad it really was. Lack of space was the first issue. The *B-59* was nearly as long as a soccer field, but nowhere was there room to bounce a ball, much less kick it. Corridors were so narrow that crewmen often snagged each other's shirt buttons as they squeezed by. Everywhere bulkheads, pipes, and fittings protruded to wallop passing foreheads. Sleeping hammocks were slung three deep in prison-like cells the size of broom closets. The food in an actual prison probably would have been more appetizing than the salty, greasy glop they spooned out of tins.

Another problem for Swarovsky was that he did not have a specific assignment on board the *B-59*, other than to help launch World War III if the opportunity arose. The ship already had three radio men. As "communications adjutant" Swarovsky filled his twelve-hour shifts listening to radio music programs in languages he did not understand. He taught himself Morse code. He read *The Brothers Karamazov*—a novel that proved to be so tedious Swarovsky found himself reading the same page over and over again without realizing it.

The bright spot of each day was the captain's morning briefing, which took place on the bridge at 0800 hours when the captain began his shift with coffee. Here Swarovsky learned that they were crossing the North Atlantic at just seven knots—thirteen kilometers per hour—in order not to outrun the twenty-two freighters they were accompanying to Cuba with a cargo of rocket fuel, trucks, and disassembled Il-28 bomber jets. As flagship of the four-submarine escort they sailed at the front of the convoy while the other subs guarded the flanks and rear. This also meant that the *B-59* carried the detachment's overall

commander, Arkhipov, an officer with the same rank as Captain Savitsky but without any particular duties that Swarovsky could determine. It was Commander Arkhipov who had so warmly recommended the Dostoevsky book. This was also why Swarovsky felt obliged to continue wading through the old novel.

After two weeks, life on the submarine suddenly became much worse. Up to that point they had been sailing on the surface, with access to fresh air. But as they neared the Caribbean, Commander Arkhipov decided it would be best for the submarine escort to continue underwater. Moscow had radioed news that the Americans had declared a naval blockade of offensive military weapons to Cuba. In the face of possible opposition, the convoy should proceed with caution.

The air aboard the *B-59* soon began to stink. There had always been the smell of oil and old socks, but now the recycled air was thick with the scent of fear. The engines that had throbbed like a metal heart through the walls night and day now beat louder and faster, pushing the ship through the depths.

At the captain's morning briefing, the radio men shook their heads, reporting what Swarovsky already knew: They were too deep to receive further orders from Moscow. The only radio signal was a garbled salsa station in Miami.

"A blockade is an act of war," the submarine's political officer grumbled. Ivan Maslennikov was too tall to stand up straight on the bridge. He had not trained with the Navy or even with the KGB. A Communist Party apparatchik from Murmansk, he did everything by the book, and as a result no one wanted to play cards with him in their off hours.

"That may be true, Ivan," the captain replied. "But the Americans are not using the word 'blockade'. They say it is not like the Berlin blockade, when we cut off all supplies. The Americans have gotten approval from their OAS allies for a military quarantine."

"Quarantine? Cuba is not sick. America itself is the disease."

Captain Savitsky turned to his first mate, who had stood the past twelve-hour watch on the bridge. "What does sonar tell us about ship positions?"

The mate unrolled a navigational chart that had been marked with colored pens. "The convoy won't reach the quarantine line for another twenty-four hours. We've just begun to pick up passive sonar signals of a dozen ships at a range of 250 kilometers. From the engine signatures, we're looking at the USS Randolph and its accompanying destroyers."

"An aircraft carrier." Savitsky sighed. "If our Navy had enough carriers they would have sent one to escort this convoy. Instead all we've got are four submarines. But we have something the Americans do not expect—a nuclear torpedo."

Ivan, the political officer, added, "It is a way to level the playing field."

"At a cost," added Arkhipov, the detachment commander said. "If confronted, we gamble all or nothing."

Captain Savitsky finished his coffee. "For now, our decision is easy. We stay the course. Any questions?"

Swarovsky nearly raised his hand. But this wasn't a school class. The air was thick with everything except oxygen. When the other officers had been dismissed he took the captain aside and asked, "How long can we stay submerged?"

"Are you not enjoying your trip, Swarovsky?" The captain gave him a lopsided smile. "I thought Varangians would be used to foul air."

Swarovsky bit back a smart reply. "As I understand it, we're running on batteries underwater. They can't last forever."

The captain's smirk faded. "We have forty hours. That will either get us past the Americans, or not. Then we'll have to go topside to run the diesel engines. Trust me, the atmosphere in here will get worse before it gets better. If we unleash Fenris, we may never come up at all."

CHAPTER 23
CONSTANTINOPLE, 907

"The barbarians are retreating!" At the railing of the palace terrace, the Imperial lieutenant chuckled with relief. Most of the Varangian ships were sailing south. A few were rowing north. Almost none seemed interested in staying to threaten the Lion's Gate. "We've frightened them away."

General Petrion pensively scratched the back of his neck, where the purple feathers dangling from his helmet itched. "I have to admit that I admire their signaling system. Those trumpets managed to spread word quite quickly among the various ships. I think the empire could use horns like theirs."

Beside him Emperor Leo scowled. "And ships like theirs. And generals like theirs."

"Your Eminence?" the general asked, ill at ease.

"Can't you see? They're repositioning, not retreating. Their light ships are swift. The horns were not issuing a command. They were relaying one."

The general opened his mouth and then closed it without speaking.

"Are my officers so old and deaf that they cannot hear? The horn signal came first from the north."

"But—that would be from the Golden Horn, behind the chain. No attackers have ever—"

Leo threw up his hands in exasperation. "I'm going back to my chambers to change into formal regalia."

"Why, Your Eminence?" the general asked.

"To prepare for any messengers that might arrive."

* * *

As a part-time Imperial masseur, Ali had walked the streets between his home and the palace a thousand times. He waved cheerfully to acquaintances and greeted passersby in Greek. They responded hesitantly, because this time the Arab doctor was accompanied by a malodorous Norwegian Viking with a grizzled beard, chain mail, and a shiny battle ax.

Thorkell slunk beside Ali, gripping his axe in both hands. His eyes searched the shadows of every doorway and alley.

"Relax, Captain," Ali said. "Constantinople is a world city. The people here have seen all sorts."

"They all look the same to me, these Greeks. And there are so many of them! This cursed city seems to stretch on forever."

"Cursed," Ali mused, latching onto the topic as if by accident. "Years ago when I was in Novgorod, I met an herbalist. A woman who said something about a cursed sword."

"You met Groa?"

"That was her name, yes. I remember her husband, a pleasant but remarkably ugly man. He had a name that sounded like he was vomiting."

"Hrolf?"

Ali stepped aside to make sure the old Viking had not actually thrown up. "An interesting couple. Then you know them?"

"Since the day we sailed from Norway together. We were among the first of Oleg's recruits in the quest to reconquer Russiya." He grunted. "Imagine. After all these years, Hrolf and Groa were rowing again on my ship to Miklagard."

"Really? They're here in the city? Do you suppose the Varangians brought this cursed sword with them?"

"Certainly. It's called Fenris. Oleg wears it all the time."

By now they were crossing the grassy ruins of the acropolis, where marble columns lay scattered like children's blocks in a nursery for giants. With no other people nearby Thorkell's nervous tension eased. Ali was such a sympathetic listener—so interested in everything—that the old Norwegian captain ended up telling him the whole story: How Oleg had bought the famed sword of the Vikings from a grave-robbing jarl. How the wolf-god Fenris was said to have made the sword both victorious and evil. How the sorceress Groa, impossibly, claimed to have helped forge the blade more than a century ago. And how she had killed the King of Sweden to save Oleg's life.

Ali nodded. "So now the sword belongs to Oleg?"

"Sort of. You see, he's promised to give it back to Groa when the Miklagard campaign is over."

"An amusing tale. Oh look! We're practically at the palace. I'm afraid you'll have to leave your weapon at the gate."

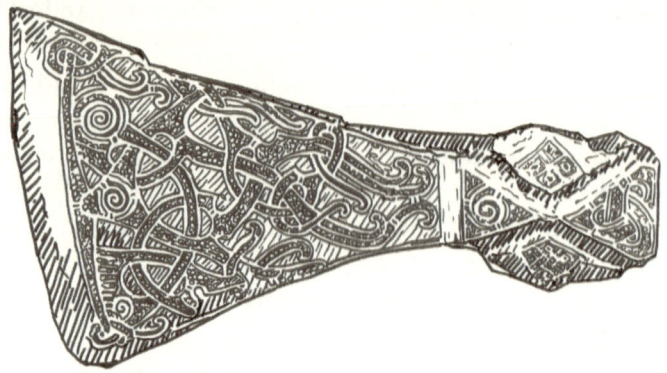

"My ax? It's my walking stick," Thorkell objected, his fears returning. "I never go anywhere without it."

"Perhaps the sentries could issue you a different cane," Ali suggested. "Come, let's go chat with Leo."

* * *

Emperor Leo was not interested in negotiating with Varangians inside the occupied Eugenios gate tower, a confined space where he would essentially be a captive. Instead he proposed that he parley with Oleg in the Strategion, a large plaza a few blocks away. Thorkell grumbled, but when he was told that both sides could bring armed troops as backup, he relented. The meeting would take place in two hours—a span of time that he was informed would be marked by the tolling of church bells throughout the city. Thorkell was surprised to learn that Christian temples did this every day, banging out the time with iron bells.

As Thorkell left the palace with Ali the sentries returned his ax. They even provided an escort all the way to the Arab Quarter, making sure the Viking ambassador was safe. Thorkell marveled that he might have won a jarldom by merely strolling through town.

The Eugenios Gate looked different—and not just because Oleg really had nailed his yellow-and-white-striped shield above the arched entry. The Varangians had torn up the Prosphorion docks and used

256

the planks to build palisades across all of the nearby streets. Rows of archers lined the tower parapet, the wall, and the roofs of adjacent buildings. Yellow-and-white banners were everywhere, some of them with Igor's double-headed eagle.

"An open square, inside the city?" Oleg shook his head. "It isn't what I wanted, but I suppose it will do. We'll take five hundred men to secure our side of the square. Thank you, Captain."

"Jarl," Thorkell said.

Oleg took a breath, flaring his nostrils.

Thorkell stood his ground, waiting for the regent to respond with the reassuring words, "Jarl Thorkell."

Instead Oleg said, "Thank you, Thorkell. Bring your crew as part of the tsar's entourage. Don't let the sorceress forget her paper list. Now you may go."

The ambitious Norwegian captain reluctantly returned to his ship, uncertain that his courage had gained him anything after all.

At the torn-up docks outside the gate Thorkell found his crew lighting a Byzantine fishing boat on fire.

"What are you doing? We're supposed to go to a conference with Emperor Leo."

"Leo can wait." Tsar Igor used an oar to push the flaming ship away from the shore. "Our first duty is to Voris."

"A funeral on water?" Thorkell now recognized the crew's somber mood as a tribute to their fallen comrade, the Tsar's closest friend. But pyres were always lit on land, even when burning a ship.

"Voris never wanted to be in Miklagard," Igor said. "I convinced him to come here against his will. His spirit deserves to be set free somewhere else."

The helmsman Gunnar added, "We couldn't very well build a fire in the city. People might misunderstand."

"And I wouldn't let them burn a ship I'd built," Hrolf put in.

For a while the crew watched in silence as the fiery ship drifted out into the Golden Horn. The tide and a faint breeze carried the boat slowly toward the unseen chain, where it would be blocked from the straits of the Bosporus beyond. But because Voris had died in battle, the smoke would carry his spirit beyond that barrier to the honored realm of Valhalla.

As Groa watched the reflected flames, she wondered why no one had thought to send ship-pyres out onto water before. The spectacle was not only beautiful, but more appropriate than burning a ship on land. Fire and water represented life and death. Mortals were not meant to burn forever. They might sail the seas of the living for a while, but eventually they had to face their doom, either rising as smoke or sinking as charred wreckage.

Why was it, Groa wondered, that she herself had been granted a second life? Was it a gift or a punishment? She had consorted with Fenris to create the Vikings' sword of power. And now it seemed she might never rest until she had undone that work. It was a relief that she would soon be able to destroy the sword. Then she could live out the rest of this life in peace.

When the last of the flames vanished beneath a pall of smoke, a distant bell tolled from the city. Then a different bell tolled, and yet another.

"That's the signal," Thorkell said, remembering. He explained to the crew that Leo had agreed to meet Oleg at a large square inside the city. "We're supposed to go join them. Groa, bring that leaf list. Everyone, gather your weapons."

"What if this is a trap?" the young tsar asked.

"That's right," Gunnar added. "We've got a strong position here at the gate. If they lure us into the city they could surround us."

"You're not the first to think of that," Thorkell replied. "Be ready for a fight."

Groa and Hrolf marched with the rest of the crew through the open Eugenios Gate. She didn't think a sorceress would be of much use in an actual battle. Hrolf was a woodworker, so at least he knew how to use an ax. The only weapon Groa had brought, aside from some mostly useless incantations and a small hidden dagger, was a rolled-up stack of paper.

Everything about the stone city was so alien that the marching Varangians constantly twisted their helmeted heads to gape in amazement. The buildings on either hand were stacked three or even four on top of each other. Why did they not collapse? How did people get to the upper stories without ladders? Nothing here was made of wood. The stone walls and even the stone street had been whitewashed until it all gleamed in the sun. The street they were following was wide enough for ten men to walk abreast, and it continued perfectly straight until it disappeared over the crest of a hill a mile away.

Their route angled away from the Arab Quarter, an older part of the city with crooked alleys and dirtier walls. Before long the street opened up on the Strategion, a rectangular field of flagstones surrounded by the marble pillars of palaces.

A red line, like a trail of blood, had been painted across the center of the plaza to divide it in halves. On the far side the Byzantines had arrayed their Imperial reservists in precise phalanxes—square ten-by-ten formations of soldiers with identical pikes, shields, and plumed helmets.

Groa saw at once that these troops would not be as easily overrun as the gatekeepers. Their shields were rectangular, and although the metal curved to encompass each man, the shields also fit together to protect the entire phalanx with a seamless defense. The round wooden shields of the Vikings seemed chaotic in comparison. Likewise, the Rus warriors carried a chaotic variety of weapons. That might be valuable for one-on-one combat, but not against a phalanx.

Groa felt fear on both sides of the square. When she tapped into the thoughts of individual men, however, she was surprised by the differences she heard. Despite all their show of unity, the Byzantine troops were anything but confident. They were reservists—mostly older men who had been left behind when the elite troops had been sent to fight in Asia Minor. Many of the Vikings, on the other hand, were actually spoiling for a fight. If even just a few of the Imperial legionnaires turned to run, the careful phalanxes would be riddled with holes. And if Russiyan warriors found those gaps, their battle axes might swing into the Greek reservists like scythes into wheat. The bloodshed on both sides would be immense.

Or did the emperor have another plan? Could he have brought out these trembling troops as bait, with stronger forces waiting to come out of hiding when the time was right?

"Igor! Get up here," Oleg shouted angrily from the center of the square. "You're late, Tsar. Bring your captain and your sorceress."

Hrolf clutched Groa's arm. "Don't go. The danger is too great. I couldn't bear it if you were to die."

She patted his big, rough hand. "Sometimes I wonder if I can die."

A look of confusion crossed her husband's face. In that moment she loosened his grip. Then she followed Igor and Thorkell through the crowd toward the red line.

The two armies had faced off a hundred feet apart. In the middle, just fifty feet from each other, Emperor Leo and the Varangian regent, Oleg, had each surrounded themselves with a few dozen advisors and a ring of warriors with shields.

Standing alone on the red line between the two forces was a bald, dark-skinned man that Groa recognized with surprise as Ali, the Arab doctor who had been such a nuisance in Novgorod.

More surprising still, Ali gave her a wave of recognition. "Well, look. The Rus have brought their woman wizard. Now we can get started. What will it be first, threats or offers?"

After this speech in Norse the Arab doctor turned and spoke for a while in Greek. Emperor Leo, dressed in silken robes and a tall white hat, sat on a golden chair carried by four men. He conferred with his generals. Then he raised his head and spoke loudly in Greek—a seemingly endless stream of bird-like vowels and bear-like consonants.

"What's he saying?" Oleg demanded impatiently.

Ali turned to face the Varangian regent. "Emperor Leo the Wise greets you, men of the north, with your storied leaders and—"

"Cut the nonsense," Oleg said. "What's he got? A threat or an offer?"

"A little of both, Regent."

"Let's hear it."

"Well, the emperor first wishes to point out that he has your men outnumbered and surrounded. Several thousand legionnaires are concealed on streets around the plaza. Your only feasible path of escape from the Strategion is the way you came, through the Eugenios Gate."

Not all of the Varangians in the plaza had been close enough to understand Ali's heavily accented Norse, but those who had began looking about with caution. Some rattled their weapons against their shields.

Oleg held up his hand for silence. "Go on, Ali. You have told us the emperor's threat. What is his offer?"

"If you choose to leave the way you came, the emperor is prepared to provide you with 30,000 silver dirhams as a parting gift."

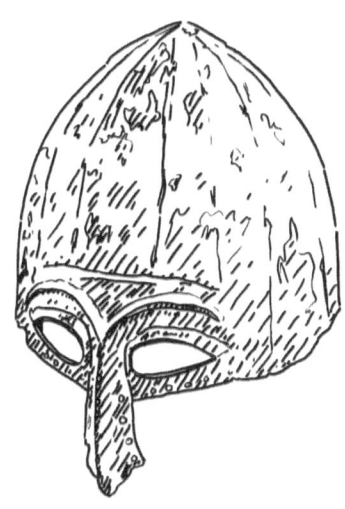

Appreciative murmurs spread amongst the warriors. Thirty thousand dirhams was an entire boatload of silver—more than any of them had seen before in one place. But divided amongst 15,000 men the treasure would amount to just two coins apiece. That would be enough to buy a few sheep or a good horse. Had they come so far for so little?

"Tell the emperor," Oleg said, "That he is mistaken. His forces have not surrounded the Rus. Our forces have surrounded his. Allow me to demonstrate." Oleg held up his index finger as a signal to his helmsman Milovic. The Slav blew a single long note on his lur-horn. A moment later the same note sounded from a different horn at the far end of the square, and then more faintly from the Eugenios Gate, and then fainter still from the harbor of the Golden Horn. Oleg held up both his hands, asking for patience. A minute passed in silence. And then the single lur-horn call returned, distant at first, but growing louder until it reached the square.

"You have just heard a signal that circled the walls of Miklagard," Oleg explained. "You have already seen how easily we captured one of your towers when it was lightly defended. At this moment we have 13,000 men poised to attack the remaining twenty-nine towers. Because most of your troops have been lured here to the middle of the city, they will be useless to protect against this assault. If I order the horn blown again, our warriors will storm Miklagard from all sides. They will have permission to pillage and burn as they see fit. The men of the Rus are eager for this command."

Oleg pointed to the lur-horn. "Shall I give the signal?"

While Ali translated this long speech, Milovic held his spiral trumpet at the ready—as if the horn might emit a dragon's fire rather than merely a musical note.

After a long, tense pause Ali translated a reply. "The emperor acknowledges that this is your threat, Regent. The Varangians are obviously brave and resourceful fighters. But the fact that you have not yet given this signal suggests you may be willing to negotiate. Leo has offered you 30,000 silver dirhams. Do you have a different offer in mind?"

Oleg threw back his head and laughed. "Put down your horn, Milovic. We're dealing with someone who knows how to bargain. I think we can do business with Emperor Leo the Wise."

Tsar Igor stepped forward. "Don't we want the silver, Uncle? You said—"

"Oh, we'll take his silver and more."

"Will we get trading rights without taxes?" It was Farlof, the knight from the Westlands.

"Trading rights, and still more." Oleg turned to the Arab translator. "Tell the emperor we will need more than just his silver. Our ships are full of trading goods. We demand the same privileges as Greek merchants. If the emperor would truly have us as allies instead of rivals, then he must also offer us respect."

"Respect?" Ali lifted an eyebrow.

Groa sensed the Arab's confusion. To him the Vikings were filthy infidels. How was he, a sophisticated medical expert with a crimson vest and pointed shoes, supposed to translate Oleg's demand?

"Respect," Oleg repeated. "Tell the emperor that all Knights of the Varangian Order will be treated in Miklagard as visiting princes, with free room and board while they trade."

"I see." Ali spoke to the emperor in Greek. Groa had the feeling that he was no longer translating Oleg's words precisely.

At length the Arab turned back to Oleg. "The emperor suggests that instead of free room and board it might be a greater sign of respect if he were to offer your knights free access to the public baths."

"Baths?" Oleg frowned. "What are these baths?"

"They are buildings with pools of water inside. Some of the water is hot and some is cold. You wash yourself there."

"Without weapons? Naked? Indoors?" Oleg was not the only warrior to wonder at the absurdity of this proposal. "Tell Leo that our knights want food and bedding."

"I see." Ali relayed this request. Soon he translated Leo's response. "The emperor wishes to know how many knights are in this elite order?"

"Fourteen." It was Farlof again, proudly holding up a silver medallion inscribed with arrow-shaped runes.

"No. Don't translate that." Oleg looked about the crowd of men. His glance fell on Thorkell, the Norwegian captain. "I have been thinking of promoting a few more of the Rus. Our campaign has proved that many of you are worthy. As one of my last acts as regent I intend to expand the Varangian Order."

Thorkell swelled with pride. Was he to become not merely a jarl, but a knight?

Ali asked, "How many knights, then, would you have?"

"Sorceress!" Oleg waved Groa forward. "How many names do you have on your list?"

She unrolled the sheets. "Six hundred and eighty-seven."

"That many, Ali."

The Arab's mouth hung open with incredulity. "You expect Constantinople to treat six hundred and eighty-seven Vikings as visiting princes? Without baths?"

"We'll see about the baths later. For now, just ask Leo if we have a deal. Or should I tell my helmsman to sound the lur-horn signal?"

Ali swallowed. "You would allow your men to destroy the city?"

Oleg put his hand on the hilt of Fenris. "My sword is named for a wolf. It is always hungry for blood."

CHAPTER 24
NOVGOROD, 1962

Fenris howled through the dreams of the world. On the night of October 24, 1962, billions shared the nightmare—red eyes, balls of flame, and the mushroom clouds of death. After a thousand years the dark god had at last been summoned to prowl the Earth. Fenris was hungry for blood.

Black clouds blotted the stars above Novgorod's kremlin square as the Knights of the Varangian Order celebrated the return of Fenris to Oleg's hand. Torches lit red banners with the triple runes of Tyr. Hundreds of hands held up their medallions as Sergei, the blacksmith, welded a giant sword onto the Millennium of Russia monument, the flame of his torch crackling like harnessed lightning.

The crowd chanted, "Hail Rus! Hail Rus! Hail Rus!"

Surrounded by the frenzied throng, heralded as a Viking princess, Helen Gustmeyer was terrified. She didn't understand Russian, but Urmas had translated enough to suggest that Helen had been lured to Novgorod for all the wrong reasons. How had she allowed herself to be caught up in such madness? The people here seemed to belong to a secret order intent on weathering the nuclear war together. And how could she possibly escape? Sweden was a thousand kilometers away, through a landscape that the Cuban crisis might light up with atomic bombs at any moment. She closed her eyes, wishing she could make time run backwards—or perhaps run forward to some safer age.

On the far side of the Millennium monument a very old woman crouched in the darkness, her eyes also closed. Groa had forgotten many of the ancient spells. Her incantations for changing time had never worked very well. Instead she would do her best to summon a different champion, a rival to Fenris.

She chanted Odin's names,

> Grim, Gangleri,
> Herjan, Hjalberi,
> Thekk, Thrithi,
> Thuth, Uth,
> Helblindi, Har,
> Sath, Svipall,
> Sanngetall.

A gust of wind spooked a flock of crows from the trees, croaking like angry frogs. That wasn't right. She would have to try again, but with what? Groa clenched her fists together, trying to remember. And in doing so she felt the ring.

Thorleif's ring. Her first husband had forged the silver band to mark his love. Two entwined dragons, embracing so tightly they seemed as one. Long ago she had hidden the ring in a millstone in Norway. It had waited there for her through the ages. When had she returned to find it? So many of her memories had dimmed with age. But the love in that ring had always been a counterweight, a balance against Fenris' hatred. Thorleif—his name itself meant "Love of Thor." She kissed the old ring now, wishing with all her heart.

The wind gusted again, carrying the last of the trees' leaves away with the crows. The chants of the Varangian Knights grew louder as they piled their torches together in a bonfire. "Hail Rus! Hail Rus! Hail Rus!"

And then there fell a drop of rain. The wind paused, as if gathering its breath. Far to the west, clouds rumbled.

By the bonfire, Professor Henrik Talin touched his hand to the scaly red scar on his bald head. Raindrops began hissing into the fire. Thunder rolled from across the city. "A storm is coming. It's time we moved into the bunkers."

Still standing beside the statue of Oleg, the blacksmith looked up at the dark sky and shook his head. "It's Thor. We've summoned Fenris for the final battle, and the thunder god has heard the call."

Suddenly a crooked flash lit the bare branches of the trees. Seconds passed before the boom arrived. And then the sky opened up, pelting the pavement with rain.

Henrik took hold of Helen's arm. "Let's get to the dungeon."

The blacksmith jumped down from the monument, blocking their way. "You're too old, Talin. The rest of us have agreed, the girl goes

with me." He grabbed Helen's other arm.

"Stop it! Let go!" Although she hadn't understood the blacksmith's Russian words, his ominous tone was clear. Helen managed to jerk her arm loose from the professor. The blacksmith's grip was harder to break. "Let me go!"

The smith guided her grimly across the square toward a basement door with a grille. Helen remembered that prison door—she had seen it in Aunt Sasha's microfilm photos. She struggled. She screamed. Around her the crowd drowned her cries with the chant, "Hail Rus!" Even Urmas smiled and waved, as if she envied Helen's good fortune.

The professor unlocked the door with a large iron key. The blacksmith dragged Helen inside. The door clanged shut to the sound of cheers. And then the crowd quickly dispersed, heading for other basement bunkers.

At length Groa tottered unsteadily from behind the Millennium of Russia monument. Rain dripped from her stringy white hair. Lightning flashed again, but it was no use. The gods she had hoped to summon for help had grown weak. She had failed. Fenris had been  loosed upon the Earth, his evil stronger than ever. Even Helen, the youngest of the Gustmeyer line, was lost.

Groa bent her withered face into her hands and cried.

* * *

A thunderous detonation shook Swarovsky out of his nightmare. All night long, wolves had been devouring the world. They had torn him apart, howling at his protestations that he should be spared. At the sound of the explosion Swarovsky sat up so fast in his hammock that he banged his head on the metal ceiling.

As the young KGB recruiter sat in darkness rubbing his head, the submarine about him still reverberated with the blast. Had the ship been hit by a torpedo? Had they felt the shock wave of a distant nuclear bomb? The air was so stale that he had to breathe with his mouth open. His skin was wet with sweat. Voices began shouting in the corridor.

Swarovsky felt for the light switch, and was relieved when the bulb actually flickered on. Quickly he pulled on his sweat-stained clothes. As soon as he stepped out into the corridor, however, a second explosion staggered him against a bulkhead. The lights stayed on, but the pressure of the blast nearly popped his ears. He hurried toward the bridge.

Captain Savitsky and the other officers of the *B-59* huddled around a bank of control panels. "Damage report?" the captain asked.

"Nothing yet, sir," the first mate replied. "It appears to have been a depth charge."

"I know that," Savitsky snapped. "But it was off target. The American destroyer is a kilometer to starboard. Don't they know where we are?"

Commander Arkhovsky commented, "Have you forgotten about their fleet's aircraft carrier? The depth charges are probably being dropped by an anti-submarine bomber."

Ivan, the political officer, wiped sweat from his mouth. "The bomber must be homing in. The next charge could destroy us."

Savitsky tilted his head. "A jet like that has sonar. If it's a Neptune bomber, the pilot knows exactly where we are."

"Then what's he doing?" Swarovsky should not have dared to interrupt. Now his question hung in the air.

In the past weeks Swarovsky had learned to read the sweeping blips of the sonar screen. Even before turning in last night for some much-needed sleep, he had noticed that their convoy of supply freighters had slowed. Apparently the cargo ships were hesitant to cross the quarantine line, although without radio contact it was hard to know what they were thinking. Savitsky had decided to sail the *B-59* ahead to scout things out. Now their sub had been surrounded by the American carrier fleet.

"Maybe the Americans are knocking on our door," Commander Arkhipov suggested. "They know we're too deep to reach with a radio signal. Maybe they want to talk."

"With depth charges?" Ivan scoffed. "That's a hell of a conversation."

The captain mused, "If the charges really are on target, then they must be small. Just grenades, really."

The political officer shook his head. "An attack is an attack. We've been authorized to respond with the Special Weapon."

"True," the commander said. "Our other choice would be to surface."

"And become a sitting duck for the destroyer's guns?"

"We'll have to surface within a few hours anyway," the captain said. "Our batteries are almost drained. The air system's off. We don't have much time to decide."

"You know what I think?" Ivan asked. "I think World War III has already started. The Americans have invaded Cuba and we've launched Castro's missiles in response. But all our missiles could do was target a few cities. We don't have enough to take out their aircraft carriers. That's a job for a submarine. It's our responsibility."

At that moment a third explosion rocked the ship. This time the blast was louder, and the pressure on their ears more painful.

The political officer pounded his palm with his fist. "That's it. I vote to fire the T-5."

"I agree." Savitsky turned to the first mate. "Turn us to face the fleet. Lock onto the *Randolph*. Prepare to launch the nuclear torpedo."

"One moment, Valentin," the commander said. "This decision requires consensus among the ship's top officers. Normally that would mean just you and Ivan. But this is the flagship of my command, so my vote counts as well."

The captain paused. "All right, Arkhipov. How do you vote?"

The commander took a labored breath. "Have you seen the results of a T-5 detonation?"

"Have you?"

"Yes. The first T-5 test failed. That was in the desert of Kazakhstan. A year later, after tinkering with the warhead, we tried out the T-5 in the Arctic Ocean, off the coast of Novaya Zemlya. We put out three decommissioned submarines as targets. Do you know what a five-kiloton warhead does when it detonates twenty meters underwater?"

The captain shook his head.

"It sends a plume of radioactive water a kilometer straight up. Then the mushroom cloud spreads out."

"What happened to the target subs?"

"Instantly destroyed. At a range of ten kilometers."

The silence on the bridge was broken only by the beep of sonar.

At length the political officer said, "Well, that's our goal, isn't it? To take out the entire carrier fleet?"

"Twelve ships. There are six thousand men on the *USS Randolph* alone. If World War III hasn't started yet, it will when that many Americans die."

The air was so thick it was hard for the officers to breathe, even with their mouths open.

"Our duty is clear," the political officer said. "We have been attacked. We have to respond."

"I still agree," the captain said. "What about you, Commander?"

Arhipov tapped his fingertips together. "The grand inquisitor asks for a decision." Suddenly he turned to Swarovsky. "What do you think, Vasiliy? You have been reading *The Brothers Karamazov*. If there is a God, would you return his ticket to heaven? Would you press the button to hell?"

The young KGB agent swallowed. He had no idea what the commander was talking about. So far the Dostoevsky novel had seemed like a meandering melodrama. Three privileged men were arguing over their inheritance and their girlfriends. Why should he worry about such nonsense? He had just spent a miserable night struggling with a wolf in his dreams. Even now the medallion beneath his uniform shirt burned against his chest, as if to brand him with the angry mark of Tyr. And his hand—what was the strange feeling in his left hand? He had never worn a ring. Now his fourth finger—his ring finger—was tingling. The sensation reminded him: In the past year he had started to consider asking Urmas to marry him. She might not be the prettiest girl in the world. She certainly hadn't seemed that way at first. But love kept creeping into his thoughts. Dreams battled against nightmares. The fate of the world was suspended by a thread. And his own fate was held by nothing more than the footfalls of cats and the breath of fish.

"Vasiliy?" the commander asked.

CHAPTER 25
CONSTANTINOPLE, 907

Sunlight slanted from a hundred arched windows across the cavernous nave of the Saint Sophia cathedral. Everywhere rays shimmered from the gold leaf of tiled mosaics, bathing the enormous hall in the golden glow of heaven—or perhaps Valhalla.

Ali Ibn al-Namid looked about at the men crowding the marble floor and the colonnaded balconies—more than a thousand Viking warriors and Byzantine dignitaries—and he cursed his own failure. His mission had been to twist the words of Regent Oleg and Emperor Leo to provoke them into battle. The wisdom of the Voice, his unseen Cordovan overlord, had brought a Varangian army to the poorly defended gates of Constantinople. The plan had been to ravage the Christian capital with a lightning bolt out of clear skies—an armada of infidels conjured from the northern wastes. Meanwhile a suicidal war of succession was consuming the Abbasid Caliphate to the south. Soon the way would be clear for a new, truer caliphate to arise in the west, bringing the Prophet's holy word to a world at its feet.

All of those plans had been undone by the word of a woman. Ali squinted across the cathedral's altar at Groa, the backwoods medicinalist from Novgorod. Her demonic, mismatched eyes seemed to see the invisible. Two days ago, in the Strategion plaza, the Viking regent had been about to sound the trumpets that would bring down Constantinople's walls. Ali had translated Emperor Leo's response as "We deny consideration of your demands."

Oleg had angrily lifted his hand to signal his armies when Groa had called out, "Wait!"

"Why wait, sorceress?" Oleg had asked.

"I suspect the translation may be faulty."

"Do you speak Greek?"

"No," Groa admitted. "But Farlof does. What did you hear the emperor say, Knight?"

The Westland chieftain hesitated, "It was hard to hear clearly. Many Greek words sound much the same. But I believe the emperor actually said, "We *deign* to consider your demands."

Ali clapped his hand to his mouth in mock horror. "Is this true? A thousand pardons! Greek is a difficult language, Regent."

And so, instead of a battle, the confrontation in the plaza had concluded with an alliance. Leo had agreed to grant nearly all of Oleg's demands. In exchange the Viking fleet would retreat to an encampment in the Diplokionion fields north of the Golden Horn. More than six hundred newly ennobled Varangian Knights would be offered free lodging within the city. In addition, Emperor Leo promised to give them the option of hiring on as mercenaries for the Byzantines. Leo had been so impressed by the warriors of the Rus that he proposed to demote his own Imperial Guard to the reserves and to replace them with a "Varangian Guard." Instead of sacking Constantinople, the barbarian warriors were to become the emperor's private shock troops!

And now, beneath the echoing dome of the largest building on Earth, the Varangians and the Byzantines were about to seal their friendship with a formal treaty. But all was not yet lost. The Voice had assured Ali that he had a longer-range plan, a backup strategy that depended on acquiring the cursed sword. If Ali failed a second time, there would be no third chance.

The treaty itself had been written in Greek on a large calfskin parchment. To fit in all of the terms the script was so small that the church patrician had to squint in the dim golden light. There were laughs from the balconies when he mispronounced Norse names, transcribed rather roughly from the runes of Groa's original list.

"Swearing to this pact are Oteg, Igon, Thor-kill, Rulav, Stemir, Far-off, Frost, Gunner, Milo-bitch—"

"That's enough," Oleg cut in. "We get the idea. Shall we seal this treaty with our blood?"

Ali translated this into Greek as badly as he dared, hoping to suggest a sword fight. But Farlof was now listening so he could translate the other way, and it was harder to introduce errors.

Leo shook his head. "We are not becoming blood brothers, just trading partners. To seal our agreement we Christians will swear by the Holy Bible in the presence of God Almighty. You of the Rus may swear by whatever relics or gods you hold most sacred."

After Farlof had translated this Oleg unbuckled his sword belt and placed the sheath on the altar. "I swear by my sword Fenris, and by the gods that have watched over me all these years—Odin, the all-seeing All-Father, Thor the thunder god, and Tyr, master of warfare."

The thirteen other original Varangian Knights followed Oleg's example, swearing by their weapons and by their gods of choice. When they were done they turned to Igor, the self-proclaimed tsar.

"Well, Nephew?" Oleg asked. "Will you not also swear?"

The young tsar clasped his hands together, thinking. "What should I swear by? I brought no weapon to this ceremony. I'm not even sure that the gods of the north have followed us here. I prefer to wait to see how our Byzantine counterparts will swear."

When Ali translated this into Greek, General Petrion of the Imperial Reserves scoffed, "You see, Your Eminence? The barbarian leader refuses to swear. He is planning deceit."

"Or he's cautious," Leo replied. "A man who sells his horse wants to see some silver before letting go of the reins."

"But we've already shown them the silver, Your Eminence."

"It's an expression, you idiot." The emperor waved to the church patrician. "Commence our part of the ceremony."

Wearing a black cylindrical hat and a long white beard, the old holy man took an incense burner from a brazier and swung it on a chain above the parchment. In a nearby apse a semicircle of bald monks began singing a chant-like hymn in minor tones. Smoke from the censor rose in a bluish plume. The incense spread the sweet, earthy musk of a tomb. The monks' echoing song could have been the call of spirits from beyond the grave.

Tsar Igor watched the smoky apparition rise through the arms of a chandelier into the nave's golden dome. Groa could sense that he was shivering inside. What was he afraid of now?

The emperor opened a gold-bound Bible on the altar, placed his palm on a page, and looked up through the wispy smoke to the *pantocrater*—a gold mosaic of Jesus Christ arching across the dome.

"I, Leo the Sixth, Emperor of Byzantium, swear to uphold the treaty we have concluded with our Varangian guests from Russiya." He turned to the patrician.

The aged cleric dipped two fingers into a basin of holy water and touched the emperor's forehead. "*In nomine patris et filii et spiritus sancti, amen.*"

General Petrion and a dozen other dignitaries repeated the ritual one by one, each choosing to place their palm on a different page in the Bible. When they were done the monks stopped their mournful chant.

Leo held out his hand to Igor, encouraging him to endorse the treaty.

The young tsar looked about, scanning the faces of the hundreds of Varangian warriors in the balconies, and he spoke in Norse to them.

"Men of the Rus! Since my father's death I have been your leader in name only. Russiya has been ruled by a regent, my Uncle Oleg. Today, with this treaty, Oleg's regency ends. Now I will truly become your tsar. The treaty gives each of you silver and the opportunity to earn more through trade. For those of you who are Knights of the Varangian Order, Miklagard is no more. From now on, honoring the customs of the people here, you will call it Constantinople. For those of you who choose to serve in the emperor's guard, this city will become a second home. But you will always be bound by a higher order—the Order of the Varangian Knights."

When Igor paused one of the men in the balcony shouted, "Hail Rus!" Soon others took up the chant. Before long the great dome thundered with the voices of Vikings.

"Hail Rus! Hail Rus! Hail Rus!"

Men stamped their feet until the walls trembled and the chandelier in the central dome began to swing. The church patrician retreated toward a pillar, his eyes white with the fear that this foreign horde might destroy his cathedral after all.

"Enough!" Oleg shouted. The old Viking raised his hands for silence, as he had done so often before.

But this time when the crowd quieted, it was the tsar who spoke, shaking his head. "Put down your hands, Uncle. Your saga is over."

"Over?" Oleg's voice betrayed both uncertainty and a touch of anger. "And how does your saga begin, Tsar? You have not yet sworn to the treaty."

Igor pointed to the altar, with Fenris at one end and the Bible at the other. "The start of a new Russiyan saga is the start of a new age.

I want nothing to do with your sword, Uncle, and its dark stories. In Constantinople I have seen the marvels of a brighter world."

Igor looked up at the *pantocrater* mosaic—a haloed man with a hand raised in peace. "Are the gods here so different from the ones in the north? Odin once hanged himself in a tree for wisdom. I'm told the Christian god was hanged in a tree as well. They call this temple Saint Sophia—holy wisdom. Someday I would like to build a hall of holy wisdom in Russiya as grand as this."

Ali translated only this last sentence, having neither the time nor the desire to convert the rest of the infidel's ramblings into Greek.

The church patrician nodded approvingly. But Groa—and everyone else—was left wondering if the tsar intended to endorse the treaty or not.

Igor walked around the altar. He passed by the sheath of Fenris. Then he stopped before the Bible. He boldly placed his hand on the parchment page and announced, "I swear to our treaty by the god of holy wisdom."

Shouts of outrage resounded from the Varangians in the balconies. The tumult grew even louder when the church patrician dipped his fingers into the basin of holy water and anointed Tsar Igor on the forehead.

Was the tsar suggesting that he would convert to Christianity? Would he expect the rest of Russiya to betray its faith as well? The prospect was unimaginable! Everyone knew how vengeful the Norse gods could be when angered.

Men surged down spiral stairs from the balconies. Oleg and the others on the main floor held them away from the tsar. Meanwhile the Byzantine entourage retreated with the Bible, the treaty, and the emperor.

Leo paused to take a last look at the chaos in the cathedral. Then he shook his head and made his way through a door that led to the calm of a monastic cloister.

Desperate to restore order, Oleg reached for the sword on the altar. But a small white hand caught his wrist with an improbably firm grip.

"Leave Fenris," Groa said.

"But—"

"Turn aside from violence, Oleg." With her other hand she withdrew a small dagger from the waist of her tunic. She flipped the blade in the air and caught it by the tip without drawing blood—a remarkable feat. Now the sharp little knife was poised to be thrown. "You owe me a life, Oleg. You promised that we would trade knives."

"Groa, I—"

"Fenris must be destroyed."

The old Viking's massive shoulders sagged. Behind him the shouting and shoving had ebbed. Calmer voices were telling the men that the tsar had merely meant to honor local custom, and was assuredly not abandoning the Norse gods. The treaty had been ratified, granting knights trading privileges. Whoever brought their trade goods to market first might get the best price. Or would they rather stay here to argue about religion?

Oleg slowly withdrew his hand from the sheathed sword on the altar, although the effort seemed to take all his strength. "What will I do with myself, Groa? For twenty-five years I have lived as a warrior king. With Fenris by my side I have never known defeat."

Groa shook her head. "Those victories were not yours. You have been a regent not just to Igor, but also to a dark god. The only victory that is truly yours is this one now—letting Fenris go."

He took the dagger from her hand. Smiling weakly, he held the blade against his palm. "This knife's hilt has the same pattern as my ring. Such an old-fashioned style. It was what Helga wanted. Two dragons."

"Embracing each other so tightly that it's hard to tell where one begins and the other ends." Groa put her hand on the altar between Oleg and the sheath of Fenris.

"Marrying Helga was the happiest day of my life," Oleg mused. "And it was followed by the worst, the day the fighting began."

"Maybe you should go back. Before the fighting."

"To Sweden?" Oleg frowned. "You can't turn back time."

Groa wasn't entirely sure of this, having once somehow bent the passage of time herself. She shifted the subject to more familiar ground. "If you stay in Russiya the tsar will always see you as a rival. You have to let him make his own mistakes, and hope that he will learn from them. Why not go back to Sweden?"

Oleg laughed. "Among other things, there is the matter of a king we killed."

"Since then you have ruled a bigger realm than old King Eirik ever knew. Your wealth and saga fame would smooth your path. In order to return to your happiest memories you may need to face down your darkest ones."

Oleg tightened his lips, willing himself not to intervene as Groa took the sheathed sword from the altar. "What about you, sorceress? If I recall there was once a beautiful young woman who suddenly wanted to leave Norway on the first ship she could find. What unfinished business did you leave behind? If I go, would you dare to sail back too?"

Groa was just opening her mouth, unsure how to answer this challenge, when a voice interrupted.

"Women aren't allowed to carry swords in Constantinople!" It was Ali, the Arab doctor, hopping from foot to foot as if his pointed shoes were on fire.

"They're not?"

"Of course not." This wasn't exactly true, but it suited Ali's purpose. "Here, let me take it."

Groa jerked the sword away from his outstretched hand. To Oleg she said, "We will talk about this later." Then she hurried through the cathedral's crowds to the door where Hrolf had said he would be waiting. Ali followed behind, calling for her to wait.

Outside in the market square, a vast plaza flanked by the Imperial palace and the baths of Zeuxippos, Hrolf stood up wearily from a marble bench. He had spent a long morning searching the city's markets for the two things he had hoped to find in Constantinople. He had learned that they could not be purchased for two dirhams—or even for four, if he used Groa's share of the silver too. Everyone said he would have to look in the Arab Quarter, and that he would need to offer a much greater treasure.

Groa nearly stumbled in her haste to thrust the sheathed sword into Hrolf's hands. "Quick, strap on the belt."

"Is this—?"

"Fenris, yes. Keep it safe. I'm told women aren't allowed to carry swords in the city."

Ali caught up with them, all smiles. "Oh there you are, Groa and Hr—Hr—" He hesitated to make the vomiting sound of the woodworker's name. "Groa's husband. I have such fond memories of my visit to your shipyard in Novgorod. You are a man of many talents."

"Not as many as I'd like," Hrolf admitted glumly.

Groa cast him a questioning look. This was a curious thing for her husband to say. And once again his thoughts were barricaded behind an opaque wall.

"Is there something you desire?" Ali asked. "Constantinople is a city of endless possibilities."

Hrolf said nothing, his expression as blank as an uncarved block.

Groa, however, said, "What we really need is a forge."

"A forge?"

"A fire hot enough to melt steel." She tried not to look at the sword, but her green eye twitched.

"I see." Ali stroked his bare chin. "Today is a Christian holy day—honoring one of their countless saints—so the Christian forges are cold. Those smiths are on the far side of the city anyway. The only forge fires you will find today are near the Eugenios Gate."

"In the Arab Quarter?" Hrolf asked.

"That's right. Not far from where your ship is docked."

Groa didn't trust him, but they would have to go in that direction anyway to reach the ship. It would be safer in the company of a local.

"Let's go, then," she said.

As they walked through the acropolis in the old section of the city Ali chattered on amiably, asking them about their voyage from Novgorod. He chuckled when Hrolf admitted that he hadn't immediately guessed the reason for building hundreds of ladders as "trade goods."

"You really could sell them," the Arab said. "But they're too long to be practical in cramped quarters. You'll want to saw them in half."

"I can't," Hrolf replied. "I lost my tools in the Dnieper rapids."

"What a tragedy! I remember you were almost as proud of your tools as you are of your lovely wife. In Novgorod you even wished—" Ali cut himself short with a wave of his hand. "But enough of that. Did you know I have become the personal masseur of Emperor Leo?"

"Masseur?" Groa asked. "What does that mean?"

"It means I have to rub him all over with olive oil."

Groa looked at him askance. "I don't suppose you bleed him, as you did Queen Danuta?"

"Goodness, no. The emperor is quite healthy. Just tense. It helps if I ease the strain from his muscles. Sometimes his secrets slip out as well."

Ali led them down a narrow stone stairway in an alley so crowded by whitewashed walls and balconies that the sky was little more than a jagged blue stripe overhead. He pointed to a low wooden door in passing. "The forge is in the courtyard of the blacksmith shop here. But first I will introduce you at the women's quarters next door."

"Why?" Groa asked.

"Why what?" Ali rapped on a narrower door. A metal plate slid sideways, revealing two eyes carefully lined with shadow. He spoke in Arabic to the woman inside. She opened the door a crack, revealing that her head and body were entirely cloaked in a gray shroud. She motioned for Groa to quickly come in.

"Where does this woman want me to go?" Groa demanded.

Ali looked puzzled. "Well, you can't go into a blacksmith shop. And you certainly can't stay on the street by yourself."

"Why not?"

Ali clapped his hands to the sides of his bald brown head as if it might explode. "You are in the Arab Quarter! It is sacrilege enough that you have been wandering around with your hair exposed. It would be impossible for a woman to walk into the shop of a strange, half-naked blacksmith. And Allah would strike you dead if you were seen alone on the street without the company of a male relative."

"I'll take my chances."

"No, you will not." Ali shook his head vehemently.

"Then we'll wait until the Christian blacksmiths are back at work." She crossed her arms and glared at him.

After a moment Hrolf put his hand on his wife's shoulder. "Let me deal with this, my love. I know you want to be rid of the sword as soon as you can. Trust me to do it for you."

Groa's mood softened at her husband's touch. If anyone could resist the wolf god, it was Hrolf. He might be gullible—even simple at times—but no one was more sincere, more reliable. Everything Hrolf did was from love.

"You promise, you'll have the sword melted down?"

"I promise." He kissed her on the cheek. "Let me do this, for both of us."

The shrouded woman in the doorway motioned again for Groa to come in off the street.

"All right," Groa said. She lingered in the doorway while Ali went back to the blacksmith's door. He rapped in a peculiar way—three times, then twice, then once. Only after the low door had opened and Ali had ducked inside with Hrolf did Groa turn to see what kind of quarters had been set aside for Arab women.

Carpets? There were carpets on the floor and the walls. More carpets hung as dividers between the entry and a second, better lit room. There, half a dozen scantily clad women sat cross legged amidst piles of colored yarn, giggling at her. Obviously Arab women did not wear shrouds amongst themselves. Apparently they drank tea while using little hooks to stitch tufts of wool into exuberant patterns of stylized gardens. The woman who had answered the door took off her shroud and poured Groa a small glass of hot tea. Unable to thank her in Arabic, and not knowing what else to do while she waited for Hrolf, Groa decided that she might as well learn how to hook rugs.

Meanwhile Hrolf had been confronted by a blacksmith who was every bit as ugly, muscular, and taciturn as himself. The big, sweaty smith led the way through a dark room to a courtyard where two boys were pumping the bellows of a smoky forge. Metal bars glowed red in the shimmering heat. Chains and scimitars hung on either hand of the little courtyard. Blue smoke drifted up four stories to a hazy sky.

Was Hrolf trembling, or was it the sword itself? For the first time in more than a century, Fenris faced a fire that might destroy it. Even gods have bad days, and this threatened to be the worst.

Hrolf began to draw the sword from its sheath, but Ali stopped him. "Not yet. Norse steel is so valuable. Constantinople is full of valuable things, if you know where to look."

"What kinds of valuable things?"

"I once told you that this city has wizards who can offer wonders. Would you like to speak with one of them now?"

Silently Hrolf nodded. And just as silently, Ali led the way up the staircase that wound about the courtyard for four stories. At the top, although Hrolf was short of breath, he gasped at the sight of the most beautiful wooden door he had ever seen, entirely covered with delicate geometric inlaid

patterns. So many tiny pieces! So many colors! Black, brown, bluish, red, yellow—and yes, even the white of Russiyan birch. The wood-worker ran his callused hand over the unbelievable artwork as if he were stroking the fur of a unicorn.

But Ali merely rapped on the door—once, twice, and then three times. Hrolf frowned when there was no reply. Ali held up his hand for patience. Eventually a deep voice from inside said a single word in a language Hrolf did not know.

"The Voice says to enter," Ali explained. He pressed a hidden latch among the inlay and pushed the door open. "After you, master ship-wright."

Hrolf ventured cautiously into the strangest and yet most beauti-ful room he had ever seen. It resembled a gigantic jewel box, entirely made of intricately carved wood. The floor was a herringbone parquet of polished oak blocks, fitted in diagonal patterns. The coffered wood-en ceiling was even more astonishing—completely hung with wooden spires that suggested the stalactites of a cave. And the walls consisted of wooden shelves lined with row after row of what looked like leather bricks.

"What is this place?" Hrolf asked.

"A library. It is a storehouse of wisdom."

"Like the cathedral?"

"Better," Ali replied, taking one of the big leather bricks down from a shelf. "Saint Sophia merely celebrates wisdom. A library actually contains it. The knowledge of the world is here in books."

As Hrolf watched in amazement, Ali set the leather brick on a round table, pulled the edges apart, and laid it flat. Inside were hundreds of paper leaves—like the stack Groa had used for the list, but sewn together between leather boards. Rows of black squiggles covered each page.

Hrolf touched the page with awe. "Are these runes in Greek?"

"Arabic, actually. My master's library has works in Greek, Latin—dozens of languages."

"Who is your master?" Hrolf looked about. "Where is the person who asked us to enter?"

"I don't know, exactly. I have never seen the sorcerer. He is known to me only as the Voice."

"Then tell him to speak."

After Ali translated this demand a low voice filled the room with a language Hrolf did not know. The woodworker cocked his head, listening, but could not figure out which direction the voice was coming from. Was it behind the bookshelves or above the pinnacled ceiling? At times the voice seemed to emanate from a large black ball spangled with silver stars—or even from the book on the table. The wooden room reverberated on all sides like a musical instrument.

When the Voice stopped, Hrolf asked, "What did he say?"

"He says that you have been to many markets today, asking for miracles."

"How does he know that?"

Ali shrugged. "Just as my master has an unseen mouth, he has unseen ears."

Hrolf sighed. "Well, it's true. I had imagined—I had hoped—that I might find what I am looking for in such a great city."

The Voice spoke again, and Ali translated. "Your wish is not for yourself. Heaven smiles on seekers of knowledge who want to help others. In this case, your wife."

Hrolf lowered his head. "I have never deserved Groa. When we met I was the ugliest, clumsiest carpenter in Norway and she was the most beautiful girl in the world. And yet she has rowed beside me all these years. I am an unskilled laborer. Worst of all, I have failed her in love. I have failed her as a man."

Ali tilted his head. "The Voice is a powerful sorcerer. He may be able to offer assistance."

Hrolf looked up skeptically.

Ali spoke with the Voice in Arabic. When the Voice fell silent Ali fetched a stool from a corner. He climbed to the topmost shelf and took down a thick book bound in red leather. He set it on the table next to the first book.

"Open it, woodworker."

"But I can't read runes."

"Just open it."

Hrolf lifted the book's cover—and was surprised to discover that it was actually a box, cleverly carved and painted to resemble a book. Inside, instead of paper leaves, was a hollow filled with folds of black velvet. A small glass vial was wrapped inside the cloth.

"What is this?" Hrolf lifted the tiny bottle, marveling that the greenish liquid inside glowed like the eye of a night animal.

"You and your wife want a child?"

"Yes. A daughter."

"A daughter?" Ali frowned. "Who would choose a daughter instead of a son?"

"Groa would. I've heard her talking in her sleep. She wants a daughter."

"Why?"

Hrolf shook his head. "I've tried to ask her during the day. Our people generally pass on their property to their sons. But Groa believes more important strengths may be inherited through the female line." He set the vial back in the box. "With me as her husband, Groa has been unable to produce any children at all."

Ali spoke for a while with the Voice. Then he switched back to Norse. "My master invites you to look deeper inside this book of knowledge."

Hrolf set the vial aside and pulled the velvet from the hollow book. Underneath was a thin panel, and beneath that a second chamber stuffed with black cloth. Wrapped inside was a smaller vial filled with red liquid. It might have been blood, except that it too glowed. If the green bottle had resembled the eye of a night animal, this one burned like the eye of a demon.

"Is it—?" Hrolf didn't dare ask aloud.

"Yes," Ali said. "Drinking some of this before lying down with

284

your wife will produce a daughter, if such a thing is possible."

"What do you mean, 'possible'?"

Ali shrugged. "How old is your wife?"

"Forty-four winters, I think." He wasn't really sure.

"You see? I am a doctor. I know that this is the age when it can become too late for women to bear children. My master offers no promises, other than this: With this potion, it will not be your fault."

Hrolf tightened his lips. "And what is your price for this sorcery?"

Ali waved his hand toward the sword at Hrolf's belt. "The Voice would relieve you of a burden."

"No. I promised Groa that I would melt Fenris down."

"Oh, we would melt the sword down. As I said, Norse steel is very valuable."

"You would destroy the sword? You'd promise to melt it in the forge?"

"Yes." Ali hesitated. "The sword would be destroyed, as such. That's what you promised Groa. But I'm sure even she would not want the steel to be wasted. It would be reforged for other purposes."

"I see."

"Then perhaps we have a deal after all. Or should I reshelve the sorcerer's book?"

Hrolf had always prided himself that his stony expression was hard for others to read. But this time the intensity of his internal battle made his brow wrinkle and his lips quiver. Enabling Groa to bear a daughter would be the greatest proof of his love. The guilt of his own inadequacy—a fear that had weighed upon him for years—would finally be lifted. But what if the potion didn't work? Groa was older than most mothers. And she often chided him for his gullibility. If she were here now, in this magical library, might she scoff at the deception of the Voice?

"No," Hrolf said, setting the red vial reluctantly back into the hollow book. "I'm afraid my answer is still no."

Ali held up a palm. "Wait. There is another part to our offer."

"I don't think—" Hrolf began.

But Ali cut him short, opening the library's outer door and shouting, "Akhbar!" The rest of what he called down into the courtyard was unintelligible to Hrolf.

Soon heavy footsteps began echoing on the courtyard stairs. The sound thumped louder with each story. Suddenly Hrolf realized he was trapped. No one would hear if he called out for help—even Groa was too far away. He put his hand on the hilt of Fenris. After all the tales about this ancient Viking sword, did he dare to use it to fight his way free? Or would it be the other way—would Fenris be using him?

The library had no other exit. When the heavy footsteps reached the landing outside, Hrolf drew the sword out of its sheath. At the same moment the door swung wide. The blacksmith filled the frame, his muscles glistening with sweat. Hrolf had half expected him to be brandishing a huge, curved scimitar. Instead he was carrying a wooden box by a leather strap over his shoulder.

Ali and the blacksmith were both looking at the sword in Hrolf's hands. Even Hrolf had never seen Fenris this close before. Wavy bands of gray and silver revealed that the blade had been forged from many twisted rods of steel. A faintly etched pattern depicted Thor and a wolf. Cut more deeply into the blade were the runes: FENRIS. Hrolf couldn't help thinking that the sword was a thing of beauty—a work of art.

Ali arched an eyebrow higher on his bald head. "It would be a pity, carpenter, to slaughter the blacksmith who brings you tools."

"Tools?" Hrolf lowered the sword.

The smith hefted the strap from his shoulder and swung the wooden chest to the parquet floor. Then he knelt behind it, pressing his palms and his face to the floor in obeisance to an unseen lord.

The Voice spoke—strange, guttural syllables that made the hair on Hrolf's back stand on end.

The blacksmith crept backwards to the doorway, his face still pressed to the floor.

Ali tapped the wooden box with the tip of his pointed shoe. "Open it, carpenter."

The plain pine chest was no larger than the sea chests of the Vikings, cheaply hammered together with square nails. Age and use had darkened the wood and left it dented. But the brass key protruding from the lock was decorated with intricate silver filigree.

Hrolf went down on one knee and laid Fenris on the floor. Then he turned the box's key and lifted the lid.

Inside was a world of dreams. Hrolf marveled at the cleverness of this trick. The chests' ordinary exterior had been a disguise. The interior was a miracle of artistic skill. Every surface had been inlaid with delicate patterns of rare woods, ivory, and silver. Large slots to the right held tools Hrolf could recognize—planes, saws, chisels, drills, and hammers—although they were small and the workmanship was foreign. Stacked on the left were thin sheets of exotically colored wood. In the middle a brass compartment opened to reveal the tiny tools of elves. Hrolf lifted out a saw no larger than his thumb.

"What is this?" Hrolf shook his head in wonder.

"It is the tool chest of an Arab inlay master. With this you could turn a Viking ship into a Damascus jewel box."

Hrolf sat back on his heels. "And the price for this is Fenris?"

"No. I'm afraid your sword is not enough."

Hrolf's heart sank. How had these Arabs known precisely what he wanted, and precisely how impossible it would be for him to acquire?"

The Voice spoke again, this time with the tone of a bargainer in a bazaar.

Ali nodded before translating. "My master is sympathetic to your plight. Because your motives are pure, he is prepared to suggest a combined offer."

Hrolf stood up. "What is this offer?"

"If you trade the sword for the vial, you may purchase the tool chest for two silver dirhams."

"Two coins!" Hrolf laughed out loud. It was a ridiculously low price. The Arabs must realize that the tools alone were worth ten times that much—if such treasures could be bought at all. But then Hrolf considered that the ordinary-looking chest had been disguised to appear worth even less than two silver coins. Sailing back to Novgorod, Thorkell's crew would laugh, thinking that the simple woodworker had spent his pay unwisely. Only Groa would know how much he really loved her. And sooner or later he would tell her the whole truth.

"Well?" Ali asked. "Do we have a deal?"

CHAPTER 26
NOVGOROD, 1962

Groa wasn't sure how long she stood in Novgorod's kremlin square that night, alone in the dark, tormented by her failure. The Knights of the Varangian Order had celebrated the reinstatement of Fenris. They had taken Helen captive. The battle to end the world had begun. Groa had decided she might as well catch her death of cold, if such a thing were possible.

Eventually, however, the rainstorm passed and an old man shuffled across the wet cobblestones, supporting himself with a cane. The dark figure twisted his hunched neck to look about, evidently confused. To his right were the sodden ashes of a bonfire. To the left, a kremlin wall. And directly in front of him an old woman stood dripping wet, a statue of despair.

"Pardon me," the old man said. "Does this city's kremlin have a dungeon?"

The man's Russian was clumsy. The words were tinted with the lilting accent of the old North. His shoulders were bent, but broad. His scraggly beard was gray. Despite the dark, his eyes were bright. On a hunch, Groa responded in Swedish.

"Have you come for Helen?"

The old man looked at her more closely. The flickering light of a half-broken streetlamp reflected green in her eyes, as well as blue. The old man sucked in his breath.

Groa asked, "Were you summoned?"

If gods could age, this might be what the thunderer would look like now. Or did the old man actually resemble her first husband? If only that clever old smith were somehow able to walk among the living again! Thor and Thorleif—she had always had a weakness for men who knew how to hold a hammer.

The man's lips opened, but he did not speak.

"Who are you?" Groa tried reaching into the old man's mind, but found layer upon layer of masks.

When he finally spoke, it was a whisper in Swedish. "Is she safe?"

"No, she isn't safe." Groa put her hands on her hips. "Helen Gustmeyer is locked in a basement on the other side of this square. She's being held by a neo-fascist professor and a fanatical blacksmith who think they can outlive the end of the world."

The old man followed her gaze. The door across the square had a massive lock and an iron grille. He nodded. "Hold my cane. I'll be back."

He walked away, leaving Groa as lost as ever. The man's cane was an ordinary black stick. She thought it might serve as a cudgel, if need be. Once, long ago, she had been handy with a well-balanced throwing knife. She wished she had one now, in case the mysterious man actually did return, and brought trouble.

Eventually a pair of headlights wobbled through the kremlin gate from the direction of Novgorod's business district. The car noisily putt-putted across the square and stopped with its engine still running. The old man got out. He began carrying something toward the dungeon door.

Groa hobbled closer, leaning on the cane. She found the man tying a rope to the door's iron bars.

"When they come out," he said, still in Swedish, "do what you can to trip up the professor. And tell Helen her pen pal is here."

"Her pen pal?" Groa repeated.

"An imaginary one, I'm afraid." The old man returned to the car. It was an ugly, boxy little sedan that sputtered like a badly tuned motorcycle when he gunned the motor. The headlights brightened. Then he popped the clutch and the car jerked forward like a startled rabbit. It was gaining some speed, heading toward the Millennium monument, when the rope behind it suddenly sang taut. An instant later the dungeon door ripped off its hinges. The car swerved onward, just missing the monument. The door bounced behind at the end of the rope, scattering sparks off the cobblestones.

Professor Talin was the first to come running out of the doorway.

Taking the advice of the "pen pal," Groa held the cane in front of the professor's feet. He tumbled onto the wet pavement. Groa decided it might be a good idea to hit the professor a few times with the stick, just to make sure he stayed down.

Sergei emerged from the broken doorway with more caution, wrapping a chain around the knuckles of his right fist. He took in the chaotic scene—the professor on the ground, Agent Veliky dripping wet, and a car careening around the Millennium monument. He muttered, "блядь."

When Helen peered out of the doorway the blacksmith quickly turned to bar her path. With the broad stance of a soccer goalie, he held out his massive arms. "Stay! You are mine."

Helen took a step toward the big man. And then, as if she were an opposing goalie booting a soccer ball the length of the field, she swung up her foot, kicking him in the groin.

The smith collapsed, writhing with his hands on his pants.

"Who's the crazy guy in the car?" Helen asked. The sedan was taking a second lap around the monument. The door behind it had swept an arc clear of trash bins and benches.

Groa stopped clubbing the professor. "He says he's your imaginary pen pal."

"Oh!" Helen brightened. "Lennart?"

"Who?"

The car slewed up beside them, its passenger door flopping open. Helen peered inside. "What the hell? You're not—"

"Get in, babe!" The old man's voice was suddenly half an octave higher.

"Hey, that's my Trabant!" the professor cried.

Helen got in, and the car started off. But before Helen could close the door Groa leapt in on top of her. For a few seconds the car veered around the square like a vodka tippler. Helen shouted, Groa squirmed toward the back seat, and the driver struggled to regain control.

When Groa finally wrenched herself upright the car was headed toward the town gate—but that portal was now blocked by a police car.

"Turn!" Helen cried.

The driver veered the car around the monument one more time. Then he aimed for the kremlin's other gate.

"That's a pedestrian bridge," Groa objected.

"Not anymore." The driver gunned the car through the arch. Beyond were bollards designed to stop cars from reaching the footpath over the Volkhov River. The car scraped both its sides on the posts. A man with a dog on a leash jumped onto the bridge railing. The door dragging behind the car caught sideways between bollards and broke loose with a bang.

"Glad to get rid of that," the driver said.

"We also lost the car's bumper," Helen said.

Groa looked out the back window. "And our license plate."

"Not so good," the driver admitted. He managed to steer the car across the narrow river bridge, through a row of bushes, and onto a road on the far shore. Finally he pulled over beneath a streetlamp, the motor still running.

"So, how are we doing? Helen, are you OK?"

She pulled the blond hair out of her face. "Yeah, I guess. How'd you get here, Lenny?"

The driver peeled off his mustache and beard, revealing a much younger face. "I wanted to tell you before, but I couldn't. I'm with the Swedish security police."

"You're a *Swedish* spy?" Helen laughed. "The Communist skateboarder? The Beatles guitarist? Was that just a joke for you?"

"No," Lennart said. "I really am a Communist. And trying to be your boyfriend has never been a joke."

"But all this time you've been like, with the Swedish CIA?"

"Sort of. I was a trainee. With everything that's happened I got promoted. It turns out my mentor, Colonel Wennerström, was spying for the Russians all along. And then you mailed me this weird pen pal letter that sent me here."

"Wow." Helen put her hand on his.

"What I want to know," Lennart continued, "Is why you've been hanging out with our old museum tour guide from Berlin."

Lennart and Helen both turned around to look at Groa in the back seat.

"Yeah," Helen said. "What's with that?"

Groa straightened the damp sleeves of her black dress. "Consider me an old friend. I once had a husband who said, 'She may be of more use than you think.'"

"Not an answer," Lennart said. "Tell us who you are or get out of the car."

Groa sighed. "Call me Frau Osterberg, or Fru Hansen, or Lifu, or Groa. I don't care. Just trust me. I'm on your side. You need all the help you can get."

Helen squinted at her. "Your picture was in the microfilms of the Varangian Order's meeting last year. Are you one of them?"

"Yes and no. Is that good enough?" Groa shook her head. "I'm too tired to make up more lies."

Helen and Lennart weighed this confession.

Groa said, "By the way, do you two have some sort of escape plan? We're in the middle of Russia, nuclear bombs may start falling, and the Varangian Order is going to send half the Soviet police force after us."

"Good points," Lennart said. "I'm an expert on rock music. Not so great yet with the espionage stuff. Any ideas?"

Helen said, "Our hitchhiker here claims to be useful. What skills has she got?"

Groa shrugged. "Sometimes I can see the future. On a good day I can slow the pace of time. I wonder if that would help?"

Given her luck with spells, Groa no longer hoped to defeat the Varangian Order. She had failed to confound their plans to rearrange the world. But she felt so protective of these two young people — Helen and Lennart, hopelessly over their heads in trouble — that she dared to conjure a wish.

* * *

There are tipping points in history, fragile moments when even a wish might change the course of great events.

Time seemed to slow down, paused as if lost in a fog, while President John F. Kennedy, Premier Nikita Khrushchev, and a Soviet submarine captain beneath the Atlantic each prepared to give the command that would launch nuclear war.

In Moscow, Sasha Andersen watched the clock in the cavernous lobby of the Kazansky Railway Station. Was it her imagination, or was the second hand ticking ever slower as her meeting with Petra Barents approached? Half an hour earlier the Kremlin secretary had frantically

292

called the Intourist travel office to say that she had changed her mind. She wanted a ticket on the Trans-Siberian Express after all. Sasha must meet her at the Kazansky station in person at noon under the big clock. Everything in the world depended on it. She must not be late!

The clock's hands pointed to 11:59. *Tick, tick, . . . tick, ... tick*

A gigantic chandelier hung above her, suspended from the lobby's cathedral-like tower. Near the top, shafts of light from dozens of arched windows cast rays across golden walls. The station reminded her of Saint Sophia, a mosque she had once visited in Turkey. That hall had been built as a gateway to Heaven. This one was the gateway to Siberia. Both stood as portals to the end of the world, where time meant nothing.

Tick . . . . tick!

"Mrs. Andersen?"

Sasha turned around, startled. "Oh, Miss Barents, it's you."

"Do you have my ticket?"

Sasha fumbled in her purse, and then held out an envelope. "The train's boarding already. You'll have to hurry."

"Good."

"But Miss Barents—" Sasha lowered her eyes. "I mean Petra. I have to ask. Why?"

In reply the secretary held out a piece of white paper.

Sasha turned the small sheet over. It was completely blank on both sides. "I don't understand."

Petra whispered, "The premier was in Gromyko's office this morning, writing a draft of an address for Radio Moscow."

"What is he planning to say?"

"I don't know. Maybe he'll declare war and we'll all die. After the premier left I tore off the blank notepad page below it. The impression of his pen is still visible. Perhaps you could—Oh!" She covered her mouth with her hand in horror.

Sasha turned where was looking, but saw only the usual lunchtime businessmen in black suits.

"Gromyko must have seen me. They've learned about my birth parents. They think I'm not pure enough."

"Petra, you're overreacting. What makes you think anyone's after you?"

"I found this on my desk." The secretary showed her a white cardboard disk printed with the insignia of three red, upward-facing arrows. Then she clutched her ticket and ran through an archway toward the trains, her heels echoing like gunshots off the shiny tile floor.

Sasha held up the notepad sheet at an angle so the windows' light raked across the paper. The Cyrillic indentations were deep. Khrushchev must have been tense when he held that pen. She strode briskly out the front door to the street and called, "*Taksi!*"

A yellow Skoda pulled over. "Where to, honey?"

"The Swedish embassy, and make it fast. There's an extra twenty rubles in it if you run all the lights."

* * *

"Damn it, where's that Swede?" CIA deputy director Marshall Carter flipped all the red switches on the armrest of his swivel chair. He might as well let every agent, secretary, and custodian in the whole headquarters hear. "Andersen! Lars Andersen! Bring me our Swedish agent on the double."

Two minutes later, his suit blown out with sweat stains, Lars was hustled across the second basement's communications center by half a dozen uniformed guards. As soon as he staggered into Carter's glass booth the door whirred shut behind him.

CHAPTER 26 ~ 1962

"Listen up, Andersen. The Swedish ambassador's on the line."

"Sir?" Lars struggled to catch his breath. "I'm not actually Swedish. I grew up in Denmark. I've been an American citizen for twenty years. My sister lives in Sweden, but—"

"But what? Do you grok their lingo or not?"

"Yes, sir."

"Good. Because our guy in Stockholm, Jay Bonworthy, asked for you specifically. He's got a message from Khrushchev for you to decode. It came by way of your wife in Moscow."

"From Sasha! What kind of code did she use?"

"Swedish. No one can figure it out. Bonworthy's not so good at it either." Carter flicked a switch. "Carol? I want you to take dictation. Type every word this man says and forward it straight to McCone in the White House. Top security, top clearance. Alert the President."

Carter took off his headset and handed it to Lars. "This ain't racquetball, Andersen. Swing for the fence."

Lars fitted the headset's wire around his head, not entirely sure which end was supposed to be in his ear and which in front of his mouth. "Mr. Bonworthy?"

"Hey! Andersen?" The Texan's voice drawled hollowly, as if from the bottom of an oil barrel. "Gotta tell ya, I'm in love with your niece Helen."

"I'm sorry, sir?"

"Your niece! What a cutie. She's proud as hell of her uncle in the CIA. She escorted me and the wife for the raising of the *Vasa*. Otherwise a big disappointment, really. That old wooden junk wasn't even from the Vikings."

Lars pushed the earbud with one finger, making the voice clearer. "Sir, I understand you have a communique from my wife Sasha in Moscow?"

"Yeah, I guess so. She says Khrushchev's going to make an announcement on Radio Moscow soon, but we've got the scoop. Somehow she got a draft of the speech. You ready?"

"Yes, sir."

"All right. Here goes."

The sounds that began coming out of the ear bud reminded Lars of a tape recorder played backwards. Then he realized that these noises really might be Swedish words, unintelligible to most actual Swedes.

All the vowels were undotted, the gliding G's were hard as rocks, and the whole thing drawled in Texan.

"Excuse me, Mr. Bonworthy, could you start again?"

"What?"

"If you could, sir. Start again, but slower, and pause after each sentence so I can translate."

"Oh, you bet."

Five minutes later a typed transcript of Lars' translation landed on President Kennedy's desk in the Oval Office.

```
Mr. President, we and you ought not now
to pull on the ends of the rope in which you
have tied the knot of war.
```

Kennedy took off his glasses and rubbed his eyes. "How sure are we that this is from Khrushchev? It sounds like a ransom note from a Nigerian prince."

"We're fairly certain, Mr. President," McCone replied. His hands were sweating.

Kennedy put his glasses back on.

```
The more the two of us pull, the tighter
that knot will be tied. And a moment may come
when it is too tight to untie. Then it will
be necessary to cut that knot, and what that
would mean is not for me to explain to you,
because you yourself understand perfectly of
what terrible forces our countries dispose.
Consequently, to avoid the catastrophe of
thermonuclear war, then let us not only relax
the forces pulling on the ends of the rope,
let us take measures to untie that knot. We
are ready for this.
```

The President looked up at the CIA director. "You know, I think it really is him. No secretary, no editor, just Khrushchev jotting down his thoughts. The tone's conciliatory, I like that. But we need actions, not words."

"There's more." McCone laid a second paper in front of the President. "This diagram was at the bottom of the page."

USA	USSR
Remove missiles from Turkey.	Remove missiles from Cuba.
Let Cuba be.	Let Berlin be.
End quarantine.	Recall ships.

Kennedy leaned forward and pushed an intercom button. "Get my brother in here. And the joint chiefs—the whole executive committee. McCone thinks we may have an offer from the Russians."

* * *

"You're nuts, you know that?" Lennart said, twisting around in the driver's seat to take a better look at the ancient woman in the Trabant's back seat. "No one can change the pace of time. How would that help, anyway?"

"It doesn't usually work," Groa admitted. "I have better luck with second sight."

Helen whistled sarcastically. "So you can see the future! That could come in handy right now. Do you hear that siren?"

A distant, two-tone police horn was in fact starting to haunt the night air.

"Here's my own prediction," Helen continued. "We're about to be arrested for assault, reckless driving, and vandalism. They're going to send us to a gulag in Siberia. Is that what you see in our future too?"

Groa shook her head, thinking. The trick to clairvoyance was putting clues together faster than anyone else.

"No," Groa said. "I predict that we are going to find something very useful in the trunk of this car."

The siren was louder now. Evidently the police car at the kremlin gate had not dared to follow them across the pedestrian footbridge. It had taken a while for the cop to drive around to their side of the river.

"Well." Lennart opened the car door. "This is one prediction we can check." He walked around to the back of the sedan. Helen and Groa followed. He took out his Swiss army knife, extracted a strangely crooked set of tweezers, and began fiddling with the lock.

"Don't you have a key?" Helen asked. The lights of the police car were beginning to flash blue in the riverside trees.

"Naw, I just hot-wired the first car I found. That's why we have to keep the engine running. Aha!"

The trunk popped open.

The streetlamp behind the car cast a cold light into the trunk, revealing a wooden fruit crate.

The crate was filled with bundles of money.

At this moment the police car pulled up sideways in front of the Trabant, blocking the street. The siren fell silent, but the blue lights kept flashing.

"Terrific," Helen said. "Now we can add grand larceny and car theft to our list of crimes."

"How did you know about the money?" Lennart asked Groa.

Groa shrugged. "The professor said the Trabant was his. He'd just cashed some gold bars and moved to Novgorod. Where else would he put it?"

The policeman opened his car door. Boots began crunching on gravel.

Helen swallowed. "What now, sorceress?"

Groa tossed two bundles of bills into the roadside grass. Then she closed the trunk and called out in Russian, "Good evening, comrade!"

"It's almost morning." The patrolman aimed a large flashlight directly into their eyes. He scanned the car, noting the scrapes and the missing bumper. "I've got a report of a damaged Trabant, possibly stolen."

"Yes, comrade," Groa replied. "We saw it."

"You saw the damaged car. Did you really?" The sarcasm in his voice was even thicker than Helen's had been. He wore a pistol on his belt, but did not yet pull it out.

"Oh yes. A very reckless driver. As he raced by he lost this." She reached into the grass and handed a bundle of notes to the policeman.

The man flipped through the purple bills in silence. There were at least a hundred of them, worth twenty-five rubles apiece. Not enough to buy a Trabant, but a lot.

"Oh look," Groa said. "Here's another. I hope you find that careless driver."

The second bundle consisted of ten-ruble notes. They were red, but they too had a quieting effect on the officer.

"Which direction did you say his car was going?"

"Toward Smolensk." Groa pointed south. "If you hurry you might catch up with him."

The policeman cleared his throat. "Thank you for your vigilance, comrades. Safe travels."

He got back into his patrol car, drove around the Trabant, and sped off toward Smolensk, his siren blaring.

Helen looked at Groa in wonder. "That was amazing. You really must be some sort of magician. What did you say your name was?"

Groa considered the options.

"Groa," she said. "Let's get going. It's a long way home."

* * *

There had been a long and heated argument aboard the *B-59* about what they would find if the submarine surfaced. Ivan Maslennikov, the political officer, thought they would be immediately bombarded by the deck guns of the surrounding American destroyers. Captain Valentin Savitsky insisted that nuclear war must have already started. If they surfaced they would be enveloped by a radioactive cloud from the remnants of Havana and Miami. The Soviet Admiralty would be broadcasting desperate orders from their secret alternative headquarters to fire all torpedoes.

Once Commander Vasily Arkhipov had made up his mind, however, he refused to be swayed. And when they finally did surface, he was proven to be right. The American fleet did not attack. They were sending word by radio that they had dropped small "practice depth charges" near the sub because there had been no other way to communicate. Meanwhile, Moscow was radioing orders for the submarines and the supply ship convoy to return home. Global thermonuclear war had been narrowly avoided by twelfth-hour negotiations between Kennedy and Khrushchev.

Most of the crew on the *B-59* cheered as the submarine curved around through the waves, heading back toward Russia. But Captain Savitsky ordered the communications adjutant into his private ready room. When the metal door clanged shut behind them, the captain burst out in rage.

"What were you thinking, Swarovsky? That was our chance! Arkhipov would have voted to fire the special weapon if you'd encouraged him."

The young KGB officer lowered his head. "I don't know, sir."

"You don't know? Well I do. You're a coward. Fenris called us to start the final battle, and you were afraid it might be unpleasant. You might have to breathe some bad air."

"No, sir." Swarovsky rubbed the fingers of his left hand. They still tingled where he had felt a strange, imaginary wedding ring. Why had he envisioned, in the dark, the mismatched eyes of Agent Veliky?

"Last night a feeling came over me, sir. I realized that letting the world end would be an act of cowardice. What takes courage is trying to save the age we are in."

The captain glared at him. "Open your shirt, Swarovsky."

"Sir?"

"I said, unbutton your uniform. That's an order."

The KGB man unbuttoned his shirt.

The captain reached out to Swarovsky's chest. He yanked loose the iron medallion hanging there. Broken links of the pendant's chain pinged on the metal floor.

"You are no longer a Knight of the Varangian Order."

"No, sir."

"Get out. Never let me see your face again."

"Yes, sir."

* * *

The sun was rising in a red pall when the Trabant crossed the Neva River bridge on the outskirts of Leningrad, leaving a trail of black smoke as it putted along. Ahead, the nearly empty six-lane highway was lined with dozens of identical nine-story apartment buildings. They looked like an army of concrete robots marching toward an apocalyptic sunrise.

"We need to stop for gas," Groa said from the back seat.

"How can you tell?" Lennart asked. "There's no fuel gauge on this thing. No tachometer, no turn signal indicator, no nothing."

"She's psychic, remember?" Helen pointed to a gas station with a food kiosk under a rusty metal awning. "Stop at that place. I'm starving."

He took the first exit after the bridge.

"Could a nuclear bomb have made the sky this red?" Helen asked.

Lennart pulled up to a pump. "It could, but this looks like smog to me. It's caused by cars with two-stroke engines like ours." He got out and lifted the Trabant's plastic hood. "Look at this. You have to open

the hood to refuel. The gas has to be mixed with oil, most of which just burns up. There's no fuel pump, so the gas just drips into the motor. The only way to tell how much you've got left is with a dipstick. This crate is a chainsaw on wheels. It's a spark plug with a roof."

"Lenny?" Helen said. "I'm still starving."

Groa suggested, "If you open the trunk, I'll use some of the money to buy food. We might as well eat hearty. We're not supposed to take rubles across the border."

Lennart fiddled with the trunk lock until it opened. Groa left for the kiosk with a bundle of fives.

Ten minutes later they were sitting at a picnic table under the awning, eating stew-filled pastries.

"I talked to the man in the kiosk," Groa said. "He thinks the Caribbean crisis is over. Kennedy has agreed to remove American missiles from Turkey if Russia pulls back from Cuba."

"Then the Varangian Order failed to end the world," Helen said.

"They'll try again."

"You seem to know things you shouldn't, Gramma."

"My name's Groa."

"OK. Tell me something you should know. Who is professor Henrik Talin, really?"

Groa sighed. "He was an assistant for your mother during the war, at the excavation in Hedeby."

"You're kidding."

"No. I think he even fell in love with her."

"How would you know a thing like that?" Helen asked. But then she added, "What happened?"

"Henrik turned out to be a Nazi collaborator. When the war ended the big-name Nazis escaped in a submarine. Henrik had to flee in a little sailboat. It must have taken him weeks to get to the Soviet Union. Along the way the sun burned one side of his face to a red scar. In Estonia he changed his name and started over as a professor of archeology."

"Why did the Varangian Order want me?" Helen asked. "My father's Jewish."

"Most of them only knew about your Viking lineage. And the professor had his own reasons."

"Like what?"

"If he couldn't have your mother, he wanted you."

"Yuck." Helen turned aside, grimacing.

Lennart leaned forward. "The Varangians will try to stop us at the border."

"We've got passports and visas," Helen said. "You do have a passport, don't you Groa?"

"Half a dozen."

"OK. Then the real problem will be the car. It's stolen, and only has a front license plate."

"We should ditch the car and take the train," Lennart said.

Groa shook her head. "Trains are watched too closely. There's only one border crossing to Finland for trains, and several crossings for cars. We should drive."

"And what will we do at the border without papers for the car?"

"We have plenty of papers," Groa said. "Our trunk has enough rubles for a lucky border agent to buy a house."

"I don't like it," Lennart objected.

"What?" Helen asked. "Is it so wrong to buy a man a house?"

"Yes. It's all wrong. The corruption, the bribery, even our stupid car." Lennart pointed to the battered Trabant as if he wanted to throw a grenade at it. "This is the problem. Germans are quite capable of building good cars. I've seen their BMWs. But the workers of the People's Socialist Factory in Zwickau have no incentive to try. The word *Trabant* means satellite. The cars are named for *Sputnik*. But they're garbage. Everything from the government factories is garbage."

Helen cocked her head. "That's not what you said when we toured Berlin."

"Maybe I've soured on the miracle of Communism. The ideology still rings true. But in practice, the socialist world is polluted with incompetence and corruption. Our Trabant is like the actual Soviet state—cheap, stinking, and badly built."

"That's pretty harsh," Groa said.

Lenny ranted on. "Even in Sweden, the man I trusted most was a fake. When we hired a maid to clean Colonel Wennerstöm's house she found microfilms with plans for the new Swedish fighter jet. My mentor was a traitor. He was Sweden's leak to the Warsaw Pact. Now he'll rot in prison."

Helen put her hand on Lennart's arm. "Both sides have spies. The West isn't immune to corruption and lies. The Varangian Order has spread their nonsense about race and hatred everywhere. Maybe that's what we should be fighting."

Lennart sighed. "I guess the original Varangians were just as bad, slaughtering people who were different, or selling them as slaves. Things never change."

Groa cleared her throat. "Actually, Oleg was a Viking with a conscience. At least, more than most. It's a shame, the way he died."

Helen looked at her from the side. "I'm not even going to ask how you know that."

"Good." Groa stood up. "We're four hours from the border, if traffic stays light. When we get there, let me do the talking."

CHAPTER 27
VOLKHOV RIVER, 907

"Do you remember?" Oleg mused to Groa as their longship sailed down the Volkhov River toward Novgorod. "You once predicted that I would be killed by my horse."

Groa wrinkled her brow. Her memory had never been good, but she did remember this. "I'm often wrong, you know. Have you worried about horses?"

"I've avoided them for years." He looked ahead, past the dozens of other ships heading toward the beach below the city's palisade. The Jarls of Novgorod had spent five months on their voyage to Constantinople, and were returning with ships full of treasure. But in that same span of time Oleg seemed to have aged ten years. He was no longer Regent of Russiya. He had relinquished his sword, Fenris. He was just another old knight, the flames of his fiery red hair turned ash-white.

"People don't use horses much around Novgorod," Groa pointed out. "That's why you had us build ships."

"Yes, of course. Still, I've wondered about your words. When you made that prediction I didn't have a horse. It worried me when Helga gave me one as a present the next day. Then it died the following morning, shot by the Swedish king's archers. Along with my bride."

"My vision should have been for Helga instead."

Oleg nodded. "I miss her. In Constantinople you said it might be awkward for me to stay in Russiya with Igor as tsar. I think you're right. I have no role in Novgorod. I have no family here, either, but Helga and I both left cousins in Ruslagen. I am ready to return to Sweden."

"Autumn can be a dangerous time to travel. Winter will be upon

304

us soon."

"We are not the only Varangians who have returned with trade goods," Oleg said. "The first ships to reach Sweden will have the market to themselves."

"I heard that." It was Thorkell, at the prow of the adjacent longship. The Norwegian captain had been made a knight in Constantinople but was old enough to be thinking about retirement. "Let me sail my ship with you, Oleg. I've a mind to sell my goods in Norway and buy an estate there."

Oleg laughed. "Only if you take your crew with you. This sorceress and her woodworker have been nothing but trouble here in Russiya."

"Agreed," Thorkell replied. "Groa? Hrolf? Are you with us?"

Groa looked to her husband. He had become cheerful since Constantinople, and his mind had cleared.

"Let's go, my love," Hrolf said. "In Norway I will build a jewel box of a palace for you and our daughter."

"Our daughter?" What was her husband thinking? When she looked into his thoughts, the image was so vivid that she blushed.

* * *

They stayed in Novgorod only one week, hurriedly settling their affairs. After twenty-five winters Groa and Hrolf had accumulated a circle of friends that were hard to leave behind. Groa was astonished by how much property they had to sell. Their house in town, the shipyard, four completed Ships in the Woods, and enough raw materials to build a dozen more. By week's end they had filled an entire sea chest with silver dirhams—an unimaginable fortune.

Hardest of all for Groa was leaving Nadya. The old Slavic herbalist refused to accept Groa's town house as a gift.

"Nerves for the city blue smoke," she said, her broken Norse as cryptic as ever. "Green bugs happy in my woods."

Groa clasped Nadya's withered hands. She knew exactly how the old woman felt. "How can I repay you for all you have taught me?"

"Twist time for luck," Nadya said. "Hearts never fly dark."

When the time came, Vlad saw them off at the Novgorod beach. The town's governor still had his handsome, shiny black hair, but he had grown fat with age. Countless children ran about him, as if they were bees buzzing around a distended old queen.

"I will go," Vlad laughed, mimicking a voice he had heard on the

Tunsberg beach long ago. But of course he wasn't going anywhere. He was merely being stupid and cruel. Groa recoiled to think she had once desired this man. Leaving him behind made it easier to leave Russiya.

Milovic, Oleg's Slavic helmsman, did not want to leave Russiya at all. He had no family in Scandinavia. Oleg asked Thorkell if he could borrow his helmsman. "Gunnar knows the Baltic. I'll pay him well. You are a skilled enough captain to steer your own ship."

And so Gunnar stood at the tiller of Oleg's ship when it set out into the Volkhov's current. Their prow was still shaped like an arrow—the Tyr-rune that had been Oleg's emblem from the first. Behind them, Thorkell's ship was fronted by the curled head of a snake. The old Norwegian had announced that he was done with the war god. Instead he had wanted an animal as his figurehead. Hrolf had complied by carving a hugorm—the zigzag-marked, venomous reptile of Scandinavia's wilds.

A day's easy sailing downriver brought them to Ladoga. Oleg was welcomed in the old fortress as a hero. That night in the town's largest hall, skalds recited saga verses about the Varangians' reconquest of Russiya years ago. After Hrolf had drunk two horns of mead he told how he had hit upon the idea of winching down Ladoga's rotten palisades to roust the Finnish usurpers. Groa was surprised that her shy, taciturn husband felt so free with words. Admittedly, his stumbling prose would never rank him as a poet. Still, she was glad that they were returning to Norway, if the change brightened his spirits so much.

The next morning, on their way down to Ladoga's beach, the crews of the two ships walked among a dozen grassy mounds. The town's chieftain recited the names and accomplishments of the Vikings buried there. Then he clapped Oleg on the shoulder and invented an impromptu verse.

> No Russiyan warrior
> Has won more fame
> Than the fearless regent
> Who retook Rurik's realm

"We consider Ladoga your true home, Oleg. It would be an honor to burn a ship for you here when the time comes."

"I don't need a tomb yet," Oleg said, shaking his head. "Still, I appreciate your offer. By the way, do you keep any horses?"

"A few," the chieftain replied. "Why?"

"Thank you for your verse, and for your hospitality." Oleg motioned to his crew. "We have far to go. Let's sail."

A west wind slowed the two longships' progress across Lake Ladoga. The headwind was even worse down the Neva River to the Baltic. A week of hard rowing left Groa's shoulders aching, but it also brought them to Karlsgard, the old Varangian outpost on the Estonian island of Hiiumaa.

Years ago, sailing the other way from Sweden to Russiya, Oleg's forces had found Karlsgard burned. The local Finns had killed Karl, the Varangian leader. Oleg had quickly rebuilt the fortress stronger than before. Wiglaf, the Geatish chief from Gotland, had staffed the post with three shiploads of his men.

Now it seemed the Geats were gone. The Finns who ran the outpost welcomed Oleg's crews as trading guests. Many of the locals spoke tolerable Norse when needed. Only later in the evening did Groa realize that the Geats had never actually left Karlsgard. The Scandinavians had intermarried, adopted the customs of their wives, and raised families that spoke Finnish.

"I remember you," a thin, middle-aged man in a blue tunic told Oleg. "You unshackled my mother when she was a hostage. You allowed my father to escape from Ladoga. At the time, I thought you would kill us all."

Oleg shook his head, uncertain who this man might be. But Groa remembered.

"You were the boy who led us to the iron bog. Your mother was—" Groa ran aground, her memory failing.

"Anni."

"Yes." Groa looked into his eyes and saw shadows. "Your mother has passed. I am sorry."

"I may follow her soon." He plucked at the tunic that hung from his narrow frame. "It seems I am wasting away. I do not know why."

Groa did. She and Nadya had battled this contagion in Novgorod. Apparently the sickness had finally reached this island, no doubt carried by traders like themselves.

"Willow bark and old man's beard," Groa said.

"What are these words?" The man's grasp of Norse was weak.

Groa explained to one of the older Karlsgard men that the symptoms of the illness might be relieved with a tea brewed from the bark of willows and the gray-green tree lichen known as old man's beard. She added, however, that there was no cure. Those who lived, would live.

After the men had spoken amongst themselves, Anni's son sought out Groa once again.

"The Varangians are healers as well as rulers. I wish for you a very long life."

"Do not wish that on anyone," Groa replied. "Wish instead to die at peace, having finished your business with the gods."

The man frowned. "Even when I understand your words, I don't always understand."

* * *

The first storm of winter set in with a fury as the two longships crossed the Baltic toward Sweden. Ice encrusted the shields along the gunwales. Spray drenched the oarsmen. Ahead lay the warm halls of Sweden, so no one wanted to turn back and spend the winter on Hiiumaa.

Thorkell was among the men who fell ill, shivering despite many layers of furs. Groa had no herbs and no tea to offer. She hoped the Norwegian captain had merely caught a cold, rather than the more dangerous contagion.

Just beyond the Åland Islands the archer Stenir died. There was nothing to do but to wrap him in a blanket and stow him below the deck boards. Like most of the others Stenir had left family in the old country twenty-five years ago. Unlike the others, he no longer had to worry about whether his relatives were still alive—or if they would celebrate his return.

The clouds broke when the two ships finally sailed into the calmer waters at the mouth of Ruslagen's fjord. The ships' yellow-and-white-striped sails billowed in the sun. With oars stowed, everyone lined the gunwales, curious to see how the homeland had changed. Thorkell unwrapped his furs and sneezed in the warmth of the sunlight.

Birch forests along the shore hid most of the view. Bright yellow leaves still clung to the white branches. Groa wondered that she didn't see more plumes of woodsmoke. The night had been cold. Where were the people?

The mystery deepened when they rounded a point and saw the beach at fjord's end. Where once an armada of sixty ships had prepared to sail, Groa now counted only three small fishing boats and half a dozen turf-walled huts.

"Hail Rus!" Oleg called out from the prow of his ship.

A dog ran out onto the beach, barking.

Even when the ships landed and the Varangians got out, stretching their legs after a cold week at sea, they were met by a single old man. He walked down from a sod hut, scratching the back of his head.

"Where are the Rus?" Oleg demanded.

The old man narrowed his eyes. "Who are you?"

"I am Oleg, from Russiya. Where are our people?"

"Oleg the King-killer." He shook his head. "Your name is unwelcome here. Why have you come?"

"We've brought trade goods. We want to find our relatives. Where are they?"

The old man waved a hand through the air as if he were sowing seeds with his fingers. "The Rus are scattered on the wind. To Uppland, Gotland, Denmark. King Björn has allowed Svea families to fill the empty huts."

"Why have we not heard this news? Our traders come to Sweden every year."

"They do not come here," the old man said. "No one stops at

Ruslagen. They all sail to the king's market town, Sigtuna."

"To be taxed by the Swedish king."

"There is a toll," the old man admitted. "But Sigtuna is closer to Uppsala. Your trade goods can easily be taken to buyers in all of the Svea realm by horse."

The word *horse* made Oleg flinch. "What about Birka, the island with a free port?"

"Birka is abandoned to robbers and snakes. Perhaps it would be a place for Oleg King-killer." The old man eyed the crew on the beach and raised his voice to speak to them. "Followers of Oleg! If you want to know the fates of your relatives you can talk to Astrid, the hag on the hill. She may even let you camp on the meadow behind her hut. But Ruslagen is no longer friendly ground for you. Sell your goods in Sigtuna and sail back to Russiya."

Then the old man turned and left.

Before long Oleg's men learned that the old man had not told them the whole truth. Astrid turned out to be the same woman who had arranged Oleg's wedding celebration in Birka years ago. She admitted that the population of Ruslagen had dwindled somewhat in the face of persecution by King Björn the Bent, and that a number of old houses had been taken over by sullen Svea opportunists like the old man at the beach. But she was happy to report that most of the Rus crewmen still had relatives in the area. The Rus were farmers now, rather than rowers. The Svea king had confiscated their ships to discourage what he called "piracy."

Oleg sat down on a stump chair. "What news do you have of my cousins, and of Helga's family?"

Astrid leaned against the wall of her hut and sighed. "Those people truly have scattered like dandelion seeds. The king left them no peace. It's a shame, because Helga had a large estate that would have been yours. She had many fine horses."

Oleg shifted uncomfortably on his stump. "What about Birka? The old man said it was full of robbers and snakes."

"That's finally what drove us out," Astrid admitted. "There were so few people left on the island, and the king refused to offer us protection. We felt safer here among the Rus. Every summer we get a few visitors from Russiya, bringing silver and trade goods. That fills the soup bowls and keeps up our spirits."

She paused, thinking. "But you have come so late in the year. Does this mean you plan to spend the winter? Or perhaps you do not intend to return to Russiya at all? You might find places to stay if you knock on the right doors."

That evening, camped in the field behind Astrid's house, the ships' crews debated their options. They had not been hailed as returning heroes. The relatives who remained sounded mostly interested in their silver. Treasure would surely open doors. It would also allow them to build halls of their own, given time. But the mood in Scandinavia had changed. Varangians were outsiders. This was not the home they had imagined.

Despite everything, most of Oleg's crew decided to winter in Ruslagen. Thorkell's crew held out hope that they would receive a better welcome in Norway.

The one thing everyone agreed on was that they first should go see Sigtuna. Or rather, everyone agreed except Oleg.

Gunnar tried to talk the old Viking around. "Sigtuna is the market that matters. That's where we'll find merchants who can afford our silk."

"It's too close to Uppsala," Oleg grumbled.

"Are you afraid of Björn the Bent?" Gunnar taunted.

"Of course not." Oleg put his hand on the hilt of his sword—and found only a dagger in a leather sheath hanging from his belt. He drew the little blade, sighing. "Even a small piece of good steel can bring down a tyrant."

Thorkell said, "We don't want trouble. We just want to trade. Come with us, Oleg."

The old Viking relented. "I'll go with you if we visit Helga's tomb on the way."

"Birka?" Gunnar objected. "We can stop there later. First we need to bring the wares of Constantinople to market."

"All right. Afterwards."

* * *

A hard day's travel—first sailing around Ruslagen's rock skerries, then rowing through the Holm narrows, and finally maneuvering up a long arm of Lake Mälaren—brought the two Varangian ships to Sigtuna. Night was falling, and a pall of woodsmoke from cooking fires hung over the settlement. Groa was surprised that there was no palisade protecting the town from the harbor. The village seemed less permanent and less safe than Novgorod.

The hungry crewmen were eager to spend their silver on the luxuries the town promised, but Oleg urged caution. "Keep your weapons handy. Do not drink—not even one hornful of mead. I want a dozen well-armed men to stay with me on board the ships. We'll take turns keeping watch."

The crews grumbled, but Thorkell agreed that Oleg's orders were wise. "We've worked too hard to risk our treasure now. The Swedes have never been friendly to the Rus. I plan to stay on my ship, and I wager I'll sleep better than those in town."

Groa and Hrolf disagreed. They did not want to spend another night sleeping on deck planks. They took a handful of coins and a couple of daggers, and ventured ashore.

Although Sigtuna lacked an entry gate, planked pathways from the beach converged at the entrance to the town's main street between two buildings. There a guard with a spear and a helmet gave them directions to three different inns for visiting traders.

The inn's food was wonderfully nostalgic—meatballs, flatbread, and lingonberry sauce. The bed was a compartment filled with straw, which seemed heavenly after life aboard the ship. Best of all, there was hot water to wash up properly.

The next day brought surprisingly summery weather. The Varangians carried deck planks up to the town's market square, where Hrolf fitted them together as impromptu tables. The sun was so bright they had to hang a sail on oars as an awning. The resulting booth, with its display of marvels from Byzantium, attracted quite a crowd. Many of the shoppers were merely curious, but others bought with a passion. By the end of the day, even after paying tax to the king's men, the Russiyan traders had done so well that the urge to celebrate was unstoppable.

And that is when the trouble began. Gunnar and two dozen of his fellow crewmen had been drinking at Krogan, the largest of the inn-halls, taking turns inventing boastful verses. When it was Gunnar's turn to devise a poem, he offered,

> Which body part
> Of Björn is bent?

His neck? His heart?
His bum? His snake?

The crewmen laughed, but the rest of the inn had grown ominously quiet. A man with a blue cloak draped over his shoulders scooted his chair back. He stepped in front of Gunnar.

"Our foreign guests forget where they are." He cracked his knuckles. "They've also forgotten to pay our tax."

Gunnar frowned. "We paid a fee for everything we sold."

"That was the king's tax, not ours. You have to pay ours before you leave."

"And who are you?" Gunnar demanded.

"I'm the man telling you that ill-mannered dogs who crawl out of a Slavic swamp and insult our king have to pay a tax if they want to leave Sigtuna."

A voice in the shadows added, "I hear they're hiding Oleg King-killer on one of their ships."

The man in the blue cloak fixed his gaze on Gunnar. "Is this true? You've brought an outlaw?"

"Oleg didn't kill your old king. It was Eirik who started the killing. The Svea kings are—"

The man's fist swung so fast that Gunnar had no time to dodge. The blow spun his head sideways. He bent over, spitting blood and teeth.

Those who did not know Gunnar would surely have thought he had been defeated with a single swing. The Varangians who did know him stood back, afraid of what was to come.

Gunnar exploded upwards from a crouch like an uncaged wolf. His right fist caught the Swede in the stomach, bringing the man's head down into the path of the left fist. The man sank to his knees with his head flopped backwards at a bad angle. Gunnar spat blood into the upturned face.

The helmsman surveyed the men in the hall. "Anyone else want to collect some tax?"

The innkeeper cleared his throat. "We don't want you Russiyans here. Get out while you can."

The Varangian crewmen quickly realized this was good advice. The locals were gathering weapons and calling for reinforcements. If it came to a battle the Varangians would be vastly outnumbered. Three of the crewmen dragged Gunnar out of the doorway, heading for the harbor. Others ran to spread word at the other inns.

Groa jerked awake, poked by a stick. A voice in the darkness hissed, "Psst! Take what you can and get to the ships! Gunnar got into a fight. Now the Swedes are after us."

Hrolf sat up so fast he conked his head on the compartment roof. "Ow! What?"

"Run, you blockhead. To the ships!"

The scene at the town's beach was chaotic. Varangians waded out to their ships, lugging chests and weapons. Locals on the beach threw rocks. Rowers with shields over their heads fumbled for their oars. Men with torches were arriving from town.

Groa and Hrolf climbed aboard the wrong ship.

"Are we missing anyone?" Oleg called out to Thorkell's ship, "How many do you have on board?"

"Forty-six. No, Forty-seven."

"And we have fifty-three. We're one short."

Groa pointed to a dark shape amid the rippled torchlight reflecting on the water. "There!"

Oleg dived in head first, grabbed the body, and began swimming back. Rocks splashed into the water about him. An arrow thunked into the ship's side near his head.

Groa shivered at this new danger. If Oleg tried to climb out he would be an easy target for the town's archers.

"Row!" Gunnar commanded.

"We can't leave Oleg and—"

"Shut up and row!" Gunnar grabbed an oar and held it out behind the ship. "Take hold, Oleg! Hang on."

The ships began pulling away from the shore, dragging Oleg and the unknown man in their wake. In the confusion, fewer than half of the oars were pulling, and even these kept crossing.

"Row! Row!" Gunnar called out, trying to get the oarsmen in rhythm.

When they were finally out of reach of the arrows, Gunnar hauled the body up over the gunwale. Then Oleg climbed aboard. "Who is it? Is he alive?"

The man who flopped onto the deck boards did not look alive. His head was bloodied and he wasn't breathing.

"Sorceress!" Oleg called out. "Over here, quick."

Groa stumbled over oarsmen and sea chests. A thin moon cast the face in a pallid light. She recognized Asger, one of the Geats who had sailed with Wiglaf to Russiya long ago. Asger had stayed to work in the forest near Ladoga, supplying wood for their shipyard.

"Give me room." She thumped her knee on his chest. The body convulsed, spewing slimy water from its bloody mouth. But Asger did not start breathing.

Groa put her mouth over his, trying to blow life back into him. All that came back was the stench of death. She sat back, wiping bloody slime from her face "He's gone."

Oleg said, "Your sorcery has limits, woman."

"I never said otherwise."

Oleg turned to Gunnar. Blood had matted the helmsman's beard. "You look like a Valkyrie passed you over, Gunnar. What happened back in town?"

"I had a disagreement about an extra Swedish tax." Gunnar's words whistled through a gap of missing teeth. "A man with a blue cloak took a punch at me."

"That would be Sigtuna's governor. You didn't kill him, did you?"

"No! Of course not. At least, I don't think so. Unless I broke his neck."

Oleg wiped his face with both hands, as if to wring away the water, and the memories, of Sigtuna.

"Where do we go now?" Gunnar asked.

Gunnar wasn't the only one weighing their options. The king's men in Sigtuna were likely to send ships. Oleg had already been declared an outlaw, and now Gunnar might face the same banishment. Thorkell would want to sail onward to Norway, his original goal. Oleg's ship, however, had no safe destination.

"The moon will set soon," Gunnar said. "We can't sail these narrows in complete darkness. We need to rest. Where do we go?"

"Birka." Oleg said. "It is time I went to see my wife."

* * *

Later that night Groa had a prescient dream.

She dreamed she was on Birka—which of course was true. The two Varangian ships had managed to find the island's beach in the predawn darkness. Most of the town's buildings had decayed so badly that it was hard to tell where the streets had once been. But one large hall near the beach remained remarkably intact, evidently repaired for use by travelers, fishermen—or, more likely, pirates. The Varangians built a fire on the central hearth. They crowded around the blaze, drying off and warming up before rolling into their blankets on the floor. Groa fell asleep curled against Hrolf's reassuring warmth.

In the dream she was walking through summer wildflowers, looking for Helga's tomb. The birch trees that had given the island its name were gone, replaced by fields of white and yellow flowers—the wild carrot and mustard blooms that brightened so many abandoned pastures in both Sweden and Russiya. Half a dozen thin white clouds crossed the sky at various angles, as if Thor had shot flaming arrows in different directions. When Groa squinted, she saw that one of the arrows was still flying, a tiny silver dot slowly writing a long, white ice-rune. To the east, an orange pall hung over the narrows at Holm, as if that unpeopled island at the mouth of Lake Mälaren now hosted thousands of hearth fires.

Even in a dream Groa had not expected to find graverobbers digging up Helga's tomb in broad daylight. There were a dozen thieves in all —young men and women wearing comical blue leggings and tight tunics. For some reason they had used string to mark the grave area into squares. Instead of digging with spades they were picking through the dirt with tiny brushes. Although this seemed ineffective, they had somehow managed to remove virtually all the dirt, right down to a skeleton at the bottom.

A man and an older blond woman were standing above the other robbers, talking. Groa crept behind a boulder to listen.

"Could the horse have been a decoy—a trick to make it harder for looters to find the warrior?"

The woman spoke in a dialect Groa could hardly understand. Whole sentences vanished into nonsense.

The man sighed and said, "If I tried to publish a theory that the warrior was female, I'd be laughed out of academia."

What did these foreign words mean?

"Let me know what else you find." The older woman with short blond hair looked at the ruins of the vandalized tomb. "There may yet be something here that ties everything together."

And then they were gone, the dream shattered by a man shouting in ordinary Norse, "Up! Everyone up. The Swedes could arrive at any moment. Let's get back to the ships."

It was Gunnar, his words whistling through the gap in his teeth.

Groa rubbed her eyes, trying to hang onto the dream.

Oleg stood in the hall's doorway, blocking the morning sun. "Not so fast, helmsman. We haven't yet decided where we are going. I came here to visit a tomb. I don't intend to leave Birka until we have honored Helga."

"Your wife's grave—" Groa faltered, unsure how much to trust a dream. "Helga's tomb may already be disturbed by looters."

"We will see." Oleg crossed his arms. "A few men can stay to guard the ships. The rest of you, come with me to pay homage to the queen of the Rus."

By daylight the abandoned townsite seemed even more desolate. The huts had mostly rotted away, leaving only an occasional stave upright. Everywhere the dry stalks of dead wildflowers waved in the brisk west wind.

Even as Oleg was leading the way up the slope behind town, Groa could already see that the tombs were not intact. There had been two grave mounds, each topped with a boulder. Now only one remained.

Oleg stood somberly at the crest of the hill, surveying the damage. Then he laughed. "The thieves dug up the wrong mound! Helga lies under the boulder to the left. She'll sit there through the ages with her weapons. That woman was the fiercest fighter I've known."

Gunnar spoke up. "Tell the truth, Oleg. On your wedding night, did you lose the arm wrestling match to Helga on purpose?"

"No! That crazy woman almost tore my arm off." He touched a knuckle to his face, drying a tear. "Later that night I learned what an accomplished wrestler she was."

The Varangian men hid smiles. Hrolf managed to turn his guffaw into a cough.

"She should have stood with us in Constantinople. Helga and I should have grown old together. We should have returned here to retire on Birka."

The west wind gusted through the dead wildflowers, bending the stalks low. No one spoke for a long time, their thoughts on the way the world might have been.

Oleg broke the spell with a sad laugh. "You know, I feel a little sorry for the grave robbers." He held out his hand to the looted mound on the right. "All that work, only to discover that they had fallen for a trap. All they found was Helga's horse."

He knelt by the pit where the horse's skull lay exposed, its teeth yellow. The skull's eye was a dark hole.

Suddenly Groa felt a prickling of fear. There was danger here, but how? She took a knife out of her tunic.

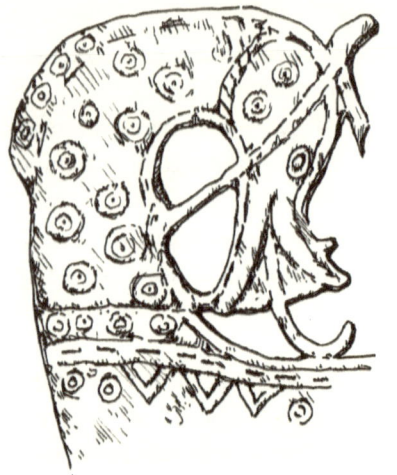

At that moment Oleg reached out as if to stroke the horse's head. A brown shape flashed and he cried out, "Ah!"

Almost without thinking, Groa threw the knife. It flipped end over end. When it stabbed into the ground it pinned a large brown snake beside the horse's eye.

Oleg looked at his hand in wonder. There were two small red dots on his wrist. Then he looked at the dying serpent. "A snake?"

"Not just any snake," Groa said, examining the brown zigzag markings on the serpent's back. "This is a hugorm."

"Odin!" Gunnar whistled through his teeth.

"Why would a snake be hiding in a skull?" Oleg asked.

"Hugorms nest in caves," Hrolf said. "Groa, can you get the venom out?"

She shook her head. "The bite is in a vein. I'd have to drain too much blood."

Oleg flexed his hand, mesmerized by the red dots. "My fingers are growing numb. What do you think, sorceress? Are hugorms as deadly as they say?"

"You are a strong man, Oleg, but the snake was large."

"That's not an answer."

Groa sighed. "I'm afraid the venom is likely to seize your heart before nightfall. Perhaps even by midday."

"Witch woman!" Oleg's gray eyes flashed like steel blades. "You foretold this. Killed by my horse, you said. And now here I am, beside Norna."

"Norna," Groa repeated. That had been the name of the horse Helga had given Oleg on their wedding night. The horse had been named for the Fates.

"You saved my life on Birka once, sorceress. Do it again."

"This time I'm afraid I cast my knife too late."

"My whole arm feels like a block of wood. You have powers, Groa. I have seen it. You are not like the rest of us. You can turn back time. Why not now?"

Her throat tightened. She looked aside, wishing she really were able to reverse time. The world about her was a confusing overlay of dreams and memories. Even now, where she saw an autumn wind bending the stalks of dead wildflowers, it was also midsummer in her memory, and the Varangians were mourning at Helga's freshly built tomb. At the same time, the strangely clad graverobbers of her dream were brushing dirt from the horse's skull.

Was it possible to turn back time, even just a little, to the moment before Oleg reached out to his horse's skull? Or, once a future was foretold, were even the gods unable to bend their doom?

"Sails! Yellow-and-blue sails!" A voice cried from the back of the crowd. A man was pointing north toward Sigtuna's fjord. The dozen ships there were still no more than dim dots. But everyone knew what they meant.

"The king's men," Oleg said. Groa heard his thought: Will I be able to fight when they arrive? Will I even be alive?

"We cannot defeat twelve shiploads of Swedes," Gunnar said, as if in reply.

Thorkell spoke. "I am sailing to Gotland and Norway. Anyone who wants passage on my ship is welcome."

A man asked, "Can you outrun their ships?"

Thorkell laughed. "Swedish tubs? Our Ship in the Woods will be on the open sea before they get to Holm."

Gunnar turned to Oleg. "And what of our ship? Where do we sail?"

Oleg held up his stiff arm, the fingers already frozen into a claw. "I am joining Helga. You will have to become our captain now, Gunnar."

The helmsman—suddenly in command after all these years—surveyed the crowd and made a quick decision. "Some of you have said you want to return to Ruslagen. We will take you there, if you want. But be warned: There will never be peace for the Rus in Sweden. After Ruslagen our ship will sail on to Russiya, for those who want to return to the true realm of the Rus."

"With winter upon us?" a man asked. "The trip here was bad enough."

"Look at the sky. If this weather holds, the west wind will bring us back to Ladoga in a week." Gunnar raised his fist. "Put your hand in the air if you are with me."

The Varangians raised their fists—some with conviction and some with reluctance. Only Oleg did not join them.

"Is your arm already dead?" Gunnar asked.

Oleg shook his head. "I would rather be buried here, with my wife."

"We have no time to build grave mounds. You have been promised royal honors at Lodaga. You will come with us."

"But I—"

"You promoted me to captain. There is no time to argue." Gunnar turned to the crowd. "We sail for Ruslagen and Russiya. Help Oleg to the ship. Hail Rus!"

"Hail Rus!" The Varangians shouted back, their fists in the air. They began heading down the slope to the beach, attempting to hustle Oleg among them.

But the old Viking planted his feet apart, growling like a wounded bear. Suddenly charged with his old strength, he shook himself loose, hurling men to either side.

"No! I came to Birka to say farewell to my wife. And I mean to do it."

The Swedish sails were closer now, but the entire troop of Varangians stopped short, deferring to the iron will of the man who had led them for so long.

Oleg walked stiff-legged to Helga's grave mound. He embraced the boulder there, laid his whiskered cheek against the cool granite, and cried. His great shoulders heaved with each heart-breaking sob.

"My love, my love, my love," he said, his voice cracking. "I would join you in your tomb if I could. My time is short, and we belong together. Once again, it seems that I must be the one who sails."

Oleg stepped back, swaying like a severed oak in the wind. Suddenly he fell to his knees, facing the gap the graverobbers had dug in the horse's mound. He pulled Groa's dagger from the dead snake. Then he yanked the hugorm out of the skull's eye socket and threw it aside. Finally, with tears dripping from his bowed head, he worked the silver wedding ring loose from the stiff finger of his left hand.

"You once told me that the gift of your horse was proof of your love. Now let Norna bear my ring to you in Valhalla. This is my proof that I guarded your dreams. We will be together at last."

Oleg dropped the ring into the dark hole of the skull's eye.

Now Oleg wrenched himself about. "Groa!" He bellowed the name with such force that the waiting Varangians cringed. "I can't get up. You and your woodworker husband will have to help me to my ship."

Groa and Hrolf took the old Viking under his arms. As they stumbled together down the slope to Birka's beach, Oleg muttered, "You were wrong about my welcome in Sweden. But you were right that I needed to come back. To face down my darkest memories. To clear my heart for the good."

Groa's eyes were damp and her voice was thick. "I failed you, Oleg."

"No, I was the one who failed. You have always been true to a higher purpose. Tyr, the god of war, is not the answer to evil."

Groa managed to wipe her eyes. "In the legends, even Tyr failed. Fenris bit off the war-god's hand."

"If there is anyone who can stop the wolf-god from wreaking havoc in this world, it will be you."

They had reached the beach. Both of the Varangian ships were ready, with their masts up and their crews in position. To the north the yellow-and-blue striped sails of the twelve Swedish longships were so close that sunlight glinted from the helmets of soldiers in the prows. The blue banner of the Svea kings streamed from the mast tops in the west wind.

Oleg steadied himself by holding onto Groa's shoulder. She knew this would be their final good-bye. She and Hrolf would sail on Thorkell's ship to an uncertain future in Norway. Oleg would sail to his own inevitable doom, and a tomb in Russiya.

Oleg clasped Groa's head in his stiff hands. He kissed the blond crest of her hair.

"Remember me."

CHAPTER 28
GOTLAND, 1962

Hi Celeste—

Helen here, writing from a frozen island in the Baltic. I wish you were real, so I could spend the winter with you on a sunny island in the Mediterranean.

This is the first Christmas I've been treated like an adult. I'm almost eighteen, for gods' sake, and I aged about thirty years in Russia last summer. The good news is that Lennart's arriving on the five o'clock ferry. He's promised to bring a surprise. Maybe a bass guitar for me to learn?

The bad news is that my favorite *bedstemor*, Grandma Kirstin, seems to be struggling. She's 86, but never seemed old until now. Uncle Lars and Aunt Sasha flew her in from Copenhagen last night, presumably using their secret agent connections to borrow a four-seat airplane for Lars to pilot. Bedstemor took some pills and went straight to bed in the villa's back bedroom. When she finally appeared for breakfast at noon she forced a smile, even though her whole face was wrinkled with age and pain.

"I want to see that tombstone." She wasn't even looking at the coffee, toast, and lingonberry jam I'd put out for her.

"Whose tombstone?" I asked, thinking it might be hers. Old people sometimes plan their graves in advance.

"The one we found in the Eskelhem church two years ago. I hear it's featured in a new exhibit at the Visby museum."

That's just like Bedstemor, to want to see a thousand-year-old rock on Christmas Eve. Even Mom couldn't talk her out of it.

Oops—I gotta run. It's four o'clock and we're all supposed to crowd into our little Saab. Dad's staying home to cook the goose, but that still puts five adults in one car. Museum first, then the ferry. What are we supposed to do on the way back, have Lenny sit on my lap? Or the other way around?

* * *

The History Museum in the ancient Gotland capital of Visby looked like a Russian farmhouse that had been built out of place, on a crowded cobblestone Swedish street. Elsewhere in the old part of town, last-minute shoppers were puffing clouds of steam as they hurried past bright window displays of Santas, snowblowers, and hi-fi stereos beneath garlands of greenery and colored lights. The museum was dark, built of flattened logs that had been painted red. White moldings framed the tiny win-

dows. The eaves had fringes of icicles, but no snow.

Mette parked the Saab, got out, and looked in her purse for the museum's key. Meanwhile Lars helped Kirstin balance on the uneven cobbles with her cane. Despite layers of wool coats and shawls, the old archeologist looked cold. Papery skin scarcely concealed the bones of her face and hands. She pressed her lips together as if to stifle a cry. No one had talked much during the short ride from the villa, or in fact since Kirstin's arrival the night before. Even Helen was quiet, waiting for Bedstemor to break the silence.

"I had a dream," Kirstin said.

Mette stopped fumbling with the door key. "A dream?"

"Yes. Last week I dreamed that I that would learn the answer to my life's work here on Gotland, on Christmas Eve."

"Mother, there's no mystery about your professional work. It's on display in the national galleries of Oslo and Copenhagen. All we have in Visby is a provincial museum."

Kirstin waved a bony finger toward the lock.

Mette tried a different key, opened the door, and turned on the museum's hidden, recessed lights.

The little group ventured into a dim reconstruction of the Viking Age, following a crooked plank walkway between woven willow fences. The entrance to a stave hall loomed up to the right, its pillars carved in a pattern of red and white beasts. Inside, stiffly posed women in brown linen dresses stirred a cauldron over a fake glowing fire. To the left, the prow of a longship emerged from the gloom, tethered to a rickety pier. A recording repeated the cries of seagulls, the creak of mast ropes, and the slosh of waves. The displays had managed to pack the ambiance of an ancient world into a single dark room.

What drew Kirstin, however, was a grassy hill at the end of the crooked path. The hill itself was merely a diorama painted on the museum's back wall. But the tombstones in front were real. The largest of them was the Eskelhem stone, cleaned and restored after lying face down in a church floor for a millennium. Eight feet tall, with a curved top and sloping sides, the gravestone depicted two scenes. Below, a square-sailed ship carried a host of warriors across violent waves. Above, they battled with swords and spears. In front of the stone, a glass window into the "hill" revealed a buried treasure of silver coins.

"Whose grave was it?" Kirstin asked.

Mette shook her head. "We don't know. The stone was moved when the church was built. It's possible the coins have nothing to do with the original burial."

"I think they do," Kirstin said. "A hoard of silver dirhams. A voyage over whitewater rapids. A battle. This could be the grave of one of the Rus who sailed with Oleg to besiege Constantinople. Someone who returned with a treasure."

Lars asked, "What's with the dog?"

"It's Fenris, the wolf-god," Helen said.

Mette cut in. "We don't understand all the imagery on this stone. The woman carrying a horn is probably a Valkyrie, bringing mead to the dead she has chosen in battle. The horse, the wolf, the man with a ring—these are less certain."

"Then there are no answers here. My dream was wrong." Kirstin turned away. She looked at the faces of her family—tense, worried, and perhaps a little ashamed. "Or wait. There's something you haven't told me. All of you, you've been coddling an old woman with half-truths for the past year. What's going on?"

"Mother, we—" Mette began.

Kirstin banged her cane on the wooden floor. "I don't have time to waste with lies." The old archeologist aimed her cane at Helen first. "You! In your letters you wrote that you left your internship at the Russian excavation because the leader was unreliable. That may be true, but I suspect there's a lot you left out. Who was the excavation leader, and what really happened?"

Helen looked down. "Professor Henrik Talin turned out to be the same Henrik who worked with Mom at the Hedeby excavation during the war."

"The Nazi? What on earth did he want with you in Russia?"

Helen explained about the Varangian Order, their belief in the power of Oleg's ancient sword, and her own escape with Lennart to the Finnish border.

Kirstin studied the girl in silence a moment. Then she asked, "How did you get across the border in a stolen car?"

Helen shrugged. "I don't really know. I mean, we did have 200,000 rubles in the trunk, and that got us past the first guards. But then at the actual border, time seemed to sort of slow down."

Now even Mette was puzzled. "You didn't tell me that."

"We'd brought this old woman along as a sort of hitchhiker? Groa, she called herself. Anyway, the soldiers just kind of froze and we drove right through."

Mette studied her daughter skeptically.

Kirstin aimed her cane at Mette. "How can you doubt your daughter when you've been hiding information yourself? What have you been up to this past year?"

"Well, we've started spraying the wreck of the *Vasa* with glycol."

"That's not what I meant." Everyone in Sweden knew about the shipyard where the seventeenth-century warship had been put on temporary display. To be permanently stabilized, the ancient wood would have to be treated with preservatives for seventeen years and then slowly dried out for another ten years.

"There's something else," Kirstin said. "Something troubling."

Mette nodded. "It's the graffiti. The three arrow-shaped Tyr runes."

Helen perked up. "That's what Professor Talin was using for his white supremacists. They must have followers everywhere."

"This may be true." Sasha's words were tinged, as always, with a slight Russian accent. "In Moscow I learned that the Varangian Order has infiltrated the Soviet military. The Kremlin is cracking down on them as militant reactionaries. Professor Talin has been arrested. His top lieutenant, Urmas Byelekov, is still at large."

Lars added, "We suspect they have other agents in Western Europe and the US. What about that Marine defector you were following?"

"Oswald?" Sasha shook her head. "A simpleton. I don't know why the US let him back in. At least he's out of harm's way in Dallas, Texas."

Helen looked at her mother uncertainly. "There were arrow-runes on an artifact in the *Vasa*. And on the podium when the ship was raised. What other graffiti have you found?"

"It wouldn't be important, except—" Mette waved her hand as she searched for the right words. "My colleague, Per Gertula, has been re-examining Bj 581, the warrior grave on Birka. He thinks it's actually the grave of a woman. It's paired with an identical grave mound for a horse."

"A woman and a horse." Kirstin looked up at the Eskelhem tombstone. "I don't suppose there's also a wolf and a man with a ring?"

"Actually, there might be. When Per brought the horse's skull to the university he noticed that it rattled. He cleaned out the skull and found a silver ring with a pattern of biting beasts. Inside the ring, someone had scratched three Tyr runes."

"Wait." Kirstin held up a palm. "How did the ring get in a skull? Did the horse eat it?"

"No. The ring wasn't in the horse's mouth. It was inside the cranium."

"Is that even possible?"

"There was a hole in an eye socket. Someone must have put the ring there after the horse was dead."

Kirstin drew in her breath. "Oleg! It was Oleg."

Helen wrinkled her nose. "Oleg is supposed to be buried in Old Ladoga. I worked on the excavation there."

"That could be, but the *Primary Chronicle* tells of a different prophecy. A seer said Oleg would be killed by his horse. Oleg ignored the warning. Years later, when he returned to visit the grave of his horse, a snake crawled out of its skull and bit him."

"That's a weird story, Bedstemor. Even if it were true, why would Oleg put a ring in the horse's eye? Besides, the person buried by this horse was female, so it couldn't be Oleg."

Mette nodded agreement. "The whole Birka excavation has been confusing. I don't know what Per should publish. The one thing his work seems to show is so disturbing that we've both kept it quiet."

"What does his work show?" Lars asked.

"It's the ring. The Tyr runes suggest the Varangian Order dates to the Viking Age. Don't you find that alarming?"

"Times have changed, Sis. Today the kooks who believe in white supremacy aren't like the Vikings. They're trying to trigger nuclear Armageddon so they can start a new world."

"But that's exactly what a Fenris cult would have wanted. The Vikings just gave it a different name. They called it Ragnarök."

Suddenly the museum lights went out. The resulting darkness was absolute.

"Sorry," Mette said. "The lights are on a timer after hours. I think I've got a flashlight in my purse."

Even the recorded sound of birds and waves had stopped. In the frightening void, the five people in the museum could hear each other breathe.

Then a distant horn moaned.

"The ferry!" Helen exclaimed. "Lennart's coming. We've got to get down to the harbor."

Mette clicked on a pen light, turning everyone into shadowy wraiths. "All right, let's go."

They found their way out of the museum, crowded back into the Saab, and drove the few blocks down to the ferry dock.

Helen bolted from the car to the harbor railing, trying to spot Lennart among the people on the arriving ship. The ferry was already churning up water as it slowed, a great white whale with a row of holiday passengers in its gaping mouth. Helen bounced on her toes, both from excitement and from the cold. She had worn only a short, form-fitted jacket that flared over her hips. No one had suggested she put on something warmer—a sign that she really was being treated as an adult.

Behind her, Mette whispered to Kirstin, "I miss the days when she used to tell me about her imaginary boyfriend, Lenny."

"But—" Kirstin whispered back. "Didn't it turn out that there really was a boyfriend?"

"That's the best part. Her imaginary Lennart was supposed to be a troublemaker. She wanted him to be a rebel, I guess. But then I found her a much more suitable boy, a university student interning with the Ministry of Foreign Affairs. And guess what? His name is Lennart too."

Kirstin laughed, thinking that this was one time when a little deception might be a good thing.

"He's not there!" Helen cried, her heart in her throat. A broad metal gangplank had lowered from the front of the ferry. First ashore were half a dozen bicyclists, followed by a crowd of foot passengers, waving greetings to their friends and relatives. Helen had hoped to see Lenny at the front of that pack, riding his skateboard. How could he have missed the boat? He had promised to come—he had even promised to bring a Christmas surprise. And now all that was left on the ferry were trucks and cars, starting their engines in the cold air.

Bang! One of the cold motors backfired, coughing black smoke out of the ferry's mouth. A big truck covered with blue tarps struggled up the ramp and turned on the lane toward town.

Bang! The boxy little car behind the truck backfired again. This time it also blinked its headlights and beeped.

"A Trabant?" Lars laughed. "Those things are washing machines on wheels."

"Lennart!" Helen vaulted over the railing. "You kept the Trabi!"

He rolled down the window. "That's not the surprise, girlfriend. Hop in and see."

She got in the passenger side, the tinny door banging behind her with the clang of a washing machine lid.

"Just like old times, huh?" Lennart's smile warmed her all the way through. It *was* like old times—driving across Finland, the two of them together with a stash of smuggled rubles, the smell of gasoline fumes, the thrill of adventure, and—

Helen sensed the presence before she saw it. Slowly she turned toward the shadow in the back seat. The old woman sat hunkered in a black shawl, her gaze a timeless juxtaposition of blue and green.

"Groa," Helen said.

"She was going to be alone for Yule." Lennart's tone was both apologetic and—strangely—a little doubtful.

"How—?" Helen began.

"It wasn't easy. I had to drive all the way to Norway to pick her up. She lives in a little backwoods village called Oseberg. I hope you don't mind."

Helen had run out of words. This was entirely the wrong sort of surprise. She had wanted to spend Christmas just with Lenny. How would she explain this uninvited guest to her parents?

Helen's unspoken question was: *Why?*

The old woman's unspoken answer was: *I am almost too late.*

* * *

The Gustmeyer family admitted Groa to their Christmas celebration more readily than Helen had expected. Lennart introduced her as a freelance agent who had infiltrated the Varangian Order and helped rescue Helen.

And yet each of the Gustmeyers harbored a reservation—a suspicion that they had seen this woman before. Sasha imagined that she had once run into Groa in a Berlin museum. Lars remembered Groa's unnerving gaze from a microfilm photograph of a dungeon doorway. Mette couldn't shake the feeling that she too had seen those mismatched eyes—perhaps in London just after the war? Kirstin's suspicions were deeper, and so troubling that she spoke very little that evening.

The warmth of Julius' welcome made up for them all. "Anyone who saved my daughter and beat that scoundrel Henrik with a stick deserves to sit at the head of our table."

"We do have room at the table," Mette said, "But I'm afraid we don't really have a spare bed."

"I am used to sleeping on wooden floors," Groa replied.

This statement—by a frail, elderly guest—seemed so unlikely that Mette had no answer.

At length Kirstin broke her own silence. "My room is the largest. I'll put out sofa cushions."

With the sleeping arrangements apparently settled, the family turned their attention to dinner. Julius insisted that Groa take his place at the head of the table. Julius stood beside her to carve the goose and pass out the plates. Lars opened two bottles of riesling from Germany's

Mosel Valley. Mette brought steaming bowls from the kitchen with pickled red cabbage and boiled potatoes in dill sauce.

After dinner they lit candles on a fir tree in the parlor and sang a few carols. Then they blew out the candles so they could concentrate on opening presents. Mette had quickly wrapped a knitted scarf as a gift for their unexpected guest, and Groa responded by presenting the Gustmeyers with a packet of homemade herbal tea.

Because Helen was no longer a child, she received just one present— a disappointing set of watercolor paints. By then it was late enough that Lars poured a round of akvavit for a final Christmas toast.

"Let's each propose a wish," Julius suggested, his cheeks already flushed from the wine. He held up his glass. "To our family and friends—may our circle continue to grow."

"I'll second that." Mette tapped his glass with a small clink. "A family is the triumph of love."

Lars said, "I'd like to toast the end of the Cold War. Someday."

"And espionage," Sasha added. "My wish is that our countries would get rid of our jobs and hire people for peace."

"That might be asking too much." Kirstin's hand shook as she lifted her glass. "I'd just like to understand things in the time I have left."

"As would I," Groa added.

Helen sipped her drink and sputtered. "I was going to toast the akvavit itself, but it tastes like spiced kerosene."

"Is no one going to toast Sweden's king?" Lennart looked around the faces and shrugged. "OK, instead let's raise our glasses to someone who's better looking. Here's to turning eighteen and finding something useful in the trunk of a Trabant."

Helen paused. "What's that supposed to mean?"

Groa said, "It sounds like a prediction you could check."

Lenny held out a key. "I got tired of picking the Trabi's lock."

Helen grabbed the key and hurried outside to the battered East German car. She unlocked the trunk and lifted the lid.

Inside was a cherry-red Stratocaster electric bass guitar with a large red ribbon. She threw her arms around Lenny's neck. "How did you know?"

"Groa's been teaching me to read minds."

"Really?"

"No, but in your case, I knew. C'mon, let's try it out on your family."

330

"I don't have to read their minds to know what they'll think of the Beatles. Or are you going to teach me old Swedish folk songs?"

In reply Lennart lifted a second guitar and an amp out of the trunk. A few minutes later they had plugged everything together in the parlor. Helen touched a string, unleashing a boom that shook the house. Feedback screeched. The older people in the room cringed, covering their ears.

"Easy, girlfriend." Lenny showed her how to play three notes—C, G, and D. "Just pluck one of those lightly at the start of each measure."

"Which one?"

"Whichever sounds best. Start with C."

Thump! Thump! Thump! Helen whanged out a series of Cs. On the fourth beat Lennart joined in with a strummed chord. And then he began to sing—not the wailing rock and roll lyrics Helen had expected, but rather a very modern love ballad.

> She was just seventeen
> You know what I mean
> And the way she looked
> Was way beyond compare.
> Now I'll never dance with another
> *Whoa!*
> When I saw her standing there.
>
> Well my heart went *boom!*
> When I crossed that room
> And I held her hand
> In mi-i-i-i-i-ne.
> Now I'll never dance with another
> *Whoa!*
> Since I saw her standing there.

Lennart ended with a jazzy riff. He took Helen's hand and they bowed together to fervent applause.

Mette stopped clapping long enough to unplug the amp.

"Mom!" Helen complained.

"*Gledelig Jul*, everyone," Mette said. "And to all a good night."

With yawns and thank-yous, the Gustmeyers retreated to their rooms. Even Lennart merely gave Helen a kiss on the cheek before heading out to a trundle bed in the poorly heated pantry. Helen wasn't ready for sleep—it wasn't even midnight! She dragged her feet up the stairs, wishing the party could continue into the morning hours.

Then she remembered the Christmas two years ago, when she had spied on the adults through the heat vents in the upstairs floor. Helen's was the only bedroom upstairs. If she didn't alarm people by creaking floorboards she could listen in on almost any room she chose. Except, maddeningly, for Lennart's pantry, which lacked a heat vent.

Helen took off her shoes, wrapped herself in a down comforter, and set out to spy on Uncle Lars and Aunt Sasha. They were intelligence agents, so they surely had secrets worth discovering. But Helen also remembered carrying a Santa Lucia breakfast tray into their bedroom one morning to find them sitting up naked in bed. That memory was still painful enough that she shuffled in her socks to the vent above her parents' bedroom instead.

Amazingly, her father was humming the Beatles' tune. Didn't he hate that kind of music? Then he actually sang a verse—with revised lyrics.

> Now, I'd rather dance with her mother
> *Whoa!*
> When I see her standing there.

Her mother responded with a suggestively low, husky laugh.

Helen hurried away from the vent, stepping on all the creaky boards she could find.

That left Bedstemor's back bedroom, where Groa had a makeshift bed on the floor. Helen assumed both of these elderly people would already be snoring. Instead they were talking rapidly—perhaps even arguing? Helen held her ear to the vent. They were speaking in an old-fashioned Norwegian dialect that made her miss parts of the conversation. It sounded as strange and as distant as a radio play from an old, crackling transmitter in far-off Norway.

> KIRSTIN: I saw you, covering your left hand all evening. Show me your ring.
> GROA: (unintelligible)
> KIRSTIN: It's the same.
> GROA: No, the dragons are facing the other way. You see?
> KIRSTIN: How would you know that? I didn't describe the

ring from Birka.
GROA: (unintelligible)

Helen strained to hear. She had noticed Groa's ring during their long drive together from Russia. The silver band was obviously one of the cheap reproductions sold to tourists in museum gift shops. Rather than recreate the detail of a genuine Viking artifact, the forgers had simply made the ring look as if it were worn smooth with age.

KIRSTIN: Your husband? Now I remember where I've seen your eyes before. At the Oseberg excavation. You called yourself Fru Hansen then. Your husband owned the farm. Superstitious locals went to you for magic.
GROA: People wanted to believe. Many still do.
KIRSTIN: No—that doesn't work.
GROA: Spells seldom do.
KRISTIN: I mean the timeline. We excavated the Oseberg ship in 1904. I was young and you were old—at least sixty. Since then it's been, what? Fifty-eight years. How—
GROA: They have not been good years. We've seen two world wars. Tens of millions died. Now this new, colder war threatens to destroy everything before its time. Fenris is loose.
KIRSTIN: Fenris? You thought we'd find a sword in the Oseberg ship. But we didn't.
GROA: The sword helped Harald Fairhair unify Norway. He buried it with his grandmother. Graverobbers stole it from the mound. Its curse fueled the Viking Age.
KIRSTIN: No one sword could have been in all the Vikings' battles.
GROA: Copies were made. One of them allowed Oleg to conquer Russia. Another helped the Danes conquer England. But I fear a third is still at large. If it were found, (unintelligible)
KIRSTIN: Why have you come to me?
GROA: The shadow of Niflheim already darkens your eyes. You have days, not weeks.

Helen drew in her breath. Was Bedstemor really so ill? How could Groa be so sure?

KIRSTIN: I came to Gotland so I wouldn't die in a hospital.

And now I know why we had to meet again.

GROA: Why?

KRISTIN: So I can tell you what you already know. You cannot be a hundred and twenty years old, much less a thousand.

GROA: My memory is poor.

KIRSTIN: In the old days, gods interacted with mortals. They intermarried. People could be promoted and gods could be demoted.

GROA: (unintelligible)

KIRSTIN: No, you were given a task. Even in the legends, the Norse gods failed to stop Fenris by themselves. Now the threat is growing. You, an old woman from a small Norwegian farm—you are the one who has been left standing in the wolf-god's path.

GROA: I am afraid to sleep. For some, sleep is death. For me, it is the horror of becoming young.

KIRSTIN: And the birth of hope. Let us both go to rest, knowing some answers at last.

The voices from the floor vent fell silent.

* * *

No matter how hard Helen tried that night, she was unable to sleep.

And yet Mette shook her awake the next morning. "Honey? Don't you want to join us for Christmas breakfast? You've been out like a rock."

CHAPTER 29
BIRKA, 907

Thorkell was right about outrunning the Swedes. The Ship in the Woods that Hrolf had designed was so light it seemed to skip across the waves, flying on the fresh west wind to the open sea.

Beyond the skerries Thorkell ordered, "Oars up!"

The entire crew raised their oars in a farewell salute to Oleg. Was the old regent still alive? Groa couldn't see him among the faces on the other ship. Gunnar, now both captain and helmsman, waved good-bye from the stern. Then he steered Oleg's ship away from them, heading north toward Ruslagen.

Even after Thorkell had turned their own ship south toward Gotland, Groa couldn't help looking back, watching the yellow-and-white-striped sail of Oleg's ship slowly diminish into a hazy horizon. So much of her life—her second, renewed life—had been tied to Oleg's ambitions. Gunnar might have been the helmsman of Oleg's ship, but she had been the helmsman of his ambition. She had thrown the knife that saved his life on Birka long ago. She had allowed him to wield a sword of destiny all the way to the halls of Miklagard. And now her prophecy, long ridiculed as foolish, had come to pass. The fates must already have known that she would throw her knife too late this time.

Oleg's life had come full circle to a full stop. She had no choice but to sail on without him. Her own Ship in the Woods now seemed a fragile leaf, alone on the World Ocean.

A chuckle beside her reminded Groa that she was anything but alone. Hrolf, her steadfast husband, was chortling over something in the old tool chest he'd bought in Constantinople. He had lifted the beat-up lid just high enough that he could peer inside.

"What's gotten into you, Hrolf?"

He closed the lid. "Nothing."

He blushed! Her husband wasn't telling the truth. For the first time in their marriage, Groa heard in his thoughts that he was lying to her. Or perhaps just concealing something.

"What do you have in there? Why haven't you shown me?"

Now Hrolf's face really was red. "You never asked, my love. It looks like such an ordinary box, doesn't it?"

He motioned her closer and lifted the lid a little.

She looked inside, puzzled. "They're tools. That's not very surprising for a tool box."

"But look! They're tiny."

"Yes—" She drew out the word uncertainly. Her unspoken question was: *Why?*

Hrolf closed the lid with a satisfied smile. She heard her husband's unspoken answer loud and clear, although she would not fully understand it for more than forty years.

I am going to make you proud, my love.

* * *

Molten metal seethed in the hellish fires of Iberia.

At the forge the Voice stood unmasked as Abd al-Rahman III. Twenty-two years after slipping out of Constantinople as a spy, he had at last defeated three rival Moorish emirs and proclaimed himself the first Caliph of Cordoba.

Beside him Ali Ibn al-Namid cowered with dread. The old Arab doctor held up his hands, protecting his face against the glare of the coals—and the demonic forces the Caliph was attempting to conjure.

"Arise, djinn of the North! Spirit of darkness, you are now bound to *my* will."

Flames leapt up about the liquid steel in the cauldron, reflecting from the men's faces as a skeletal glow.

"My lord," the doctor objected. "I fear the Varangians' demons are not like ours."

"The djinn are all one race, created by Allah on the day before men. Some inhabit bodies and some reside in objects. The djinn we captured in Byzantium was cast in a sword."

"Isn't one enough, my lord?"

"Not if the Caliphate is to conquer the infidels of Europe." Abd al-Rahman lifted his arms and commanded, "Pour the metal!"

336

A team of men in black shirts tilted the cauldron, spilling a thin river of fiery red into a series of ceramic troughs. The flaming liquid hissed and crackled sparks before settling into its new form—three new bodies for a single evil god.

"When they are wrought into shining blades, these manifestations of the Varangians' djinn will open a new front in our battle, harrowing the Christian world from the North."

"Now, my lord? While rebels still challenge the Caliphate from within?"

"The ablest spies, and the most insidious saboteurs, infiltrate their victims slowly. Our Norse demon has already waited ages. Time passes at a different pace for the djinn. I will gift a sword to the Varangians once every twenty years. Each generation will bring a fresh wave of pagan terror to weaken the Christian kings."

"The carpenter who brought us the sword called it Fenris. That name was etched on the blade in the Varangians' stick-writing."

The Caliph was a short man, with white skin and blue eyes, but in the glow of the forge he loomed large. "The new swords will be exact copies, with identical lettering. Belief in the djinn gives the demons power."

"The Varangians say Fenris is a wolf that will devour the world. Does that not alarm you, my lord?"

Caliph Abd al-Rahman III stroked his black beard. "Perhaps the world must be devoured before a purer age can begin."

* * *

Even when Hrolf lay dying after a life of eighty-eight winters, he hesitated to tell Groa his secret. Instead he squeezed Groa's wrinkled hand, recalling one of their brightest moments together—Groa's triumphant return to the Tunsberg inn that had been her home.

"Do you remember the look on Solveig's face?"

Groa squeezed his hand in return, blinking back a tear. She did treasure the memory of that day, arriving in Norway aboard Thorkell's proud ship after twenty-five winters in Russiya. All that time she had plotted her revenge on Bjarne, the one-handed liar who had usurped her house—and on Solveig, the slave-maid who had tormented her with cruel pranks—and on Jarl Bork, the nobleman who had dug into Queen Asa's burial mound to sell a stolen sword. All that time she had vowed to reclaim what was hers, the inn that had been her first husband's blacksmith shop.

On the morning of their arrival Groa and Hrolf had worn their finest clothes, blue satins bought in the markets of Constantinople. At the harbor they had hired three men to carry their chests of silver and tools. Townspeople emerged from their houses to watch the wealthy strangers parade up Kingsgate. But Tunsberg had changed in the intervening years, and so had Groa. The peace imposed by King Harald Fairhair had obviously not brought prosperity. Without the plunder of Viking raids, Norway was a poor land with rocky soil. The inn itself was smaller than Groa remembered, and much shabbier. The wattle walls bowed outward, the dried mud flaking from bare willow withes. Rotten shakes in the roof had been patched with straw. A young man dumping slop in the street called through the open door, "Mom! Guests are arriving!"

A moment later Solveig appeared in the doorway—a tired, old woman trying her best to look cheerful for the wealthy travelers. But then she saw Groa's mismatched blue and green eyes, and she knew. The day Solveig had dreaded had finally come.

"These aren't guests," Solveig told the young man, her expression wooden. "It's her, the one I warned you about. It's Groa's granddaughter."

In that moment Groa's youthful feeling of triumphant revenge shifted to a more mature mood. Sympathy? Perhaps even regret. These people had suffered too. How much of their sorrow was her fault?

"Solveig, this is my husband Hrolf," Groa said. "Where is Bjarne?"

"Dead." Solveig stood in the doorway, blocking her way. "Bjarne freed me when we married. We had two children before he died. Now this inn is all we've got. You can't dare to throw us out."

"We'll see." Groa pushed past her.

Hrolf followed, curious to examine the inn his wife had boasted about for so long. He sized up the dirt-floored dining room with the experienced eye of a craftsman. He walked through the sooty kitchen to a courtyard surrounded by derelict sheds and a stinking privy. A round granite rock stood in the middle of the courtyard—apparently an old millstone.

"It's not like I remember," Groa said beside him. "This place has become a worthless ruin."

"I'm afraid you are right," Hrolf replied slowly, thinking. "The structures here have no value. But the location is excellent. The property lies on a busy street very close to the harbor. I wonder if we could rebuild?"

Groa looked into her husband's mind—and reeled at the scale of construction projects already underway there. The man who had built more than four hundred ships had, with a single stroke, demolished the courtyard sheds. In their place a two-story U-shaped building was rising from the ground, its beams fitted together with intricate joinery. Then the inn itself vanished, replaced by a three-story boarding house. The inlaid wooden designs of a jewelry box decorated every beam and doorway. The silver hoard in their sea chest was simultaneously dwindling, but the rebuilt inn would be magnificent.

"Excuse me, my lady," a girl's voice interrupted.

Groa turned, and was stunned to discover that Solveig had regained her youth—perhaps by the same mysterious magic that had transformed Groa long ago? Somehow the tired old innkeeper appeared to have become a fresh-faced slave girl of twenty.

Instead of taunting Groa, as had been Solveig's old manner, the new version of Solveig addressed her with quiet respect.

"Forgive me for speaking up like this, my lady. I'm told your grandmother was treated badly in this house. My mother always said you might come back to claim your inheritance. We've worked so hard. My brother cooks. I serve and clean. Only the poorest travelers stay here, so we often go hungry ourselves. Please, my lady, don't make us leave."

As Groa listened she kept seeing Hrolf's palatial, three-story boarding house hovering in the air. An inn of that scale would need staff.

Hrolf cleared his throat, as he often did when about to make a suggestion. "If we rebuilt the inn, there might be room for Solveig's family."

And so it was that Solveig stayed. Groa never entirely trusted her old tormenter, but Solveig's children—and later, their children—became the family that Groa and Hrolf had always lacked.

The new inn that rose on the site became the marvel of all southern Norway. Hrolf proudly showed visitors his work—ornate half-timbered walls, whittled designs on the handrails of spiral staircases, and entire woodland scenes pieced together from scraps of colored wood.

Travelers went out of their way to stop in Tunsberg. As a result, news arrived there from far and wide. Groa learned, for example, that Jarl Bork had been charged with treason. The surly nobleman had emigrated to Iceland rather than face King Harald. There Bork had eventually been killed while his men were raiding a neighbor's farmstead.

The news from Russiya came mostly from Eskel, a lanky Geatish trader who had returned from Novgorod on Thorkell's' ship. Eskel had gone ashore at Gotland, intending to take Asger's body to his family there. But all of Asger's relatives had either died or moved away. So Eskel used some of Asger's treasure to raise a tombstone for him depicting their voyage to Byzantium. With the rest of the silver Eskel bought a ship and started plying the trade routes of the Baltic. Almost every year he stopped in Tunsberg to exchange news and to admire the improvements Hrolf kept making to the inn.

On one of Eskel's first visits he reported that Gunnar had died.

"Gunnar?" Hrolf asked across the dining table, surprised. "I thought Oleg's helmsman was unkillable."

"We all thought so, after seeing him fight in Miklagard and Sigtuna." Eskel stretched his long legs under the inlaid table and leaned back with a horn of ale. His price for news was dinner. Since Groa and Hrolf owned an inn, they were only too glad to reward him with feasts in the upstairs room reserved for special guests.

"What happened to Gunnar?" Groa asked. "Not the straw death, surely. He was a fighter, always quick to anger."

"Too quick, this time." Eskel took a drink and wiped his trim brown beard with a hand callused by years of rowing. "You remember when we left him, Gunnar was taking Oleg's body back to Russiya for burial?"

"Yes."

"His ship got back to Ladoga just in time for the first hard freeze of winter. Gunnar reminded the Ladogans that they'd promised to build Oleg a big grave mound. The local chieftain said the offer had been made in summer, and not when the ground was frozen. They honored Oleg by blowing lur horns and reciting saga verses. They burned his body in a ship. But the Ladogans refused to build the actual mound until the following spring."

Groa sensed what was coming. "Gunnar picked a fight with them, didn't he?"

"And for once, he lost."

Groa and Hrolf exchanged a somber glance. Eskel's news was not always good.

Several years passed before Eskel returned, this time with a ship-load of strange trade goods—pewter pitchers from England, gold brocade from Africa, and ceramic tiles from Italy. The news he brought was just as unusual.

"I have sailed around the world," Eskel boasted. The gluttonous Geat's words were hard to understand because his mouth was full of ox-blood sausage.

"Around the world? Then is the World Ocean circular?" Groa asked.

"The route I took was. It's like this plate of sausage." Eskel drew a circle around his plate with the tip of his knife.

"Careful!" Hrolf exclaimed. "That tabletop took me a year to piece together."

"It took me longer to sail around it. You see, Europe's like this sausage in the middle. After my crew sailed to Russiya we rowed the rivers to the Black Sea and just kept going—to Greece, Sicily, Iberia, Mercia, and back." At the mention of each place name Eskel stabbed the tip of his knife into a different part of the table around his plate.

Hrolf winced with each mark. Still, he hesitated to take a knife away from a hungry Viking.

Groa made an effort to intervene. "What about Persia and China? Did you visit them too?"

"No, Persia's over here and China's here." Eskel stabbed his knife into the table in front of Hrolf and then Groa.

Groa put her hand over Eskel's and squeezed it with surprising strength.

"Ouch!" Eskel said.

"Stop stabbing the table. Instead tell us what news you learned on your voyage."

The Geat let go of the knife and resumed eating with his fingers. "In Russiya everyone misses Oleg. Tsar Igor is an incompetent fool. He started building a Saint Sophia church in Kiev, but had to stop when the jarls threatened to revolt."

"Why would Igor want a Christian church?" Hrolf asked.

"It's a fad among the Varangian Knights. Hundreds of them have been fighting for the Byzantines. They've helped the Christians reconquer a lot of Sicily, southern Italy, and even parts of the Levant. Some have allowed themselves to be baptized. Emperor Leo lets them loot, so they've gotten rich."

"Is that what lured you to the southern sea?"

Eskel shook his head while drinking from a horn, and as a result ale dribbled into his beard. Since his last visit the once-trim beard had grown into a rope-like appendage that dangled nearly to his plate.

"My idea was to trade between Muslims and Christians. They've divided the Mediterranean into two separate markets. I thought outsiders like us might sell to both sides."

"Judging from your cargo, your plan worked."

"Actually, they all pretty much tried to kill us. A fast ship helps. We spent a month in Iberia as prisoners of the Emir of Cordoba. He had a doctor who said he knew you. Ali Ibn-Something?"

Hrolf drew in his breath. "Ali Ibn al-Namid? What was he doing there?"

"Translating between the emir and us."

"Why did the emir take you prisoner?" Hrolf asked.

Groa added suspiciously, "And why did he release you?"

"He just wanted news. He insisted that we tell him what we knew about every king, jarl, and outlaw in the North. The doctor wrote it all down, using squiggles on paper leaves. The weird thing was that we never saw the emir's face. All that time, he was just a voice behind a screen."

"A voice?" Hrolf paled. To Groa's surprise he suddenly changed the subject. "Tell us the news from England."

"There's not much to report." Eskel gathered his beard in one hand and pulled—a gesture that helped explain its rope-like shape. "They're still using King Alfred's system, dividing the country in half. In the east, people in the Danelaw speak Norse and follow Nordic law. In the west everything's English. It seems to work. The Danelaw keeps outsiders from attacking. But traders like us were welcome on both sides of the island."

Eskel licked his fingers and leaned back from the table with a belch. "I met a duke in Oxford you'd like. He loves travel."

"You should tell him to visit Tunsberg," Groa said.

"I did." Eskel winked. "I raved about the place. It never hurts to send a little trade to friends."

* * *

Eskel paid his final visit to Tunsberg thirty years later. That fateful day turned out to be Hrolf's last among the living—and Groa's too, in a sense that even a sorceress would not have predicted.

To be sure, Groa had noticed omens. Hrolf had been short of breath that morning. His eyes had been cloudy for a year or so. Groa wanted to believe this was the murkiness of age, rather than the shade of Niflheim. Besides, everyone was too busy that day to worry. The inn was completely full for Tunsberg's autumn harvest festival.

The Duke of Oxford and his young wife, Eowin, were the most illustrious of the guests in town, having sailed from England with a retinue of guards, ladies in waiting, and musicians. Groa gave them the entire third floor of the inn, a suite the Duke insisted they share with Eskel.

Groa wasn't the only one who puzzled over the two men's friendship. The Duke was a clean-shaven gentleman of fifty winters who wore colored satins and jeweled rings. Eskel had degenerated over the years to a ragged scarecrow of a man, with a filthy beard that hung from his chin like the hawser of a ship's anchor. The Duchess, a delicate flower no older than twenty, avoided sitting or standing anywhere near the old Geat.

Nonetheless, the Duke and Eskel spent the afternoon watching festival games together like boys on a picnic outing. The Duke tried his hand at an archery contest and came in third. The Duke urged Eskel to attempt the swimming competition, a trial that involved holding one's breath as long as possible underwater. Eskel lost, but he was a good sport, laughing when the Duke admitted it had been a trick to make him take a bath.

Groa understood the men's friendship better that evening when the Duke's musicians accompanied the singing of an English saga.

The inn's second-floor banquet room had been set for the feast, with twenty plates on Hrolf's inlaid table. The old carpenter proudly showed the Duke and Eskel his latest addition to the room—a bay window fitted together with pieces of actual glass. Imported glass was so expensive in Norway that beads were treasured and glass goblets rare. Holes in house walls were called "windows" because they let in wind as well as light. Here, however, Hrolf had filled the opening with little circles of blown glass, so clear that people at the banquet table could look out across rooftops and see longships in the harbor below.

The young Duchess said nothing, apparently unimpressed by the novelty of a glass wall. At that point Groa realized that the Duchess hadn't spoken all day. Was the lovely Eowin mute? All through dinner the Duchess maintained her silence. Even when Solveig's grandchildren brought in platters of apple-stuffed duck and asked if the Duchess was pleased, she merely smiled. And so Groa was astonished when, as the plates were being cleared away, the Duke stood up, clapped his hands for attention, and announced that for their entertainment his wife was going to sing a saga.

Hrolf blinked, obviously confused as well. "Sagas are spoken, not sung. And they're never recited by women."

"We have different customs in England, master carpenter. Please, permit us to demonstrate." The Duke pointed to the old Geatish trader seated beside him. "Your friend Eskel has achieved some fame in

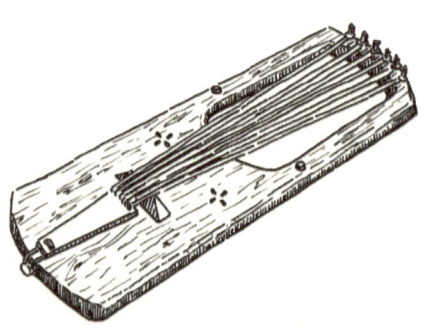

England with his performance of *Beowulf*. Eowin and my musicians have been looking forward to accompanying him."

Hrolf blinked again. "Eskel is secretly a skald? Is this true?"

The Geat chuckled. "Not exactly. You'll see." He stood up from his chair and shook his shoulders to loosen his tunic.

Then he struck a dramatic pose and nodded.

The Duke's musician responded by strumming a musical instrument that resembled a long hollow box with strings.

After a series of four chords, the Duchess stood up and spoke.

Hwæt!

Was this a word, Groa wondered? It certainly wasn't Norse. Nor was the verse that followed.

We Gardena in geardagum,
þeodcyninga, þrym gefrunon,
hu ða æþelingas ellen fremedon.

Groa realized that Eowin had been silent all day because she only spoke English. Her husband and the others in their retinue were older, and presumably had learned Norse from the Danes in the Danelaw.

As the Duchess recited the English verse, Eskel began dancing about on his long legs, variously miming expressions of surprise, amusement, and horror. It took Groa a while to figure out what Eskel was doing. He was acting out the verse in pantomime.

Together the strummed chords, the foreign song, and Eskel's gesticulations created a spectacle unlike anything seen before in Tunsberg. Because many of the English words were close to Norse, and because Eskel acted out the saga so well, Groa was able to get the drift of the story. The poem was about a Geat like Eskel—if Eskel were a fearless warrior king named Beowulf. In the saga, the hero traveled to Denmark to vanquish some monsters. Then he returned to Gotland, where he died slaying a dragon.

Sprawled dramatically on the banquet table in mock death, Eskel translated Eowin's final words.

Wiglaf then became the king,
And long the land was ruled by him.

Cheers greeted the conclusion of the epic. The Duke called for a bucket of ale. He dipped the drinking horns and offered toasts in honor of the performers. A blurry moon was shining through the glass circles of the window by the time Eowin, her ladies, and the musicians retired for bed.

With just four people remaining at the table—Eskel, the Duke, Hrolf, and Groa—the conversation took a darker turn.

"There actually may be a monster in Denmark," the Duke said. "Something is wrong there."

Eskel nodded in agreement. "The Geats never used to fear the Danes. Every island in that land had several petty chieftains. But this new one, Gorm, keeps winning battle after battle. He's on the verge of conquering all of Denmark. The man has uncanny luck."

"Uncanny?" Groa had also heard of Gorm, a minor Viking from a fjord on the island of Zealand. "You suspect sorcery?"

The Duke spun his empty drinking horn. "Denmark was once the homeland of the Angles. Our English king still has spies there. They report that an Arab caliph from Iberia sent an emissary with a present to Gorm's wedding."

Eskel looked up, surprised. "The Caliph of Cordoba? He held me prisoner years ago. He was an emir then. I remember he asked about the chieftains of the North. What kind of present did he send to Gorm?"

"The spies aren't sure," the Duke said. "The gift was kept well hidden. Since that day, however, Gorm has won his battles with a shiny new sword. Foes who see its blade do not live to tell their stories. Rumors have spread that the steel is engraved with a runic name."

"Fenris?" Hrolf breathed the question.

"That sword was destroyed," Groa said. "And it was old, not shiny. But there might be other sorcery at work. Arab wizards are not like ours. They tap into strange powers."

The Duke sighed. "If I weren't Christian I might be tempted to try my own luck with Arab magic."

"You?" Groa studied the Duke. "Why?"

The Duke did not reply.

After a moment Eskel repeated an old adage in verse.

> It is a time-tested truth
> That a man in possession
> Of a noble title
> Must be in want of an heir.

Groa understood. "The Duchess is not your first wife."

The Duke nodded somberly. "I have tried before. A healer suggested travel might help. I took my first wife on honeymoons year after year. With Eowin, I have finally realized the fault is mine."

"Once I wished to bear a daughter," Groa admitted.

The Duke looked up. "That's what Eowin wants. She's even picked out a girl's name. Now I fear I have become too old to hold out hope."

Hrolf had been quiet since the discussion of the Danish king. Now the old carpenter cleared his throat—a noisy rattle that made Groa turn in alarm.

346

"Hrolf?"

"I have something." He pushed back his chair.

"Are you all right?"

"Something that may help." Hrolf lowered himself stiffly to his knees. He reached under the banquet table, pressed a panel on the inlaid pattern of the base, and opened a hidden cabinet. Inside was the battered old toolbox from Constantinople. He dragged the box out and hefted it to the table. Then he carefully unlocked the latch and lifted the lid.

"Itsy bitsy tools?" Eskel laughed. "The Duke isn't some broken toy you can fix with an elfin hammer."

Undeterred, Hrolf lifted the top tray of tools aside. A reddish glow from the space beneath cast the old woodworker's blocky face with an eerie flush. He reached inside and withdrew a small glass vial, half full of an iridescent liquid.

"What on earth?" Groa asked.

"It is an elixir to help in fathering a girl-child. I was too cautious, and only used part." Hrolf held the little bottle out to the Duke. "Perhaps you will have better luck."

The Englishman pulled the vial's stopper and sniffed. "Where did you get this?"

"In Miklagard. They say you can find anything you seek in Constantinople."

"All right, then!" Eskel laughed again. He sloshed the bucket of ale. "We've enough to wash down some magic goop with a last round."

The Duke hesitated. Groa could hear his thoughts arguing amongst themselves like law speakers at a Thing meeting.

Hrolf, however, seemed eager for a drink. He held out three empty horns—his, Groa's, and Eskel's. The Geat poured each of them half full.

"Come on, old man," Eskel admonished the Duke. "Or can't you hold your horn up straight tonight?"

The Duke's mental arguments stopped short. He emptied the vial into his drinking horn and held out the horn for Eskel to top off with ale.

"To life!" Eskel said.

The four of them tapped their horns together and drank.

"And now to bed." Eskel winked at the Duke. "Good night and good luck to us all."

* * *

Groa knew it wasn't just the drink that made Hrolf stumble going down the spiral stairs from the banquet room that night. All evening her husband had been shaky, with a sheen of perspiration about his lips. Now he sat on the bottom step, crumpled against the wall, his face ashen. He had seen his fetch and was being called to Niflheim, the realm of the dead.

"I'll go get Solveig's children to help," Groa said, although she knew this would not help.

"No." Hrolf's speech was broken by shallow breaths. "You. Just you. Our room."

Hrolf had lost weight with age but it still took all of Groa's strength to help the stocky carpenter through the empty kitchen to the courtyard. Moonlight cast the millstone in pale blue, as if it were a second, closer moon. Beside the ancient stone rose the dark prow of their "flagship"—a private bedroom Hrolf had built using strakes from old longships. Groa had wanted a retreat separate from the main inn, yet close enough to keep an eye on things. The ingenious old woodworker, with a touch of whimsy, had constructed a ship-shaped annex behind the kitchen. He had joked that he knew more about building ships than bedrooms.

Groa pushed the door open with her shoulder. A fire had already been lit on the hearth by one of Solveig's conscientious family members, chasing out the chill and the shadows. Hrolf staggered along the curved wall and sank onto the straw tick of their bed closet. Groa sat beside him and held his hand.

"Are you sure I shouldn't call Solveig's children?" Groa didn't dare to add the obvious: *So they can say goodbye.*

"It would just hurt them more." Hrolf closed his eyes—and for some reason, he smiled. "Do you remember?"

"Remember what?"

"The look on Solveig's face when you returned from Russiya? She had treated you so badly before."

Groa squeezed his hand, blinking back a tear. "Everyone makes mistakes when they are young. Now it's time to forgive."

Hrolf tried to nod, but instead coughed—a nasty rattle that left him weak.

"Just rest," Groa said. "I'll put some herbs in tea to help."

348

"No. Come here."

She bent closer. His eyes rolled back, as if he were looking up through clouds.

"I need to tell you. The tools. The potion. They were for you."

"Oh, Hrolf. It wasn't your fault that we had no children. I had no idea you wanted a child so badly."

"I wanted you to be proud of me."

"I always have been."

"Then will you forgive me, my love?"

Groa stopped, struck by a foreboding. This was the dark spot that she had never been able to read in his thoughts. The darkness went back to an alley in the Arab quarter of Constantinople.

"How much did you pay for the tools?"

"A mere two dirhams!" Hrolf sputtered a laugh. "The entire chest cost two silver coins."

"And the potion? Where did you find that?" Groa had dealt in sorcery long enough to recognize quackery when she saw it. A glowing red elixir that promised fertility was the perfect example of a wish-fulfilling ruse.

"From the same Arab wizard. The Voice."

"What voice?"

"Ali's master. Above the blacksmith shop." Hrolf clutched her arm. "They promised to melt the sword down, like you wanted. They destroyed it. But why waste good Norse steel? Why not let them reuse it? I didn't know they would recast it as a new blade."

He sank back, his strength sapped by the exertion.

With horror, Groa saw the truth he had kept hidden for so long. The price for the potion had been Fenris.

"It was all for you, my love. Everything has been for you." Hrolf lifted his shaking hands in supplication. "Do you forgive me?"

"Yes." Groa gritted her teeth. And yet: No!

Hrolf gasped, his eyes suddenly wide. Before him an enormous door began to open—an unbelievably beautiful door, inlaid with colored wood and gems. But beyond that door lay a hall of mysteries he did not want to see. He had struggled to shut out the horrors of the unknown for so long. His heart was tired. Love was all he had wanted—love and peace. He leaned back, closed his eyes, and let his heart come to rest.

* * *

Groa paced the room long into the night, glancing at Hrolf's corpse each time her path along the curved walls took her past the bed closet. How could such a good man, with such good intentions, have done something so terrible?

She had spent two lifetimes trying to undo the curse she had allowed the wolf-god to create. Now the sword that "vests the Vikings' fate" had fallen into the hands of an Arab ruler. For some reason the caliph had reforged it and gifted it to a Danish king.

King Gorm's unlikely victories were almost certainly indebted to Fenris. His success was as hollow as Oleg's had been in Russiya. She had wanted the Viking fury to end at Constantinople. Because of Hrolf's misguided love, the disease had been allowed to infect Denmark. She knew the contagion of violence would spread. Evil always did, given a chance.

What could she do? She was old. She could no longer summon the strength to stop Fenris. Crones can't stand in the path of gods.

Groa stopped in front of the hearth fire's smoldering embers, struck by a sudden thought. A wisp of smoke rose before her like a ghost. Years ago she had spent the night in this same courtyard. Then too she had despaired of hope. She had slept on the millstone, tormented by strange dreams. In the morning she had awoken with her youthful

strength restored.

She looked at her dead husband. Then she yanked away his feather comforter, rolled his cold body to one side, and pulled the straw tick out from under him. Before leaving, however, she looked back at her husband with a sigh.

Tenderly, she straightened his body on the bare wood. She crossed his callused hands on his chest.

"Goodbye, Hrolf. You loved me too well."

Groa carried the bedding outside and spread it on the granite millstone. Then she paused again, struck by another tender memory.

She pulled the straw mattress aside and reached down the stone's central hole, curious to see if the ring she had dropped in years ago might still be there. Time had filled the hole almost to the top with debris. Rather than dig she decided to leave the ring for another age. Thorleif, the husband who had forged the silver band for her, had made the mistake of forging Fenris. Hrolf, her second husband, had built treasures for her out of wood. But he had allowed the cursed sword to be forged anew.

Groa was as tired of husbands as she was tired of life itself. She climbed up onto the stone, pulled the feather cover over her, and closed her eyes. As she drifted toward sleep she thought: People are fools to wish for youth.

* * *

This time there were no wolves in Groa's dream. The correct god came to visit, but he did not do what she wanted.

First she noticed the ravens circling the moon above the courtyard. The two big birds looked down at her and cawed—raspy croaks like strangled laughter. Behind them the stars began to shift, coursing through the sky as if they were stitching dark threads into a mysterious tapestry. If only she could figure out what the needles of light were weaving! Constellations of ships? Runic verses of fate? The future itself?

Meanwhile, either the millstone was growing or she was getting smaller. Her aches vanished and her limbs straightened. She felt younger. But why could she no longer reach the edge of the millstone?

The ravens perched on the inn's topmost gable. There they grew together into the silhouette of the All-Father. The raspy caws deepened to the mischievous chuckle of Odin, the all-seeing, all-knowing prankster.

Groa looked at her hands. They were too small, with slender fingers. She had not merely become young. She was a child. Worse yet, the back door of the inn had banged open and one of the guests was coming her way. What would they think if they found a girl out here at night? The person walked on past, crossing the courtyard to the outhouse. In the moonlight, Groa recognized the face of Eowin, the Duke's young wife. By now Groa's arms had shrunk to the pudgy limbs of a baby. She was too young—altogether too young! Her memories were unraveling like a dropped skein of wool. And now the nightmare darkened, leaving her adrift in a moonless sea.

The last sounds Groa heard were a laugh from the rooftop and the footsteps of Eowin returning from the privy.

* * *

Wails of anguish and cries of alarm woke the guests of the Tunsberg inn the next morning. Solveig's grandson Ragn had gone to light a fire on the hearth of the "flagship," and had discovered Hrolf dead in the bed closet. Before long all three generations of Solveig's family were there, mourning the loss of the man they called grandfather—the steadfast carpenter who had rebuilt the inn as a monument to love.

The last to arrive was Solveig, an ancient, bald woman with a bent back. She surveyed the scene, her eyes dry. "Why is Hrolf laid out on a bare bunk?"

"That's the way I found him," Ragn said.

Solveig prodded the body with a piece of firewood. "There are no obvious wounds. It's made to look like a natural death."

"Of course it's a natural death," Ragn protested. "You're old, but Hrolf was even older."

Solveig lifted her chin at the boy's impertinence. "If it's so natural, where's his wife?"

The others in the family looked at each other. Where was Groa, and why hadn't she reported her husband's death?

Ragn's sister rushed in from the courtyard, breathless. "Come outside! Look!"

Solveig led the others out the door. By then most of the inn's guests had come down to the courtyard, curious about the commotion.

"What's going on?" the Duke demanded. "You've woken up half the town."

"Hrolf is dead," Solveig replied.

The Duke drew in his breath. "Dead? How? Where?"

"We found him in his bed closet." She squinted at the Duke. "Weren't you and that Geatish trader with him late last night? You may have been the last to see him alive."

The Duke bridled at Solveig's accusatory tone. "The master carpenter looked fatigued when he retired for bed, but he seemed well enough. His wife must be heartbroken. They were such a close pair. Where is she?"

"No one's seen her."

Ragn's sister hadn't wanted to interrupt, but now she asked, "Don't you want to see what I found?" She lifted the feather comforter from the millstone. "See? Groa left her clothes here."

Solveig and the others crowded around to inspect this unusual discovery.

The Duke wrinkled his brow. "Those really are the clothes she wore last night."

Ragn added, "And this is the bedding from her room."

"She must have been distraught by her husband's death," the Duke said. "Still, it's hard to imagine her dragging the bedding out here and taking off her clothes. The only way out of the courtyard would be through the inn. I suppose in the middle of the night people might not notice a naked woman."

One of the guests stifled a laugh.

The Duke gave the man a stern look. "Do you have another explanation?"

"Ha!" Solveig said. "I'll give you an explanation. Groa was a witch. Her grandmother vanished from this same courtyard years ago. Her name was Groa too. Theirs was a wicked lineage. It's a good thing they left no heirs. Witches can disappear whenever they choose."

"Witches?" The Duke raised an eyebrow.

"In a good way," Eskel put in. "I'm not sure about English witches, but Groa certainly wasn't wicked. She was a sorceress, and one of the best. Sometimes she could foretell the future. Often as not, she could heal the sick."

"Only the guilty run from a crime," Solveig said. "Hrolf is dead, and now Groa is gone. Draw your own conclusions."

Eskel shook his head. "If Groa has left, it wasn't to run away. She was a woman with a purpose."

"Be that as it may. Her claim on this property has always been weak. Now the inn belongs to me." Solveig waved her hands to disperse the crowd, as if she were shooing flies and not people. "Go back to your rooms, all of you. Ragn, you and your brothers can see to building a pyre for Hrolf. The rest of the family had better get to work on breakfast. You'll have time to weep when the chores are done."

Gradually the crowd left the courtyard, saddened and dissatisfied. Finally, only the Duke and his wife remained.

"I don't understand," the Duke said, examining the tunic on the millstone. "Why would Groa leave her clothes here? Where would she have gone? And why? Nothing makes sense, and yet the people here seem content to carry on as before."

"Maybe she really was a sorceress," Eowin said.

The Duke turned to his wife. "Do you know something about this mystery? You went out here last night to use the privy. It was just after we—you know."

"I do indeed," the Duchess replied. The corners of her lips turned up ever so slightly. "I was thinking of you at the time. I did notice two big crows on the roof, cawing. That might have distracted me, because I otherwise didn't see anything out of the ordinary."

"But—" the Duke searched for words. "We've been caught up in a tragedy. A carpenter has died and his wife has mysteriously gone missing. Why are you smiling?"

"Because last night it worked."

"What worked?"

"Something happened. It all came together. You were passionate, and then—I don't know. I just feel like we are going to have what we've always wanted."

"You're pregnant? How could you know so soon?"

She shrugged. "I just know. We're going to have a daughter. And we'll give her the name I chose. Lifu is here, inside me."

"By Christ's holy wounds—if only this could be true." He embraced his wife cautiously, as if she were now made of thinly blown glass. Her skin was warm, her cheeks flushed. He leaned back, looking at her. "Let's go back home to England. I'm tired of these cold northern lands with their pagans, witches, and mysteries. What do you say?"

Eowin opened her mouth to answer, and found the words were already there.

"I will go."

Epilogue
Tønsberg, Norway, 1962

Groa shivered in the cold night air, walking the dark country road from Oseberg toward the first streetlights of Tønsberg. She should have been in bed, but how could she sleep? She should have been glad to stretch her legs after sitting for seven hours in a Trabant, but her old body ached all over.

Groa hadn't talked much during the long ride from Gotland. Helen and Lennart had sat in the front seat, excitedly discussing their futures, full of possibility and hope. Sometimes, Groa thought, it is better not to know.

Night had long since dimmed the sky by the time the car finally drove up the dirt lane to the Oseberg farmhouse. Helen had begged for a tour of the neighboring burial mound, where her grandmother had once excavated a Viking ship. Groa had sent the kids off to explore the grassy hill on their own with a flashlight. While they were gone she lit a few lumps of coal in the fireplace. Then she took an old bottle from a cupboard and sprinkled crystals on the fire.

Three blue flames had appeared —not one, but three. Somehow the Caliph of Cordoba must have reforged Fenris into three swords. If one was in London and one in Novgorod, where was the third?

Helen and Lennart returned from the excavation laughing and joking. They asked if there was anything they could bring Groa before they left for Stockholm. Was there anything she needed? Anything at all?

Groa had shaken her head and let them wave goodbye.

But as soon as they left she had thrown a blanket over her shoulders and had set out on the seven-kilometer walk to town.

Fenris vests the Vikings' fate.

The old verse echoed in her head as she trudged the road, its asphalt cracked by winter freezes into an inscrutable map—a ragged tapestry. The Viking Age had lingered the longest in the coldest corners of the world, banished to Iceland and Greenland. The third sword would be there. The world would not end in fire, but in ice.

No one noticed the crone hobbling beneath the streetlights of Tønsberg. No dogs barked as she walked around the base of Castle Hill. No wolves howled as she passed the harbor. No ravens laughed on Kingsgate. Groa had been left to stand in the path of evil by herself.

After all these years, only the central part of the old inn was still standing, converted to a whaling museum. The back courtyard was a field littered with anchors and whale skulls.

Groa found the old millstone, its worn granite surface nearly flush with the dead grass. At first she thought the stone must have sunken with time. Then she realized that a thousand years of soil had left the ground higher.

She spread the blanket on top of the circular stone. The night was cold. Groa shivered. The fight to stave off Ragnarök called for someone with the vigor of youth.

She closed her eyes, wishing for one last chance.

AUTHOR'S NOTE

While it would be inappropriate to include footnotes in any historical novel, readers may be interested to know which portions of *The Ship in the Woods* are historical and which are novel.

Throughout the book, Karen Sullivan's pen-and-ink drawings depict actual artifacts from Sweden, Russia, Byzantium, and Germany.

The story in the Viking Age chapters is based on the *Primary Chronicle*, a history of the Rus written in Kiev in 1113 AD. This Old East Slavic manuscript, also known as the *Tale of Bygone Years,* tells of Russia's Swedish founder, Rurik, and his successors. Oleg served many years as regent for Rurik's young son Igor. The chronicle implies that Oleg was a relative of Rurik's, but probably not a blood relative. Perhaps a brother in law? To fill in the story I have invented Oleg's brief marriage to Helga. I also created a host of other Viking Age characters, including Groa, Hrolf, Vlad, Gunnar, and Thorkell.

Both the *Primary Chronicle* and texts from the Byzantine Empire document Oleg's attack on Constantinople in 907. The details of his advantageous treaty with Emperor Leo VI are genuine. The sources have little to say, however, about why Oleg's forces were so successful. I take the liberty of suggesting military tactics that allowed the Vikings to broach the city's harbor chain and scale the walls.

The *Primary Chronicle* is very specific about Oleg's peculiar death—that a seer prophesied he would be killed by his horse, and that he was later bitten by a snake in the dead horse's skull. The chronicle suggests that Oleg died in Russia about five years after the siege of Constantinople. I have placed Oleg's death in Sweden the same year as the siege.

The politics of the Byzantine Empire, the Abbasid Caliphate, and the Caliph of Cordoba are portrayed with reasonable accuracy, although

I admit to many embellishments—notably the Arab doctor Ali Ibn al-Namid and the reforging of Fenris.

The chapters set in the 1960s follow the course of the Cold War closely—the building of the Berlin Wall, Lee Harvey Oswald's defection, and the Soviet submarine that nearly launched a nuclear torpedo during the Cuban missile crisis. Lars and Sasha are fictional CIA spies, but Colonel Stig Wennerström really did smuggle Swedish secrets to the Soviets, and Nikita Khrushchev's message to President Kennedy is genuine.

Sweden's most impressive archeological find may well be the seventeenth-century warship *Vasa*, rediscovered by Anders Franzen in 1956 and lifted from Stockholm's harbor on April 24, 1961 before an audience of thousands. Almost as newsworthy was the revelation that the famous Viking warrior's tomb on the island of Birka, identified as Bj 581 by Hjalmar Stolpe in 1889, actually contained the skeleton of a woman. Bioarcheologist Anna Kjellström announced this finding based on her analysis of the bones in 2014. For dramatic purposes I credit the discovery to my fictional archeologists, Mette and Per, in 1961 while work is continuing on the *Vasa*. I have also separated the grave into two tombs. The actual burial included two horses in the same chamber as the woman warrior.

Although the Varangian Guard was in fact a battalion of Viking mercenaries fighting for the Byzantine Empire, there is no record of an "Order of Varangian Knights," nor of a secret society using three runic letters as their identifying talisman, nor of the rings, swords, and medallions suspected of having special powers in this novel.

Many ages, however, have faced the very real threat of nationalistic groups promoting racial supremacy. In a metaphoric sense, Groa is right: The evil of Fenris is still at large.

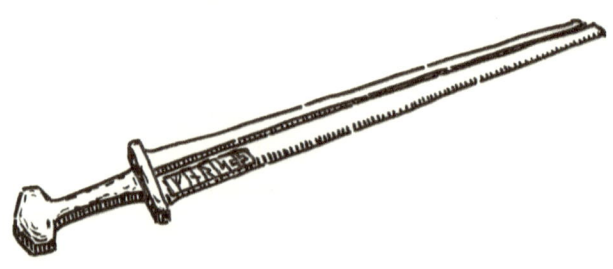

WILLIAM L. SULLIVAN

The author of six novels and more than a dozen nonfiction books, Sullivan grew up in Salem, Oregon. He completed his B.A. degree in English at Cornell University under Alison Lurie, studied linguistics at Germany's Heidelberg University, and earned an M.A. in German at the University of Oregon. He reads in a dozen languages, including Swedish, Danish, Norwegian, and Old Norse. He undertook ten voyages to Scandinavia and Russia while researching Nordic sagas and Viking history for *The Ship in the Hill, The Ship in the Sand, The Ship in the Woods,* and the planned conclusion to the series, *The Ship in the Ice.*

Listening for Coyote, Sullivan's journal of a thousand-mile hike across Oregon's wilderness, was chosen by the Oregon Cultural Heritage Commission as one of Oregon's "100 Books," the most significant books in Oregon history. Summers he writes at the log cabin that he and his wife Janell Sorensen built by hand in the wilds of Oregon's Coast Range, more than a mile from roads, electricity, and telephones. The rest of the year they live in Eugene, Oregon, where he volunteers to promote libraries and literature.

A list of Sullivan's books, speaking engagements, audio books, and favorite adventures is at *www.oregonhiking.com.*

The Rulers of Sweden and Russia

Sweden

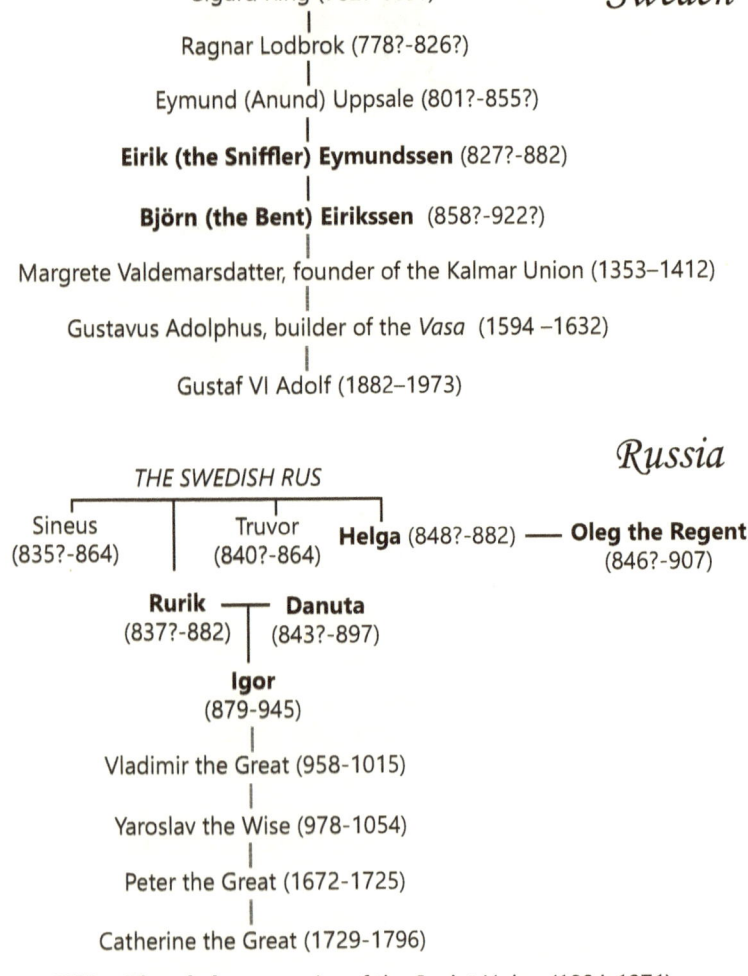

Sigurd Ring (762?-803?)
|
Ragnar Lodbrok (778?-826?)
|
Eymund (Anund) Uppsale (801?-855?)
|
Eirik (the Sniffler) Eymundssen (827?-882)
|
Björn (the Bent) Eirikssen (858?-922?)
|
Margrete Valdemarsdatter, founder of the Kalmar Union (1353–1412)
|
Gustavus Adolphus, builder of the *Vasa* (1594 –1632)
|
Gustaf VI Adolf (1882–1973)

Russia

THE SWEDISH RUS

Sineus (835?-864)   Truvor (840?-864)   **Helga** (848?-882) —— **Oleg the Regent** (846?-907)

Rurik (837?-882) —— **Danuta** (843?-897)
|
Igor (879-945)
|
Vladimir the Great (958-1015)
|
Yaroslav the Wise (978-1054)
|
Peter the Great (1672-1725)
|
Catherine the Great (1729-1796)
|
Nikita Khrushchev, premier of the Soviet Union (1894-1971)

SWEDEN
in the Cold War
(1961 A.D.)

Uppsala

Roslagen

Norrtälje

Sigtuna

Stockholm

Birka

NORWAY
(NATO)

Area
Enlarged
Above

ÅLAND

Oslo

Oseberg

Stockholm

HIIUMAA

SWEDEN
(Neutral)

Ferry

Göteborg

Visby

GOTLAND

Kalmar

DENMARK
(NATO)

Copenhagen

BALTIC SEA

Ferry

Hedeby

WEST
GERMANY
(NATO)

GERMAN
DEMOCRATIC
REPUBLIC

Berlin
(Divided)

Warsaw Pact

N

0   150 Miles
0   150 Km

EUROPE
in the Viking Age
(907 A.D.)

N

0   1000 Miles

Inset map (Area Enlarged Above):

BALTIC SEA

Lake Ladoga

Neva R.

Ladoga

Novgorod

Volkhov R.

Holmgard

Lake Ilmen

Pskov

Loviat R.

RUSSIYA

Dvina R.

Portage

Zarkhov

Portage

Dnieper R.

Rapids

Smolensk

Main map:

FINNS

Area Enlarged Above

Volga R.

NORWAY

Sigtuna

Tunsberg

SWEDEN

Novgorod

Portage

DENMARK

Dvina R.

ENGLAND

RUSSIYA

Hedeby

SLAVS

Dnieper R.

FRANKISH REALMS

Kiev

BULGARS

EMIRATE of CORDOBA

Rome

Constantinople
(Miklagard)

Black Sea

Cordoba

SICILY

BYZANTINE EMPIRE

ABBASID   CALIPHATE

Damascus

Alexandria